HAVE THE MEN
HAD ENOUGH?

Margaret Forster is the author of many successful
novels, including *Lady's Maid*, *Mother Can You
Hear Me?*, *The Memory Box*, bestselling memoirs
Hidden Lives and *Precious Lives* and most
recently, *Over*, and several acclaimed biographies,
including *Good Wives*.

Margaret Forster

HAVE THE MEN HAD ENOUGH?

VINTAGE BOOKS
London

Published by Vintage 2004

22

First published in Great Britain in 1989 by
Chatto & Windus

Vintage
Random House, 20 Vauxhall Bridge Road,
London SW1V 2SA

Addresses for companies within The Random House Group Limited can be found at: www.randomhouse.co.uk/offices.htm

The Random House Group Limited Reg. No. 954009
www.randomhouse.co.uk/vintage

A CIP catalogue record for this book
is available from the British Library

ISBN 9780099455646

Penguin Random House is committed to a sustainable future for our business, our readers and our planet. This book is made from Forest Stewardship Council® certified paper.

Printed and bound in Great Britain by Clays Ltd, Elcograf S.p.A.

for
Annabelle and Marion
whose mother gave me this title
and a great deal besides

Hannah

Have the men had enough?
Never mind the men.
Which men?
Hurry up, the potatoes will be cold.
I'd love a potato.
Then take one, Grandma.
Have the men had enough?

Always the same. Every week, every Sunday. All of us crowded round the table, Grandma wedged in between Bridget and Paula, Bridget of course laughing at everything Grandma says and Paula not even smiling, and moving away, ever so slightly, when Grandma plonks a hand flat in the gravy as she searches for her fork.

Have the men had enough?
Yes, thank you, Mother.
Who's Mother?
You are, go on, Mother, help yourself.
Hold the plate steady.
Steady the Buffs.
Go *on*, Grandma.
Have the men had enough?

7

Always the same. Dad desperate to fill his face, but patient, good-humoured, coaxing Grandma along and Adrian impatient, resenting the ritual when he's just in from football and starving and not disposed to care about Grandma's feelings, as dear Bridget well knows so she drags it out and encourages Grandma to peer round the table and fuss on until eventually Mum calls a halt and piles her plate and then it starts, the next little song, the next refrain:

> Pass the salt.
> Grandma, everything's covered in salt.
> It's salty enough.
> Salt's bad for you.
> It hardens the arteries.
> Hers have been silted up for years.
> Adrian!
> Pass the salt.

Who does it irritate more? Hard to say. Mum long ago stopped seeing this passion for salt as an insult to her cooking, in fact I think it gives her a kind of malicious pleasure to watch Grandma totally ruin the food, watch her covering the delicate slices of delicious herb-scattered chicken, the crisp roasted potatoes, the bright green leeks (Grandma loves leeks but not the way Mum does them, barely tossed in lemon and butter, she likes the hell boiled out of them), covering all of it heavily with salt.

> Pass the salt.
> It's in front of you.
> Stick it in her hand.
> Stick it in her mouth.
> Adrian!
> It'll ruin her taste-buds.
> She hasn't got any.
> Pass the salt.

Finally, when the salt has fallen like scurf, Grandma is satisfied. She eats, with her hands, Paula concentrating hard on her own plate, Bridget cooing and praising and expertly pushing the pota-

8

toes out of the gravy, and we all hurry to eat before the inevitable, before Grandma says the chicken is tough, which of course it isn't but who can bother saying this when it's melting in all our mouths that very minute, and then she takes her bottom teeth out (the top set are already out, lost sometime between breakfast and lunch and likely to turn up any place from the peg basket to the biscuit tin). She uses them as a scoop, grating them through the shallows of the gravy to fish out a potato, and Adrian laughs and Dad smiles and Mum moves her face not a muscle and Paula closes her eyes and Bridget snatches the teeth, rushes to the sink, sluices the teeth, rams them back into Grandma's mouth.

Any pudding?
You haven't finished your lovely dinner.
Throw it in the waste bin for God's sake.
Hannah!
Give it to me, come on.
Adrian!
Any pudding?

Bridget takes a bit of the chicken, all cold and ruined by the gravy which only Grandma has because she won't eat anything not sodden with thick, dark gravy, and Adrian leans across and spears the potatoes knocking aside Dad, who is grappling for one of the drier ones, and Mum removes the plate and plonks down in front of Grandma a bowl of her very special absolutely beautiful apple trifle, which takes half a pint of double cream, a certain sort of apple, sponge which Mum makes herself and loads of time to concoct and we adore it. She puts extra cream on to make it even more sloppy for poor Grandma's gums. The spoon is put in Grandma's hand but since she is likely just to shove her mit straight in the cream and begin a plastering job on her face, Bridget has arranged a napkin under her chin. Bridget oohs and aahs and keeps telling Grandma, 'You Are Certainly Going To Enjoy This Mum,' and praising my own Mum for making it, reminding Grandma that Jenny has made it specially for her. Grandma takes one mouthful and we brace ourselves and, yes, she spits it out, face contorted with disgust, miserable with disappointment.

It's sour!
Mum, it is not.
Put some sugar on for her.
It's drowned in sugar.
Just give her straight sugar.
Adrian!
It's sour!

Mum already has it taken away and passed on to Dad who couldn't give tuppence that Grandma, in spitting it out, has spat into the bowl and flecks of saliva are spotting the cream. Mum substitutes a bowl of ice cream, chocolate, with chocolate sauce, heavily sweetened, on top of it. Grandma says it's lovely and begins applying it to every crevice of her skin but getting a good deal down the hatch too. Bridget watches her adoringly, pleased she is quiet and content at last. It's nearly over, the weekly ordeal, the worst of all similar ordeals in the week. We all relax. After the main course we all have a salad before the pudding, a huge green salad with a garlicky dressing. Grandma does not usually want salad but doesn't like to be left out so Mum makes sure that she goes through the motions of serving Grandma who sometimes does take a bit of green pepper or a sliver of celery and plays with it, but not today; today she most graciously declines and says so clearly that she has had an excellent sufficiency that we all laugh, nicely. Only one more ritual to go.

Has anyone a cigarette?
Not yet, Mother, we're still eating.
Have it with your tea, Grandma.
Wait till I've left the room.
Charlie!
It's her only pleasure, Charlie.
Has anyone a cigarette?

That marks the end, really, unless anyone is foolish enough to have dallied over their salad and not got on to the pudding. Dad takes his with him, not at all put out by Bridget's reprimand. Bridget of course smokes, as does Paula actually, surprisingly, so she

10

naturally doesn't mind Grandma filling our house with smoke. Mum hates it but ostentatiously holds her peace, knowing that Dad's protest is enough. Well, he does get bronchitis often – smoke is bad for him. Adrian has already gone out. He disapproves of smoking, being your sporty health-freak type. We can do without his self-righteousness. Paula has left the table and sits in a corner of the kitchen, thoughtfully opening the window beside her before she has her own cigarette. Grandma shivers melodramatically and announces darkly that there is a draught from somewhere and Bridget, who stays at the table to smoke companionably with her, covers her shoulders with a tartan shawl. She doesn't bother turning to look at Paula. Paula isn't really a smoker – it's seventy-five per cent letting the cigarette burn and only a few puffs. But Bridget – wow. It's quite frightening, the intensity, the sheer power of the deep drags, the apparent absolute disappearance of the smoke. I used to think she was a magician: I'd get all excited about where it went and Dad would say it wasn't a trick, that some nice little containers called lungs collected it and that if Bridget could take them out and look at them she'd find they were covered in tar. It was all beyond me, especially as Grandma, quite sharp then, would immediately protect Bridget from her mean brother and say either A Little Of What You Fancy Does You Good or There Is No Harm In It. Bridget is an addict. If she can't find her cigarettes it's pitiful to see her. She is frantic, unhinged, almost hysterical. Now, Grandma is never like that. She's an elegant smoker which, for a woman lacking elegance in any other way, is odd. She has good hands, long-fingered, narrow-palmed, and a pretty way of holding a cigarette. Bridget talks with a cigarette in her mouth. I've even seen her drink with it there, but Grandma never does. She smokes slowly, knocks ash off neatly, is relaxed. Bridget is right: it is, next to tea, her one remaining pleasure. And she has the tea now, a big yellow pot of it, strong and dark, though she says repeatedly she hates strong tea. Once, Mum believed her and prepared her finest Darjeeling, poured into a sweet little rosebud-covered cup. Grandma almost had a fit at the 'coloured water'. Weak tea to Mum is half a pint of water to one tea bag and strong is a whole tea bag in a cup. Weak to Grandma is a whole tea bag in a cup and strong is six in a half pint of water. In her

11

mug – Grandma is only comfortable with large workmen's mugs – there are three heaped teaspoons of sugar. It is fascinating to watch three more go in, be languidly stirred, tasted, smiled over.

Here we go. 'Right,' Bridget says and stands up. Grandma slowly begins to stand up and asks where are we going and she thought we were going to have lunch. Bridget sits. Grandma sits and says she's hungry. Mum tells Bridget to for heaven's sake go and then we have several cross conversations.

> Where's she going?
> She'll be fine, Bridget.
> I don't know why you fuss.
> It's worse than leaving a baby.
> Do you think I won't look after her.
> I'll go, then if –
> Where's she going?

She's gone. Paula's gone too, five minutes after. Paula has told Bridget she will stay until Grandma has settled, as if it made any difference since Grandma no longer knows who Paula is, but Mum pushes her out, impatient with this dithering. Mum has endless sympathy for Paula, which no one else has, least of all Bridget, and protects her.

Mum says at least Paula tries, at least she comes, which is more than her dear husband Stuart does. And think, Mum argues, but never persuasively enough for Bridget, think what trouble it causes for Paula, think what she has to put up with from Stuart. Stuart gets left with the children and that, says Mum, amounts to a statement on Paula's part – she, Paula, is prepared to leave her children on Sunday lunchtimes in order to have lunch with Grandma. It is, Mum claims, amazing. Bridget only laughs. Bridget says Mum is getting carried away, that Paula only does it to *spite* Stuart. Mum says Paula wouldn't even attempt to do that, she hasn't the nerve, and she adds that in a strange kind of way Stuart is secretly pleased Paula makes this weekly pilgrimage: women should, women are supposed to keep the family together. Mousy, scared-looking little Paula with her funny fly-away hair and her old-fashioned stiletto heels is actually doing the right thing.

And now Bridget has gone too, probably gone to bed with the newspapers and her fags, and Paula has gone back to Stuart who will on no account come and go through this charade, not ever, except for Burns' Night when he softens (his brother Charlie, my dad, mutters that he only appears on Burns' Night because he is very partial to whisky, not to please Grandma). Adrian is out, Dad is in front of the television waiting for Match of the Day to start, happily trailing his finger round his empty pudding bowl (and Grandma's). Mum loads the dishwasher, tidies the kitchen, and I re-fill and re-fill, re-sugar and re-sugar Grandma's mug. She asks me if I know any poetry and I say no, not a line, and she clucks her tongue and says something about they told me you were dead, Heraclitus. I decide not to be provocative and merely encourage her to recite more. Yards and yards of dismal-sounding rubbish come out. It makes Grandma very happy indeed – the tea, the sugar, a biscuit and poetry. Life is not too bad. She's forgotten Bridget.

Then Mum helps her up and I take the other side and Grandma is so happy to be half-cuddled between us that she does a little dance as we walk through to the living room and Dad says that's a good Highland Fling and Grandma says she thinks she'll go to the Highlands. We lower her onto the sofa as she asks us to mind her legs, which are sore, then Mum puts a pillow at her head and I fetch the crocheted blanket, crocheted by Grandma in her heyday, a lovely thing in violent colours, and Grandma sighs and says it's nice to get up in the morning but it's nicer to stay in your bed. She closes her eyes. The match starts with a roar. Grandma says that men and their football are the very devil and the dirty boots and the filthy clothes and is the water heated ready and men must work and women must weep. She's asleep. Mum dashes for her coat and runs through instructions while she puts it on: Keep her covered, remind her about the loo when she wakens, only one more cup of tea or she'll wet the bed and Mildred will give up. Dad grunts. Mum goes.

And I am here, in my room, wondering. What I want to know is:

Why don't more people kill themselves when they get old?
Why do relatives not kill old people more?
What is the point of keeping old people alive anyway?

13

Haven't the women had enough, as well as the men?
Will somebody please tell me?

*

There's the doorbell. It won't be for me. It's four o'clock and it will
be Bridget. Mum will answer. Bridget will come in. Grandma, still
on the sofa, will be furious with her and ask her where in God's
name she's been. Bridget will say resting. Grandma will laugh,
satirically, laugh and exclaim to heaven that some people have all
the luck and that if she could have five minutes to rest it would be a
damned miracle. In a minute, Mum will shout for me. There –
'Hannah, Hannah' echoing up the stairs and Grandma complaining
at the damned noise, has nobody any consideration?
   I get Grandma's coat, awful bumpy old tweed thing, luridly
checked in yellow and black. It's too small, it seems to me, to go over
her alarming bulk especially since she has put two cardigans on, one
she knitted herself in what she proudly refers to as Factory Wool,
but Bridget says it will do. Bridget hates spending money as much as
her brothers do and Grandma is in complete agreement. So we
struggle, Bridget and I, to force Grandma into the coat. It's not
really funny. No sooner is one arm in than Grandma turns round
and it comes out and the coat is in danger of being put on back to
front like a straitjacket. Not a bad idea. Hannah! Just a joke,
Bridget. We get it on and Grandma whispers, on cue, that she wants
to go to the bathroom (she never, ever uses the words lavatory, loo,
lav or toilet). I whistle. Bridget strips the coat off because there's no
chance of Grandma getting her knickers down while it's on. I wait,
perfectly understanding no chances can be taken. Grandma, luckily
in this situation, has a very strong bladder. If she says she needs to
go, then she needs to go. We have a downstairs lavatory, to which
Bridget leads her, then waits patiently outside. A minute or two
passes. I lounge in the hall, idly looking at a photograph of
Grandma which Dad has framed in an old mahogany frame. Taken
circa 1946, I think. Grandma is sitting with baby Bridget on her
knee and her two boys, Charlie and Stuart, either side. She looks so
pretty, her hair curly and wild, her flowered dress open at the neck
to reveal a long, slender throat, the one I've just tried to get a scarf

14

round, to cover the knotted veins and loose scrag. Down the hall, the lavatory door opens very, very slowly and Grandma peeps out.

Are there men about?
No, Mum. The men are all gone.
Don't worry Grandma, I'll keep watch.
Have you been, Mum?
Are there men about?

She hasn't been, of course, but then she goes and Bridget puts her thumb up. Then the washing of the hands begins, the long, slow, careful soaping and rinsing, though Grandma does not let the water run, good heavens, no, she uses only an inch or so, with the plug firmly in. When she's finished her Lady Macbeth stunt she will leave the little bit of water and invite others to use it. Out she comes, on with the coat again, and this time Bridget and I manage it quite easily. Grandma is looking at the same photograph I've been studying. She says she's sure she knows that person. Bridget is so amused she's happy to delay. She teases Grandma, asking her if she thinks the lady pretty, if she thinks she's a good-looker and she howls with laughter when Grandma sniffs and says she looks a hussy, she needs her hair combed. At this rate we'll never get home.

It's ridiculous to call it home. Grandma's home. It's a flat, in the next street to ours, just round the corner. Dad pays the rent. It's on the ground floor of a double-fronted house and theoretically Bridget has the right-hand side rooms and Grandma and the helpers have the left. Up above, but quite self-contained with their own staircase, are two male actors who bother nobody and are very quiet. Bridget has a kitchen, a bathroom, a bedroom and a sitting room and Grandma has the same except there's a sofa-bed in her sitting room which is really another bedroom where the helpers sleep. But half the time Bridget is in Grandma's room and the other half Grandma in hers and it annoys Dad. He says it's a farce maintaining, so expensively, a separate flat for Grandma. He says we could sub-let Grandma's flat and use the money to pay for the helpers. But Mum calms him down. She tells him it's necessary for Bridget to be, in theory, entirely separate, that she needs this reassurance psychologically.

15

Grandma enjoys the short walk home. Every person we pass is hailed as a friend. Don't I know you, Grandma calls across the street and is ignored. She walks so slowly she hardly moves, examining the ground for money if she is not distracted by people. If she sees a silver wrapper, there's no chance of getting her past it: it must be picked up, turned over and eventually put in her pocket in case it comes in useful. She says how quiet it is, over and over, sighing, and then if a car door slams or we hear a siren in the distance she winces and says bloomin' noise. Meeting children is fatal. Grandma's face lights up. ''Ellaw, 'ellaw,' she croaks, like a parrot, bending to the frightened child's level, not realising how weird she looks. She asks either if they know any songs or if they would like a sweetie and Bridget loves it, denying angrily that any child could be the least bit scared of Grandma.

Bridget says we are home. Grandma stands stock still, amazed. We guide her in, to her own kitchen. This contains the clock her father won in a bowls competition, a picture of Bonnie Prince Charlie she got as a wedding present, some brass ornaments she collected herself, and her china cabinet with what is left of her wedding china in it. These objects were brought down from Glasgow when Grandma was brought down. They're supposed to make this strange kitchen homely. They fail. Grandma hasn't the slightest idea where she is. All she knows is that the doors are in the wrong place, the bed has gone from the wall, and she can't find the fire. Still, it looks very nice. Mum painted the walls a deep, warm yellow and covered the floor in brown and white checks. There's a table, with a patterned PVC cloth on it to catch Grandma's spills, and the usual cooker and fridge. The Social Services have provided a special chair which is easy for Grandma to get in and out of. Mum was annoyed about that, Bridget triumphant. Mum said we could go out and buy Grandma any chair in the world, for heaven's sake, so why all this hassle (which Bridget made a meal of, it's true) to get the DHSS to fork out.

The kitchen is warm, too warm. Dad usually mutters that it's like Africa and that Grandma's own kitchen was always freezing, that she never had any heat on, that she would not approve of all this heat, that she's spent a lifetime cowering in the cold. Bridget says she

16

certainly has, tight-lipped. Grandma loves the warmth now, there's no denying it. She acts, on a fine September early evening, as though she has come in from the Arctic. Bridget settles her in her chair and gives her a cigarette and meanwhile I've made the tea. Bridget puts the radio on and we talk over it. I would very much like to leave at once – but that's not how it works. I wait, every week, for Mildred to arrive. Mum used to do it but recently, as the going's got tougher, she's got tougher. She tells me to do the handover and adds it's not much to ask. That's true. How could I object to handing my own Grandmother over to the woman who looks after her on Sunday nights?

Sunday is Bridget's night off, one of her two. The other is variable, according to what dear Mildred will agree to and sometimes she announces that she is Hard Pressed For Time In My Own Life Which Is Not Easy Either and then Mum stays. Mum hates staying. When she voices this hate I say Dad should stay, that it's Dad who is Grandma's son whereas Mum is only her daughter-in-law. This exasperates Mum who snaps at me that Dad cannot possibly stay because Grandma's smoking brings on his bronchitis and anyway how could he dress and undress her and take her to the lavatory in the night. My answer to this is that female nurses do all that for male patients and Mum's comeback is that Dad isn't a nurse and it would be embarrassing for Grandma. These niceties defeat me. I notice Dad doesn't argue. He says he'll do it but never does.

The bell goes. Mildred has her own key but on Sunday evenings she always rings the bell because she knows I'm here. Bridget stubs her cigarette out and scarpers, with a quick goodbye to Grandma. She says the same thing every week – I have to go to work – and Grandma tells her to work hard and bring the bacon home. Bridget's door, across the hall on her own side, closes. She locks it. Grandma is fiendishly clever in the night. She could burgle anyone and get away with it. When she stayed with us she'd go from room to room, quite silently, managing to open and close doors without disturbing us. Now, of course, she thinks it's morning and the whole point is to disturb people and get them up for work. If Bridget didn't lock her communicating door Grandma would find her way to her bed and shake her awake at 3 a.m. But she doesn't shake Mildred.

Who would? Who would dare? Bridget can't bear to think of how Mildred deals with Grandma waking her three or four times a night. Mum asks her has Grandma got bruises? No. Has Grandma been all right in the morning? Yes. Well then, what is Bridget worried about?

Bridget is worried about Mildred and so am I. Mildred comes in now and says to Grandma, 'Hello, Mother.' Grandma looks contemptuous. She turns to me and says nastily, 'Who is she talking to?'

Mildred has a thing about belts. She has three coats, a tweed one, a cloth one and a raincoat and they all have belts which Mildred straps viciously round her fat middle. They must be so uncomfortable but then comfort never seems to be high on Mildred's list of priorities. She makes no concessions to it. She wears her grey hair in a bun which is not only secured by a fierce-looking elastic band but is further anchored with incredibly long, wide steel hairgrips. Mildred reminds me of a jeep, all squat and solid, all weight and rigid lines. She used to be a bus conductress and though she retired long before they came into use she sees Pay-as-you-enter buses, with drivers only, as the true indication of the decline of our civilisation. She treats Grandma exactly like a passenger on a bus and I'm quite surprised she doesn't give her a ticket when she leaves. Right now, she's unbuckling her belt and taking her hat off and her coat off and bustling about claiming her territory. Eventually, she plonks her short, stout body down on the chair just vacated by Bridget and asks Grandma how she is today. Grandma, staring disdainfully into space, says she is very well thank you but she has to be going, the men will be coming in and there is their dinner to get. Mildred laughs and says, a gleam in her eye, that it's bath night tonight. I say I'd better be going. Grandma says she'd better be going too and starts mouthing she'll go with me and making faces. Mildred says I should trot along and enjoy myself as I'm only young once and that she'll soon sort Grandma out: we'll have those things off in no time and give your back a nice scrub, eh, Mother? Grandma is appalled. I'm beginning to feel like Bridget.

Often, I say goodbye and kiss Grandma and slip a comforting peppermint in her mouth and then I go out and close the inner door and the outer door and I make a few noises of walking away along

18

the gravel path. But I creep back and crouch near the window and listen. I don't know what I expect to hear. Hard to hear anything, really, with the radio on. Mostly I hear Mildred droning on. I can't make out the words but the tone is acceptable. She isn't shouting at Grandma, anyway. I walk home, thinking how wrong it all is. Grandma should be living with us. But I can't help thinking, thank God, she isn't because it would be awful. But at least she is not in a Home and never will be, Bridget says. Mum says nothing. Dad says the present system costs as much if not more than any Home. Mildred gets £30 a night. Susan, who comes every morning, gets £2.50 an hour. Lola who comes three afternoons, gets £2 an hour (she only sits and chats whereas Susan does things). It is all ridiculous, Dad says, and not as though it gave anyone peace of mind.

Peace of mind. I would say Dad and Stuart and Adrian seem to enjoy peace of mind where Grandma is concerned. Dad hasn't got peace of mind about the money he's forking out but that's different. He doesn't worry about Grandma. Mum lies awake at night, fretting. Bridget is screwed up all the time with anxiety and pain. The pain is because she alone truly loves Grandma. More, she adores her, thinks she's quite wonderful, is her champion. She can't see a single one of Grandma's faults. I'm talking about before, of course, when Grandma was herself. I love Grandma but not to that extent. Since I love Mum more, I can see, could see, Grandma is capable, was capable, of some meannesses. She was sly and devious and sulky and childish, in many ways, long before she reverted to being like a child. But Bridget saw only Grandma's kindness and warmth and cheerfulness and sense of humour and bravery, all true, and most of all her hard life. Bridget says Grandma got most of the custard pies around flung at her. And they were mostly flung by men.

It's hard to get far questioning Bridget about these custard pies and the men that threw them. How can my Grandfather getting killed be a custard pie he threw? That's fate, isn't it? Bridget says she means before her father was killed. Apparently Grandfather gambled, dogs and horses. Grandma had hard times with him. Bridget does not enlighten me about them. Dad says he can't remember them and he doesn't know how Bridget knows because she was only six months old when their father was killed. Dad says, to Bridget's face, that she romances. Bridget says she does not, she says she knows things Dad does not, things Grandma told her. Mum thinks Grandad was probably just your average working-class husband circa 1930s.

The house smells of Grandma when I go in. The smoke, but it's Bridget's and Paula's smoke too, but also a strange, musty, close smell, not exactly unpleasant – Grandma is kept very clean, but she smells of being old. Just old. She's forgotten her tartan shawl. I pick it up from the sofa and bury my face in it. Mum comes in and says to give the shawl to her, it needs washing, that she shudders to think how many times Grandma has blown her nose on it and mopped up tea and used it to wipe dishes. She will wash it in Lux flakes and rinse it in Comfort and hang it in the garden to dry in the wind. In fact, she'll help Grandma to wash it and hang it out her-self tomorrow, she'll love that. It's perfectly true. Grandma is passionately happy scrubbing things. I look at her, when Mum has her standing at the sink up to her elbows in suds, and I can always see Mum is right. Washing is women's work. It doesn't take Grandma back to backbreaking days of unremitting labour, when she had to heat the water in a copper and stand in a freezing wash house, oh no, it takes her back to a house full and never a lonely moment and a sense of purpose. Grandma believes firmly in the good old days and no amount of evidence produced by Adrian, our statistics expert, can persuade her otherwise.

Adrian comes in. He's gloomy. He sighs, throws himself on the sofa, then jumps up as though stung. He holds out his hand and there are Grandma's top teeth, some toast still stuck to them. I laugh. Mum takes them. Adrian tells me it's not funny, it makes him feel sick. I tell him he's a tender flower to be made sick by a set of false teeth. Adrian says he can't help it and that he wishes he didn't have to watch Grandma eat, it's so disgusting, she doesn't close her mouth and the food swills around and he feels like vomiting. It isn't even just because she's ill now either, he goes on, her manners were always awful, it was always horrible eating with her and then those mighty burps, they make him feel sick too. Mum says nobody enjoys it but surely he can rise above it one day a week, especially since he never sees her otherwise whereas at least Hannah helps. Adrian is indignant, claims he helps too. Didn't he clean Grandma's windows, dig her garden, drive her to the clinic to see the chiropodist? Good heavens, he can't be accused of not helping, what else do we want him to do. Mum says he could visit her, like Hannah does. For ten minutes every day, just pop in when she's alone and make her a cup of tea and chat. Adrian says she doesn't like men, that last time he dropped in she bolted him in the kitchen and he had to wait for Lola to arrive and let him out. We laugh. Very funny, he says.

Dad shouts down from the sitting room. Bridget has just telephoned. Lola can't come tomorrow afternoon, her little girl is ill. Mum says Oh God. Dad yells that Bridget cannot possibly get off work, they are two nurses short on her ward as it is. Mum says oh God again. I know she's going out tomorrow, nothing important, just pleasure. *Just* pleasure. So I say I'll go, not to worry. I'll go straight from school and stay until Bridget gets home. Mum kisses me. Two minutes later, Bridget rings me. She says thanks, petal, you've saved my life.

*

I arrive at Grandma's at four o'clock. She calls nothing today thank you as I shout hello from the front door. That means she's in a good mood. If she's in a bad one she grumbles that she'll hello me and where the devil have I been. She's standing at the sink with a cut lemon in her hand. What she does is squeeze the lemon juice onto her face to improve her complexion, a tip she read many years ago in the *Sunday Post*. It's preferable to the eggshell tip. Grandma also read that when you've used a fresh egg you should wipe the inside with a finger and coat your face with what's left on the shell. Usually, she coats it with small pieces of actual shell which harden and are difficult to get off. Grandma's complexion, her skin, is beyond the benefit of all tips. Her face is like W. H. Auden's, millions and millions of cragged crevices and all the colour of a used tea bag. I make her tea, light her a cigarette, remove the lemon and sit her down. I say I've just come from school.

21

Do you like school?

No.

I loved school.

Why did you leave at thirteen then?

Everyone did.

No they didn't. Your sister stayed on.

I loved school.

So you say.

Do you like school?

That's that one over, theme song for the day Number One. Luckily, we're interrupted by the radio or I might have got bad-tempered. Grandma loving school is fishy and gets fishier. Her three brothers and her sister all did stay at school. Her family, by the time Grandma was born in 1908, was nothing like as poor as when her sister Annie stayed on at school, so it's nonsense to say she had to leave for economic reasons. Yet Grandma is intelligent and well read so there's no question of her not being clever enough to stay on and follow Annie's example. What went wrong? She loved school and left at the first opportunity and went as a maid to the manse and there had her greatest day when she took tea one morning, to a visitor, to that Eric Liddell man, the Scottish one in *Chariots of Fire*. He left her sixpence.

But Grandma has picked up a horror story on the radio. A rape. A thirteen-year-old on her way home from school was raped three times each by two boys who took her to a nearby waste ground . . . I switch the radio off.

Isn't that terrible!

Don't listen, then.

Dreadful, dreadful, did you hear –

I don't want to hear.

Two of them, three times –

Grandma, forget it, please.

It's getting worse, the world's gone mad.

It has *not* got worse, we just hear more about it.

Isn't that terrible!

22

Grandma subsides into a favourite quote about man's inhumanity to man which leads inevitably on to Culloden. She tells me I would not believe the things that happened at Culloden, it was terrible, terrible. She rolls the word beautifully, stretches it out like a song. The need to distract her from her misery, real misery, prods me to action. I ask her if she fancies a wee walk. She brightens, gets up by herself, says she's a little stiff from rugby but she likes a walk. Her father took them for walks in the Highlands. The dreaded coat slides on easily, she is so immersed in her story. They went to the Highlands every summer and, oh, what a long journey and, oh, how excited she was and, oh, how she saved comics for weeks before, knowing they'd sit for hours and hours on the train. The holidays were great, the weather great, all the people in the village they went to great, asking you in for cups of tea and exclaiming when they heard you were Charlie Cameron's daughter. Grandma laughs and laughs, telling me, becomes animated, acts out accents and expressions.

I think I'll go to the Highlands.
Go, then.
I'll need someone to go with.
Go with Bridget.
My cousin's asked me to go with him.
Go with him, then.
It'll all have changed.
The Highlands never change, only the people.
I think I'll go to the Highlands.

I don't see why they don't take her. Bridget says there's no point, she's looking for the faces she knows and they won't be there and it will confuse her more. Dad says it's too far. Last year we went to Greece, the year before to California, but the Highlands are too far. I would quite like to go, to see Grandma's heritage. Dad says her heritage is the slums of Glasgow (Bridget says not slums, for heaven's sake) and the Highlands are all romancing. Well, I'd like to investigate the romance for myself. Anyway, we walk, only round the block, and Grandma still goes on about her father and his walking and her mother saying he would exhaust them and reminding him his daughter's legs were shorter than his. But Grandma was the most like him and quickly grew to have very long legs. Her mother feared she might become a giantess. She used to make Grandma stand up in front of visitors so they could inspect her height and be awed. Another odd story. I am only five foot seven and I am taller than Grandma.

I decide to put in ten minutes in the corner shop, our ever open Indian general store. Grandma is very pleased. She loves all shops. Most of her life seems to have been spent humping shopping home, great bags of it. Mum's methodical ways are a mystery to her. Every day Grandma drove herself mad wondering what to get the men for their dinner and every day she trudged out and ended up bringing back much the same things. Potatoes, carrots, onions and mince. And tea and sugar, naturally. Pounds and pounds of sugar. Sugar for porridge, sugar for tea, sugar to make jam, sugar for puddings, sugar for cakes and sugar sometimes for just sticking fingers into and sucking. When Bridget and Dad cleaned Grandma's Glasgow rooms out they found thirty-one two-pound bags of sugar. And precious little else.

I manoeuvre Grandma down the aisle in the crammed shop. The Indian woman on the till smiles and nods. They like to see me with my Grandma, it is right and proper that I, the young one, should be looking after her, the old one. They approve. Grandma reads the prices out, scandalised, especially by the price of her beloved sugar. She cannot believe it, in the name of God, she exclaims all the time. Her voice is deep, rough, guttural. She once told me she used to worry about it. Her mother convinced her she was going to be a giantess and she convinced herself she was going to be a man. Her Glasgow accent is broad, the dialect strong. People around here find Grandma hard to understand when she's in full flow. I wish Dad had her voice but he has only the faintest trace of Scottish vowels and Bridget has none at all. Only Stuart is recognisably Scottish but then he was twelve when they moved south for those years in Newcastle.

Newcastle is where Grandma went when her husband was killed. She had no choice, Bridget says. She had no money, not even to pay the rent. She went to her sister Annie's even though she had two brothers still living in Glasgow. Bridget says neither of them offered her a home. Dad tells her to be fair, for God's sake, how could either of them have offered a woman with three young children a home when one of them only had two rooms and four kids himself and the other was in the navy and not even married or with any kind of home. Anyway, Grandma went to sister Annie's and Annie was kind and welcoming. Her husband was not. He found Grandma and children very hard to take and according to Bridget gave her 'cold charity'. Dad won't say a word on the subject even when goaded by Bridget. He only says he liked Newcastle better than Glasgow. He didn't want to go back to Glasgow but Annie died and that was that.

Grandma whispers she wants some ciggies. She hasn't any money. Up to recently she had a handbag but losing it and worrying about it caused her and all of us such distress and trouble that Bridget put it away. Grandma misses it. Since she still has hysterics about where it can be, I don't see anything is gained by not letting her have it. But I have money, not that I will need it.

I want some ciggies.
Fine. What brand?
I haven't any money.
I have. How many? Twenty? Two packets?
Five.
Packets?
Ciggies. Five will do.
They don't sell them in fives, Grandma.
In the name of God.
I'll get twenty. Which brand?
I want some ciggies.

I smile at the Indian woman and we pass the till. I have Grandma's cigarettes in my pocket and have extracted five which I roll up in silver paper and present to her. She gives me a squeeze, clutches the cigarettes tightly. She says it's getting dark. It isn't but I agree. She says she must get her washing in, the men's overalls will be dry, damned awkward things to wash. She stops at a lamppost and recites that we are very lucky to have a lamp before our door and the lamplighter will soon be here and this gets mixed up with bairns cuddling doon at night. I am so bored by the time we get in again. I switch the radio on. Grandma turns round and round like a dog chasing its tail and then faces me. She asks me where I've been all day, bloomin' cheek, she's been waiting and waiting and where is that Bridget? I say at work and Grandma snorts with emphatic derision. A fine story, she says, when she know she's gallivanting. All the same, they're all the same, all after the men. Except her.

Here we go. No songs, no poems, no anecdotes, no reminiscing now. Black sulk sets in. She trails off, closing the door behind her. I take a book out of my bag, *Bleak House*, one of Grandma's favourites and hell as a set book. Grandma has read all Dickens six times or so she boasts. Certainly she's very knowledgeable and makes lots of Dickensian catch phrases her own. I'm not going to follow her through but I listen with one ear. She's probably pulling all the towels out of the airing cupboard and throwing them around. Well, they're easily put back. Or more likely in the lavatory tearing sheets of loo paper into microscopic bits. Makes a mess but who cares. Bridget, I suppose. Bridget will say Grandma must not be allowed to do it because it's a shocking waste and Grandma herself would be upset if she realised because she hates waste. Grandma used to say all the time how she hated waste, if anyone left so much as a bit of gristle. My smart reply used to be so did I and that Grandma had wasted her life and *that* was the only sort of waste that was wicked. Grandma just used to stare and ask if the girl was mad.

After half an hour, when Grandma has not re-appeared, I go in search of her. Bridget will be back soon and I want Grandma in a good mood so that it looks as if I've been doing a good job. No Grandma in the bedroom. Oh, God. It's not unknown for her to escape and be found wandering, streets away. Bridget will give me hell. But she's in the bathroom, scattering Vim everywhere. I lead her back to the kitchen gently. Tea, a cigarette, nice harmless music on the radio. Bridget is even earlier than she hoped. She bustles in. Grandma's face breaks into a great smile. Bridget kisses her.

What I cannot decide is:

Do I think this is a touching scene?
Do I think it is nauseating?
Do I think Bridget is a heroine?
Do I think Grandma is lucky?
Do I think it is normal or sick?

Jenny

I was soundly asleep when the telephone rang but then at three in the morning most people would be. We do not have an extension in our bedroom, but I heard it ringing downstairs. I lay, listening, carefully checking the people in the house. Charlie, Adrian, Hannah – we were all safely in bed. It could be a wrong number. Or it could be Bridget. Most unlikely, but it could be Bridget. I slipped out of bed and down the stairs, mind racing. Maybe Grandma was dead. Oh, God, the relief if she were – quietly, painlessly, in the middle of the night. All problems solved, neatly. I was practising what to say, arranging the funeral, consoling Bridget, assuring her it was the best thing that could happen in view of what we were told lay ahead, doing all this in my head as I lifted the receiver. It was indeed Bridget but my mother-in-law, Grandma as she likes to be called by all, was not dead. She was very much alive but on the floor. Bridget told me to wake Charlie up and send him along; she could not get Grandma up and needed him. I said I was on my way and put the receiver down before she could argue.

Hanging behind the kitchen door was my old raincoat and in the cupboard under the stairs my wellingtons, so I had no need to go back to the bedroom and risk waking Charlie up (though I doubt if I would have done). Bridget does not understand. He needs his sleep. She is contemptuous of his need compared to hers. Is Charlie on

28

shifts, responsible for the lives of a whole ward of patients? No, he is not. Does he spend two nights a week with his mother, being wakened, sometimes every hour? No, he does not. Charlie sleeps deeply, undisturbed, every night and as far as Bridget is concerned his job does not compare with hers in its demands, this sleeping of his does not need protecting. But it does. Charlie is a broker, specialising in metals. He makes decisions involving thousands of pounds and hundreds of jobs every day of his life and is under constant pressure. Bridget has always refused to understand her brother's job – he is 'something in the city' and gets handsomely rewarded for it and he is not serving society as she is or even as Stuart is. She is disappointed in him and wishes he had become a teacher as Grandma hoped.

At least it is not cold as I slip out of the house, as silently as I slipped out of bed, and hurry along the street. All the lights are on in Grandma's flat. Bridget does not credit Charlie with any generosity in renting that flat. She sees it as guilt money, for not taking Grandma in, and it is. But Charlie did not have to rent that flat. He could have insisted on Grandma being put in a Home. He did not have to co-operate with Bridget, whatever the moral pressures. Stuart, the eldest, did nothing but then, in that respect, Bridget lets him off the hook. Policemen are not rich, not like 'something in the city'. What Bridget doesn't see is that money does not solve every-thing. True, Charlie can afford to rent the flat but he handles the maintenance too and that involves a great deal of trouble. The flat has ancient plumbing, cracks in the ceilings, all kinds of problems crop up and Charlie deals with them all. It takes time and effort and not just money, as Bridget imagines. Charlie is sick to death of that flat.

I have my own key so I had no need to ring the bell. I saw, as soon as I entered the bedroom, that Bridget was hysterical. If an old lady fell in her ward – not that Bridget is on a geriatric ward – then Bridget would be a model of calmness and have her up in no time. But now her face was contorted with anxiety and her professional expertise had deserted her. Grandma was lying on the floor, be-tween bed and wall, looking perfectly cheerful and comfortable. She was singing 'Hey, Johnny Cope' in a sort of murmur, alternating the

29

tune with the occasional whistle. What on earth was all the fuss about? Bridget had put a rug over her and a pillow beneath her head. She told me she didn't think anything was broken but the crash had been violent, she couldn't be sure until Grandma's limbs had all moved without causing her pain. I said, I suppose a little acidly, that Grandma would be bound to make a loud noise when she fell because she was so heavy and that she looked pretty comfortable to me so why not leave her until the morning. Bridget said she couldn't. Susan must not find her like this in the morning. Susan comes at nine o'clock, an hour after Bridget leaves on Tuesdays. Grandma is left in bed and Susan gets her up and gives her breakfast.

Of course Bridget is right. I felt ashamed. Susan certainly would be alarmed. And there is a deeper point which Bridget reminds me of: as long as Grandma is a cheery old dear who is just 'a bit funny', then Susan is happy to oblige, but she made it plain when we took her on that she didn't want to have charge of an invalid. I told Bridget not to panic, we had no proof that this was anything but an isolated incident. And then we set to, trying to get Grandma up. I took her shoulders and Bridget tried to straighten her legs but Grandma roared at us both ferociously. We were in such an awkward position, trapped in a very narrow gap. But the main trouble was that Grandma did not want to get up and would not co-operate one tiny bit. She told us all decent folk were in bed. She asked us if we wanted to kill her. She requested confirmation that she had never hurt a fly. We got her into a sitting position and then rested. She eyed both of us and burst out laughing and shouted, 'Look what the cat brought in.'

I ordered Bridget to go away. With her there, Grandma was never going to make any effort. The minute she had gone I closed the door and then came and stood over Grandma, quite threateningly, I suppose. I pulled the blanket off her and Grandma immediately shivered and moaned that it was cold. I agreed. I invited her to get into bed with me and got in myself and pulled the blankets up, saying aloud how cosy it was, oh how comfy Humphrey. Grandma began to struggle. She got herself in a crouching position and then clutched the side of the bed and very, very slowly (I held my breath) levered herself up. The minute she was upright I was out of her bed in a flash and had pushed her in. She closed her eyes and smiled and said, 'Night night, sleep tight,' and went straight back to sleep.

Bridget thanked me. She had listened at the door, of course. I rather despised her for not trusting me. Does she really think I would hurt her beloved mother? I told her not to worry. She apologised for telephoning at such an hour and I said she did the right thing. We sat and drank tea and I could not help it, I had to seize the opportunity and ask. 'Bridget,' I said, 'how far do we have to go before you give in?' She did not pretend not to understand. She held her mug of tea tightly, just as her mother does, and avoided my eyes, just as her mother does, and said, 'If she didn't know me. If I couldn't look after her properly. Maybe then.' Then she lit a cigarette and inhaled deeply and raised her eyebrows and made a funny face. Emotion embarrasses Bridget, as it does her mother, as it does Charlie and Stuart. The McKays do not hold with emotion, any emotion. I have never seen any of them cry. At moments of extreme grief or stress the most they ever do is go silent, quite silent.

Maybe Mr McKay was different but who knows? Certainly not Grandma. She cannot even remember her wedding day, it made so little impact. Any tales she tells about her husband are derogatory in a mild way. She relates how the children were sick one night and she was sick herself and 'he' never moved, never stirred, and them 'all hollerin' and cryin'. Then she laughs, admiringly. Or she recalls being in hospital with her varicose veins, loving the rest, and 'he' came into the ward and said she would have to get up and come home, the children needed her, and there were no clean clothes, and the Sister came up and shouted at him to have consideration for his wife. Again, Grandma always laughs at this point, uproariously, as though telling a joke she loves, and she ends, gasping, by repeating 'consideration!' She wants a united front against men when she tells these stories. It annoys her when I will not conspire to agree that all men are selfish and inconsiderate. I tell her how tender her own son is with our children when they are sick and how loving and protective when I am ill but she ignores me. If I remark, as I used to do the first hundred times I heard these stories, that her husband

31

sounds a brute, she is most indignant. 'Not at all, not at all,' she says, 'he was just a man.'

He died young anyway. Bridget was born in 1945, the year her father was killed in the war. I have to remind myself, now that Charlie and I have celebrated our Silver Wedding anniversary, that Grandma was only married thirteen years, only half the time I have been married. She has been a widow forty-three years, roughly three times as long as she was married. So is it surprising she can hardly remember her husband? Well yes, if you look at what she *can* remember. The doctor has explained it to us: the long-term memory remains after the short-term has gone. Grandma cannot remember what she had for dinner an hour ago but she can remember every detail of what she ate on the train journeys to the Highlands in the 1920s. And it makes her happy. It does not seem to worry her in the least that she cannot remember her husband's first name or the colour of his eyes or what he liked and did not like. He remains in her memory as the subject of a few unflattering anecdotes and, if she has to sum him up, she is content to say he was 'a man's man'.

Stuart can probably remember him best of all, since he was eight when his father went off to the war and twelve when he was killed, but Stuart is taciturn on that subject as on most. Stuart does not go in for memories. He is our silent, practical, solid brother, perfectly suited to being a policeman. How Grandma loves him in his uniform. Bridget in her nurse's uniform, Stuart in his policeman's, what more could a mother ask? Charlie in his suit does not impress though she admires his general smartness. Stuart does not want to discuss anything, ever, regarding all forms of discussion as 'soft'. He thinks Charlie is mad to pay for Grandma's flat and foot the bills and generally manage her affairs. He let it be known, in an uncharacteristic outburst of at least four sentences, that he thought Grandma should be in a Home, that Home should be in Glasgow and a Council Home. Grandma had paid her taxes and was entitled and that was that. Her mind had gone and nothing could be done and he was very sorry but facts were facts and could not be dodged. She was better off with her own kind. How Bridget blazed! What Grandma was entitled to, she shouted, was love and patience and kindness, the very qualities she had lavished on Stuart himself. Her mind had *not* gone, she knew her family and that was a fact they could not dodge. And she was not better off in any institution. Bridget invited Stuart to just tell her how many Old People's Homes he had been in, because she, Bridget, had been in scores and not one was good enough for a cat, never mind her mother. Stuart said he washed his hands of it all. That was five years ago and he has stuck to his resolution.

So maybe Grandma's husband was like Stuart: handsome, dependable, unimaginative and boring. Maybe she married him for the same reason Paula says she married Stuart: because he inspired confidence and pestered her. Grandma uses those words – 'He pestered me.' She used to say, when I first became her daughter-in-law and dug deep into family history, 'I couldn't get rid of him. Mind, I could have had all the men but I was never bothered. I didn't fancy them, but they never stopped pestering.' Well, if Mr McKay was like his son Stuart then nobody would be allowed to pester once married to him. Grandma was twenty-four when she married. Not excessively young, but there must have been plenty of time to pick and choose, and to be picked and chosen. 'Don't marry young,' Grandma tells Hannah all the time, followed by, 'Always keep a hundred pounds to yourself.' Hannah laughs and asks what for and Grandma says, 'So you can always run away.'

*

Charlie was furious in the morning. Not, as you might think, because I had gone instead of him but because I had gone at all and because Bridget had rung in the first place. 'If she's going to start that,' he said, 'then I've had enough.' I went through Bridget's reasons, pointing out, as she had rightly pointed out to me, that if Susan found Grandma on the floor – but Charlie cut through all that. What concerned him, he said, was the future. It was time Grandma went into some sort of Home and the sooner Bridget faced up to this the better. 'Bridget,' I said, 'will never, ever, put your mother in a Home.' Charlie said, 'If I withdraw my support and you do too, then she'll have no alternative.'

It was the truth, but hardly worth stating. He would never withdraw his support and neither would I. How could we? Bridget already bears the brunt: compared to her we do hardly anything. What do I do, after all: I bring Grandma along here for two hours three times a week; I shop for her; I do her laundry; I look after her on Sundays; I supervise the helpers. What does Charlie do: he pays the bills and looks after the flat. But Bridget, Bridget sleeps with her two nights a week and lives beside her, always on the alert. Her life is dominated by Grandma. And most of all Bridget suffers, whereas we do not. We suffer tedium and irritation and boredom. Bridget suffers real pain. She cannot bear to watch Grandma disintegrate, to see her helpless and lost, wanting only the love of her family. 'Men,' Bridget says with Grandma about Stuart and Charlie and now even Adrian, 'Men.'

*

Today I rang Dr Carruthers. It was Charlie's suggestion. Dr Carruthers is a geriatrician. He has already seen Grandma, when she first came to live here. Bridget says he is useless but grudgingly admits he is highly thought of among her colleagues. She resented him being brought in, saying there was nothing wrong with Grandma that a few weeks' loving care could not put right, but Charlie insisted. It was Charlie the neighbours had rung because only Charlie had been thoughtful enough to leave a number with them. 'She's wandering at night,' they reported, breathless with the weight of their own virtue, 'wandering up and down the street in her nightie at two in the morning. Anything could happen.' And she shouted, opened her front door and shouted pointless things like, 'Awa' wi' you all.' Her milk bottles piled up on the doorstep and newspapers were never taken from the letter box. So Bridget went up and was shocked. There was food everywhere, a trail of buttered toast across every surface and puddles of tea poured onto the carpet and cushions. Then Charlie went up and together they brought her down from Glasgow because Bridget could not bear it. It seemed to her the only solution and no amount of Charlie's reasoning could persuade her otherwise. It would never have happened, Bridget said, if she had not left home.

And that was the point. She had left home, at the ripe old age of thirty-five. She had finally made her break for freedom, a trifle late, and the guilt was awful. She had left Grandma alone and thought of herself for once and the hurt inflicted had been cruel. Not that Grandma stood in her way. There were no scenes, no recriminations, absolutely no attempts at moral blackmail. Grandma was courageous, which only made it worse. She encouraged Bridget to go. She told her to enjoy herself. She announced firmly that she was independent. Bridget, in desperation, said she did not really want to go but would be promoted. She would be a Sister, if she went south, a Sister in the children's ward of a very famous teaching hospital. She only wanted to go for the experience and then she would return. Grandma told her to go and do well for herself. Bridget's parting words were that Grandma had to promise that if she wanted Bridget to come back, then she would write and tell her so. Grandma said there was no need for that, 'Get awa' wi' you.' But she did ask. After five years of loneliness, five years in which Bridget went back to Glasgow only for three separate weeks a year, Grandma said to Bridget, 'Remember you said I had to speak up if I wanted you home?' Bridget told me she felt faint at the dreaded words and could only nod. 'Well,' Grandma said, 'your bed needs warming. You've been gone a long time.' And that was it. Bridget blustered, said if she left her job the ward would suffer, that she couldn't just walk out, it was not like an ordinary job. She would come back as soon as she could decently leave and as soon as a comparable post was vacant in Glasgow. Grandma was satisfied.

I do not know if Bridget even went through the motions of either giving notice here or applying for a post up there. I suspect she did no more than run an eye over Appointments Vacant in the *Nursing Times*. But she marks that moment when Grandma asked her to come back as the beginning of her mother's decline. If she had gone home, she is convinced things would have been different. That is why Charlie called in Dr Carruthers. He wanted to know if Grandma was ill or merely depressed. Bridget, with all her medical knowledge (though she had never nursed the elderly since she finished training) could not tell us. She thought Grandma might have had 'a little stroke' but there was no evidence of this. Grandma's own doctor told Charlie it was unlikely. Dr Carruthers agreed. He came and spent an hour with Grandma on his own and then he wrote a report.

Bridget said she could have written it herself, it was so obvious, but we found it helpful. Grandma, the report said, was suffering from moderate senile dementia. She knew her name, her age, the names of her children and grandchildren, and where she was living. She could feed herself, toilet herself and walk unaided. But her sense of time had gone. She did not know the date or the year or who was Prime Minister or Queen. She did not know whether she had eaten today or not. She had no sense of direction. The prognosis was carefully worded: with the family support she was getting it was perfectly possible that the dementia might get no worse for several years. Charlie rang up Dr Carruthers to ask the crucial questions: was it inevitable that eventually it would get worse? Yes. And how long did the process usually take? Five years. What happened after that? Death.

The first thing Dr Carruthers asked me today when I finally got through to him was how long it was since he had seen my mother-in-law. It was four years. 'She's done well then,' he said. I agreed but I said we felt there was a change, and we would like her re-assessed. We made an appointment. I checked the rota first – oh yes, we have a rota, it is essential – to make sure Bridget would not be about. Bridget would know what we were up to. And we were, because then I rang the only Home I had ever heard spoken of with any respect. I asked if I could look round with Charlie. It was extraordinary how, just by making two appointments, I felt I had achieved something. For too long we had bowed to Bridget's passionate conviction that her mother could never go into a Home. We had never even looked at one. We accepted her word, her word which was all the more impressive because she was a nurse, that all Homes were appalling. We needed to see for ourselves. I feel pleased that I am acting and not just thinking. But I also feel guilty, for going behind Bridget's back, and apprehensive. Suppose Dr Carruthers confirms that Grandma is much worse and likely to deteriorate rapidly? Suppose we find that this Home I have made an appointment to visit is a good place? What then? What will Bridget say? What dreadful quarrels are we moving towards? What right have we to do what we are doing?

Hannah

Must be something going on, both of them grim-faced, whispers every five minutes, mysterious phone calls, Mum jumpy. Whatever it is, it passes over Grandma, as most things do. She looked sweet when I came in today, sitting at the kitchen table with a pile of potatoes to peel and a bowl of water to wash them in. She loves scraping potatoes. She has such strong wrists and she holds each potato so surely, almost caressing it. She doesn't look so sweet now. The idea is supposed to be that she scrapes the potato, puts the scrapings on one side onto a piece of paper, dips the scraped potato in the water and then pops it into the waiting pan. No chance. I eat my doughnut and drink my hot chocolate and watch. The potato is scraped all right but then the scrapings are put into the pan and the knife in the water. 'Where's my bloomin' knife?' Grandma asks. 'Who's pinched my knife?' I take it out of the water and hand it to her when I've dried it. She starts to eat the potato and asks Mum if she has any sugar. Mum puts a bowl of sugar in front of her and Grandma dips the potato into it and sucks it and beams. I say to Mum I've got masses of homework and such a headache.

> I never had headaches at your age –
> What a daft thing to say.
> Hannah!

37

How can she possibly make a statement like that?
Just ignore her.
It gets hard.
I never had headaches at your age.

Well, lucky old you, I say to her but if you didn't have headaches, which I do not believe, then you must have had bloody awful toothache. Grandma says language as Mum says Hannah. I carry on, annoyed, fed up with humouring Grandma. Your teeth must have been rotten from the beginning, I tell her, with all that disgusting sugar you ram into yourself, ugh. Grandma mimics me, thrusts her face forward and repeats ugh, ugh and then asks who stole my scone. I fidget with fury.

Have you got a flea?
No I have not. More likely you have.
Hannah!
Well, she's always scratching.
She can't help it.
She can't help anything according to you.
Have you got a flea?

Then we have the saga, about her mother and how she had a phobia about fleas and would make you take your clothes off if you scratched so that she could minutely inspect you. I remember when we went to the Highlands etc. etc. I mimic her this time, saying I remember, I remember. It is a mistake.

I remember, I remember the house where I was born.
Oh god, not that crappy poem.
It's a lovely poem.
It's rubbish.
Mr Fairfax taught it to us.
What a pity he couldn't have taught you a good poem.
I remember, I remember the house where I was born.

She does, just. Can't remember where my Dad was born but she remembers the rooms in Glasgow where she lived till she was twenty. It sounds hell. Two rooms and one kitchen, each with a bed in an alcove, and seven of them, three boys and two girls and their parents, no bathroom or inside lavatory. She speaks of these Buildings lyrically. Dad took us once, just to look at the outside. Great tall dirty buildings, no gardens, no greenery, narrow streets and at the back the wash houses and lavatories, all communal then, not used now, and over everything the shadow of the bing, the slag heap, where Grandma says they 'had good times' playing. Great. But why on earth I want to attack her memories I can't imagine. Let her keep them, paint them, embroider them, wrap them in glittering paper, why should I care.

Adrian slams in. He kisses Grandma. She beams up at him.

> Have you worked hard?
> I'm worn out, Grandma, a twelve-hour shift.
> Of sitting on your arse.
> Hannah!
> Somebody has to bring home the bacon.
> I can't see it will ever be you, you wimp.
> Have you worked hard?

Grandma tells Mum to give the man his dinner, he deserves it. Adrian sits down while the kettle boils and chews some of Grandma's raw potato. She looks at him admiringly. Adrian looks how Grandma thinks real men should look. Grandma is appallingly sexist. Men should be tall, men should be broad, men should be strong. If I ask her why, she says feeble things like 'for working'. It's no good asking what if a man is a hairdresser or a dress designer or a vicar, what if his work needs no physical strength? Grandma just says it will come in useful all the same. Adrian meets with her entire approval. He looks disgusting but Grandma adores him. Adrian is tall, Adrian is broad, Adrian is strong. He doesn't look like Dad, who is rather slight and weedy, but like his dear Uncle Stuart. Adrian looks tough. He isn't, he is a rotten coward in my opinion, but he looks tough. It makes me feel ill just to look at him – all brawn and, however brilliant his exam results, virtually no brain.

Adrian slobbily asks Grandma if she would like a cup of tea. I point out that there are two cups of cold tea untouched in front of her. Grandma glares at me and says she was just going to drink it and yes she would like some fresh. Adrian makes it with the maximum fuss. Then he says he had better go and rest before the next shift. Grandma says he's done well and he's a fine worker and to get his head down at once and she'll wake him for his dinner. Very slowly, when he's gone, she gets up and lifts the pan of water into which she has mistakenly put the potato scrapings. She carries it carefully to the sink while Mum and I watch. Slowly she puts it down, accurately, on the draining board and then starts searching. Neither of us ask what she is looking for. We know she wouldn't be able to tell us. It becomes quite fascinating watching as drawer after drawer is opened, cupboard after cupboard inspected. She is in a trance. Probably she's already forgotten what she was looking for, but no. She locates a sieve. That's it. Back she goes to the sink and strains the potato scrapings through the sieve then lifts the pan onto the cooker. She sighs with contentment and tells us the soup will not be long, it'll be ready when the men come in.

She is quite exhausted. She staggers and both Mum and I rush. I am ashamed; I wish I had not snapped at her. I take her next door and settle her on the sofa and stay with her. She murmurs 'the bairnies cuddle doon at nicht' and goes to sleep. But only for five minutes. She complains her back aches. I get a hot water bottle and wedge it against her shoulders where it pains her most.

> All women have bad backs.
> No, they don't. It's all that carrying you did.
> The bairns have to be carried, the shopping has to be carried.
> You should have looked after yourself.
> Ours not to wonder why, ours but to do or die.
> Oh Grandma!
> All women have bad backs.

I must not attack her again. I pick up a book. Grandma sighs and yawns and says it is very quiet, are they all in their beds, there aren't many people here tonight, where have they all gone to? Who, I ask. Them, she says. Who's them, I insist. The men. Which men? The men. Then she says we are best without them anyway.

It is a silly thing to say but I am always doing it, always trying to force Grandma into *thinking*. Nobody else does. They all say to

40

humour her, ignore her, go along with her but nobody ever says make her think. I've had it explained, this senile dementia, and I've looked it up myself and I understand it but it still seems to me that, just as exercise helps the body, whatever condition it's in, then it must help the mind. It must, surely. So I often try to exercise what is left of Grandma's mind. I ask her what she had for lunch. She says nobody gave her any. I say they did, what was it. Mince? She guesses. I say I have no idea. She states it was mince, confidently. I ask what kind of mince was it. She says it was done with carrots and onions and a few wee potatoes. She gets quite animated, describing the flavour the mince had, searching for the right words. It may all be made up but she has enjoyed describing the mince. I comment that of course she made mince dishes a lot and she agrees she did and I ask why and she says it was nourishing and cheap. I say how hard it must have been, with no money, feeding her family. She sits bolt upright suddenly, indignant.

> I had plenty of money.
> Oh, Grandma, you did not.
> I always paid my bills.
> I know you did but —
> And we had food in our bellies and a fire.
> I know but —
> I had plenty of money.

Amazing. She won't have it that she scraped and saved and performed economic miracles with the little she had. It is no good being sarcastic and saying, well, of course you had so much money you could buy a mansion and have a Rolls in the garage and how many weeks a year did you say you went to Monte Carlo for? She just repeats 'plenty of money' over and over.

I like Grandma whistling. She has her hands behind her head now and, for her, looks comfortable, given that she is the most awkward-looking person in the world. She sits, usually, on the corners of chairs and then is surprised when they tip over. Even in bed she screws her body into odd shapes, 'all to one side like Gourock' as she puts it herself. But now she is quite relaxed, lying on the sofa, pillow at her back, hot water bottle behind her shoulders, whistling 'Charlie Is My Darling'. It soon tails off into aimless notes. Sometimes no sound comes out, the lips remain pursed, and then she resumes. Where she lies she is facing the window looking out into the street. All she sees is the houses across it and a little sky above. She stops whistling to comment, 'Not many there tonight,' and then carries on until the next thought occurs to her and she says, 'I don't think I'll go to church tonight, I've a bad back.'

She's Scottish Presbyterian, as you'd expect. It's an awful religion. Grandma used to take me when I was little and I was terrified – all bleak and dour and colourless. If I want to annoy Grandma, I say so. I say if I was religious, I'd be a Roman Catholic and have some beauty and glamour. I don't know about Grandma and church anyway. She is fond of telling me she always went to church, always. If I ask her why she just looks astonished and clicks her tongue in exasperation and tells me not to be silly. Trying to get Grandma to talk about religion is like trying to get her to talk about love or, worse still, sex. It is indecent, it is not a suitable topic of conversation, it does not *need* talking about. I don't attempt it this afternoon. I upset her enough earlier but that is one of the few advantages of Grandma's dementia, she forgets bad things at once as well as good things. Now, I just want her to be comfortable and to whistle.

Sometimes, in moods like this, I can catch her eye and know she is *sane*. Everything has to be right, as it is now. She is comfortable, the room is quiet, the sun is filtered through the leaves of the tree outside and splits into fragments of light which mesmerise Grandma. Mum is in the background, moving about in the kitchen. There are delicious smells as something cooks in the oven. And I am sitting in front of Grandma so she can see me and know she is not alone. I have my feet up too. I pretend to be reading a book. And I look up and stare at Grandma and for a moment she catches my eye and I hold my breath. It is there: sanity. If I move, if I speak, if there is an unexpected noise it will go. What can I do with it? It is so precious. I want to scream for Mum to come quickly and look, *look*. She is *there*, she really is, she knows, she communicates, what shall I do? I smile. Grandma raises her eyebrows. Then Mum drops something, there is a bang, Grandma blinks and she has gone.

The whistling has stopped. Furtively, I watch Grandma from

behind my book. She has swung her legs down and is inching herself towards the edge of the sofa. My instinct is to jump up and help her. My experience tells me not to. She knows, at this moment, what she wants to do and it is better to let her get on with it. She is almost on her feet, finally makes it. She stoops, lifts up the shawl that has covered her and begins to fold it. She loves folding. Mum gives her the washing to fold and she does it beautifully. She folds and folds and when the shawl is in the smallest possible square she gives it a triumphant pat. Then she drops it. She says she must be off, the men will be in for their tea etc. She says her mother will be looking for her. I know not to remind her that her mother died thirty years ago. She wouldn't believe me anyway, she'd ask me if I had anything else ridiculous to say while my mouth was warm.

Now she is walking round the room, lifting objects up and examining them. She is searching for a cigarette or as a poor substitute a mint imperial. She will find the mints in due course. She is near now, slowly opening the desk drawer, peering, fingering, closing it. Next stop and she's there. Ah. Beside the flower jug, in the wooden box Dad brought back from Egypt. She prises open the lid and sees the mints. She pauses, looks round. I read my book studiously. Gently she takes the packet of mints out, the cellophane making a crinkling noise which makes her freeze for a minute, and slips it into her cardigan pocket. She continues round the room and ends up where she started. She asks me if I am coming for a wee walk. I say no, and that Bridget will be here soon. Grandma asks where the devil Bridget is anyway.

> I haven't seen that Bridget for ages, the hussy.
> She spent the night with you, Grandma.
> She did not, the nonsense.
> She lives in the same house as you.
> Listen to the child.
> Bridget sees you every day.
> I haven't seen that Bridget for ages, the hussy.

She shuffles off, finds the door, goes through it. There is a long silence. She will be looking in every room, maybe even transferring the mints to the toe of a wellington. There is no need to do anything.

Mum comes through, asks where she is. I say wandering. Mum sits down and sighs. I ask what's going on, what's the sighing for and the funny atmosphere. She tells me about Grandma falling in the night and how she thinks we should be getting prepared. For what? For Grandma going into a Home, Mum says. I laugh. It's such a waste of energy. About twice a year we go through this one and nothing ever happens. Nor should it. I agree with Bridget. For heaven's sake, Grandma's happy in her own way. All this 'strain' Mum and Dad go on about is absurd. What strain? I can't see it. It isn't as if she's living with us. If there's any talk of strain, it should be from Bridget and there never is. Mum is a kind person but she seems to have a block on this one. Grandma isn't an intolerable burden as far as I can see, yet Mum acts as if she is. It disgusts me.

I suppose it shows. Mum colours. She says she hopes I know how fond she is of Grandma. I say I do (do I?). But we have to think of the future and of Bridget's future. Bridget's future? Yes. If Grandma does not go into a Home while she is reasonably fit, then she won't get into one when she becomes impossible to look after. What is this, I ask, what are we talking about? Schools? Mum says it is like schools. You have to get your name down. Oh, excuse me, I say. What is this, are we talking about private schools, private homes? I'm sorry but I thought we were proud of having no truck with private education, private health. This, Mum says, is different. The State provision for old people like Grandma is limited. This is getting too deep for me, I say sarcastically, and I don't think I want to talk about it. Who does, Mum asks, and looks miserable.

Grandma comes in, her skirt pulled up round her waist after a clearly successful visit to the loo. She looks lost, she is lost. Mum springs up, adjusts Grandma's skirt, suggests a nice cup of tea. She leads her into the kitchen. Nobody could accuse Mum of not being tender with Grandma, of not treating her, at all times, with immense consideration, of not showing she cares. But watch Bridget with Grandma and any fool can see the difference. Bridget is rude, she is cheeky, she tells Grandma off sharply on occasion, but she is *natural*. Mum is not. Her attentions stink of effort. There is nothing effortless about her solicitude. She is thinking that Grandma would enjoy it, appreciate it, love it if she did x, y and z. So she does it. And

Grandma does enjoy, appreciate and love this evidence of being valued. But she also distrusts it. It is too obvious. Instinctively, Grandma can see through it. No matter if Mum bakes her favourite gingerbread, trails to a special shop for the only kind of mint imperial she likes, knits a cardigan in violent violet, Grandma's favourite colour – it is Bridget, who never bakes, tries not to shop and can't knit, it is Bridget who gets the smiles.

She gets them now. In she comes, still in her uniform, all bustle and noise. Grandma's face is radiant. She says hello, pet, are they good to you, and Bridget says no, they damn well aren't . . . Mum seems to shrink, become invisible. Bridget is having hysterics over something Grandma said to her last night. She wrinkles her nose and throws her head back and laughs as she tries to repeat this gem. Mum smiles politely, unable to see the joke. I'm not sure I can see what's so funny myself but it doesn't really matter. It's nice to think Bridget and Grandma can have such good times. I wish we did, I mean I wish we had that particular kind of good time, that we had the fun Bridget sometimes has. Bridget often says she'd rather have an evening with her mother, in the right mood, mind you, than with anyone else in the world. Bridget is still telling us what terrific form Grandma was in, as though she was a race-horse. This makes me smile, thinking of Grandma as a horse but a big lumbering cart-horse not a race-horse and that makes Bridget think I am appreciating the jokes she's relating, the ones Grandma made. Mum still isn't smiling. Bridget finishes the saga and asks Mum doesn't she find it funny. Mum shrugs. Bridget flicks ash and tosses her head and says well she thought it hilarious.

Then they start talking in the way I hate. Bridget, lighting her fag, asks how 'she' has been and Mum says 'fine', 'she' has been quite cheerful this afternoon and so they go on, talking about Grandma as though she was an inanimate object. It is outrageous. I have told them both. But still they do it, every day that Bridget collects Grandma. They do not attempt to include Grandma in their chat, they talk about her and over her, discussing what she's eaten and how many times she's been to the loo as though she was a baby. It is Bridget who insists Grandma is perfectly normal and yet there she is, treating her like an idiot. Who can blame Grandma for getting querulous and in the end shouting for a ciggie? In the end, Bridget gets up and I fetch Grandma's coat and off they go. Mum wishes Bridget good luck tonight but Bridget says she has swopped with Mildred: she needs tonight off. Mum looks at her significantly. Bridget smiles and says no, nothing special, only going out for a meal. With? Mum asks. Yes, Bridget says. Then have a good time, Mum says with, it seems to me, great emphasis.

Bridget's personal life is shrouded in mystery. I don't understand it. Surely, in this day and age, no one thinks it necessary to conceal the fact that Bridget is having an affair? It's crazy. Yet, when I ask, I get shrugs and am told it is Bridget's business, ask Bridget. But I somehow can't. It embarrasses me, it never comes up naturally. How *can* I be so crass as to ask my aunt if she has a boyfriend? Why doesn't it just emerge? If she has, why is he not part of our life? Why have I never seen her with a man or found a man in her flat? Men are sometimes referred to, it is true, but always to do with work. None of them are ever produced. Bridget is forty-three and unmarried. She always seems perfectly cheerful about this, never bewailing her lot or going misty-eyed over children. Though I do remember that when Paula had Alistair, and Bridget was holding him and I said to her, being young and thoughtless, would she like her own baby, Bridget did look odd before saying she had plenty of babies at work and all the cuddles she could use.

What I wonder is:

Did Bridget not get married because of Grandma?

*

This time, it's me that hears the telephone. Ringing and ringing, nobody moving. I get up, go downstairs. Mum's door is closed. Mum likes it open, Dad likes it closed. I lift the receiver. A lot of panting. Oops, I think, about to replace it, obscene phone call, but then Mildred speaks, the awful Mildred. She says Grandma is on the floor and she can't lift her and the doctor said to her only last week, Miss Bronson he said, Miss Bronson you must not lift so much as an iron with your back – I break in. I'll be right there, I say. She tells me no, to wake my Dad, a young girl like me should not be out in the street in the dead of night or anything might happen and she will not accept the responsibility which she has been too quick to do all her life, accept responsibility that is, such as for Grandma, which many people would not, and she is going to have to re-think that, indeed she is – What an old bat she is. I scribble a note, just in case Mum hears me go out and take Grandma's key from the hook behind the door. It has a heavy brass tag on it saying 10 Downing St. In the days when Grandma was at liberty in charge of a handbag she was always losing her key so Dad took the real address and name off it.

Mildred is in a state of righteous indignation. She is more concerned about what she has 'been through', as she puts it, than anything that has happened to Grandma. She looks terrifying in a dressing gown of lurid plaids and with her hair concealed under a thick black net. She tells me at once that Miss McKay is *apparently*, apparently (sniff), not in. Or not answering. She has knocked on Miss McKay's door, because that was the understanding when she assumed responsibility for Grandma at night, it was clearly stated by Miss McKay that she would be just across the hall in case of emergency. This was an emergency, and was Miss McKay across the hall? Well, if she was, she had locked herself in and was not letting on. When I could get a word in, I said maybe Bridget was on night duty, she worked so hard at the – No, Mildred flashed back, and flourished a rota pointing out that on Wednesdays Miss McKay was off. I had not yet got to Grandma. I said to Mildred that I was here if my aunt wasn't and that I had come at once and where was my Grandmother. Mildred stalks ahead. Grandma is on the bath-room floor, curled up. At least Mildred has covered her with a blanket. Grandma is snoring. I smile. Mildred is livid, tells me that it is no laughing matter, young lady, that it is three in the morning and some people need their sleep and are not paid for this sort of thing. I say it seems a shame to waken Grandma. The bathroom is warm. Can't we just leave her? Mildred is appalled. *Leave* her? On the *floor*? Where do I get such ideas from. So we waken the poor old soul. Mildred is all for brute force, one of us either side and a good old yank, but I have learned from Mum. 'Time to get up,' I whisper, and, 'the men will be late for their work,' and, 'it's seven o'clock and the porridge not made.' Slowly, grumbling and groaning and complaining about bloomin' men, Grandma heaves herself up with the minimum of effort. We walk her through to the bedroom and tuck her up. It was easy, really. Dealing with Mildred is much worse. I know I must apologise, I must grovel and be smarmy and praise Mildred's competence and grossly exaggerate what she has gone through and thank her very, very, very, very much. I know helpers are hard to find and that, whatever else she is, Mildred Bronson is utterly reliable and would be almost impossible to replace especially at short notice.

On the way back down the road I meet Mum, running. She screeches to a halt and grabs me, says I should have woken her, that I shouldn't have gone, and had Grandma fallen? I say, yes, and tell her what happened, minimising Mildred's indignation. We walk back into the house together. Mum hasn't asked where Bridget was. I go straight back to bed. It is hard to get to sleep. I can foresee the next day's discussions.

> If Grandma is going to fall every night then Mildred will leave.
> If Mildred leaves somebody else must be found.
> If someone else is found they must be told the truth.
> If they are told the truth they may not want to do it.
> I begin to feel like Mum.

★

Mildred has given notice. In writing. Full of 'owing to' this and that and 'unforeseen circumstances'. Unequivocal. Dad said he would offer more money to cover what Mildred referred to as 'night disturbance prejudicial to the health'. He did. She took the greatest pleasure in turning down the extra £10 a night. She told Dad that an agency would not consider charging less than £50 a night.

Bridget is furious, livid. She sits in our kitchen raging. I come in from school, make myself some tea, shrink into a corner to shelter from the blast. 'Bloody damned cheek,' Bridget says to Mum, smoking manically. 'Prejudicial to the health! My God! Let her spend one night on my ward and see about her health. What a fuss, what a silly fuss, making a drama out of nothing.' Mum says nothing, she knows better. No point in arguing with Bridget, no point in being fair and urging her to consider Mildred's position: she is old herself and only took the job on to keep Grandma company, not as her nurse. Gradually, Bridget winds down. Mum says she has put notices on all the local newsagents' boards and she is sure we will get plenty of replies because we've offered £40 a night. Bridget winces. 'If Mum knew that she'd have a fit,' she says. Mum shrugs, says that is the going rate, that Bridget mustn't forget 6 p.m. to 8 a.m. is a long time not counting the night disturbance. Bridget sighs. She says she'd do it herself if only she wasn't on night shifts sometimes. Nobody says anything. Mum is not going to say she will do it. Dad has said she mustn't. He has talked about forcing Bridget's hand. I think, looking at my aunt, that I wouldn't like to force her hand. Bridget is tough, Bridget is strong, Bridget is a match for anyone. She exposes our hypocrisies, our faint-heartedness, our downright lies.

At least Grandma's not here. It is one of Susan's days. We all like Susan. Susan's a bit younger than Mum but looks older. She's stupid and lazy but she likes Grandma and Grandma likes her mainly because she's black and has a baby. Susan thinks Grandma's sweet. She tumbles chaotically into Grandma's flat each day, always smiling, whatever her tale of woe. She sits and gossips and her baby crawls round messing everything up and delighting Grandma. Who cares if sometimes Susan brings two, even three babies, and that it is obvious she is being paid, by us, as a babyminder? Who cares if she doesn't do the light housework she's supposed to do? Who cares that she feeds Grandma toast, jam and tea and precious little else? But on the other hand we do have to care that Susan is as unreliable as the awful Mildred is reliable. Susan is a slattern. She's as careless as Mildred is precise. She arrives late, often, and this matters because Grandma is on her own. Mum has tried to get Susan to see the seriousness of her unpunctuality but she always makes such exotic excuses for it that Mum dries up. Susan's whole life is a soap opera and Mum is outflanked from the start. As Susan says, she always does get there in the end (and implies that it's over dead bodies half the time).

Unfortunately, just as I'm finishing my tea and Bridget has quietened down to a sad, resigned state, Stuart arrives. I'm the one who opens the door to him. It's his day off, so he is not in uniform. I think, on balance, I prefer him in it. He wears such terrible clothes.

Grandma says he is always smart, that both her sons are smart. It's a kind of miracle to her that this is true. But, whereas Dad's smartness is inoffensive and a joke and only for work, Stuart's is a weapon. His stiff, shining white collars and knife-creased pressed trousers and brushed blazers with brass buttons – they are all designed to overwhelm his opponent. Stuart stands there, mountainously smart, cutting smart, and I almost jump clear. He comes into the kitchen, fills it, nods at Bridget, nods at Mum, and plonks himself down, trousers hitched at the knees as he sits. He asks how things are with everybody.

Bridget glares, Mum speaks. She tells Stuart there's a little bit of a crisis at the moment. She outlines it. Stuart shakes his head and says he told us so, and he has washed his hands of it. Several times. Mum tells him we will find someone else and mentions the advertisement. Stuart asks how much. Mum tells him, he winces, hides his eyes with his beefy hand, and says anybody will be able to spot we are mugs, we'll be taken for a ride, to the cleaners and several other clichés. It is, says Stuart, criminal. That is what it is as well as pouring good money down the sink and his mother in her right mind would turn in her grave. Bridget says Mum is not in her grave, that is the point. We are trying to keep her out of it. Her tone is acid, just on the edge of open contempt. Stuart is caught. I see he hasn't the courage to say we should not keep his mother from her grave, that nice cosy little grave where surely she will be so terribly comfortable, but he's reluctant to let his little sister score a victory, especially a moral one. So he says he stands corrected, that it was only a manner of speaking and Bridget knows it. Mum breaks in. She says there is no other way, it is no good moaning about the money, that we are lucky to have it. Bridget says if it wasn't for Charlie's money she doesn't know what we would do. We would all have to take turns with Grandma and how would Stuart like that, how would Paula like it?

But Stuart is not upset by this implied criticism of his wife or by the deeper attack on himself. That's the only thing I like about Stuart: he makes no excuses, sees no reason why he should. He knows he is not cruel. He doesn't hate his mother, he doesn't wish her to be unhappy, but he thinks, as he constantly repeats, that she has 'had her day' and should be 'packed off'. Stuart's heart doesn't break when he looks at Grandma, he doesn't melt as Bridget does. He sees everything in practical terms. There are no confusions. And, as for Paula, he always says don't bring Paula into this and that it's not her pigeon. Bridget usually replies smartly that no it's not her pigeon it's her mother-in-law: Grandma is Paula's mother-in-law like she is Jenny's mother-in-law. That, says Stuart, is Jenny's business. Today, Stuart simply says that as Bridget well knows he wouldn't take any turns and he hasn't come to go over old ground again. He has come, it appears, to ask Mum a favour. He wants to take Paula to a conference in Birmingham. There is a police conference and she can come along. Will Mum have Alistair and Jamie? Mum says of course. Bridget asks what the hell Paula wants to go to Birmingham for? Stuart gets up, thanks Mum, Bridget asks if he is going along to see Grandma. Stuart says no, she doesn't know who he is so what's the point. Bridget says she would know who he was, as she knew who Charlie was still, if he visited her often and regularly. Stuart says he doubts it but that she can have her own way if she wishes, he's not bothered. Then he leaves.

Pig, Bridget says, pig, he was always a pig, he is in the right job. Mum says, 'Bridget!' Bridget groans, rubs her forehead wearily, asks, 'What is the *matter* with him?' Then, when she has lit another cigarette, she says, 'Of course, it's Paula.' Mum leaps in, says it's wrong to blame Paula, that Stuart is fifty times the stronger of the two and Paula has no influence whatsoever over him. Bridget says 'precisely' and that she should have, that men have to be brought to understand almost everything where feelings are concerned, that Charlie only does what he does and acts as he acts towards Grandma because of Mum. Mum denies this vehemently. She asks how can Bridget equate Charlie with Stuart. Bridget says she doesn't but that still she doesn't believe Charlie would be as supportive without Mum's influence. I think about chipping in because of course Bridget is right, Mum is forever tutoring Dad who is indeed not like his big brother but on the other hand not the most naturally imaginative or sensitive of souls. But I keep quiet. Mum can handle this herself, which she does. She points out how like Grandma Charlie is – kind, benign but, like Grandma, oh yes like her, unemotional and a blocker-out of anything nasty. All Mum does,

51

she says, is unblock him emotionally and he does the rest himself. Bridget, determined, as on so many occasions, to have the last word says, defiantly, that Stuart has nothing to unblock and Paula would need to give him a transplant. Mum says she is defeating her own argument.

I leave them in the kitchen, tired. All that energy going into these arguments, backwards and forwards. I know they have to do it, the problem is not invented, but why do they have to do it all the time? They make Grandma sound like a great big stone they are all carrying on their backs. I can't stand it. She is only a poor, nice, harmless old woman and yet on and on they go. Surely it doesn't have to be like this. In other countries, other societies, old women just sit in the doorway, don't they, watching the world go by, a bother to no one. Grandmas just muck in. Nobody puts them in flats on their own and spends a fortune having them looked after. Very well, I say to myself, kindly answer these questions:

> Do you think Grandma should be living here, in your family?
> Yes.
> Would you like her to be living here?
> No.
> Well, then, smart-ass.

*

The phone never stops.

> 'Ello.
> Yes?
> 'Ello, is job please, I do it.
> What? What's your name?
> Is for job, I do it, the forty pounds, I want.
> Can I have your name and address?
> I come now?
> Can I have your name and address?

What do they think they are doing, these people? Nobody seems to give their name, it is no use Mum saying I must write that down first then their number and address. I don't have conversations with

52

them. The pips go in a second and they haven't got telephone numbers and I don't know what to say. I only seem to get the foreign ones and how could we let someone look after Grandma if her English is so poor she can't even handle a phone call?

Mum has a list. It's depressing. Fourteen calls in a day and most of them hopeless. Girls of fourteen, women of eighty, all dying to sleep the night with Grandma and pocket forty smackers. No experience, not the slightest idea of what the job entails. 'We're looking for someone motherly and kind,' I hear Mum say. Everyone, but everyone, is both kind and motherly. They know they are because everyone has always told them. 'But what about your husband?' I hear Mum ask when, hurrah, someone is the right age and respectably married and a mother too. 'And what about the children?' Oh, the husbands will not mind, four nights is nothing (and four times forty in cash a very great deal) and as for the children, the husbands will be there and the children never wake and really it is ideal. Mum turns against married women. She and Bridget decide they want an unmarried woman of between forty and fifty. A divorcee is acceptable and a widow perfect. Grown-up children excellent but anything under eighteen not. Neither of them wants anyone who has a full-time job but part-time is all right with Mum though not Bridget. Bridget wants Grandma to be any applicant's sole concern. Mum says she is being a trifle ambitious. The list of fourteen is whittled down to four:

Mrs Monro (47, divorced, no children, works three half days cleaning, *loves* old people)

Cathy Gibson (40, divorced, one son of twenty, afternoon job as dental receptionist, *loves* old people)

Mrs Callaghan (52, widow, no job, three children all grown up and not living with her, *loves* old people, especially those who wake at night because she is an insomniac)

Mrs O'Malley (60, Irish, married but no children, husband night watchman, loves old ladies because they remind her of her mother).

Mum says I can stay for the interviews if I like but I am to keep quiet. She says it will actually be helpful having my opinion and

Bridget agrees. Mrs Monro is due at 4 p.m. By 4.15 she has not turned up. A bad start. Bridget is depressed already. But Cathy Gibson arrives early, at 4.25 for 4.30, and that is a good sign. Not much else is. Cathy Gibson never stops talking. Neither Mum nor Bridget gets any of their cunning questions in. She is quite bright, well-dressed and, as Bridget says afterwards, too good for the job. She can only be after the money. She asked not a single question about Grandma, nothing. All she did was boast. She left as Mrs Callaghan arrived. Mrs Callaghan is promising but is she fit enough? She is very fat and out of breath and generally exhausted-looking. But she has a nice smile and seems gentle and does ask about Grandma and tells us she used to work in an old people's Home, one Bridget has heard of. She seems to understand about dementia and volunteers bits of information which show she takes an interest. Mum asks her if she thinks she could lift Grandma. Mrs Callaghan looks hesitant, says it would probably take her a little time but she thinks so. She is used to lifting. As soon as she has gone Bridget says it would be the blind leading the blind. Mum sighs. Mrs O'Malley is a fraction late but apologises, says she got the wrong number. She doesn't look sixty. She is tall, strong-looking, definitely strong-looking enough to lift Grandma, very forthright, a bit clipped in fact, shades of dear Mildred here. Turns out she was a nurse so she and Bridget chat. She, too, knows about dementia and makes sympathetic noises. Mum asks her why she wants the job. Mrs O'Malley looks straight at her as she says she will not deny she needs the money. Her husband, the night watchman, does not earn much and she has failed to get any job she goes for because she is too old. Nursing agencies do not want people over sixty and anyway she is not up to it any more. Four nights would be perfect, it would be a godsend. Her own mother lived with her until she died, God rest her soul, five years ago. She still misses her, God bless her.

After she has gone, with Mum saying she will let her know tomorrow, Bridget is doubtful, to Mum's astonishment. Mum says what more does Bridget want? Mrs O'Malley is ideal, much better than Mildred ever was. Bridget says she thinks Mrs O'Malley looks hard. She would not feel easy leaving Grandma with her. She has met those sort of nurses before – martinets, everything done by the clock. Bridget, Mum says, we cannot pick and choose. Mildred leaves on Monday. What are we going to do if we don't take Mrs O'Malley? Bridget shrugs. She says she could take time off if necessary until someone better turns up. Mum asks where they are going to turn up from. Bridget doesn't know but says she is not leaving her mother just with anyone. Mum is silent, but clearly angry. I say how about letting Grandma meet Mrs O'Malley, here, arranging for Mrs O'Malley to call round when Grandma is here. Then we could see how she handled it. Bridget beams, Mum beams, good idea, Hannah. Fortunately, Mrs O'Malley is the only one of the four on the telephone. Mum rings her, the appointment is made, same time tomorrow when Grandma will be with us.

*

Grandma looks so sweet. Bridget washed her hair last night, before Mildred arrived, and it looks startlingly white and beautiful. She is wearing her blue dress, the one Mum bought her for Christmas, the one that she feels important in. She preens herself a little, smoothing down the fabric with admiring, tentative hands. Her thick old nails gleam with bright pink polish. I don't like Bridget plastering Grandma's nails with polish: it's tacky, yucky. But Grandma likes it. Every now and again she spreads her fingers out and puts them, fan-like, across her cheek and says skittishly, 'Anyone seen my milkman?' Then she laughs and laughs and says that's what the young housewives used to do. No point in either trying to sort that one out or contesting it.

So Grandma, I swear, knows something is up. She can smell it in the air, feel it in the atmosphere all around her. She is expectant without knowing why. We are all tense, Bridget, Mum and I. We jump when the doorbell goes, jump so obviously that Grandma looks scandalised and says 'in the name of God'. Mum goes. She brings Mrs O'Malley in. This could be worse than a Foreign Office test. It's been agreed that we will let the candidate make all the running. Bridget will say this is my mother, Mrs McKay, and Mum will offer her tea and then she's on her own. Bridget says her bit, Mum offers tea, Mrs O'Malley declines.

No tea? No tea? Dear me, what's the matter with you?

I've just had tea, Mrs McKay, thank you.

Well, have some more.

One cup's enough, thank you.

What a funny woman, one cup's enough.

You're fond of tea yourself, Mrs McKay?

Everyone's fond of tea that knows what's good for them.

That's true.

How's your mother?

I beg your pardon, Mrs McKay?

How's your mother? I haven't seen her lately.

She's – er – well, she's passed on.

Get away! You never know the minute. And I was only
   speaking to her yesterday.

That's a nice dress you're wearing.

Thank you. I bought it last week, terrible price.

It suits you.

I like red, always did, it's cheerful.

Yes.

Do you fancy a cup of tea?

No, thank you.

No tea? No tea? Dear me, what's the matter with you?

Mrs O'Malley is doing well if only she can have the sense to
capitulate and at least pretend to drink tea. She does. Good.
Grandma beams. She is gracious to Mrs O'Malley now. She engages
her in conversation about the weather, how freezing it has been (the
heat wave finished only a week ago, our Indian summer) how
dangerous the icy pavements still are. Mrs O'Malley has got the
hang of it. She does not actually accept the lies but she goes
along with them, does not challenge them. Bridget watches Mrs
O'Malley's face intently: one flicker of expression revealing she's
got Grandma down as a loony or is laughing at her and that will be
that. In the end, it's Grandma who gets up to go, saying the men will
be in for their tea. Mrs O'Malley goes.

Mum says come on Bridget, she was marvellous. Bridget says yes,
she was bright enough but there is still something she does not like

about Mrs O'Malley. Maybe she's a drinker. A drinker, Mum echoes, amazed. Her nose was a little red, Bridget says. Mum says what rubbish, that Bridget is determined to find fault. She, Mum, wants to snap up Mrs O'Malley at once, we would be crazy not to. Bridget won't actually agree. She starts moaning about the hell of breaking people in, getting Grandma used to them. Mum is silent. All right then, Bridget says, I suppose she's as good as anyone. For that money, she should be.

Relief all round.

Jenny

Yesterday Bridget was upset. She sat down quietly, in itself unusual, and clasped her hands and told me that Grandma had been in a strange mood last night, that she had not quite known how to cope. She had seemed distressed all evening and when Bridget had asked her what was the matter she had said, 'Everything is black.' Bridget said it frightened her how calmly this was stated. She had asked Grandma to explain, to try to say what she meant. Did she mean she could not see? Was something the matter with her eyes? But no. Grandma had paused, and then said, 'I'm doing things I shouldn't do.' Bridget said that though these words might sound innocuous they had made her heart pound – just the misery of knowing that her mother realised something of the state she was in, that she was not protected from that horrible knowledge. Bridget said she had never thought Grandma had any insight into her own condition. The only other thing she had said before she fell asleep was 'Isn't life disappointing?'

Today has been the first day I have not seen either Grandma or Bridget for a whole week. I am ashamed to feel so relieved. The to-ing and fro-ing and all the tension while Mrs O'Malley settled in has been ridiculous. Bridget works herself up into a dreadful state over nothing. I told her I would introduce Mrs O'Malley into Grandma's flat and acquaint her with Grandma's ways but Bridget insists on doing it. Then she flies here to relate yet another instance of Mrs O'Malley's insensitivity or stand-offishness. Because Mrs O'Malley is basically not a talkative woman, Bridget has labelled her stand-offish. She says she has listened at the door and Mrs O'Malley sometimes does not speak to Grandma for twenty minutes at a time. At least Mildred spoke, if just to harangue Grandma. This silence, Bridget alleges, makes Grandma miserable, she *looked* miserable when Bridget went in the first day after Mrs O'Malley had slept there.

I really ought to have learned to ignore Bridget's complaints. She cannot help making them. Hannah asked the other day, in some distress I thought, why Bridget seemed so excitable, she said she felt exhausted from just being in the same room. There is no answer to that kind of why but then the analytical Hannah, at seventeen, is expert at putting those kind of questions. It upsets her that Bridget is upset, she feels for her, realising how much she loves Grandma. I suppose that is why she attacked Adrian even though he was only asking what she herself had asked.

All Adrian said was that he did not know why Bridget was behaving like a maniac. This was after she had rushed in demented, shouting that 'that bloody woman, Mrs O'Malley,' had just rung her up to ask her if there was any vaseline anywhere because she had discovered a little sore patch on Grandma's bottom and wanted to put something soothing on till the doctor could see it. 'Bloody show off!' Bridget roared. 'As if I didn't *know* there was a sore patch, as if I wasn't dealing with it, I'm a *nurse* for chrissake, implying I don't know my job, implying I neglect my mother –' And Adrian looked up from his supper and merely said, 'What are you yelling about, Bridget? How could Mrs O'Malley know you knew? What's wrong with asking for vaseline? You're paranoid.' Hannah dropped her knife and fork and told him to shut up, he was a lout and stupid and what the hell did he know and Bridget was quite right, it *was* showing off, being virtuous: Mrs O'Malley was making sure Bridget realised how goody-goody she was. Adrian told her not to be so silly, Bridget said Adrian didn't understand, Hannah said he had never even tried to –All our meals this week have been like that. 'I wish Bridget wouldn't come while we're eating,'

Adrian said and I agreed. Hannah almost wept with shame at our callousness.

And in the middle of all this I have had Grandma seen again by Dr Carruthers and we, Charlie and I, have visited the Green Valley Home.

Dr Carruthers agreed Grandma has deteriorated. His little tests, the same he applied three years ago, show she has become much more severely demented. She does not know how many children she has and can name only Bridget. She does not know if she has any grandchildren. She does not know if she has eaten recently or what she ate. She could not recognise a comb, a brush, a jug. She cannot put her shoes on or a cardigan. She is disturbed at night. But, said Dr Carruthers, she is still not really severely demented. She is continent, she can walk and talk. I found myself asking him what I did not want to know, asking him if it was inevitable that my mother-in-law would become incontinent, unable to walk, unable to speak. He said it was, quite inevitable.

I had never realised that. Bridget with her talk of 'little strokes' had made me think Grandma was not actually suffering from senile dementia. She had not told me anything of the progress of the disease. She had led me to believe, or I felt she had, that with loving care it could be arrested, go into remission, that Grandma might not ever, as Bridget put it, 'get really bad'. She must have meant that she might die first of something else, if we were lucky, if *she* was lucky. Hearing Dr Carruthers hardened my resolve: Charlie is right. We cannot wait. If we wait too long then, when the time comes, we will not be able to get Grandma into a good home. Who takes the incontinent, the wheelchair-bound, the mute? Precious few, I should think.

I want to act now, to protect us all. And yes, I am afraid, afraid of what it will do to us all if we keep Grandma in our midst to the bitter end. But the Green Valley Home is impossible. It was highly recommended by so many people who swore their elderly relatives were blissfully happy there, never better looked after, wished they had gone there years ago, a pleasure to visit. I had been told, countless times, of the waiting list to get in, of the high fees not deterring applicants because it was such a high calibre place. I cannot wait to see again some of these people who raved about the Green Valley Home. They are either blind or deaf or wilfully wicked. Did they not see the six beds in a room, all jammed together? The lack of pictures, of any decoration, anything personal? Did they not see, at eleven in the morning, the twenty chairs in a circle in a silent, dark room, each with a motionless figure slumped on it? Did they count the lavatories, only two of them, both up flights of stairs? Did they not smell the urine, certainly not masked by disinfectant? Did they not hear the silence, the lack of activity? Did they not sense the utter despair? Maybe they did and told themselves it did not matter because Grandma or Grandad was past it, it did not matter because everything is the same to them. As long as it is clean (it was) and warm (it was) and the staff are kind (they appeared to be), then *that* was what mattered.

We came out numb. Charlie had gone through the motions, simply because we were there, of finding out things, like costs, length of waiting list, method of entry. They have no vacancies and the waiting list has twenty-four names on it. They do take the moderately demented – I heard Charlie hurriedly claim Grandma was only moderately demented – but not if they are incontinent. We drove home too depressed to talk. I did not have to convince Charlie. It is out of the question, not an option. What, then, is? Charlie has heard from someone at work of another home, outside London, but if it was so far away we could not visit every day. Would we visit every day, Charlie asked, horrified and I said that of course we would. One of us, every day. It would be the least we could do.

Dr Carruthers has mentioned a Day Centre near us, a mere five minutes' drive away. He says it is excellent and that Grandma would enjoy it, for the moment anyway. Later, she would not be able to cope but he thought she could, at the moment, just. She could go three days a week, all day, from ten in the morning to five in the evening. It would relieve the pressure on us, he said sympathetically. So Charlie and I went there, greatly dreading it. And it is lovely, we were so surprised, so relieved. It is like a nursery school only full of old people. There is a garden, an internal garden in a courtyard, full of shrubs and greenery. As we went in we could hear singing, lusty singing, and smell coffee. In one room some old people were painting, in another making pastry. It looked too good to be true. Charlie became quite excited and I hated bringing him down by pointing out that a Day Centre may be very nice but it does not help in the long run and it is the long run I am concerned with. The days are in fact no problem. We have Susan and Lola, we manage days very well. But still, I agreed, it is worth a try.

Except that Bridget does not think so. When we suggested it, she was immediately suspicious. Why had we gone there? Why had we not told her? Why had she not been invited to go with us? What was going on? We were forced to mention Dr Carruthers and then she was furious all over again because we had thought fit to call him in without her permission. Charlie took exception to that. He said he had no need to obtain Bridget's permission, what on earth was she talking about. Bridget managed to make a stab at an apology. She had not meant to put it like that. She said it was just that she thought we were all in this together. Charlie said he was afraid that was the point: we were not together any more. He told Bridget she must begin to face facts and the facts were that sooner rather than later their mother would have to go into a Home. Was it not better that she went into one now? Bridget said no and got up and left.

Charlie first took me to his home on New Year's Eve, without warning. There was a party going on. The rooms seemed packed with people and Grandma was standing in the middle of them all, laughing and clapping her hands as someone played the bagpipes. It was such a shock to identify her as Charlie's mother whom I had thought of as small and slight and blonde and elegant. Grandma was big, tall and big, and very dark-haired, and elegant was the last word anyone could apply to her. I had thought she would be shy and rather retiring like Charlie and here was this extrovert, boisterous, jolly woman. Charlie did not seem like her son, except for his laugh which, in timbre and tone, matched hers exactly – a strong, thick laugh, very infectious. But when I saw Bridget that night I recognised her as Grandma's child at once. I saw her across the room, among a crowd, smoking, glass in hand, her arm round some man's shoulder (her uncle) and I knew she must be Charlie's sister. I knew because she had the same spirit as her mother if not the same looks.

Charlie does not have it and neither of course does Stuart. Grandma and Bridget have a wild air, an untamed look to them, Bridget more so than Grandma. They are arresting, there is a hint of danger in them both and yet neither has ever done a dangerous or even an unconventional thing in their disappointingly ordinary lives.

Bridget got up and left. Bridget is so alarming. I, in her position, could not have walked out. It was like a declaration of war. She just got up and left in one energetic burst of speed. Charlie was furious. He hates confrontation, always feels bested by Bridget. And I was furious with him. He should not have brought up the subject of a Home at that point, it was tactless, especially when we have not found a Home. He said he was sick of Bridget, that she was a bully and he was tired of it. She acted as though she was the only one with the right to say what should be done. I said, 'Bridget loves your mother, Charlie.'

That is the difference. It is what gives Bridget the right which Charlie so resents. She fights her mother's corner, he does not. I know Charlie cannot stand up and say he loves his mother. He does not *not* love her but, if his love is analysed, it proves to be a token emotion. He likes his mother, he is greatly concerned with her welfare, he pities her, he admires her, but he does not *love* her as he loves his children, as he loves me. Nor is he loved by her, which has a great deal to do with it. Grandma would never use the word love of anyone but, if pushed, she would say she loved all her children the same, as any decent woman should, and had no favourites. She loves Stuart, Charlie and Bridget, all equally. Nothing would ever make her admit there is a difference in the interpretation of the word love when applied to Stuart or Charlie or Bridget. But the difference is so huge that there is no connection. Grandma loves Bridget with an all-consuming emotion, fiercely, completely, beautifully; she loves Charlie affectionately, distantly; she loves Stuart as a memory. And they all know it. Grandma gets back what she gives, it is as simple as that. She is lucky. Many mothers do not.

'Now what do we do?' Charlie asked, as soon as Bridget had gone. He knew the answer. Nothing. There is nothing we can do. But it occurs to me that there is one hope. Bridget likes to keep her personal life enigmatic. Nobody is supposed to know about her love affairs, though heaven knows why because they are perfectly commonplace. She stays with no man very long but she is not promiscuous. Her affairs are brief and few and far apart. But they are very intense and explosive, like Bridget, and invariably end in tears. Grandma knows nothing of them, or so Bridget thinks. Certainly, in her present state, she knows nothing but whether she has always been so naive I do not know. When I first came into the McKay family, there was nothing Grandma wanted more than for Bridget to get married, preferably to a doctor. 'The men buzz round her like flies,' Grandma told me with satisfaction. (I think she meant bees, not flies, bees round honey, but maybe not.) 'She won't look at them,' Grandma said, then, even more triumphant, 'sends the lot of them packing.' Five years later, after Adrian was born and Bridget held him so adoringly when we took him north for Grandma's inspection, the tune changed. 'Would you not think it time to settle down?' Grandma began.

I don't know if Bridget was having troublesome love affairs then. I only know her intimate history from when she moved to London and was out of Grandma's patch. She did not confide in me – Bridget, like Grandma, scorns the giving of confidences – but when her little secret came out, and I was supportive, she learned to trust me and ever after took care to inform me what was going on. The Indian student came to Bridget's flat when I was there. Bridget was so angry, he was so apologetic. She had finished the affair but he could not let her go. He cried and I groaned for him, knowing tears to a McKay meant the case was lost before it was stated – silly boy, to have known Bridget and not known that. They are all boys, her lovers and, while saying she is not ashamed of this, she clearly is. Very ashamed and embarrassed. She can almost faint at the mere idea of Grandma knowing. Her current lover is twenty-two to Bridget's forty-three. Nobody would believe it. It appals Charlie. Stuart does not know and neither do Adrian and Hannah. Bridget is emphatic, she does not want them to know, it is none of their damned business, she *hates* people knowing her business.

Naturally, I have met Karl. Bridget would prefer that I had not but, now that I have, she is quite glad. I may not be a confidante, although I am willing at any moment to become one, but I am the nearest thing she has to a friend and she can trust me. It is touching to sense her eagerness to find out what I think of Karl while she announces defiantly that she does not care. It was a great relief to me to find I liked him. He is no wet-behind-the-ears callow youth caught in the strong Bridget's clutches. Quite the contrary. He seems much, much older than twenty-two and has none of the brashness of youth. In fact, his ponderous manner and slowness are what age him, just as Bridget's vitality keeps her young. It is easy to add ten years to Karl's age and deduct ten from Bridget's. But this is not what Bridget wishes to hear so I never say it. It is too obvious, would appear ingratiating. And it is not really relevant to the relationship Bridget has with Karl. If I were going to argue that age does not matter it would be a great mistake to appear to be falsifying those ages.

I am not quite sure what Karl does or where he lives or how Bridget met him. She does not like giving such information and I feel guilty about wanting to know. All I do know is that the affair has been going on for almost a year which is a record for Bridget. She is surprised herself, surprised she has not become bored (it has always been Bridget who has grown tired of her young men, not the other way round). Karl is with her all the nights she is not with Grandma and some of the ones she is. I suppose Bridget envisaged some catastrophe and felt she had to prepare me, just in case. So she asked me what I thought about Karl sleeping with her while she was staying with Grandma. The idea was startling. I imagined Grandma shuffling into Bridget's bedroom on some merry midnight wander and seeing a man's head on the pillow beside Bridget's. But then all she was likely to do was mutter 'bloomin' men' and shuffle off again, not sure whom she had seen. So I said that I could not see that it made any difference – if Bridget was comfortable, why shouldn't she have her lover there? That is, if he was also comfortable.

Bridget told me, only a few weeks ago, that Karl wanted her to go on holiday with him. He wanted to take her back to Germany, to his home in Berlin, and then to the Black Forest. She was both excited and terrified by this suggestion. 'Imagine!' she said again and again. 'Imagine! Imagine what his mother would think!' I said I thought it was a sign that he had perfect trust in his mother and so should she.

Why not go? She hadn't had a proper holiday in years. She could go for a month and, before she said it, I would say it: What about Grandma. Well, what about her? We would look after her. I would share Bridget's nights with Charlie, it would all be quite simple. Bridget said nothing. She reported later that Karl was becoming more and more persistent but she did not appear to be cross about this.

So, as I explained to Charlie, Karl could be our trump card. Charlie says I am getting carried away. I am. I even see Bridget married, which is silly. And I see her visiting Grandma in a pleasant Home three times a week. Grandma, in this dream, is sitting in a comfy chair chatting to some other sweet, white-haired, smiling ladies and there are flowers everywhere and a kettle is whistling and everything is bright and cheerful . . .

Hannah

Alistair and Jamie stare at Grandma. She makes faces, makes a playful grab for them. They jump. God, I hate these two, they aren't human, they're witless and dumb. Neither of them speaks to Grandma, neither of them speaks at all, much. Grandma sniffs and says it is very quiet, where is everyone, what's wrong with these two, who's stolen their tongues. She says people used to ask her mother if her father was dumb and she laughs at the memory. Alistair and Jamie take the opportunity to edge away, away from their grandmother, nearer to the TV, the beloved TV which they know and love more than their grandmother. Grandma realises someone has gone. She looks around, sighs, gives up, turns back, sees me.

> Do you know any poetry?
> Nope.
> What do they teach you in school?
> Not poetry.
> Why not?
> Dunno.
> Do you know any poetry?

I don't feel like arguing today, don't feel like giving Grandma any mental exercise. She looks sulky. Her hair isn't brushed. Who was on last night, who got her ready this morning? And her cardigan has a stain on the front, tut tut, what will Sister Bridget say about that. Grandma sees the chocolates. Paula sent them with Alistair and Jamie, my God. They are for Mum, for having Alistair and Jamie. Mum doesn't like chocolates. Grandma does. No use saying they're not her favourite sort, *all* chocolates are her favourite. Her hand goes out, slowly, creeping across the kitchen table. It takes all of five minutes for her to secure the box and draw it to her. She asks me if I want a chocolate *in* my tea. I say *in* my tea, ugh. She says what's wrong with that, hoighty-toighty, try it and see. She'll just have one, anyway, since she's bought them, bloomin' awful price too, you're just as well with a bit of toffee, lasts longer. She is all the while opening the box of Terry's All Gold, with infinite care, no haste. There is a little padded bit of paper on top of the first layer. Grandma fingers it.

> You could make a blanket out of this, so you could.
> Small blanket.
> If you had a few, saved them, stitched them together.
> If you had a thousand, yeh.
> I hate waste.
> What waste?
> You could make a blanket out of this, so you could.

She eats chocolates four at a time, mingling flavours, regardless. I show her the chart, thinking it will amuse her – it worries her. This, I say, showing her, is a walnut whirl and this is a hazelnut cluster and this nougat. Which do you want. She says they are all nice. She bites one, bites another, rams them in, cheeks bulging, says, with open mouth awash with chocolate, that none of them are much good but she will manage, she will make them do, she hates waste.

Mum hurries in, scolds me, says 'she' will not eat her supper now. I say I can't see it matters; Grandma doesn't eat it anyway, she just messes it up and wastes it. Grandma repeats she hates waste. She reaches for another chocolate, Mum snatches it away, Grandma looks shocked and struggles to her feet. She says she's going, she knows when she's not wanted, the very idea. Alistair chooses that moment to come in search of a drink, sees Grandma's chocolate-smeared face and says indignantly that the chocolates were for

Mum not Grandma, he's got cigarettes for Grandma. Grandma is livid, the cheek, the *cheek*, telling her whose chocolates they are when she's bought them. With all the self-righteousness of a five-year-old Alistair says, shrill, piercingly, that his mummy bought them. Grandma says in the name of God, Mum tells Alistair not to worry, Jamie comes in and starts to cry, Grandma tells him to stop bawling, Jamie bawls harder, as hard as his three-year-old lungs can, which is very hard indeed, Grandma shouts she cannot bear the noise, it is a mad house, what has she done to deserve this, she has led a blameless life.

Walking down the road, Grandma asks if we are going to the hut. I ask what hut – she gestures vaguely, says the usual one. I play safe, say I do not think so. This hut has begun to feature heavily in Grandma's stream of consciousness. Nobody knows what this hut is, not even Bridget. She usually mentions it in the evening, she is always wanting to go there, but where would there be a hut in a Glasgow childhood? It sounds rural, as though she was thinking of a summer house. When I have said I do not think so, she is depressed. She sighs, looks miserable, trudges into her flat. As I take her coat off, she says she thinks she will just go home, starts trying to get her coat back on.

> I think I'll away home.
> This *is* home, Grandma.
> It might be to you but it isn't to me.
> You've lived here five years.
> Get away.
> Don't you like it here?
> I think I'll away home.

Mrs O'Malley arrives, is very brisk. At least she doesn't call Grandma 'Mother' as the odious Mildred did. Grandma glares at her, makes faces behind her back at me, mutters about being sick of bloomin' strangers. Mrs O'Malley is unperturbed. She makes tea, puts it in front of Grandma, adds sugar, asks would she like a biscuit. Grandma says she hates biscuits, waste of money. Mrs O'Malley silently slides a custard cream across the table. Grandma munches it, splattering crumbs as she continues to abuse the very existence of biscuits. I say I'd better go now. Grandma gets up and says she'll get her coat. Mrs O'Malley tells her to sit tight and she'll get it and then she shows me out. She tells me Grandma will be fine, she will soon forget. How true, oh wise one. I see what Bridget means. Mrs O'Malley is competent, even skilled, in the management of Grandma, but there is no warmth, she does not really connect with what's left of Grandma's mind. And Grandma senses this. Increasingly, when Mrs O'Malley is about to arrive, Grandma wants to go home.

I tell all this to Mum on my return and she says beggars cannot be choosers. Sorry, I'm sure. She is giving Alistair and Jamie their tea. I hardly speak to them. They may be my cousins, but I don't like them, feel no obligation. I hold it against them that they are not nice to our Grandma. Jamie is quite an attractive child. I would like to see him on Grandma's knees, cuddling her, his arms round her neck. And, instead, he jumps if she speaks to him. Mum is impatient with me. She is exasperated. Jamie is only three and hardly sees Grandma, it's not his fault and really I'm being most unfair. True. As Grandma would say, I blame that Stuart. Why hasn't he brought his children up differently? Maybe he did his others, his older ones. Stuart's divorce is said in family lore to have devastated Grandma in her heyday. Mum says in many ways Grandma cast Stuart off before he cast her (Bridget says that is complete nonsense). Stuart has two other sons, both older than Adrian. I have met them once, at a wedding. Grandma is said to have been fond of them both, to have seen them regularly until they were ten and eight and the divorce took them away from her. She does occasionally ask where Stuart's boys are and it is clear she doesn't mean Alistair and Jamie. Stuart keeps them away from her. He says it is not right to frighten them, not fair to expect them to cope with a mad Grandmother. Bridget says, menacingly, that his time will come.

Mum tells Alistair and Jamie I will read them a story. I certainly will not. Luckily, Adrian comes in. He is quite willing to play football with them. Up and down the almost dark garden they go, screaming, yelling, Adrian like a great cart horse. How Grandma would love to see, to hear. That is what boys are meant to do. She feels secure when football is mentioned in any shape or form. Work and football, those she understands. Instead, she is sitting with Mrs O'Malley, vaguely uneasy, waiting, longing for delivery. It is *not* right. I say so to Mum. Mum says if one more person brings *right* into anything she will scream. I accuse her of preferring to look after loathsome Alistair and Jamie to looking after Grandma, lovely Grandma. She looks me straight in the eye and says, 'You are quite right. I do prefer looking after Alistair and Jamie. So?'

And she does. Listen to her, putting them to bed, the shrieks from the bathroom, the laughing, the chasing up the stairs and now the hush as she reads to the little darlings all cuddly in their pyjamas, smelling so sweetly of soap. One, two, three, aaah. Well, it isn't like that putting Grandma to bed, I admit. No fun in the bath with her. We can't get her into the bath, haven't been able to for months now, not even with all three of us – me, Bridget, Mum. She won't bend her legs, she's forgotten how to step into a bath or anywhere else. It's all-over washes for Grandma and pretty disgusting, yuk, the secrets of that flannel. When we wash her hair she screams we're murdering her. Close your eyes, we say, and she opens them wide. Bend forward, we urge, and she tilts her head backwards. No wonder we take turns, no wonder we only do it once every two weeks. And no one can read anything to Grandma. She interrupts from line two or wishes someone would turn the radio on or goes to sleep or gets up and goes away. Why do I blame Mum for preferring to put to bed the odious Alistair and Jamie? I am getting like Bridget.

That's a terrible thought. I don't want to be like Bridget. Oh, I'm quite happy that I *look* a little like Bridget. She has quite dramatic looks, with all that very black thick hair and strong colouring, and from her Jane Fonda figure nobody would know Bridget was forty-three. I'm glad to be quite tall like her instead of small like Mum and I would like, when I am her age, to have an absolutely flat stomach instead of Mum's plumpish body. There is nothing wrong with Bridget's looks. But I do not want to be *like* her. She is frenetic and exhausting and it makes people nervous and tired. What is she like on her ward? I can't think. Maybe, in the hospital, she is different. And that's another thing: I don't want Bridget's sort of life. She works nearly all of it and, however satisfying that is, I want something else too. Bridget has no other interests except work. She isn't even interested in her flat, has no domestic instincts. She never cooks, never decorates. She never goes to the theatre or to the pictures. When she's not working she just seems to sleep. Grandma is her only out-of-work interest. She has no friends except us. I would hate her life. I would hate Mum's too but I would hate Bridget's more. Neither of them ever does anything different. Both of them chug along on fixed lines.

Mum says if it wasn't for Grandma her life would be just opening out. *She* says she says this without bitterness or resentment or because she is making excuses, but I don't believe her. How would her life be opening out? Where would it be going? What would she be doing with three hours three afternoons a week, alternate Saturdays, and every Sunday. She says that is not the way to look at it. She is tied, she says, by the responsibility. She is the back-up. Bridget works, Charlie works, she is the one at home without whom the system would not operate and this means she cannot go back to work as she would like to do. Her face flushes as she goes over how many times she has had to step in and take over because Susan doesn't turn up or Lola is ill. She thinks I'm unfair, that I fail to appreciate what she does, that I underestimate her contribution to Grandma's welfare. She says that instead of being so self-righteous, I could help more myself. I ask what about Adrian?

Adrian does nothing and my dad hardly anything. They both protest that, of course, they care about Grandma etc. etc. but they do nothing for her. Adrian, teasing of course (oh, of course) says it's women's work, that Grandma doesn't like men looking after her. He says he does his bit in providing that background Male Presence she finds so comforting and asking her if his tea is ready. And he laughs at her jokes and her antics. I hate the way he does that. Grandma shows off when Adrian is there, getting sillier and sillier, and his laughter is patronising. He treats her like a Good Turn and is only seconds away from presenting her to his friends as My Batty Grandma from the Funny Farm. Why can't he do something useful like collect her on the days she comes here? She would like to walk down the street on her tall grandson's arm. Why can't he sit and make her tea for an hour if he's so fond of her?

What I think is this:

If, as Mum says, we are all in this together
   then there has got to be a fairer sharing out of labour.
If Grandma finds the Male Presence comforting,
   then give her more of it.
If she gets more of it, she might get over
   her general fear of all men.
Then the women would be freer.

*

Alistair and Jamie are still here. I'm glad to get out of the house and go to Grandma's. It is not our day but Lola has rung to say she doesn't feel one hundred per cent. Mum mutters who does and her face falls. Lola is getting more and more inclined to ring up at the last minute and tell us she's indisposed. She whines. She lists all her ailments and drives Mum mad. Really, Lola is hopeless but she's the longest-serving helper and Grandma is used to her. She is Spanish and every time she arrives at Grandma's she says good afternoon in Spanish first and Grandma cracks up with delight and repeats it and tells Lola how she is descended from survivors of the Spanish Armada. Ships are supposed to have been washed up on the coasts of Scotland and the sailors married and that is why Grandma is so dark. Lola gets this saga every time and every time she manages to respond appropriately. For that alone she is valuable. But Mum suspects she is phasing herself out. Lola is really too good to be looking after old ladies, too talented. Twice last week Grandma spilled tea over herself and Lola actually had to do something for a change – she made a meal out of having to change Grandma. She likes to talk to Grandma but that's all. And she's not desperate for the money, as Susan is. Lola's circumstances are mysterious, but we don't get the impression she is worried about finance. We think she sees her afternoons with Grandma as a kind of charity work; it makes her feel good. The paltry sum she gets is beside the point. Bridget thinks she's a pain.

Mum says it's up to me. I can stay with Grandma for two hours or bring her along. It's my choice. I think I'll stay there. This will mean

73

deadly boredom for two hours and it's not as good for Grandma — she benefits from the short walk to our house and the excitement of going out, anywhere, is beneficial too. Also, at home it's easier for me. I can slope off. Stuck in Grandma's kitchen, there's no escape. There's no possibility of real conversation and five minutes will seem like five hours. But I will put the radio on, and pretend to be listening to it and Grandma will talk all the way through but be indignant if I tell her to listen properly. Television is useless. She thinks anyone on the screen is real and shouts hello and waves and is furious when they don't wave back. She says she wishes they would go away if they're just going to treat her like dirt.

I put my key in the lock. It won't turn. I try again, check it's the right key. It fits and does in fact turn but it doesn't open the door. I push, the door gives slightly in the middle, enough for me to realise it's bolted top and bottom. At first, I'm alarmed. I've read about burglars bolting front doors as soon as they get into a house. The thought of Grandma confronting a burglar . . . I go round the side of the house, to the back door, for which we have a key, too, kept on the same Downing Street key ring but rarely used. The back door opens, to my relief. I start shouting, 'Grandma, it's only me, Grandma, it's Hannah,' as I go in, not wanting to frighten her because I'm coming from the wrong direction. There's no sound. The back door opens into a little hall, with Grandma's internal kitchen door opening off it. I try to open the door but, though a crack appears, I can't push it open. I know there are no locks on this door, no bolts. Then, with my ear to the crack, I hear breathing. Grandma is surely behind that door. What is going on? 'Grandma,' I keep saying softly, over and over, 'Grandma, let me in, it's Hannah.' Eventually, she replies. She says someone has put a lot of rubbish in front of the bloomin' door and it isn't her fault, bloomin' nuisance, they're all the same these days. There's some scraping and clattering and the door opens wide enough for me to see Grandma's cross face. The minute I see her, I relax. Adrian would laugh. She does look funny, brows furrowed, mouth screwed up like a prune as though she's about to give someone a prim kiss. I get one arm round the door and dislodge a cushion and then I can just squeeze through the wider opening.

74

I stare in amazement at the barricades. Behind the door I've just come through Grandma has pushed the kitchen table and on top of it wedged a chair, and keeping the chair in place are two cushions (three, but I knocked one down). In front of the other door, into the living room, she has piled a footstool and another chair and several pans. I dismantle them. Grandma says she doesn't know what someone has been doing but when she gets them will give them *biff*. In the living room the door into the bedroom is open but the other, into the body of the house, has a wonderful collection of goods blocking it. There's a shopping trolley, the sort that has wheels, into which Grandma has put a cabbage and a bag of potatoes, and a coat stand, one of those heavy wooden ones you see in restaurants, and then a great many coats. I remove it all and go into the hall. Grandma doesn't follow. She whispers that I should be careful, that she has heard men, and that there's no knowing. I want to check the front door. It's a very solid, old door and there are two sets of bolts, one running horizontally at the top and one vertically at the bottom. They're both rammed home. I struggle to unbolt the door, marvelling at Grandma's strength. It's so long since the bolts have been used that the paint scrapes off as I tussle to get them back.

It takes me twenty minutes or so to sort everything out and return things to their places. I wonder if Susan came? It's no good asking Grandma. Maybe she has been on her own for four hours instead of one, maybe that's the explanation for the panic she must have felt. And was there a man? Did someone call? Did someone look through the window? I try to find out. I ask Grandma if she has had a gentleman caller.

There's men about.
Did a man ring your bell, Grandma?
What bell?
The door bell.
I haven't got a door bell, a knocker's good enough for me.
The knocker, then, did a man knock on your door?
Which door?
The front door.
I haven't a front door, what are you on about?

The back door, then.
What about the back door?
Did a man come to it?
There's men about.

There are other signs of agitation. The tea pot has cold water and an ice cube in it. There's a puddle of washing-up liquid on the floor in front of the sink. Sugar is scattered in a long trail from cupboard to fridge. I realise it's very cold and feel the radiators. They're freezing. I go to the boiler and find it's been turned off. I say, aloud, that the heating has been switched off and how cold it is and Grandma says 'Cauld blaws the wind frae east to west'. Reciting Burns puts her in a good mood. She says listen to this, it will make you cry, and she launches into 'Highland Mary'. I say it doesn't make me cry, it makes me laugh it's so maudlin and awful. Grandma says get awa' wi ye but she's happy. She suddenly says what pretty blue eyes I have and I know that is a cue for 'The Blue-Eyed Lassie'. I'm right. She asks me if my name is Anna. I say nearly, come on, you know what it is, it's Hannah. Grandma says that's a pity because she knows a very nice poem about Anna which would just suit me, 'Anna thy charms my bosom fire' – pause for Grandma to have hysterics – but it is no good if I am not Anna, what about Jean, there's a lovely one about Jean, Bonnie Jean. 'There was a lass and she was fair . . .'

I've got the heating back on. I've made some hot, sweet tea and found a biscuit. Grandma's flat is now tidy and she's settled in her armchair with her feet up and her tartan shawl over her shoulders. I feel shaky. Grandma is perfectly all right and everything is fine and nothing has happened and she's already forgotten but I feel shaky. She's never done this before, she's never barricaded herself in, and I hate to think of the fear which must have prompted it. It's not right that she's on her own and afraid. I drink my own tea, thinking, worrying, feeling like Mum, and then, as I look up, straight into Grandma's eyes, there's one of those moments. We stare at each other, there's real contact, and yet again I'm helpless, *what can I do with it?* Quickly, before it goes. I don't speak but Grandma herself breaks the spell.

Are you married may I ask?

Grandma! Of course not, I'm seventeen.

Plenty of girls are married at seventeen.

Not today, they aren't.

I'm o'er young, I'm o'er young, I'm o'er young to marry yet –

Is that another stupid Burns?

You watch your mouth.

Sorry.

I'm o'er young, 'twad be a sin to tak me frae my mammy yet –

And she marries him and dies I bet.

Wrong, she does not.

Makes a change, then.

But if ye come this gate again I'll aulder be gin simmer, sir. The hussy.

Sexy Burns.

Don't be disgusting.

Sorry.

Are you married yet?

She doesn't know me. This is the first time she hasn't known me. I ask her my name and she says I must be in a bad way if I don't know my own name. Clever. I ask her what her name is and she says it's none of my business and she doesn't hold with all this first name carry on, it's ridiculous. I wish Bridget would come. I wish I had taken Grandma along home, but it's too late now. So I sit it out, watching the clock. Grandma is desperate to talk. She asks me how my family is and I ask which family and she says as many as you've got. Cunning. I ask her how *her* family is. She says she doesn't know, they're all good but she hardly sees them. Bridget arrives, like a whirlwind, all flying hair and nurse's cloak. Grandma's face lights up, as it always does. At least she knows Bridget.

Bridget has brought kippers for supper. Grandma says she had kippers for lunch and she's tired of kippers, kippers, but she'll eat them up if there's nothing else. Bridget reminds her that she is the cleanest kipper eater in the world and Grandma agrees and wonders why everyone can't clean a kipper like she can. She says to Bridget, nodding in my direction, has she got a kipper to spare for her friend here. Bridget looks startled and asks which friend, does she mean Hannah? Grandma says of course she does, who else, she's not daft, they don't need to come and take her away yet, she just wants to be left in peace. And she shuffles off, mouthing she needs the bathroom. I relate the afternoon's drama to Bridget. Bridget is an annoying person to tell things like that to. Instead of discussing Grandma's mental condition and responding to my alarm, what she does is concentrate on who the man can have been. Was it a window cleaner or the gas man or someone collecting for something . . . It makes me scream. Bridget is emphatic that there must have been some man, that Grandma's paranoia could not have been triggered off by nothing. When I say it seems to me that this is the point, she *is* imagining things, Bridget is quite sharp with me. I am fussing over nothing and *of course* there must have been some man around, good heavens her mother isn't mad, only a little confused. She thanks me rather stiffly. I tell her Lola may not be coming tomorrow either. Bridget rails against the useless Lola, money for jam, should be ashamed of herself. I say Mum thinks she is going to give up. Good, says Bridget, she's a pain, good riddance.

I think about Bridget's attitude on the short way home. She feels Grandma is slighted. Bridget can't bear her to be criticised. She wants everyone to praise, adore, love and worship Grandma and most of all to agree she's only a little bit confused which is perfectly natural in view of her age. Of course, Grandma is all Bridget has to love. It's no good saying she has us; it isn't the same. Bridget is all to Grandma and Grandma is all to Bridget. What will happen? How long can Bridget go on pretending? Mum says until there is a crisis and, when I ask what would you call a crisis, she refuses to elaborate. What does she mean? Does she mean Grandma might come to some harm? Or harm others?

I have to tell them what's happened when I get home, though I would rather not. I tell them at supper, when Alistair and Jamie are in bed. The first thing Mum asks is why I didn't tell her at once, good heavens that was four hours ago. Dad says that is it, the sign he has been waiting for, and surely even Bridget will recognise it. I say she does not. Bridget said it was nothing. Mum looks at Dad. Dad sighs. He says he will go and see Bridget. Mum says good, but no scenes please. Mum tells him to try for a compromise, to suggest Grandma goes to the Day Centre each afternoon or at least on Lola's afternoons if Lola goes on being unable to come. Mum tells him not to rush it, to remember how very sensitive Bridget is. Dad mutters that he's getting rather bored with Bridget's sensitivity. Adrian, who hasn't spoken, only wolfed his food, chooses that moment to say, 'Poor Dad.' What, I say, What? Poor *Dad*? What about poor Grandma, poor Bridget? Mum tells me not to start, Adrian says Dad never gets any sympathy, and Dad says thanks Adrian.

Dad goes to see Bridget. I time him. If he's gone longer than half an hour then there has been a row. He's gone ten minutes, comes back cheerful. Mum is astonished. Bridget has said we can take Grandma to the Day Centre if we want, if *we* can't manage (Dad says that was the emphasis) each afternoon but that she knows what will happen: it will be a lot of fuss for nothing. And she, Bridget, is not going to have anything to do with it. She will neither take nor collect Grandma. We'll soon see, she has warned Dad. But Dad sees this as a victory. He's very pleased with himself, looks for applause. Mum gives it but not enthusiastically. She's suspicious. Bridget has agreed too readily and also what does she mean, we will soon see. But she says Dad has done well. She will ring tomorrow and arrange to take Grandma next week. Dad says she'll love it, bit of a sing-song, lots of company, pots of tea and bikkies, there will be no keeping Grandma away.

*

Mum begins the soft-soap. She tells Grandma she's going to take her out tomorrow. Grandma, who's sitting at the kitchen table as usual when I come in, says that will be very nice, she hasn't stepped a foot out of doors for a month. Mum, who has read far too many dopey psychology books, asks Grandma where she would like to go. Grandma answers very promptly, the Highlands, my heart's in the Highlands, my heart is not here, oh it's lovely up there, we used to go on the train etc. etc. Mum says it's a bit far. She says she thought Grandma might like a bit of company. Grandma says she only likes her family. Mum says she knows this lovely club.

You're better in yer ane hame.
But you get bored, you say you do.
East west hame's best.
It would only be to give you a break for a couple of hours.
I'm fine as I am.
It would give you a change.
You're better in yer ane hame.

Mum is silly. Fancy trying to tee it up. Hopeless. Mum thinks she's cleverly sowing the seeds of acceptance but she's doing no such thing. I ask, quietly, if Grandma had barricaded herself in. Mum says no, she was fine. Bridget says she slept exceptionally well, never even got up. Mum remarks that Bridget didn't actually add 'so there' but it was implied. As if, Mum said, she wouldn't be pleased Grandma had slept, as if it was some sort of competition. She's upset. I tell her Bridget doesn't mean to hurt her. Mum snaps that she knows that perfectly well, thank you. Grandma asks where *is* that Bridget, the hussy. I say at work. Grandma snorts, says a likely story, she's gallivanting, don't try to fool me. Always the same, you bring them up decent and they gallivant.

She's a wash-out, that Bridget.
Don't be silly, Grandma.
You mind your mouth.
Bridget works like a slave and she's devoted to you, you
    couldn't do without her.
I can do without anyone.
You couldn't do without Bridget.
She's a wash-out, that Bridget.

Now I'm being silly. No good trying to persuade Grandma that Bridget is at work and, when she's not at work, she's with her which is another kind of work. She's going to sulk now. She's saying she's going to go, she doesn't like being where she's not wanted. She says she's left on her own, the last rose of summer left bloomin' well alone. Oh, let her wander off, Mum says.

She wanders, muttering. She pockets two fifty pence coins lying on the dresser and then finds Mum's handbag and becomes absorbed, minutely examining the contents. Alistair and Jamie come in, dropped off after school by a friend of their mother's. It is their last day with us. Paula and Stuart will collect them tomorrow. Grandma's eyes light up. She tells them they are both bonnie laddies. They stand in front of her, impassive, desperate to get away. Grandma touches Jamie's reddish hair and he flinches. She asks him what his name is and he whispers it. Grandma is delighted. She leans on the dresser and declaims, with extravagant gestures, guying herself and the poem, 'Thou has left me, ever Jamie'. When she gets to the line, 'Aften hast thou vow'd that Death only should us sever', Jamie bursts into tears. She's disconcerted, bends to comfort him, to embrace him, and he screams and beats at her with his little fists.

I swoop, Mum swoops. I put my arm round a bewildered Grandma and lead her away. Mum picks up Jamie, Alistair trailing behind, and takes him into the kitchen. Grandma asks what is the matter with the puir wee soul, is he not well? I say no, he isn't, he's suffering from Stuartitis. Grandma says what in God's name is that, is it catching, and I say only for the cold-hearted. Grandma says cold hands warm heart and I take her hands. They are hot. I ask if hot hands mean cold hearts. She says hot hands mean can I have a cup of tea. We laugh. Jamie has stopped crying. I ignore him as I make Grandma's tea. I try hard to see Grandma from a small boy's point of view. If she was familiar, if he had grown up seeing her every day, then he would not be frightened but she is not truly familiar, he sees her only six or seven times a year, and there's no denying that to a stranger Grandma can be alarming. She's large and shambolic and she likes to get close to people and thrust her dark, heavily furrowed face into theirs, and her whiskers tickle. Then her voice probably frightens Jamie most, so deep and rough and Scottish. But I accept no excuses. Surely even a child can sense Grandma's kindliness, her gentleness.

Grandma drinks the tea. She sighs with pleasure. Then a strange expression settles on her face, part alarm, part surprise. She munches a biscuit, her eyes vacant, her thoughts far away. I pick up a book. Then Grandma starts to heave herself up saying the men will be in for etc. etc. I ignore her. It's an hour before Bridget is due. Grandma, on her feet at last, stands stock-still. I watch her out of the corner of my eye. She turns round and round. Then she says why do folk leave wet flannels on seats, is there no end to it. This is a new one. I put my book down. She's still turning and suddenly I see a dark patch on the back of her dress. Alistair has come into the room, edging round the wall. His eyes widen and, before I can stop him, he shrills out, 'Grandma's wet herself!'

Jenny

Charlie maintained that just because Grandma had wet herself once, only once, there was no need to tell the Day Centre people this. He preferred, in any case, to describe it as Grandma forgetting to go to the lavatory and I agree that is preferable. Bridget said at once, 'Something must have upset her' and of course it had. Children crying, whether in anger or misery, always distress Grandma. It was easy to connect the unfortunate incident with Jamie to the accident. And Hannah should not have given Grandma more tea, but then she was not to know Grandma had just drunk three large mugfuls. As Bridget lost no time in saying, it was all a fuss about nothing.

But it was not, it is not. Every time something new happens the complete picture changes. Incontinence is to be dreaded. Grandma is not a baby. She cannot be easily lifted and changed when she is wet – it is a performance. All her clothes have to come off and it takes hours. Will the helpers do it? The first time it happens, will each and every one give notice? Bridget is outraged at the suggestion that changing Grandma may prove distasteful, that dealing with wet knickers is not something Mrs O'Malley or Susan or Lola wish to do – but then Bridget is a nurse. I am not. I find it quite distasteful myself. It is not something I want to do myself, frankly.

But we did not tell the Day Centre people. They had told us they could not take Grandma if she was incontinent and we had said, truthfully at the time, that she was not. Maybe it would never happen again (just as Grandma has never barricaded herself in again since that time Hannah found the doors blocked). And if it did, well, then, that would be that. I made sure, the first afternoon we took Grandma to the Day Centre, that she had had no tea for two hours and that she had emptied her bladder. She knew something was about to happen even though I had given up trying to prepare her. She was nervous, kept clearing her throat, said as I pulled her coat on that, since it was snowing, she thought she would just stay at home. I pointed to the October sunshine flooding through the windows and the blue sky. I told her it was a lovely day and an outing would do her good. She said right-o, resigned.

Charlie drove, with Grandma in the front seat beside him. Charlie talked away, Grandma was silent, as though going to her doom. Unfortunately, as we drove up to the front door of the centre a dormobile-type van was unloading several old people, some severely handicapped. Grandma watched, horrified, as a woman bent double over a walking-frame inched her way through the door and another, clearly disabled by a stroke, her mouth all to one side, was half-lifted in by helpers. Grandma said she did not like to see old folk, the poor things. As we waited, the next person out of the van was a man, quite sprightly, who turned to one of the helpers and beseeched her for a kiss, which she gave him, laughing and calling him a sexy old bugger. Grandma shuddered. She said if there was one thing she hated, it was familiarity and men, they were all the same.

Grandma can walk perfectly well but to show solidarity we walked either side. We overdid it. Charlie exclaimed over the indoor garden and the pretty fountain and I went into ecstasies over the posters on the walls and the comfortable chairs and we both urged her to listen to the distant singing. She said not a word. We were unsure where to take her but a woman in a pink overall came out of an office and smiled and nodded and asked if this was Mrs McKay. Thank God she gave Grandma her full, formal title. She said she would take Grandma along to hang up her coat and then maybe she would like a nice cup of tea. We gathered we were meant to go.

Charlie kissed Grandma and said he hoped she had a good time. When I tried to do the same Grandma hissed in my ear, 'Don't leave me – there's men about.' The woman in charge was very good. 'You're going to be with me, Mrs McKay,' she said, 'and I'm not a man, am I?' Grandma was embarrassed and said she had nothing against men. And they went off down the corridor.

I wasted the next two hours. Charlie went back to work and, when I had dropped him off at the tube, I drove home and worried. There was no one in at that hour, just me, and I longed for Hannah who understands Grandma's pathos and the curious way she can blackmail us emotionally without meaning to do so. It was far worse than leaving a child in school for the first time. A child *has* to go to school, a child's future is all bound up with the relationships it will make in school. But Grandma did not have to go to the Day Centre and she is no longer capable of making any relationships. It is no good persuading myself that she is there because she will enjoy it, as Charlie obstinately chooses to believe. Bridget is right, she is there for our convenience and as a stepping-stone to a Home. It feels wrong. But nevertheless I was full of hope as I went, alone, to collect her. I deliberately went early so that I could catch Grandma unawares, just as I used to go early for my children and peep through the classroom door. Wandering round the Centre it still felt as friendly as when we inspected it and I was again cheered. Grandma was in a room singing lustily. I saw her sitting in the centre of a half-circle of women and men singing 'Afton Water'. I waved. She ignored me. The woman in charge brought her out to me. She said Grandma had had a lovely time and my what a good voice and she would look out some other nice Burns' songs for next time. Surreptitiously, as I put Grandma's coat on, I checked to see that she was dry – she was. Victory.

I felt elated as I drove Grandma home. It had been managed, a whole afternoon in a strange place and no disasters. Next time, knowing how well it had worked, I would not worry about imposing this routine on Grandma. It was so much better for her than being stuck in her flat. I took her straight to her own kitchen and waited for Mrs O'Malley, trying all the time to talk to Grandma about the Day Centre. She denied she had been anywhere, didn't know about any singing and became irritable at my attempts to remind her. Mrs O'Malley said she looked exhausted. Am I becoming as paranoid as Bridget or was there a note of censure in her voice? If so, it is absurd, and I am not going to let it depress me. Charlie was pleased to hear this, even more pleased to hear the session had gone well. He said that in no time at all we would have Grandma there every day and it would be a weight off our backs. I said he had better not repeat that in front of Bridget.

If Grandma is a weight, then I have lifted her on to my back deliberately and Charlie knows that. I didn't have to become so involved with her – no one asked me, least of all Bridget. I could have done a Paula, visited her once a week, kept my distance. It is not as though Grandma even likes me. She classes me with Paula as far as liking goes. And she was as against my marrying Charlie as she was against Paula marrying Stuart. Neither of us was suitable for her beloved sons. I involved myself so heavily with Grandma because she is worth it. She is a good woman who has had a hard life and she deserves care and kindness. What is good in me responds to what is good in Grandma – that is the link. But I do not love her and I am not close to her and when we were both younger I could not stand either having her in my house or being in hers. We clashed, our personalities clashed quite spectacularly.

Hannah, on the other hand, does love her grandmother (which is why she is so popular with Bridget). It is not good for Hannah any more to have so much to do with her Grandmother. Bridget was furious when I said so to her, when I warned her that should Grandma become incontinent, then I would not allow Hannah to change her. 'Why ever not?' asked Bridget. 'It's too disgusting,' I replied, determined to be honest. 'Well, you are a precious little flower,' Bridget sneered. 'Good heavens, I'm surprised you can survive in the world at all. If that's the most disgusting thing your Hannah is going to have to do in her life, then she'll be very lucky, I must say.'

When Grandma used to come and stay with us years ago, soon after we were married, the first thing she used to do was wash her underwear. She would arrive in the evening and first thing in the morning she would be standing in the kitchen washing her knickers.

'Just rinsing out m'breeks,' she would whisper. It took her half an hour. Squeeze, in a tiny amount of hot water, rinse, in an equally small amount of cold, then wring with those ferociously strong wrists and take out into the garden and pin in the middle of a washing line. Did she only have one pair, I used to wonder? No, she had three: one pair to wear, one in the wash and one spare. It was such a paradox: on the one hand she hated, and was deeply offended by, any reference to natural functions, especially to going to the lavatory, and yet on the other was obsessed with knicker-washing during family breakfast and derived great satisfaction from watching her knickers blow in the wind in full view of us all. And again, though appalled by nudity, Grandma had a passion for absent-mindedly 'stripping off', as she put it, if it was hot. She would sit in our garden and proclaim she was roasting alive and very slowly she would start taking her clothes off. Once, when Grandma was down to her vast vest, Adrian said, 'Ugh' and she was black-affronted (her favourite expression of outrage). She asked him what the devil was the matter with him and had he anything else unpleasant to say while his mouth was hot. Bridget, of course, told him he was a horrible little boy and then encouraged her mother to bare her all.

Her legs were, are, the worst. All of Grandma's life is written in her legs. She once had her hideous varicose veins surgically removed and the scars are horrific. Then there are the burns. She still cannot talk about the burns because Stuart was burned too. I have tried and tried, this long time after, to get her to tell me exactly what happened but it pains her so, and I have to stop. She closes her eyes and shakes her head and winces and says sssh, sssh. Not even Bridget knows the whole story, but then Bridget was not even born. Charlie was, he was four, but he says he can't remember a thing — typical! Piecing together scraps of information gleaned from older family members all I know is that Grandma spilled a pan of boiling water over herself and Stuart, aged six. She scalded her own legs from knee to ankle and Stuart's from thigh to knee. Luckily, he was wearing those long, grey-flannel short trousers fashionable for little boys then or his burns would have been much worse. Hers were more serious. She had only lisle stockings on and these absorbed and made more damaging the boiling water. Of course, there was no one in the house — which was not a house but a few rooms in what were called the Buildings — except for four-year-old Charlie. There was no telephone. There was no one she knew who had a car. She sent Charlie to find a neighbour but no one was in. He came back and she had taken Stuart's trousers off and covered his thighs with butter. Her own legs she ignored. Then — and this is the part I cannot stand — she somehow shuffled to a bus stop with the screaming Stuart and boarded a bus to the hospital. On the bus she passed out. If it had not been for the wretched butter, Stuart's injuries would have been relatively slight, but it set up an infection. He was in hospital for two weeks and had a skin graft. She was there three weeks and her skin grafts did not take properly. If it were possible, which it is not, I would like to tell everyone who wonders why I am so 'devoted' to my mother-in-law that story.

Hannah knows it, of course, and she knows all the many other tales of Grandma's heroism and her hard life. Since Grandma has never moaned or complained and is utterly convinced that all of the past was wonderful, it is only now that Hannah is beginning to piece things together. She gets angry and asks why Grandma put up with all the things that happened to her, and the only reply I can offer is that she had no choice. Nobody asked her, or any other person, if they thought they *could* suffer before the suffering arrived. One of Grandma's most scathing remarks used to be, 'We could all have a nervous breakdown if we wanted — nervous breakdown indeed, well I never.' But that, to Hannah, is the mystery: why did Grandma not just break down under the weight of accidents and deaths and every variety of misfortune? Why did she not scream and roar and run yelling into the street when she was burned? Why did she wait for a bloody bus? Why, when her husband was killed, did she not lie in bed and weep? Is it bravery, that kind of bravery peculiar to women, the kind for which there are no medals or glory, or is it stupidity? Who can say? Not Grandma, not I. It is a puzzle Hannah will have to work out for herself.

*

Mrs O'Malley rang while we were having breakfast. Grandma had had a very disturbed night and she just thought we ought to know. Also, she had wet her nightdress, but luckily not the bed. She just thought we ought to know that, too. She made it quite clear that she was not complaining about this – 'It is what I'm paid for,' she said – so that was an improvement on Mildred, but she did wonder if maybe it was because the Day Centre had been too much for her. I said maybe it had been, that it was only an experiment anyway. Mrs O'Malley promised to report at the end of the week on how Grandma was.

Charlie had come with us on the first day only as a gesture of family solidarity. I took her on my own today. I went along early, to allow for taking her to the lavatory and getting her coat on and manipulating her into the car. Susan was still there. She usually leaves at 1.30, after giving Grandma her lunch but although it was nearly quarter to two she was sitting at the kitchen table drinking tea and talking to Grandma. It was a quite deliberately set-up scene. Susan had her hand in Grandma's and was talking to her in a crooning, sickly-sweet way, as some people cannot help doing to babies. 'You've got lovely hair, darlin',' she was saying as I let myself in. 'It's just like my mammy's was afore she died. Aw, I loved my mammy,' Susan was saying, 'just like I love you, darlin', you sweet thing you, your Susan loves you and treats you nice, eh?' There was a pretend jump as I walked in and an utterly false, old Southern 'I do declare, Missus McKay,' straight out of *Gone With The Wind*. One baby was smearing jam over the other's mouth – they sat side-by-side in a twin buggy, strapped in, the jampot between them and sodden rusks matted into the rug over their knees. 'These is my nephews,' Susan said. 'Mrs McKay here, she does love kiddies don't you darlin'?' Grandma rolled her eyes and Susan laughed, pausing only to tell me what fun they had sure been having.

Bridget thinks Susan steals. She maintains it is Susan who takes the cigarettes and that they don't get lost at all. I really cannot bear it when Bridget starts on this. I dare not say, 'What does it matter, anyway?' Bridget sees this 'stealing' – we are talking about a few cigarettes a day – as an act of aggression towards her mother. She thinks it is monstrous of Susan and is always wanting to 'have it out' with her. Or lay a trap. I refuse to discuss it – Susan is welcome to the cigarettes, if indeed she is taking them. Bridget also suspects the babies she brings with her are fed on Grandma's sugar, Grandma's biscuits, Grandma's jam. I pointed out that as I paid for them and I did not care, there was no need for Bridget to do so. Bridget said it was the principle. Grandma *never* stole and she was poorer than Susan. But then, as we all know, Bridget sees her mother as perfect.

I told Susan where we were off to. Her face went grave. 'She won't like it,' she said, shaking her head. 'She's happier here. You don't know how they is treated there, no sir.' I said I did know and that Grandma had loved it and it gave her some company and an outing. Susan turned to Grandma and said, 'Did you like the Day Centre, darlin'? You can tell Susan.' Grandma asked who Susan was. Susan did another full-bellied laugh. 'She says that to me sometimes,' she gasped, clutching her great belly. 'She says who is Susan and I say Susan is *me* and I've been lookin' after you every day nearly for three years and you say who is Susan.' Grandma said she looked after herself. 'Of course you do, darlin',' Susan said. Grandma said was anyone going to make a cup of tea or did she have to make it herself as usual but, oh yes, we would want a cup when she had bloomin' well made it.

Susan helped me get Grandma ready. I could have done without the help. The more Susan talked, the more confused Grandma became until she was sure Susan's so-called nephews were Susan's own children. 'Give them a penny,' she told me. I said they would only put money in their mouths. 'Then give it to their mother, where's my bag, I've plenty of money, the poor bairns.' I gave Susan ten pence. She ostentatiously slipped it back to me. It was hard to know which would be more embarrassing, accepting it or insisting she kept the wretched coin. Finally, we got outside and Susan trundled off, the 'nephews' screaming now that they were deprived of jam. The screaming worried Grandma and I wished Susan would get a move on and round the corner where she would doubtless have her own way of stopping the noise.

When we pulled up outside the Day Centre, there was plenty of room. We were either ahead of or behind the van delivery of disabled attenders. But, although there was nothing at all in sight to alarm her, or even to indicate what this place was, Grandma refused to budge. She said her legs were stuck and she would have to go home. It was no good saying that if her legs were stuck here they would be stuck when we got home – such subtleties of reasoning were a waste of time. I stood looking down at her, the car door wide open, thinking. Grandma said it was bloomin' cold and she wished people would shut the dratted door because they were letting the heat from the fire out. I fingered the ten pence piece Susan had returned to me. Grandma was staring straight ahead, rigid. Carefully, I bent down and placed the coin about a foot from the car door. The sun made it shine most satisfactorily. Then I stood back. The shadow of my presence removed, Grandma turned to see where I had gone. The coin stood out quite unmistakably on the dirty pavement. 'Oh!' she exclaimed, and pointed. 'Look at that money – somebody's dropped it, will we take it to the police station?' I did not move. I said, 'It's only ten pence, not worth picking up.' 'In the name of God!' Grandma raged and struggled to be free. She swung her legs out of her own accord, muttering that it was all right for some, easy come, easy go, but if you looked after the pennies the pounds would take care of themselves and she never thought to see the day when silver wouldn't be worth picking up. I gave her a helping hand up and steadied her while she bent to pick up the ten pence. She clutched it triumphantly. 'Will we take it to the police?' she asked. I closed the car door and without replying led her into the Day Centre where she approached each person she met in the corridor with the coin asking if it was theirs. Her face was flushed with the excitement of it all. I left her with the same woman as the day before.

On the way home I pondered on Grandma's love of money. She was the least greedy of women, the least avaricious, but she had, where money was concerned, a certain Scrooge-like attitude – there is nothing mean-spirited about Grandma, she would give anyone who needed it all her help without stinting, but she likes to handle money even now, to handle it and gloat over it and appreciate its worth. Probably, if she hadn't had this character trait, she would have gone under during the worst stages of her widowhood. Bridget is always wondering how on earth Grandma managed on her miserable widow's pension, how did she keep out of debt and never beg? There were her elastic savings of course, the hundred pounds she had when she got married. She would laugh and say their father married her for her bank balance, and in the thirties it was indeed quite a sum. But this hundred pounds, in her own account of how she brought up her family, was like the loaves and fishes. Everything, it seemed, came out of these savings. She had a genius with money, far beyond the grasp of most women of her class and education. Charlie, who, it goes without saying, knows where he inherited his own financial flair, was astonished to discover how very well his mother had managed her pitifully small nest-egg when he took over her affairs. She had a few useless war bonds which she ought to have cashed but otherwise she had bought Premium Bonds and had won small sums with them and then invested her winnings – £50, twice – in National Savings Certificates. She liked to handle money and to handle figures. Nothing made her angrier than contempt for finance. 'Money makes the world go round,' she used to say and when, being provocative but meaning it, I would say surely it was love that made the world go round she would say, 'Don't you believe it.'

It was just possible that dropping a coin outside the car door would always get Grandma out of it but the thought of such endless subterfuge wearied me. Everything is becoming a game – games to get her up, games to feed her, games to make her go to the lavatory. Playing games to that extent is depressing. As I drove home, I wondered if games, tricks, could do any damage. What was Grandma saying when she announced her legs were stuck? She was saying, in the only way she knew how, that she did not want to go to the Day Centre. Was this something she should be helped to overcome? Or, instead of responding with sleights of hand, should we respect her wish? Charlie was the only one with no doubts. When I tried to discuss it at supper, he said of course it was better for Grandma to have company, to be occupied, to be watched over, to be somewhere light and bright instead of stuck in her kitchen on her own from 1.30 to 3.30 until I collected her. He said, with conviction, that it is in her interests to go to the Day Centre – she isn't safe, alone any more. She needs only to trip and fall and lie there for two hours for us to realise this.

It is a funny thing, but Grandma never has fallen. I do not believe that she fell when Mildred found her on the floor – I think she chose to lie down because she forgot how to get into bed. She has never fallen during the day. She is large and ungainly and unbelievably clumsy but it is quite remarkable how this has never led to her falling or breaking things. She used to say it was because she was so slow and that may indeed be the explanation. She does do things very, very slowly, with great evident anxiety. Her own rooms used to be a maze of potential traps – all kinds of objects awkwardly positioned – but she never fell into them. My fingers would itch to clear out all her junk and make more room for her but she would not hear of it. She liked clutter. Her flat down here is much better designed – there are no standard lamps with trailing wires of the lethal sort she used to love – but, even so, she drags bits of furniture into different places, never happy until getting from one end of the room to the other is an obstacle race.

I find I think about Grandma all the time now. I daydream, I worry, I envisage the future. It would really be much better if I had her here, as usual, drinking tea, or not drinking it, and rambling on. As Bridget would say and Hannah endorse, what is all the fuss for?

Hannah

Adrian and I take Grandma to the chiropodist at the clinic. She, the chiropodist, would come to Grandma's home but it makes an outing for Grandma so we keep taking her. And it is what Mum calls a nice little job for Adrian. He does the driving. (Adrian is *very* proud of having passed his driving test first time last year.) He does the driving but for reasons unknown to me he cannot do the taking-into-the-clinic-and-divesting-of-stockings. Mum says Grandma would be embarrassed if Adrian took her stockings off. It would mean fiddling with suspenders – Grandma cannot be parted from her suspenders – and Mum says that is too much to expect. I can't see why but Mum also keeps saying Grandma would mind. How this could be proved I don't know. But I go as well, to be the stocking-taker-offer. Women's work, again.

Adrian has no idea how to get Grandma into the car. He just stands there, helpless, saying why can't she sit down and Grandma stands, equally helpless, and they stare at each other and Grandma asks Adrian if his name is Duncan. He says no, of course, and she says that's a pity because she knows a poem about Duncan Davidson that puts her in mind of him and it goes etc. etc. I say if we stand here any longer, we'll miss the appointment. Then I show off. I point to the floor of the car and tell Grandma to pick that sweetie up, it's going to waste. She bends slowly and, when she's nearly there, reaching into the front of the car, I put my hand on her head to protect it from getting knocked and I push her bottom sideways and she half-falls into the car and I lift her legs to join the rest of her. Mission accomplished. Adrian is aghast. He says I'm cruel. I tell him to shut up. He hasn't the faintest idea of how to manage Grandma.

He drives slowly, as though he had a cargo of porcelain. Grandma asks how long will it take. Adrian says five minutes. Grandma is startled. She says it's a deal quicker than the train. I tell her she's going to the clinic to have her feet done. Grandma says her corns are terrible but there's no point in having anything done because the damned things just grow again and it's a waste of time. By now we are at the clinic. Easier getting her out than in. Even Adrian can do it. A group of his friends is passing as he helps Grandma out. When one of them says 'hello' Grandma shouts 'hello' too and the friend laughs.

> How's your mother?
> Sorry?
> She thinks she knows your mother.
> I *do* know his mother, and his father.
> Bad luck, Grandma, Luke hasn't got a father.
> What nonsense, everyone has a father.
> Luke's mother doesn't know his, he was a test-tube baby.
> Adrian!
> Poor wee soul, you never know the minute . . .
> Come on Grandma, concentrate.
> The cheek of it.
> Hi, Adrian.
> Hi, Ben.
> Hello, hello, how's your lady friend.
> Pardon?
> How's your mother?

Adrian is sweating, but the friends pass on. By now Grandma is on the pavement and upright if not yet walking. We then have the exaggerated shivers as she complains about the non-existent, terrible cold. This is followed by a similar performance of gasping and blowing as she complains about the awful heat once we are in the clinic. Adrian says he'll wait outside. Why not, I say to him, God knows you've done your bit.

Grandma does enjoy the clinic, there's no doubt. She nods and smiles at the other two people waiting and assures them she knows their mothers. They both, one man, one woman, stare at her blankly. They are old too, but clearly in full possession of their mental faculties and proud of it. Grandma whispers, perfectly audibly, that they are a miserable lot, she doesn't know what is the matter with them, but never mind. She starts to sing 'Green Grow the Rashes', and when she gets to the line, 'My arms about my dearie O' she puts her arms round me and I put mine round her and we both laugh. She's still in high good humour when her name is called. She struggles up, quite excited, and I go with her and take her stockings off for the chiropodist. Her feet are like deserted battle grounds. They are covered in discoloured lumps and bumps, the flesh stretched over them scaly and blue. Her toes bear no resemblance to any toes I have ever known. They are huge and twisted into strange shapes. I could cry looking at Grandma's feet but she is looking down at them affectionately.

I sit outside. I suppose the chiropodist wouldn't mind if I stayed but when she asks would I like to wait outside, I always obey. I can hear every word. The chiropodist asks Grandma if she's been having any trouble at all with her feet. It seems a stupid question to me when she's confronted with all the evidence of the trouble Grandma has with her wretched feet. I wait to hear Grandma begin on the litany of foot trouble, but no.

No trouble at all, thank you.
Not with this big corn?
Don't you bother with it, I've had it years.
I think I can ease it a little.
They all say that, they're all wrong.
Did you walk here?
I did, I like a wee walk.
Are your shoes comfortable?
They are, lovely shoes, I got them at the Co-op.
Have you lived in London long?

96

I've never lived in London, never left Glasgow.
(*−long silence−*)
Does this toe joint hurt?
Sometimes but I just bash it.
Walking doesn't cause any problems?
No trouble at all, thank you.

I go back in to put the stockings on. The chiropodist explains to
me what she has done and what she will do next time. She refers to
Grandma as 'she' and 'her', as though she was an idiot. When it
comes to putting Grandma's shoes on, I have difficulty. They're very
old shoes. They're made of brown leather, the sort that are laced
and have good strong soles. The leather is very worn. In fact, there's
a small hole, rapidly widening into a tear, where Grandma's largest
bunion is pushing through. The chiropodist watches. She says
maybe 'she' needs some new shoes. Grandma flares up. She says
these are good shoes, they cost a fortune, there is nothing the matter
with them. I'm sweating. Grandma is not helping. She holds her foot
rigid, won't even attempt to bend her toes. One shoe is on and laced
but I can't get her left foot into the other. All this pushing and
shoving is useless. Grandma is getting angry. She starts kicking her
foot deliberately so that the shoe flies across the room.

One, two, buckle my shoe.
Grandma, behave.
You mind yourself.
You mind *yourself*, keep your foot still.
I like a wee jig now and again.
Not when you're putting your shoes on.
We need a fiddler, though.
Well, there isn't one.
Where did my father's fiddle go? Who stole it?
I haven't the slightest idea.
Look, then.
Grandma, don't be ridiculous, keep your foot still, *please*.
One, two, buckle my shoe.

The chiropodist has retrieved the other shoe and comments
sympathetically that she does feel sorry for me. Now *I* am angry. I

97

snap at the chiropodist. Then I hand Grandma her shoe and I stand up and I tell her that if she doesn't hurry up, the men will be in for their tea and nothing ready. She proceeds to put her own shoe on, stumbling only over the tying of the laces which I bend and do quickly.

When we get home, I say to Mum straight away that Grandma must have new shoes, that her shoes are in a terrible state, that it's no wonder her walking is deteriorating. I put Grandma's slippers on her feet and then I flourish the offending shoes under Mum's nose. Mum says I'm not telling her anything she doesn't know. She has taken Grandma to a shoe shop and there is no such thing as a shoe which will fit her appallingly misshapen feet. But she will mention it to Bridget and see if she has any ideas. Adrian chips in. He says how about men's trainers? I scoff but Mum nods. Adrian brings his new trainers and tries them on Grandma. They appear to go on quite easily. She looks so funny, sitting on the sofa with Adrian's white trainers plonked on the end of her lisle-stockinged legs. We're still laughing when Bridget arrives. Grandma is laughing too, she knows she's a good turn. She has taken the tea cosy off the tea pot – the tea cosy she crocheted herself years ago and loves to see on the tea pot, so Mum tries to remember to put it on – and she has put it on her head because she says she can feel a bloomin' draught. She has one ear poking out of the hole for the spout and the other out of the hole for the handle. The vivid reds, blues, greens and yellows of the tea cosy stripes straddle her large head. Adrian is crying with laughing and I am almost as bad. Then Bridget arrives. She snatches the tea cosy off Grandma's head. Grandma yelps and tells her to get lost. Bridget's face is red and angry. She *hates* Grandma to be a laughing stock even though Grandma loves to be the cause of mirth. Bridget says, 'Mother!' furiously and also yanks off Adrian's trainers. Now Grandma starts moaning her feet and head are both cold. Bridget grabs the tartan shawl from a chair and ties it round Grandma's head. She looks around and finds Grandma's shoes and forces them on. Mum looks annoyed. She says to Bridget it was only a joke. Bridget says some jokes go too far. Mum makes an exclamation of irritation and goes into the kitchen. I start to speak but Mum motions that I should say nothing. Really, Bridget is very odd.

For some reason Mum appears nervous. She tells Bridget she will notice that Grandma isn't wearing her own knickers. She had a slight mishap at the Day Centre and they provided a spare pair and Mum has just left them on for the rest of the day and anyway there wasn't time to change them between collecting her early from the Day Centre and our taking her to the chiropodist. Bridget says she knew it, she was always against that place, it just upsets Grandma, but still Mum rambles on. She tells Bridget that she has discovered the Day Centre has its own chiropodist so Grandma could get done there and they also have a hairdresser and they could wash her hair and save us the trouble. It's a mistake to say this. Bridget repeats 'trouble' several times as though she does not understand the word. She says it's news to her that any of these *simple* tasks constitute *trouble*. Mum says she, Bridget, knows what she means perfectly well. Grandma asks if anyone is going to make a cup of tea, she is parched, she has had none all day. Mum says she's had four cups since she came home. Grandma says she has not and Bridget says, 'Come on Mother, we'll go on home and you can have as much tea as you like.'

*

Everything has suddenly gone wrong. When I say this aloud Mum says it's not sudden. It's been coming for a long time and it was inevitable. Mrs O'Malley has gone back to Ireland. That's the first disaster. The tale is that her brother's wife has died and she has gone to look after the children. There was no notice given but then, if it was a genuine drama, there wouldn't be. The second catastrophe is that, just as Mum has got Grandma used to the Day Centre, they have said they are very sorry but they can no longer take her. They cannot cope either with the incontinent or the seriously confused and they are classifying Grandma as both. Mum is more humiliated than anything else. She feels the Day Centre may think she was trying to pull a fast one, trying to get them to take Grandma on false pretences when truly the incontinence and the level of confusion are new. Adrian laughed when he heard and teased Grandma about getting expelled from school. Grandma said she loves school and she has certainly not been expelled and she is the star pupil and she never stays off and once her mother had to strap her to the bed when she had the flu because she was determined to go to school and she loves school etc. etc.

But far worse is that Bridget is ill. She rang Mum this morning and said she couldn't get out of bed. Mum flew along, all memory of being annoyed by Bridget a few days before (and the atmosphere had lingered) forgotten. Grandma was in bed, Bridget was in bed, the same bed. Grandma had got up three times in the night and Bridget had slept with her to settle her. Mum said Grandma was loving it, all cuddled up to Bridget, but Bridget was white as a sheet and in agony. Bridget has awful rheumatism. Since she's a nurse, Mum says this diagnosis cannot be queried but that the fact is Bridget has never seen a doctor about it, or not for years. This rheumatism swells the joints of her legs and does something or other to her back and the result is that she finds all movement almost impossible. But it has never been so bad. Bridget has always managed to limp on. Now, she can't manage to do that and she definitely can't manage to look after Grandma. Mum more or less forced her to go through the hell of moving into her own bed in her own flat though Bridget swore she could not move and did not wish to. Mum said she would have Bridget carted off to hospital otherwise. So Bridget limped into her own bed with Mum's help and Mum packed her round with hot water bottles and, to Bridget's fury, rang the doctor. The doctor came. He said, yes, Bridget had severe rheumatoid arthritis and must stay in bed until the tablets he gave her began to ease it.

So that's it, chaos. It only needs Susan to pack it in and we're sunk. And there are two people to look after now, two dependants. Strangely, Mum is quite calm and very efficient. She says her hand is forced and in a way this is a relief. She says Karl would love the chance to look after Bridget but that she dare not ring him, even if she knew his number, because Bridget would never forgive her. Karl? Karl? I can't believe it. Mum realises she's said something she shouldn't. She tells me to forget it. How *can* I forget it. I'm riveted. I demand to have this explained. I beg to be told who on earth this Karl is. Mum says he's Bridget's boyfriend. Good God. I ask why she keeps him secret, what's wrong with him? Mum says nothing, he is charming, though as she has only met him once or twice for a few minutes, she can't really judge. She reminds me that Bridget doesn't like people to know her business. I riposte that I, her ever-loving niece, am hardly 'people' and a boyfriend is hardly 'business'. There's no denying it, I'm hurt. I thought I was Bridget's friend. Why should she exclude me from this friendship of hers?

Mum says, at supper, that we must plan. Dad says we must ring some sort of agency, this is London, there are scores of them, he's always reading about them. Mum asks who for, Bridget or his mother, and to do what? Dad says whatever needs doing, *he* doesn't know. Mum says that's what she wants to discuss. First, what about this very night? Susan has been prevailed on to come back in the evening, she's there with Grandma now, but she leaves in half an hour. Who will spend the night with Grandma? There is silence. I say I will. Mum says I will be up and down all night and won't be fit for school. Dad says he will, then. Mum says he'll be up and down all night and not fit for work. She says it's obvious, she must do it but that she's not prepared to do it every night. Dad says no one wants her to, that we must get someone else at once and did Mum keep the addresses? Mum asks what addresses? Dad says the addresses of those other women who were interviewed when we took Mrs O'Malley on. Mum says no. Dad says how careless and they argue. Then Dad says, never mind, he's sick to death of these kind of precarious arrangements and either we have to get someone to live in, full-time, a proper housekeeper and companion, or Grandma will have to go into a Home and that is that. Mum says that's a very fine speech and means nothing, that Dad *knows* housekeepers and companions are almost impossible to get, though he's bloody well welcome to try and, as for Homes, haven't they looked at Homes, haven't they, haven't they?

Have they? I didn't know. Adrian looks pained and says he didn't know and that, frankly, it doesn't seem right to him to put dear old Grandma – he gets no further. Mum screams *I am sick of people telling me what is right when there is no right*. We are all shocked. Dad says Mum is getting overwrought, and she says certainly she is. All she's heard so far are criticisms and half-baked suggestions. Nobody is facing the facts. Dad says right, we will face them. He personally will spend tomorrow on the telephone and find a temporary, full-time carer for Grandma. He agrees he hasn't the slightest idea how he will do so but he vows he will. And as for Bridget, that's easy, he will ring Paula. Paula is at home all day, she does nothing, she can do anything Bridget wants. Mum says Bridget won't like that and Dad says Bridget is in no position to be choosy. Paula is family and calls on us when she needs to, so she must expect to be called on too. Adrian says he can drive over and pick Paula up before he goes to school, since she can't drive and Stuart may not be able to bring her if he is busy. Dad's pleased. He says that's a constructive suggestion. I say that since tomorrow is Friday and I have no school on Saturday I can sleep at Grandma's tomorrow if Dad fails to find anyone. Mum says, under her breath, that he will fail all right and Dad says that's a generous offer. Mum goes off to Grandma's at nine o'clock and Dad goes with her to run Susan home because Susan has said she can only come in the evening if she's collected and delivered.

In about half an hour I ring Mum just to ask how things are. She says fine. Bridget is comfortably tucked up for the night and requires nothing. Grandma is ready for bed and is reciting 'The Lass o' Ecclefechan'. She wants more tea but Mum is not going to give her any, no matter how much she sulks, because she's convinced controlling fluid intake will cure Grandma's disturbed nights. Mrs O'Malley, and before her Mildred, gave Grandma tea to please her, to keep her quiet. Mum says she'd rather give her whisky. I ask why don't you, it might knock her out. Mum says, as a matter of fact, Grandma doesn't like whisky. She enrages people who offer it to her by saying she'll drink it, though it's horrible, and then spitting it out – that drives Stuart crazy. Grandma only likes egg-nog. In the background, as Mum talks about alcohol of one sort or another, I can hear Grandma saying that strong drink is raging, wine is mockery and he who is deceived thereby is not wise.

Dad means to do his bit. He has already rung Paula who says, yes, both boys are at school in the morning and, of course, she would come to look after Bridget but unfortunately she cannot because she has no transport because Stuart's car is giving trouble and is in the garage and the cross-country journey by bus and tube would take her so long she – Dad cuts in and says Adrian will pick her up and take her home. Paula is obliged to say in that case it will be fine. Now Dad is making lists. He's going through the local paper and the Yellow Pages and he's copying out numbers of people to ring. He also gets me to make a notice for our newsagent's board saying 'Emergency: Companion wanted for old lady for minimum of one month, live in, £250 per week.' Such money! Dad says, before he takes it round to put through our newsagent's door so it can go on the board first thing, that it would be cheap at the price. But he agrees, Grandma would faint if she knew. The way to look at it, he says, before I go to bed, is that we're lucky to have the money to solve our problem.

It doesn't. It doesn't seem to solve anything much, the money. When Susan arrives, Mum comes in from Grandma's, looking awful. Grandma woke her at one in the morning in a great state of excitement to tell her she had heard there were lovely cauliflowers in the market and, quick, let's go and get one. She woke her again at half past three to say someone had thrown a bucket of water over her, damned cheek, and Mum had to change the sheets and Grandma. At half past five, when Mum was in the deepest of sleeps, Grandma literally shook her awake saying she would be late for work. So Mum had stayed up. She sits now, with her hands fast round a cup of coffee I have made her, slumped in misery and asking what is the point. I go to school. When I come back, Dad is on the telephone, hoarse with all the calls he has made, a nursing agency will send someone but they will charge £10 an hour, extra at the weekend, and they can't guarantee the same person each night. If the nurse has to make any meals, it's extra again and they aren't obliged to do so. It will come to £100 a night, Dad thinks. He has stopped talking about money solving problems. Now he's ringing a Home he's been given the name of, St Alma's. They say they have no vacancies but Grandma can go on the waiting list if they think she's suitable. Dad must bring her for an assessment. He says he's fed up, he's had enough.

What's so awful is the way they act as though it's Grandma's fault. How can she help it? You would think someone was waging a personal vendetta against them. I can't help wondering whether they love Grandma at all. If they do, they have a funny way of showing it. I'm quite glad, at eight o'clock, to get my things together and go. The mournful atmosphere is depressing. Dad walks along with me. He's giving Susan a lift home. We don't talk. It doesn't suit Dad to have to think deeply. He's a man of quick decisions, not given to pondering. It frustrates him not to be able to do a spot of quick thinking, snap his fingers and solve things. I can't see anything of Grandma in him except for his sense of humour – they laugh at exactly the same things – and this hatred of emotional difficulties. That's what Grandma is at the moment, an emotional difficulty. Dad wants to be like Stuart. He wants to say that since Grandma hardly knows who she is these days, putting her in a Home is only sensible, but Dad knows that's dodging the issue. He knows Bridget is right, that Grandma deserves better. And he hates knowing it.

Susan has her hat and coat on and looks a little agitated. Mum has already said she has a horrible suspicion that quite a few 'nephews' have been left on their own so that Susan can oblige and make a great deal of extra money. Susan's sitting with her hand over Grandma's, patting it. She says Grandma has been looking for her mammy, poor old lady. Grandma says who's the poor old lady, she hopes nobody is referring to her, she's got plenty of money etc. etc. Susan sighs lugubriously and stands up. Grandma says good riddance and makes a silly face behind Susan's back. Dad hurries Susan out, saying over his shoulder that I'm to ring if I need him and maybe I could just look in on Bridget for ten minutes.

Have the men gone?
They have, Grandma, all one of them.
Thank goodness, bloomin' nuisances.
Why?
Why what?
Why are men nuisances?
Oh, for heaven's sake.
No, really, Grandma why are men nuisances?
Always wanting their teas.
Is that all?
All what?

104

Is that the only reason men are nuisances?
Who says so?
Says what?
Men are nuisances.
You do.
I like men, always did.
Then why are they nuisances?
Who?
Men.
Have the men gone?

I make some tea, only a small amount as instructed by Mum.
There's to be no more.

Not many people tonight.
Where?
Here.
Why would there be?
It often gets crowded.
Who with?
Them.
Who are they?
Are you daft or something?
This is your kitchen, why would it be crowded?
It isn't crowded.
I know, that's what I said.
Not many people tonight.

I put the radio on, some vaguely classical music. Grandma is so
bored. She asks if we'll away to our bed. I say why not. She finishes
the tea and asks if I've put the cat out, she hasn't seen it for a while.
She asks if I've bolted the doors, there are funny men about. As I
take her through to the bedroom, and start undressing her, I wonder
if anything has ever happened to Grandma to do with 'funny' men.
Nobody would ever be told if it had. Grandma would keep whatever it was a secret. She says talking about nasty things only makes
them nastier. All of twentieth-century psychology rejected in one
sentence. Mum says Grandma's life is full of great black holes,

105

bottomless pits of silence. That's the sort of fancy description Grandma laughs at most. But it's true.

I don't often dress or undress Grandma. I follow Mum's instructions. The secret is to sit her on the edge of the bed and keep talking, keep her attention away from what she's doing. So, as I start unbuttoning the first of her two cardigans, the lurid violet one which she knitted herself with the knobbly buttons, I tell her how tired I am of the way the boys in the sixth form treat us girls. I elaborate on their grossness, how brutal they all are, how they throw their weight about and have no sensitivity or delicacy, and the cardigans, even the brown courtelle one underneath which has hellish, small, tight buttons, the cardigans are off in a trice. The jumper under that has to come over Grandma's rather big head. I take care to be relating a particularly diverting anecdote about a boy called Alan, who pushed into the dinner queue in front of me, as I pull the wretched jumper over her head. Her 'Did you let him?' is muffled but the jumper is off. Now we're down to the vest. I pause at the vest. Grandma has night vests and day vests. I really don't think I want to remove Grandma's vest. Who will know? She is looking at me adoringly, her almost lashless eyes blinking as though the light was bright. I realise she wants to know whether Alan succeeded. I tell her I bashed him and she laughs so hard she nearly falls off the bed. I leave the vest on. I slip Grandma's blue flannel nightdress over her head and then slide her skirt down to her huge hips. She's such an extraordinary shape down there. She puts her own hands on her stomach as I persuade her to stand up and says feel my belly, I hope I haven't a growth. The skirt is off but not the knickers. Well, I can't leave those on. I fumble under her nightdress and find the elastic and yank. Grandma says leave off. The old suspender belt she is devoted to since Bridget burned her corsets is almost embedded in her flesh. I have the greatest difficulty releasing it. What stupid, stupid clothes. What Grandma needs is a track suit. I'm going to tell Bridget that.

The nice bit is tucking Grandma up. She adores getting into bed. The electric blankets, under and over, have been on for half an hour and her bed is roasting. She clambers in and sighs with contentment and screws her eyes up in ecstasy and murmurs it is heaven, it is bliss, it is all she wants. Her white hair on the pink pillow looks so pretty and her face relaxed and happy without that old, ugly body attached to it. She says why don't I get in with her. I say I've got some homework to do. I sit beside her for a while wondering why she can't be allowed to say in bed forever. It's the only place she wants to be. Mum has warned me not to be fooled. She says that when I leave the room, with Grandma vowing she never wants to leave her lovely bed ever again, I will barely have time to settle myself in the kitchen before Grandma will be padding through. She's right. It's unbelievable, but she's right. I'm barely settled in a chair with *Bleak House* before Grandma does appear. She says she didn't hear the alarm and she knows she's late and none of those bloomin' men up for their work yet. I take her back to the bed she swore she never wanted to leave. We go through the same performance again. This time I stay with her, holding her hand under the covers, until she snores.

It's only nine o'clock. I go across the hall to visit Bridget, tapping on the doors as I go in. Bridget is lying in bed reading. She gives me a lovely smile. It's such a contrast to be looking at Grandma's face *young*. I make some coffee and take it through to Bridget and sit down on her bed. She says, mimicking Grandma, I'm a little angel and won't go to the bad fire now. I entertain her with an account of putting Grandma to bed, she entertains me with an account of Paula doing her Florence Nightingale stunt. Bridget says Paula even washed the television screen when she cleaned the flat. Paula, she says, hadn't had such a good time for years, what with finding stale bread in the bin and the fridge door broken, because Bridget forgets to defrost it and it jams, and heaps of cigarette stubs stuck in unlikely places. Bridget says she almost offered Paula a peg for her dainty nose. But then she adds hastily that Paula was very good and did some shopping too and made her a lovely meal and really it *was* good of her.

I badly want to ask Bridget about Karl but I daren't. It's not that it's impossible to imagine Bridget with a man, not at all impossible, but what I can't imagine is Bridget *sharing*. She's independent, I've grown used to thinking of her as a person entirely self-sufficient. How would Bridget be with another person? A person on the same level as herself, not someone of whom she was in charge. Would it be, is it, a relief for her to lean on someone else? To be told what to do? To be planned for and organised and taken charge of? But maybe it isn't like that at all, maybe Bridget keeps this Karl secret because hers is an affair of grand passion. Goodness what would Grandma say? And maybe that's the explanation – Grandma would not like Karl whatever he was like. What I want to know is:

> Does Bridget hide Karl from Grandma?
> Is Bridget afraid Grandma will not like Karl?
> Is Bridget afraid Karl will not like Grandma?
> If Bridget had to choose which would she choose, Karl or Grandma?

*

I'm up before Grandma. It counts as a victory. I'm just thinking how lucky I have been, unlike Mum, how fortunate not to have been disturbed when I realise I may have slept through Grandma's wanderings. I left the kettle on the cooker top but when I go into the kitchen it's on the floor and there's a puddle beside it. Suppose Grandma has been standing there in the night trying to make herself a cup of tea, and me asleep. I bend and investigate the puddle nervously. It's only water spilled from the kettle. I can't decide whether to leave Grandma or go through to see that she's safely tucked up. It's only eight o'clock, not an hour at which I'm usually up on a Saturday morning. I decide just to peep round Grandma's bedroom door before I make myself some coffee. I peep. Grandma's not there.

I walk into the bedroom saying, 'Grandma?' but there's no sign of her, no response. She must be in the bathroom having trouble with her famous bowels and not wanting to be embarrassed. She isn't. I fly through the flat to the door that leads into the hall, terrified in case Grandma has got out and is looking for Bridget, but that door is locked and the key removed as I left it. This is ridiculous. I go through the flat calling and looking stupidly behind chairs and in cupboards. No Grandma. I'm a little frightened while telling myself not to be so silly, nothing can have happened to her. Then, as I come back into the kitchen for the third time I see a face peering in at the window. Oh, my God! I shout, 'Grandma!' rush to the back door and fling it open and she's standing there, blue to the lips, standing shivering in her nightdress with nothing on her feet, standing with a crust of bread in her hand and little bits of it torn up and scattered round her on the ground. She says, 'The poor birds.'

It's only when I'm trying to warm Grandma that she starts to feel cold. How long has she been out there? I have no idea. I'm going to have to tell Mum where I found Grandma and confess that I don't know how long she stood in that cold garden. Surely it can't have been long. She would have tried banging on the window or the door if she had been there long, surely? I feel so guilty. I tell Grandma she must not go out in her nightdress, ever.

I wouldn't dream of it, the idea!
You've just done it.
Watch your mouth.
I found you feeding the birds in the garden in your nightdress and with nothing on your feet.
Poor birds.
Poor you, standing outside almost naked.
I wouldn't dream of it, the idea!

But she appears terribly pleased with herself. She sings away as I make her porridge and every now and again, she says top of the morning to you. She drinks a big mug of tea with relish, saying it's nice and sweet and that she's a devil for sweet things. She asks what are we going to do today, shall we away a walk, she likes a walk, her father used to etc. etc., and her mother told him etc. etc., and suddenly there's a new bit tacked on to the end. She tells me she had three aunts, all tall, who used to look like sailing ships as they crossed Glasgow Green. Isabella, Annabella and Mary. All tall, with long cloaks billowing out and they were like sailing ships. There is a silence. I bring the porridge to Grandma and look at her and she looks at me. Her eyes are clear, she is *sensible*. We hold each other's gaze for a few seconds. I murmur very, very quietly, locking her gaze into mine, I say softly and encouragingly 'Isabella, Annabella and Mary?' and she repeats the names and says they were her father's sisters, none of them married, and when the last one died they left her a hundred pounds and she was always glad of it and wished she had not laughed to see them crossing the Green in their old-fashioned cloaks. I hardly dare put the porridge down but the minute I do that's that. She asks if her mother is back from church yet.

Susan isn't coming because it's Saturday. Dad is coming instead and we will take turns, all weekend, unless he finds some assistance – an hour each, the four of us, a continuing rota. Tomorrow we'll take Grandma to our house as we always do. Dad breezes in, pleased I've made the porridge. At least Grandma always knows who he is though, when Adrian is there with Dad, she sometimes asks him who his friend is. Dad has some tea himself which pleases Grandma. She says she was just about to fry some bacon, would he fancy some? Dad says, yes, please. He's already deep into the sports pages of the newspaper he has brought with him. He'll spend his hour drinking tea and reading his paper and will hardly address a word to Grandma, but then she seems quite satisfied with this arrangement. I give her a kiss and go.

★

There's been an applicant for the job of caring for Grandma. Mum says as I go into the kitchen that the phone rang as soon as Dad left. I say good and Mum says she doesn't know if it's good or not. It's a girl of only twenty, not much older than me. I say that I manage perfectly well so why should this Cynthia not manage too? Grandma likes young people. Mum says Cynthia is coming round at two o'clock when Adrian will be on duty and we three, Dad, Mum and I, can all interview Cynthia. She lives just round the corner and she's a student, studying anthropology. She says she's looked after her own grandmother. She would be quite happy to move in full-time if we like. Mum doesn't like the sound of this: she thinks it's too willing by half.

Cynthia arrives on time. She's quite different from the middle-aged to elderly women we have used so far. She looks even younger than twenty and is very attractive – short, almost punky, blonde hair, stylish clothes, bright smile. She is unmistakably middle-class. What on earth would Grandma make of her? She tells Dad her father and

110

mother are both doctors. This goes down very well: Cynthia is definitely onto a winner there. Her home is in Stratford-on-Avon. She agrees she wants to care for Grandma for the money. Then it turns out her up-market parents are divorced and there are arguments about who should pay her grant. She is having hard times. Mum runs through what Cynthia will have to do: make Grandma's supper, sit and chat to her, undress and wash her, put her to bed. She stresses that Grandma can do nothing for herself and asks Cynthia if she realises what that means? Cynthia answers intelligently, as you'd expect. Mum says she may get woken several times a night or not at all, how would Cynthia cope with that? Cynthia says she doesn't need much sleep. Dad jumps in to ask when Cynthia could start. She says tonight. Dad looks at Mum, Mum hesitates, Dad says shall we give it a trial run? Cynthia says fine. Dad says, ok, try it for tonight and tomorrow, no commitment either side and we'll discuss it Monday.

When Cynthia has gone, Mum asks Dad who is going to tell Bridget. Dad says Bridget doesn't need to know, she's out of the picture, so stop fussing. If it turns out satisfactorily, then we'll tell Bridget. He's firm. Mum seems to me pleased that he is. Then he says he has made an appointment to go and look at St Alma's. He says he wants Grandma's name down now, even if she is manageable for another year. It will be no good, Dad says, when a real crisis comes, trying to find a Home then. He has had enough of all this uncertainty, he wants the security of some kind of back-up. Bridget need not be brought into it. Mum says she doesn't like the thought of going behind Bridget's back. Dad sighs. He says this fear of Bridget is absurd. Who *is* Bridget to dictate what should be done about Grandma? He is Grandma's son, he foots the bills, and bloody big bills they are too, and this gives him rights, surely? So, will Mum kindly shut up about Bridget.

Adrian comes back from his shift glowing with virtue. He says he's had a lovely time, no bother. Grandma and he watched the racing on television and drank cups of tea and she was fine. He then says he really doesn't know why we don't just have Grandma living with us, that it would be a lot simpler and cheaper and he wouldn't mind at all. Mum just looks at him and says, 'I beg your pardon?'

Adrian repeats that it seems silly to him that Grandma doesn't live with us. He adds that we all act as if she was some horrible ogre instead of a lovely old lady. We could still have helpers, he says, but if Grandma was actually under our roof, wouldn't it be better? She would like to be part of a family, that's what she wants really. Adrian finishes up with a real gem by saying he doesn't think old people should be shoved off, it's a shame, in his opinion.

Mum is fighting to keep control. She clasps her hands together in front of her to keep them from trembling. She is *so* angry with Adrian and he has no idea. Very quietly, she says in theory his idea is perfect. Yes, Grandma would love to be in the bosom of her family but, in fact, she would not like to be in this one but in Bridget's. Adrian unwisely interrupts to say Bridget hasn't got a family. Mum resumes, her voice not as quiet. She says that is precisely the point, that the only family Grandma wants to be with is Bridget and Bridget is a single woman who works and therefore that is not feasible. Grandma, as Adrian well knows, spends all her time wanting Bridget and without Bridget she is restless and discontented. It may have escaped Adrian's notice but a great deal of time and effort and money is being spent trying to give Grandma as much of what she wants as possible without wrecking other people's lives. Adrian jeers – 'Wrecking? Wrecking? How would having Grandma wreck a life, anybody's life?' Mum takes a deep breath. She asks Adrian if he's blind and deaf. She asks him if he's aware of how much help Grandma needs, how she's a danger to herself, how she has to be watched and guarded *all the time*. And the nights, Mum says, almost shouting now, does Adrian even begin to imagine what it's like getting up three times in one night? Adrian becomes surly and aggrieved. He says all he meant was that Grandma could live in the same house and we would still have all the help. Mum almost screams *I do not want Grandma in my house all the time*. Well, I wouldn't mind, mutters Adrian, if I was a woman and at home all day like you, doing nothing: I wouldn't mind at all. And he goes out.

I tell Mum just to ignore him, he's a pig. Mum says Adrian is only voicing her own inner thoughts. She says she struggles with this one all the time; that it's monstrous that she doesn't want Grandma to live with us. Hoping to distract her from this kind of silly remorse, I say it's just such a pity Bridget is not married with a family because then there would be no problem. Mum smiles enigmatically and says no problem, eh? I ask if she thinks there would be one. Mum says she sometimes wonders. She says she doesn't think any husband of Bridget's would ever have been able to stomach Bridget's relationship with Grandma. He would always have felt excluded and he would never have been put first. And then, Mum says, slowly, there's Bridget herself. It's true she loves and admires her mother passionately but the sheer intensity of this adoration is a dead weight. Bridget once told her, Mum says, that it was when she was young that she craved Grandma's love and Grandma never gave her what she wanted. She knew Grandma loved her but she wanted to hear that she did and Grandma never told her, she didn't cuddle or kiss or use endearments and Bridget yearned for them. When they came, they came too late, when Bridget was grown up and out in the world. Mum says it was so sad, listening to Bridget. She said she hadn't realised Stuart was the apple of Grandma's eye for so many years and Bridget the one taken for granted. So, in a way, Bridget is giving now what she never got herself and she knows it. Bridget sees expediency in Grandma's devotion to her.

It seems a good moment. I ask about Karl. Who is he? Does Bridget love him? Why doesn't she live with him? Mum says I must ask Bridget, just as she said before. Maybe, she says, it would do Bridget good to be pressed on this subject. Maybe she wants to bring Karl out into the open but doesn't know how to do it. Ask her, Mum encourages. Is he handsome, I ask? Mum smiles. She says it depends what you call handsome. I tell her not to be annoying. She says, well, perhaps you would think him handsome. He's tall, taller than Bridget, and rather heavy. Not *fat*, I scream. No, not fat, heavy, well-built, like a rugby player, a bit like Stuart. O, ma Gawd, I say. And he has blondish hair, very short, almost a crew cut – O, ma Gawd, I say again – and a square face with incredibly blue eyes. He is quite impressive, Mum says, and his English is excellent. You mean he's *foreign*, I exclaim. Mum says he's German. I'm getting quite excited by now, it sounds as if Bridget's secret lover is no wimp, no boring ordinary dreary character, it sounds very much as though there are elements of Romance and Mystery. Mum has forgotten that she wasn't going to tell me anything. I ask if this hunky Karl is married. Mum says no. Well then, I say, why on earth is Bridget not living with him? Mum says she has said too much already.

It's my turn to go to Grandma again. I decide that my being five minutes late won't hurt Grandma and I let myself in to Bridget's instead. Because she is ill and in bed and I have the key, I never think of waiting for her to answer the bell, which I just ping to let her know someone is on the way. When I go into the bedroom there's a man sitting by the bed. Of course, it's Karl. Bridget seems to let out a small groan and to half hide under the covers. Karl stands up and holds out his hand and says he is Karl, a friend of Bridget's. I say hello, I am Hannah, Bridget's niece.

What I want to know is:

How old is he?

Jenny

There is in my head a vision of the sort of Home I want for
Grandma, the sort that would be perfect in my eyes if not in her own
or Bridget's. It would be small enough to be intimate and yet large
enough to provide variety – a Queen Anne house, perhaps, with
only two floors and a door in the middle with rooms either side of
the hall. Everything would be light and bright but not institutionally
sterile – I envisage pretty wallpapers and soft pastel colours rather
than blinding white everywhere. It would have an old-fashioned
kitchen with an open fire and a big table and several rocking chairs.
There would be no dormitories. Each old lady would have two
rooms and her own bathroom and only share at meals and for
company in a communal sitting room. There would be one member
of staff to every inmate, their own personal helper. Families would
come and go whenever they liked and stay overnight if they wanted.
There would be some sort of entertainment every day, visiting
choirs and the like, and the best of all the activities on offer at the
Day Centre.

We pulled up outside St Alma's. No Queen Anne house but a
perfectly attractive post-war, double-fronted mock-Tudor dwell-
ing. The paintwork had been freshly done – a good sign, said
Charlie, who is absolutely determined to find good signs – and the
brass knocker on the front door gleamed. A woman in a pink-

spotted dress opened the door, beaming. Charlie beamed back – another good sign. We went first into the Matron's office. Fresh flowers on her desk, a worn but colourful rug on the polished wooden floor, pretty blue curtains at the window. She said first she would tell us about St Alma's and then we could tell her about Mrs McKay. Both exchanges of information were quickly made. Matron seemed to me a little too eager to emphasise how caring her staff were and Charlie a little too keen to enlarge on his mother's sweetness. He said nothing about the beginnings of incontinence, the waking at night or the paranoia. Then Matron took us on a tour of St Alma's and, on the whole, it was very cheering. There were no silent circles of old women in dingy, cold rooms. Wherever we went, people were active and talking and there was a general atmosphere of bustle. One woman seemed to be having a birthday party. Her relatives, or those I took to be her relatives, were clustered round her chair, holding out a cake with nine candles on it. Matron stopped and explained it was Kitty's ninetieth birthday and that she was St Alma's longest resident. 'She's been in ten years come March,' said one of the relatives, 'and she *loves* it here, loves it, don't you Kitty?' Kitty did not speak or show her love for St Alma's in any way.

We moved on to the bedrooms. No dormitories but three to a room. Each bed was so arranged that there was, as Matron pointed out, some slight feeling of privacy. Certainly, the furnishings were attractive. Matron said each lady had at least one of her own pieces of furniture in her bedroom – usually some small antique she particularly valued. I raised my eyebrows at Charlie behind her back: which 'antique' from her Glasgow Buildings would Grandma take with her? We inspected the bathrooms, all very clinical, and Matron showed us with pride, the sit-in showers and all manner of latest equipment designed to help the old and disabled bathe in comfort. It struck me how very confident Matron was, how much she enjoyed showing people around, and how, by contrast, we were nervous and ingratiating. We criticised nothing, only praised. In the garden, Charlie went into positive raptures, even though, since it was nearly November, there was very little to see. Matron described how nice it was for 'the old dears' to potter about the garden if there was any decent weather. She said the roses were beautiful.

We ended the tour back in the office. Matron asked if we would like coffee or tea but, as we had agreed beforehand, we declined. We said we had to get back, life was difficult at the moment. Matron nodded understandingly. Then we got down to the negotiations. Charlie said he had no doubts at all, he would like his mother put on the waiting list. Matron said it was not quite so simple. Mrs McKay would have to be assessed, as she had explained on the telephone. She could arrange for someone to come and make the assessment at Mrs McKay's home or we could bring her here. Charlie hesitated. I could see him wondering which gave us a better chance of getting his mother accepted. I used his pause to ask Matron what kind of things were assessed, what St Alma's was looking for. She described the problem: St Alma's wanted pleasant personalities, people who would get along with other people. It was no good admitting anyone so deeply rooted in their family that they would never accept a substitute. And, although most of the old people they had were a little confused, they did not accept the severely demented since it put too much of a strain on the other occupants. Of course, if while at St Alma's they degenerated into severe dementia, then they would not be turned out; other arrangements would be made.

I really felt we might just as well forget it. It did seem a pleasant enough place but Grandma had about as much chance of getting in as she had of getting into a Cambridge college. But Charlie was most persistent. He made an appointment for his mother to be assessed in her own home, and cross-examined Matron yet again on how long she would be on the much desired waiting list. Matron took a sheet of paper out of the drawer. We held our breath. She said St Alma's had only fifteen residents and at the moment there were fourteen on the waiting list. Charlie's face! He managed to pull himself together sufficiently to ask, with no false delicacy, what the 'turn over' was like. Matron flinched and became a little stiff in tone. She said that if Mr McKay wanted her to be brutally frank – and even a fool could see that Mr McKay did – then she could tell him that this year they had admitted six new residents 'as vacancies occurred'. Charlie brightened slightly. She made him even happier by adding that the waiting list did not stay the same as, often, when the time came, ladies whose names had been put on the list did not need the place

117

any more. Charlie asked if he would be right in thinking the average lady waited a year? Matron nodded and said, roughly speaking, roughly speaking. Charlie's last request was for the price. Matron pushed a brochure towards him. St Alma's was, she said, reasonable at £300 a week.

All the way home, Charlie did mental arithmetic out loud. £2.50 an hour for Susan during the day equals £37.50 a week plus £3 extra for her evenings equals £12 so that equals £49.50 for Susan in an ordinary week; but, then, there was £2 an hour for Lola who normally did ten hours so that was £20 a week which made it approximately £70 a week but of course the real expense was the nights and five nights a week at what we'd paid Mrs O'Malley meant £200 a week added to the £70 equalled very approximately £270 a week and he hadn't even begun on light, heat, rent, bloody hell, St Alma's was a *snip*. I just let him ramble on, only half listening to this run-down of expenses which was followed by a calculation of how much Bridget and I saved by also helping. It was all a pipe dream. Grandma would never hoodwink an assessor, she would never make St Alma's prestigious waiting list. It was too late, we had waited too long. A year ago, yes, but not now. There must be places for the severely demented but we had not found them and if we did I felt instinctively that they would not be like St Alma's. After all, when I asked Dr Carruthers if he could recommend anywhere he said, 'Recommend? No, there's none I'd actually recommend. A few I could suggest as tolerable, perhaps, but none I'd recommend, not for your mother-in-law, not at this stage. A psycho-geriatric ward in a mental hospital is really the only option apart from the individual private care you're giving her now – that's the best thing, really, if you can manage it, keep her in her own home.' Oh, he was so very pleased with us for doing that, the *right* thing, keeping her in what passes as her own home though she doesn't have a clue where she is.

I found myself wondering what happened to Grandma's own mother. I remembered asking Grandma herself, when she was *compos mentis*. She was always telling me that she was not like her mother – it seemed very important to her that I should understand this. She emphasised that her mother was small and quick and sharp, whereas of course she herself was tall and slow and sleepy.

118

She told me she was like her father and was proud of it. Her mother told her she should have been a lad and people in the street said to her father that he couldn't say she wasn't his. It took some probing to discover, even then, the fate of her mother. If I remember correctly, Grandma's mother died in a Home of the same senile dementia from which she is now suffering. Grandma did not tell me this – *she* told me her mother was 'well looked after till the end' without specifying this end but Bridget suspects differently. Grandma's past is full of contradictions but Bridget was once told by some relative that Grandma's mother was found wandering in her nightdress in the snow and was 'put away'. Bridget thinks this must have been during the time when Grandma was in Newcastle, widowed, with three children and no money. She can hardly be accused of neglect. If her mother did die in a Home, I don't think it would have been like St Alma's.

I think Grandma was afraid of her mother rather in the way she used to be afraid of me. I, too, am small, quick and sharp. Grandma used to watch me helplessly while I made a cake or did the ironing – any simple job – and groan at what easy work I made of it. She would say it took her all day. I would point out the advantages I had – the Kenwood mixer, the lightweight steam iron – but she knew, and I knew she knew, that these had little to do with what she was admiring and envying. Admiring, envying, even praising but, and this was the point, also disliking and being repelled by. Grandma slightly resented super-efficiency and it also made her laugh, she mocked it. She liked most of all to identify with people, to be able to say, 'You're just like me, what a mess,' and she could not say that to me. I made her despair. 'Is there anything I can do to lend a hand?' she would ask, then add, gloomy and aggrieved, 'I suppose you've got everything done as usual.' I always had. Later, when I learned wisdom, I would deliberately leave jobs for her to do, jobs I would never even have thought of doing but knew she liked. Drains, she was an expert at cleaning drains. She believed a gallon of boiling soda should be put down the drains every week and would happily slosh about outside sluicing the drain covers and poking about with a stick to free any fragments of dirt. Wherever she worked she collected clutter, surrounded herself with implements, fell over them, lost them, but in the end did whatever she had to do perfectly, leaving the site of her labours immaculate.

I was glad, as we drove home, to think of St Alma's having a garden. Grandma, who had grown up in the Buildings, loved gardens. One of her many quotations was 'A garden is a lovesome thing, God wot' (and always she would ponder on the meaning of 'wot', however many times it was explained). She liked to put a man's shoes on, any man's, and tie a scarf round her head and get out into the garden where she had not the least idea what she was doing. She would trudge up and down in her Old Mother Hubbard shoes poking at the ground with a hoe and then bending in her agonisingly slow way to pick up stones. She was happy in the garden but also worried. She knew she did not have it under control and could become frantic at evidence of any plant beating her — that's how she would put it, 'This damned thing is beating me.' It was really better for her if someone else gardened and she acted labourer, or better still if she could be persuaded to sit and watch and supervise. She was willing to go into the garden at the first hint of warm weather. It was, still is (except she can't stay anywhere for long now and feels cold when it is blazing hot), one of our few points of contact. I, too, like to be in the garden whenever possible.

Charlie should be our biggest point of contact but he is not. Grandma always wished I had not married Charlie. She did not like my effect on him. She thought, although never said so, that I was much too dominant. She saw me as bullying Charlie as she believed her mother had bullied her father. I only had to say briskly, 'For heaven's sake, Charlie, stop daydreaming and get that letter off — go on, *now*,' for her face to assume an expression of horror. She believed Charlie to be delicate — there was a long tale, frequently told, of his almost dying of malnutrition at six months — and she thought he should be encouraged to take things easy. I appeared to want him to jump all the time. And if he and I had rows when she was with us, she would hide in a corner, be almost offended when half an hour later we were amicably chatting to each other.

Once, twenty years ago, perhaps even longer, we had a scene in the street. Grandma, who was not even a Grandma then, had taken ages and ages as usual trailing round Woolworth's looking for a left-handed potato peeler. Charlie and I got impatient. He made the mistake of saying this was ridiculous, and urged his mother to hurry up. She walked out of the shop and into the street saying she was going back to Glasgow, that she knew when she was not wanted. It was very embarrassing. We hurried along on either side of her, begging her forgiveness, begging her to stay, offering our apologies. We were so alarmed and frightened by her sudden, totally unexpected fierceness. Of course, she stayed, it blew over, was never referred to again. It struck me only recently how extraordinary it was that a mature woman could behave like that. I would never, in such circumstances, be so childish. And Charlie was ashamed of her as he was on so many occasions. Just as Stuart was indifferent, Bridget proud, Charlie was often ashamed and she sensed it and in some way blamed me, not Charlie. Everyone will. The organising, organised daughter-in-law who brought it all to pass. There will be nothing I can do about it.

*

I hardly slept the first night Cynthia spent with Grandma. I lay and worried and the more I thought about it the more outrageous it was to leave Grandma with Cynthia. And I had lied – not directly, but by implication. When I went in to see Bridget and she asked who was looking after her mother at night I told her not to worry and said we were, we were taking it in turn, all of us. Bridget was mollified. She said she would soon be better and would make it up to us. And then I took Cynthia in to Grandma. It slightly alarmed me that she had no kind of overnight bag, nothing. She had a book in her hand, and a Walkman and that was all. Where was her nightdress, her toothbrush, a hairbrush, a towel? It seemed so odd, to me, but when I got home and mentioned it to Hannah she laughed at me – so old-fashioned to imagine staying the night meant paraphernalia. And it is true, Hannah's friends come and stay the night and have nothing.

I went through all the routines with Cynthia, showed her where everything was. Unfortunately, Grandma was in a bad mood. She glared at us, said, 'Not *more* of them,' and did a lot of in-the-name-of-God-ing. Cynthia did at least make an effort. She asked Grandma how she was and when Grandma grumbled that her bloomin' back was sore but nobody cared and she'd told that doctor and he just said there was nothing he could do for her, bloomin' cheek, Cynthia was very good. She had the cunning to request a full report on Grandma's ailments and offered to fill Grandma a hot water bottle to put at her back. But, as I left them together, I felt nervous. Cynthia is only a girl, self-confessedly in this for the money. Bridget would kill me. I made absolutely sure that the door into the hall of the house was locked. As it turned out, everything was fine in the morning. Cynthia was up, dressed and Grandma quite happy eating her porridge when I went round. I was so relieved that when Charlie said we should accept her offer to do it for a month after the trial weekend was over I agreed. It was very fortunate indeed that we did not quite get to the point of asking her.

Cynthia cannot after all have been so clever. A clever person in that situation, knowing that her charge was surrounded by an obviously concerned and involved family, would never have taken the risk which Cynthia did. It was surely on the cards that one of us might pop in unexpectedly, especially during the trial period. How could she be so silly? I left Cynthia with Grandma the second evening at six o'clock, saying Susan would be doing the next morning. I told Cynthia that if Susan did not arrive by nine, she was to ring me at once. Cynthia smiled and nodded. I advised her to put Grandma to bed about nine thirty and not to give her tea after seven (Grandma, hearing this, said she would make herself as much tea as she wanted, the very idea). When I left, Grandma got up and said she would come with me, but there was nothing unusual in that. I sat her down again and left. But half an hour later I remembered I had forgotten to tell Cynthia about the arthritis pills Grandma needed to take every other night. I rang and got no reply. I thought maybe Cynthia was busy doing something with Grandma. I waited and rang again – still no reply. So I went round, round to the back because I knew I had locked the hall door. The curtains were not drawn and through the window I saw Grandma standing in the middle of the room, a finger to her lips, looking petrified. No Cynthia. I let myself in, thinking Cynthia would be in the bathroom or Grandma's bedroom, perhaps putting the electric blanket on already. But she was not. I came into the kitchen calling Grandma's name and she stumbled over and clutched me and thanked God I'd come. Her heart was thudding as she stood against me and there was a thin film of sweat over her brow. I took a deep breath, calmed Grandma and made her tea and lit a cigarette for her. In a minute her panic had subsided. Then I tried the door into the sitting room which also served as a second bedroom. It was locked. I hammered on the door, though not too violently because I did not want to frighten Grandma again. High up on the lintel we kept a spare key (because at one stage Grandma was forever hiding keys). I thought perhaps the key might be in the lock on the other side but, no, I was able to fit and turn the spare one. Inside the room Cynthia was sitting with Walkman headphones on. On the bed lay a young man, also wearing headphones. The room was full of smoke, sickly sweet smoke. Both had their eyes closed.

I stood there dumbfounded, just staring, for a full couple of minutes. I waited to be heard and seen but neither Cynthia nor friend moved. The room was in darkness except for one small lamp. I snapped on the overhead light. The man blinked, opened his eyes. He didn't move or look alarmed. Slowly, Cynthia turned and what I could not forgive was that she did no double-take, gave no sign of consternation. What she did was smile and remove her headphones and stand up. 'We were just listening to a tape Greg's made,' she said, 'just for five minutes. He dropped in to let me hear it – quite exciting, making it himself. He hired a studio.' And then she said – the effrontery of it – she said, 'Everything all right? Did you want something?' I asked her to go, at once. She was indignant, wanted to know why. I said the fact that she didn't appear to know why was an indication of her unsuitability. I said I had found my mother-in-law very frightened and the door between them locked and a strange man here. I said she had been engaged to look after my mother-in-law, not lock her out. She then said it was truly only for a few minutes and she had locked the door because Mrs McKay kept interrupting; it was just to hear the tape quickly, there was no harm in it. I told her to go, at once. She said it was ridiculous; she had done nothing wrong. I said I was not prepared to discuss it. Luckily, I had my purse on me. I took out £30 and gave it to her. She said that actually it was supposed to be £40 a night and if she left now she would lose a night's pay and she thought she was entitled to it because she was not leaving of her own accord. I said she could go and discuss that with my husband but please would she just get out.

I was trembling with fury and guilt. If I had not come along . . . But, as Charlie said later, that was an unlikely train of thought. Maybe Cynthia was telling the truth, maybe her friend had only come to play a tape and would have left soon and she would have come out and put Grandma to bed perfectly well and kindly. It would not have excused her behaviour but there was no need, as Charlie argued, to read dreadful intentions into it. Clearly, Charlie thought I had been melodramatic, even that I had acted hastily, and this angered and upset me even more. He did not seem able to empathise with poor Grandma at all, could not grasp the nature of her distress. The most important thing to her is security – she must be made to feel protected – and nothing would threaten her sense of security more than strangers locking doors behind them. Charlie said I couldn't possibly know what she felt and that is true, nobody can, but I know terror when I see it. Charlie pointed out that Grandma has been in a similar state with *no* cause, which again is true, but we cannot help that, whereas we *can* help leaving her with untrustworthy people. Charlie said the sooner we got her into St Alma's the better: he had had enough.

I stayed the night with Grandma, glad to, really, glad to make amends. I read Burns to her and joined in her recitations and let her have as many cups of tea as she wanted even if it was going to mean a wet bed or being up six times in the night. We listened to a Scottish play on the radio and I did not mind a bit that Grandma talked all the way through. I sat on her bed till she went to sleep and was still there, reassuring, when she woke with a start after ten minutes. She asked if her mother was in yet and I said yes and if her father had gone to work and I said yes and if the children were asleep and I said yes. She gave a great sigh of contentment: all was well in her world. Sleepily, she gave me four verses of 'Man Was Made to Mourn' before she fell asleep again. I tucked her up securely. When she woke me at two in the morning because she needed change for the milkman whom she could hear coming, I did what Bridget does, I got into bed with her. I could not actually bring myself to cuddle up to her, as Bridget does, as she likes, but I lay as close as I could and held her hand and that was enough. She did not waken again. She snored the rest of the night away and I lay there wondering who would do this for her at St Alma's. What a hope. All she could respond to, all that meant anything to her, was tenderness and that kind of intimate care would be entirely lacking if we took her to St Alma's or any other Home, however good. We would deprive her of all that was meaningful.

It was so lucky I stayed the night. At seven o'clock Bridget came in, all cheerful, feeling much better. She pinched Grandma's cheek as she stood looking down at her, still in bed, and said, 'Have they been good to you, pet?' just as Grandma does and Grandma laughed and I was so *proud* to have her in such a happy state and for Bridget to see it. And Grandma, always crystal clear in the early morning for the fleetest moment, said distinctly, 'Jenny's been a treasure so she has.'

How can we 'put her away', as she would call it? *How can we?*

Hannah

Grandma is here again, as she has been every day this week. Mum's at screaming point. All Dad's fine phone calls have achieved nothing in the end. Cynthia isn't talked about and neither is the agency woman who came two nights. Bridget is better so Mum had to tell her about this woman Dad had got, from an agency called Lifeline, and she was appalled. I don't suppose the woman had a chance with Bridget popping in and out all the time to see Grandma wasn't being maltreated. This confused Grandma so much that naturally she wouldn't go to bed and of course she got up about six times and wet the bed in spite of it. By the third night Bridget was back doing her stint. What is going to happen when we get to her two nights off I don't know and neither does anybody else. Meanwhile, Lola has given up, as expected and Susan has said she can only do mornings. So Grandma is here again.

A woman from this Home under consideration, St Alma's, is coming in an hour or so to assess Grandma. Bridget doesn't know but Mum says firmly that she's not trying to conceal this plan. Oh, yeah? Not much. Mum and Dad want to get Grandma on this waiting list without Bridget having the faintest idea and then they'll present her with a *fait accompli* when the time comes. They're being sensible, no doubt about that, very sensible. I follow the reasoning. But whether it'll do any good is harder to work out. Mum has appealed to me to help. She wants me to be here when this woman comes, she wants me to help 'keep Grandma rational'. Now that *is* a laugh. There's nothing rational about Grandma, how can there be? Mum insists that I know what she means. Sometimes Grandma can appear perfectly charming and civilised and even bright and at other times she's loony. But how on earth does Mum think I can help to make it one of her better days? And what I want to know is this:

> Is it right to make Grandma seem saner than she is?
> Is it right to get her on any waiting list under false pretences?
> Do I even *want* her to be on a waiting list?
> Whose side am I on?

*

The woman – 'call me Jean' – is very pleasant. About forty, plumpish, spectacles, moon-like face but sharp eyes, plainly dressed in grey and white, laughs rather too much and easily. The laughing goes down well with Grandma who asks this Jean if she knows 'The Laughing Policeman' which is one of Grandma's favourites. Grandma starts to sing, or rather to laugh, the song and ends up paralytic. She says she likes a good laugh. Jean says she does too. At least this has put Grandma in a good mood. She's looking quite perky. Jean asks her how she is.

> Fine, except for my back. And yourself?
> Oh, I'm fine.
> You've got over your trouble then?
> Which trouble were you thinking of, Mrs McKay?
> You mean you've more than one?
> Haven't we all?
> Oh, I look on the bright side myself.
> That's the best way. (*Pause.*) Have you lived here long?
> Depends what you call long.
> Well, how long have you lived here?
> Longer than you think.

Oh, Grandma is on form. This could go on hours. I smile surreptitiously at Mum, who looks away. We haven't had Grandma like this for a long time. She's smart, she's fencing, she's going to give nothing away. A basic cunning and intelligence is going to put her on her guard. Is Jean up to it? Jean tries again, asks if she has always lived here.

> No, I was born in Glasgow.
> When did you leave?
> When I was twenty.
> And where did you go?
> To Perth.
> You worked there, did you?
> I did, and bloomin' hard. I've worked hard all my life, nothing wrong with that.
> No indeed *(Pause.)* Could you pour me some more tea, Mrs McKay?
> *(Incredible tension on the part of Mum as Grandma looks for the teapot, locates it, grasps the handle, and to our astonishment does indeed pour tea for Jean, spilling it only slightly.)*
> Will you take sugar?
> Yes, please.
> *(Grandma passes Jean the biscuits. Mum knows, I know, that she thinks it's the sugar but Jean thinks it's an extra and reaches for the sugar herself when she's taken a biscuit.)*
> Thank you. You haven't drunk your own tea, Mrs McKay.
> It's too hot, and it isn't polite to blow on it in company.
> It's very nice tea. What sort is it?
> Brooke Bond. I get it at the Co-op.
> Is there a Co-op near here?
> Just up the road.
> So you do your own shopping?
> Who else would do it?
> I thought maybe your daughter-in-law –
> Oh, I can do my own shopping, I hope.
> You find it easy to get about?
> I take my time, slow and steady wins the race.

Everything's going so well. Grandma's enjoying herself. She's positively sparkling. She looks so jolly in her bright red jumper and

128

her Fair Isle cardigan and tartan skirt – nothing vacant or sullen or lost about her. Can it last? Jean is laughing less and looking more reflective. She clearly knows she hasn't got Grandma's measure exactly. She asks Grandma how many children she has. We hold our breath again.

Three.
Girls or boys?
Two boys and a wee girl.
And your husband?
Oh, I had a husband, good heavens, I had one of those.
Are you a widow, Mrs McKay?
Aye.
When did your husband die?
He didn't die, he was killed in the war.
I'm sorry.
It was a long time ago.

Grandma has got everything right but unfortunately the very words 'war' and 'widow' and 'killed' have caused one of those strange, violently sudden changes of mood we dread. Her face clouds. The film comes down over her eyes. Has Jean noticed? Then Grandma starts struggling to get up. In one way this is good. She mouths she wants to go to the lavatory: Jean will know she is not normally incontinent. I take her. Presumably while I'm gone Jean chats to Mum. Grandma takes hours in the loo muttering 'bloomin' bowels'. When she comes out she's sour. She says she wants to go home. I tempt her back into the kitchen with promises of tea. The minute she sees Jean she glares and pulls back and tells me she doesn't like strangers. But she goes and sits down docilely enough. At least Jean has seen she can walk on her own, surely that scores highly. The minute Grandma has sat down, she starts to get up again.

I'd better go, the men will be in for their tea.
You're expecting someone, Mrs McKay?
My father will be in from his shift soon and my mother will be looking for me to get the tea. (*Pause. Jean's face is a study.*)

Grandma has found her coat. I don't know whether to help her or not. She tries to put it on and fails completely. Trailing it by the sleeve she pulls the coat behind her as she shuffles off into the sitting room. Mum says quickly that of course this isn't her own flat, that if she was in her own place she would have no trouble with direction. Jean says Grandma is obviously confused but not too much so. She says maybe a trial would be a good idea then we could all be sure she was suitable for the waiting list. Mum brightens. Jean gets out an appointments book and says how about for the day, a week on Wednesday? Just bring Grandma along and leave her for the day, she'll enjoy it. Before she leaves, Jean says, carefully, that of course getting on the waiting list is not in itself a guarantee of admission when the time comes – if applicants have – er – deteriorated since they were assessed, especially if the assessment was quite some time ago, which it might well have been considering how long the waiting list is, then – er – Mum says she understands.

Jean says goodbye to Grandma and Grandma says hello. While Mum walks Jean to her car, I sit with Grandma. She's on the sofa facing a large oil painting which hangs on the opposite wall. It's a beach scene, two adults and four children on a beach, an impressionistic sort of thing. The children are building sandcastles, the adults lying prone. It's all fuzzy yellows and blues. Grandma's waving at it. She's saying 'yoo-hoo'. I plonk down beside her and look. One of the children in the picture is facing to the front. It's a girl of about four. She has one arm in the air, to attract attention, I guess. Grandma is waving at her.

Has she had her tea?
Who?
The wee lassie, she looks hungry.
It's only a picture, Grandma.
So?
Well, you can't feed people in pictures.
Why not? I suppose they get hungry like anyone else.
Don't be silly.
You mind your mouth.
You *know* it's a picture Grandma.

130

So?
Stop waving. Why are you waving?
At the wee lassie. Has she had her tea?

I can't stand it, can't just laugh, treat it as a joke. I bounce up and turn the painting to the wall. My stomach churns. I go and tell Mum when she comes back in. Mum doesn't turn a hair. She says Grandma has been doing this for a while. Mum says it's worse with photographs. She kisses them and says they're cold, surely I've seen her? No, I haven't. Bridget comes in, much earlier than arranged. Mum goes white at the near squeak. Bridget asks sharply, where Grandma is. I tell her she is through in the sitting room waving at pictures. Bridget says first, oh that's nothing, and second what's she doing on her own. She bustles through, all noise and chatter. I stand in the doorway and watch. Bridget cuddles Grandma and then lights a cigarette for herself and another for Grandma. She asks Grandma how life's treating her. Grandma says terrible, she's seen nobody for weeks, they're all a wash-out, she's like the last rose of summer left etc. etc.

Where've you been anyway?
Working, Mother.
A likely story, gallivanting more like.
Oh, now, Mother!
With your fancy man.
Is that what you think of me?
No, you're a good girl, mind you stay one.
Don't you worry, Mother.
Where've you been anyway?

Bridget tells Grandma a story about a little boy in her ward with a harelip and the operations he's going through. Grandma is enchanted. She makes noises of consternation, of sympathy, of outrage, of distress. She says the world's a cruel place and man's inhumanity to man etc. etc. In short, she's quite cheered up.

We go through the performance of getting Grandma into her coat and bidding goodbye as though she's off to the North Pole. Bridget draws it out even further by chatting to Mum and forgetting to

131

concentrate on Grandma who promptly uses the opportunity to take her coat off again. This happens several times. Finally, Bridget goes off down the street, Grandma complaining of the bitter cold (on this mild afternoon) and prophesying snow. How odd they look, Bridget so tall and upright and dramatic in bearing and colouring and Grandma so bent and bowed and shabby and grey. I watch them. When Grandma stops, I know why: she wants to pick up some bit of rubbish. Bridget is patient. Stop, start, stop, start. Hours and hours it seems until they disappear round the corner. What I want to know is:

> How can Bridget stay so cheerful?
> How can she forsake Karl for Grandma?
> How does she manage to spend any time with Karl at all?
> Why does she not want to spend more?

*

At nine o'clock Mum says Grandma's phone is out of order and so is Bridget's. Since Bridget is with Grandma tonight this is of no consequence but on the other hand Mum wants to remind Bridget that she's taking Grandma to buy some new shoes tomorrow and will Bridget please see Grandma has her thickest stockings on and is ready for Mum to collect at nine o'clock. Mum has fixed up to take her to a local shop when there will be no one else there and the assistant will have all the time necessary to cope with Grandma. Mum says she's even forgotten to tell Bridget Susan isn't coming in the morning. I say I'll pop along and tell her. My head swimming with all Mum's boring, trivial arrangements and counter-arrangements, I go along to impart this vital information to Bridget.

I know Grandma is likely to be in bed or about to go to bed so I just rap on the window to let Bridget know there's someone coming and then, as I let myself in, I call out softly. No reply. They'll be in the bedroom. I pad in, go through to Grandma's bedroom, hoping I won't give them both a fright, and peep round the door. The curtains are drawn, the light out and I can hear Grandma snoring before I see her white head on the pillow. The bathroom door is open: no Bridget. I go back to the kitchen and then I notice the

132

phone is off the hook. Bridget must have been answering it when Grandma needed her. I replace the receiver then lift it again, checking. The tone sounds fine. Bridget must have gone into her own flat for something. She'll be back in a minute but I don't want to wait. I go through into the joint hall and knock on Bridget's door and go in, calling out. I am halfway across her living room when a door bangs and Bridget hurtles into the room, wrapping a dressing gown round her. I point to her phone and say Grandma's receiver was off too and Mum's been thinking both phones were out of order. Bridget distinctly says, 'Shit,' and then smiles and says, 'Caught in the act, eh?' I'm the one who blushes. I deliver Mum's idiotic message and turn to go away. Bridget follows me. She says, hurriedly, from behind me, that she was just going back into Grandma's, that I must not think she was going to leave her all night, there was no harm in going back to her own flat. I say of course there isn't, I didn't think there was, no need to explain. Bridget doesn't say please don't mention this to your parents but I know she wants to. She goes back into Grandma's side of the house as I go out of the main door.

What bothers me most is the phones being off the hook. Oh, I can see *why*. If Grandma's phone rang and no one answered it would eventually waken her and she'd be alarmed to find she was on her own. And if it rang and wasn't answered the caller would wonder where Grandma's companion was. So it makes sense. Bridget's receiver being off makes distinctly less sense. Bridget taking her phone off the hook seems to me to indicate she wasn't going to be in her own flat just a short while. She was going to be there a long while and didn't want to be contacted. And why should she? Grandma is asleep, she's safe. Why shouldn't Bridget go into her own flat and do whatever she wanted? Well, there *are* reasons I could think of, that Bridget would certainly think of, if it was someone else doing it. Obvious reasons. The carers have always had it impressed on them that Grandma must never, never be left. It's not just that she's a danger to herself but that she would be so frightened. What would Bridget say to that?

Bridget would say she would hear Grandma. Even through several thick, old doors? Even then. And, anyway, Grandma would

133

just go back to bed. What if she didn't, what if she wandered into the hall? Well, then, she would try Bridget's door and go in and that would be fine. Why do we employ people to stay all night then? Well, because Bridget must have some privacy, she must shut herself off some time and not have the responsibility.

I don't tell Mum. I just tell her that the phone had got knocked off the hook somehow. I say I delivered the messages. I say everything is fine. But I can't help thinking what a comfort it would be to Mum to have proof that Bridget is less than perfect. And Dad would crow.

*

Adrian sits in his filthy track suit and starts taking his muddy trainers off in the kitchen and Mum screams at him and I think what a pity Grandma isn't here because she loves the sight of Adrian after football – it is *manly* – and she loves hearing Mum yell at him – that is womanly. Adrian says he's just seen Bridget in the street with a man, who is he, what is going on? Mum refuses to tell him till he has got some newspaper and put his shoes on it and dropped his track suit trousers there too. Then she says it isn't really any of his business but in case it comes up in conversation Bridget has a friend called Karl. That's all. Adrian asks if she's going to marry him. I say don't be stupid. Adrian says why is it stupid, it would be *normal*. Bridget should be married, he would like to think of her married, it would do her good, she could stop work and have kids and Grandma could live with her. We stare at him. Mum says, 'Adrian, Bridget is forty-three, she is unlikely to have children, and she loves her work.' Adrian says he's sorry he spoke and stumps off.

When he goes I say to Mum that I know what Adrian said is ridiculous but does she think Bridget might marry this Karl? Mum says no, she doesn't think so. Bridget isn't the marrying kind and there's no evidence that Karl wants to marry her. But he wants to take her home, to Germany. Mum it turns out has been encouraging her to go. I ask what about Grandma? Mum raises her eyebrows.

*

It's strange looking at Grandma and knowing she's completely ignorant of her situation. She doesn't know about Homes and carers and being an emergency. I suppose that's the only kind part of what's happening to her: she doesn't know. Does she? Sometimes, I sense a kind of panic coming off her. She will hold her head, touch her face, as though checking they're there and if she sees her own reflection she appears transfixed in horror. She will turn and turn till she staggers with dizziness, frantically looking for something. I think she has glimpses. I think she sees into her condition momentarily and the world spins. I don't think she's completely oblivious all the time.

Adrian says, as we eat, that he plans to take a year off and go to Australia next year.

> I've been to Australia.
> Have you, Grandma?
> Of course she hasn't.
> You, mind yourself, I have so.
> When?
> Years back.
> Who did you go with?
> Thingymajig, he's dead now.
> Did you have a good time?
> Very nice, thank you. The stations were very clean.
> That was Canada, Grandma, you have been there.
> They were very clean there too, lovely.
> Anyway, I'm going to Australia with Kevin.
> I've been to Australia.

I don't know why Mum had to deny Grandma had ever been to Australia. It only upsets her. Where's the harm? But Mum says it's bad for Grandma, that a distinction has to be drawn between a downright lie, which Grandma really knows is a lie, and an exaggeration. Grandma has never been anywhere near Australia. The furthest she has been is Canada, ten years ago, to visit one of her brothers. Otherwise, apart from that big adventure, she has never been out of the British Isles. Adrian, who likes to string Grandma along, asks her if she can give him any advice about going to Australia.

135

Take plenty of tea.

Don't they have tea, Grandma?

Not what we'd call tea. And TCP.

TCP? To put in the tea?

Adrian!

For the bites, they midges is terrible.

Did you get bitten?

Bitten alive, bites galore, lumps like hens' eggs.

So it was very hot?

Roasting.

How did you get there, Grandma?

Bus.

Bus, to Australia?

Well, we took a ship to Canada then a bus to Australia.

I think you mean America, Grandma.

Australia.

I think you mean that trip you went on, to New York, remember?

I remember it fine, it was Australia, and we should've taken plenty of tea.

By now Adrian is openly laughing. He says he's going to suggest to Kevin that they take a bus to Australia via Canada, hah hah. Grandma is quite pleased at his hilarity. She nods, smiles, whistles and says she liked Australia. I really don't know why Mum gets so irritated by her innocent enjoyment. But she does. When Grandma, as usual, reaches yet again for the salt, saying she's a devil for salt, Mum snatches it away and says she will not see good food wasted because it has had half a ton of salt ladled on it. Grandma is hurt. She says she hates waste etc. She says anyone who has lived during the war time never wastes a thing.

I've lived through five wars.

Five, Grandma?

Five.

The First World War, the Second World War, which were the others?

The Boer War, that was terrible.

136

(Pause. Nobody is exactly sure when the Boer War was.)
But not as bad as the Crimean, oh, it was awful.
Now Grandma you aren't *that* old.
Hundreds and hundreds of them killed like flies.
And the fifth?
I forget now.
The Falklands! That would make five wars.
I've lived through five wars.

The memory of all the wars she has lived through, real and imaginary, depresses Grandma. She says it as a boast in the beginning and then, the more she repeats it, the more real it becomes and the more miserable it makes her. She never talks about my grandfather being killed in the war. She can state it as a fact but that's all. I don't even know which battle he died in or exactly how. But these memories of surviving wars must surely be connected to that event. Poor Grandma. She's staring vacantly ahead, crumbling a bit of bread in her strong hands, thinking about war. But she never cries. Occasionally, watery eyes but tears never fall. It suddenly strikes me how extraordinary it is that my grandmother never cries. I have never seen her sob. Mum is hit by remorse. She jumps up and puts the kettle on, even though we haven't had pudding yet, and finds a tin of Grandma's favourite digestive biscuits. She even smears a couple of biscuits with butter, which is how Grandma likes them and Mum hates them. Anxiously, she puts them in front of Grandma with a mug of tea. Adrian has stopped laughing. We all watch Grandma, willing her to cheer up. Her sadness is tearing at me, *I* could cry. She nibbles at a biscuit, picks it up and dunks it in her tea. Mum doesn't even wince though crumbs and butter float messily around the rim of the mug. Grandma gulps, says nice tea, that she once had a friend who *could not* make tea and how she dreaded going to her house, but, and she takes another gulp, this is very nice tea if only she had a ciggie. A ciggie is produced. She lights it herself, a miracle, she draws on it and then suddenly throws back her head and laughs and says do we know 'The Toad Eater'? We say no but tell us Grandma, tell us and she recites, 'What of earls whom you have supt, And of dukes you dined with yestereen, Lord, a louse,

137

Sir is still but a louse, though it crawls on the curls of a Queen.'

That's all that it takes: a cup of strong sugary tea, a digestive biscuit, a cigarette and a bit of Burns. It's really very simple to make Grandma happy. Or what passes for happy. Mum relaxes. She says when we were small she used to feel such power because she knew that if she tried hard enough she could always make *us* laugh. Now, she can't. But she can make Grandma happy. Grandma breaks in to say there's no point in being miserable, that she abominates miserable people, all frozen-faced. You can always laugh, Grandma says, and looks round for confirmation of this gem. Can you? I don't think so. But in the circumstances, considering Grandma has only just emerged from the slough of despond, I decide not to take her up on it. It's not the right moment for mental gymnastics. When Bridget arrives we're still on pudding and Grandma is very happy. She has managed two helpings of chocolate mousse as well as her digestives. There'll be none left for Dad when he gets in.

I can see Bridget sizing up the scene as she comes through into the kitchen. Grandma is between Adrian and me and because of the slight contretemps, which Bridget of course has not witnessed, we are both being excessively protective. Adrian actually has his arm round Grandma's shoulders. She is being skittish, looking up at him and saying she always fancied a handsome man and a thousand a year. I am spooning in chocolate mousse with the greatest patience. A cigarette steams gently on an ashtray. There is a large yellow tea pot at Grandma's elbow. I see Bridget taking it all in and being pleased and happy at this evidence of how we love and care for Grandma. I see her wondering why it can't always be like this. She sits opposite Grandma who takes some time to notice her.

You've taken your time.
I've been working, Mother.
That's what they all say. Anyway, I'm not
    bothered, do what you please.
Have you been having a nice time?
What's it to you?
Mother!

138

Bloomin' cheek.
Oh well, I'll go away again.
You do that, who cares.
Aren't you coming home with me?
What home? Don't talk nonsense.
Your own little but and ben.
Are you mad?
I've come to take you home.
You've taken your time.

Bridget thinks we'll all be flattered. Grandma says repeatedly she wishes Bridget would leave her alone, even that Bridget would take herself off to wherever she came from, and curses people who disturb her just when she's comfortable. Bridget plays this up. She says Grandma obviously has no time for *her* and wants to be with *us*. Mum hardly smiles at that and doesn't reply. Bridget says would Adrian do her a favour? Could he just walk Grandma along and take her in while she has a word with Mum?

It's odd that she asks Adrian and not me. I soon see why. There is a certain amount of tension between Mum and Bridget. Often, I feel they're sparring. Both of them like me to be there, as though I, by my watchful presence, keep them in order, prevent them saying things they might regret, force them to shape their words so as not to startle me. Neither of them want the freedom that privacy would give them and they both want a witness. Bridget never beats about the bush, that's one good thing. Now, she says outright that she's thinking of going with Karl to Germany, a proper holiday. Mum says how lovely, you should, good idea. Mum says all the right things but rather too emphatically. Bridget says she'd like to go soon, while it's still autumn, before the nights get too dark and all chance of sun has gone. But what about my mother Bridget asks? No Mrs O'Malley, no Lola, only Susan. How will we manage? Mum says that will be our problem. She says doesn't Bridget trust us? Bridget says of course she does. Mum says very well then, book your holiday.

I grow bold. I ask where Karl lives. Bridget says in Berlin. She wishes she could speak even a word of German, she's hopeless at

139

languages like Grandma. She tells me Grandma once went to night classes to learn French and German. She only wanted to be able to understand the odd foreign words she came across in books. She got on quite well with French but couldn't manage the German and swopped to Fancy Salad classes. We discuss how awful it is that the English are so bad at foreign languages, a disgrace. Bridget says Karl can speak five languages and is tri-lingual. He can switch between German, French and English effortlessly. I feel that's my cue. I ask what Karl does. Bridget says he teaches foreign students, he teaches German as a foreign language and is going to travel the world doing it. At the moment he's working in some language school in Kensington. Bridget makes a Grandma-type face of derision. Why? Why does she mock what her lover does? I ask her how she met Karl. She says the way she meets anyone, in her hospital. Karl visited a child in her ward, a little German boy who was the son of a friend of his. The child was very ill, Karl came often. Bridget shrugs, again makes a face but I'm not sure of what. She just doesn't want to talk about Karl: it makes her squirm. Mum says why not bring Karl here for a meal. Bridget shakes her head, grabs for a cigarette. Maybe one day, she says, but not yet. Not until she 'sees'.

Sees what? She sounds like Grandma, tailing off to avoid having to explain. She says she'd better go or Adrian will wonder what has happened to her, but she doesn't go. Something obviously remains unsaid. Mum knows it. Mum probably even knows what it is. Finally, after some chat about work, Bridget makes a huge effort. She stands up, abruptly. She says that the thing is she would really like to have a word with Charlie, that she had expected him to be at home too. Mum says he's working late, won't be back until nine, but won't she do, she can pass on a message, surely? Bridget knows perfectly well that speaking to Mum is the same as speaking to her brother, only better. But every now and again she makes a point of selecting Dad to speak to because he is Grandma's son and so theoretically Grandma is more his concern. Bridget has no concept of a true partnership — she ought to have, knowing Mum and Dad, but she pretends she hasn't. She wants to speak to Dad about Grandma and it must be something offensive or she would say it to Mum.

Bridget can't decide. She fidgets, stubs out her cigarette, walks to the door, stops. She says it's silly really. She says she just wanted Charlie to promise he wouldn't do anything drastic when she goes away: wouldn't, won't . . . what? She can't bring herself to say the words whatever they are. Mum doesn't help. She stands there looking innocent. Bridget says she realises it might be inevitable in the end, she does admit there has been a deterioration, but she wants Dad to promise not to make any hasty decisions about Grandma when she's away. Mum says, smoothly, that she's sure Dad would never make any decision hastily. She asks again, and I do think this is pushing it, if Bridget doesn't trust us. Bridget is obliged to repeat that of course she does. At last, she goes, running. Mum turns to me and says I'm looking very disapproving. I say I don't like to see Bridget being cheated. Mum pretends to be shocked – cheated, she queries several times, cheated? *You* know, I say, you know you're planning to try Grandma in a Home and you're just waiting for Bridget to be out of the way. You *know* she was trying to pluck up the courage to say she wants Dad to promise he won't put Grandma in a Home while she's away. Mum says she doesn't *know* any such thing. If things get difficult, if we cannot manage to look after Grandma without Bridget, then we might be driven to trying her in a Home on a temporary basis. But Mum insists there are no actual plans.

She tells Dad as soon as he comes in. He says he will promise no such thing, should Bridget work herself up to ask him, and that she has no right to ask anyway. He just wishes she would get herself off: he's had enough of Bridget. Mum says he'll soon eat those words when he has to fill in for his sister. A single night almost killed him when Bridget was ill – how will he cope with three a week. Dad looks appalled. He echoes, three a week? Mum says there are seven nights a week. She'll do three, he will have to do three and maybe Hannah will do one. Dad says why not bring Grandma here, wouldn't it be easier? Mum says no, it would not. She would fall down the stairs, she would never find her way to the lavatory at night. The only hope is to keep her in the same surroundings where she instinctively follows the same patterns. The whole house would be disrupted every night, if she were here. Dad says this is unbelievable: here we are in London unable to get one old lady adequately cared for, it is *ridiculous*. He wonders aloud what is wrong with the unemployed that they don't want to earn such easy money. Mum laughs. She says he sounds like Mrs Thatcher. Dad says he feels like her. He is sick to death of coming home and having to face the problem of who can look after his mother when he knows, he just knows, there must be hundreds glad to do it. Mum says he's always been unrealistic, why can't he understand that Grandma has no job appeal. It's *boring* to be with an old woman who can't even carry on a proper conversation. People don't want to do it and why should they. Dad says for the money, the excellent cash-in-hand tax-free money, get it?

The trouble with Dad is that he takes all this as a personal attack. The more Mum points out the difficulties, the more sulky and aggrieved he grows. Dad is kind, he's gentle, he wants Grandma to be well looked after, but he's not sentimental. In his own way he could be as ruthless as Stuart if it weren't for Mum. She is his troublesome conscience and he resents her taking on this annoying role. I can see, anyone can see, he wants Mum to be with him against Bridget. If Mum would give the OK, Dad would have Grandma in a Home in a trice. I think. If he could find such a Home. He's bored by the whole business but he doesn't agonise, that's the difference. He thinks it's tedious, not heart-breaking. Adrian's heart is actually more touched than Dad's.

Adrian comes back from his indoor football five-aside and sighs. Mum says he's tired. Adrian says it isn't that and sighs again. Dad looks up from his paper and asks what all the heavy sighing is for. Adrian says he keeps thinking about Grandma. Dad goes back to his paper. Adrian, addressing Mum and me, says he hasn't been able to get it out of his mind all evening. Grandma looked so sad in her flat, she didn't recognise anything, wanted to go home and when he said this *was* home she said it didn't look like it. Adrian says it isn't fair, she shouldn't be on her own like that. Mum says Grandma is never on her own for more than an hour. Adrian says he thinks even that is too long. I could hit him. He enjoys this, our Upper Sixth friend, conscience of the caring male. He does nothing but, oh, how his heart bleeds. Yet he is affected by Grandma's plight, much more so

142

than Dad is. Mum says if he has any bright ideas about what to do, then they would be welcome.

Adrian is still thinking. Must be a record for him. He says he knows this is an awful thing to say but, when people are in the state Grandma is in and there's no hope, why don't they – you know – why don't they – I mean it sounds terrible, but . . . I finish for him. Why don't they get put down, I suggest. He nods. Dad puts his newspaper down, suddenly willing to enter into this discussion. He says that's what should be done but can't be. It's against the law. It would have an appalling effect on society if old people were bumped off. Adrian interrupts to say he didn't mean *old* people just old people whose minds had gone. Dad says it doesn't make any difference qualifying it, it would still be dangerous, people would still invoke the Nazis and their extermination programmes. Adrian says he's read of some country where it's done. Dad says what he has read about is euthanasia in Holland and that the Grandmas of this world do not fit that solution. The Dutch agree to put to sleep people who ask to be put to sleep and whose relatives agree. Think about it, Dad says. Grandma can't give her permission and, if she could, she wouldn't, not ever. And neither would her family, he adds after a significant pause. Adrian asks him if *he* would. Dad twitches his newspaper. He says not quite yet, no. Adrian asks Mum. She says she wouldn't count, being only a daughter-in-law. Adrian tells her not to cheat, to answer anyway. Mum says yes, she would. Dad looks at her from over his newspaper. Adrian says that, of course, Stuart would, he'd be first in the queue, and Paula, if given a vote, would just follow him, so that would be three and a half consenting adult relatives. Adrian says isn't it depressing.

That's what it is, depressing, depressing. Nobody asks what I think. Adrian doesn't say what he thinks. It's all pointless anyway. We don't have any Dutch system here, even if Grandma qualified. We just go on and on being proud that we let people stay alive to the bitter end. This is called the sanctity of human life, I think. Great. You lose your brain and the rest of you is somehow sacred. Dad is excelling himself. He's making a speech. He's telling Adrian that, so long as Grandma has any pleasure in life, he would not want to put her to sleep (note: he does not say 'kill'). As long as the quality of

Grandma's life is reasonably good, then no one has the right to end it. And he would not want to. Those, says Dad, are the guidelines. Mum says there's another. Dad looks surprised. He asks what it is. Mum says so long as the damage caused to other people's lives does not get to be too high a price to pay, *then* Grandma's own life should not be brought to a close. Adrian asks, quite intelligent for him I think, who decides that? Who judges what the damage is? Who sets the price? Exactly.

We go to bed gloomy. I can't sleep. In my mind I am drawing up lists:

Quality of Grandma's Life:
    She is secure (but does she know she is?)
    She is well fed
        warm
        clean
        comfortable
    She gets some fresh air
                exercise
                entertainment
                love
                affection

But:
    She is often lonely
                frightened
                confused
                bewildered
    She can hardly do anything for herself
    She is in a way a prisoner
    She can't really communicate with anyone
    She has no hope

Pleasures in Grandma's Day:
    She enjoys jokes
                Burns
                the sight of her family especially Bridget
                tea

144

    biscuits
    cigarettes
    hot water bottles
    electric blankets
    mint imperials
    chocolates, especially Duncan's Walnut Whirls
    sun
    the garden
    children
    cats

Pains in Grandma's Day:
   She suffers from getting up
                      her back
                      her legs
                      failing eyesight
                      her bowels
                      her gums
                      her corns
                      headaches
                      heartburn

Damage to other people's lives:
   Mum's: Grandma causes her worry
              costs her about 15 hours a week in time normally (but
                 things are rarely normal)
              responsibility of shopping
                            doing laundry
                            occasional cookery
                            transporting to Day Centre
   Dad's: hardly any in time
              financial burden (about £250 'normally' a week plus
                 £20 for bills 'normally')
              boredom of Mum nagging
   Adrian's: virtually nil – slight worry which is good for him
   Me: ditto
   Bridget's: two nights a week
                  three evenings a week

Saturdays
lack of any freedom to run own life
aggro due to tension with rest of family
enormous emotional burden

I thought I'd finished the lists, but here is another:

What does Grandma give in return for what she gets?
Gives Dad: nothing (but *has* given a lot)
Gives Mum: support in arguments
some pleasure (because Mum likes looking after
her)
appreciation (sometimes)
Gives Adrian: laughs
Gives Me: laughs
amusement
affection
memories I like
Gives Bridget: devotion
admiration
intimacy
LOVE, LOVE, LOVE

Who gives most to Grandma?
Bridget

Who gets most from Grandma?
Bridget

Who would never, ever, kill Grandma?
Bridget

Jenny

At least I have managed to buy Grandma some new shoes. Bridget thinks it was a waste of effort but she cannot deny Grandma is thrilled even if she moans about the cost (and that is knowing only half of it). They are men's shoes, not quite the trainers Adrian suggested, but very nearly. They have thick rubber soles with good heels to support her weak ankles and soft leather uppers with wide openings. Because the corn, or bunion, on her left foot is enormous she needed a bigger shoe for that foot so I bought two pairs. Yes, I did, I don't care about the so-called waste. Bridget was scandalised, said I could easily have padded the other shoe but I did not agree. Grandma now has two well-fitting shoes and walks better for it.

She also has a track suit. The more I thought about Hannah's remark, the more sense it made. After the shoe buying, which was not the ordeal I had prepared myself for, I took Grandma next door into a sports shop and bought her a dark blue men's track suit in that thick, fleece-lined cotton material. The jacket has a zip up the front, very easy to get on and off, and the cuffs are elasticated and fit snugly. The waist of the trousers is quite loose and goes over her bulging stomach nicely without cutting into it. Again, the ankles have elasticated bottoms so they don't flap and get in her way. It is so sensible, so practical. With one of her own jumpers underneath she is warm and twice as comfortable as she ever was. It has been hell for months now getting her in and out of her old skirts.

But I admit there is one disadvantage: the track suit is so easy to get on and off that Grandma can do it herself and that is bad news. Yesterday I went round at three o'clock and she was wandering around in her vest and knickers complaining about the terrible cold. It was indeed cold – this is the new thing. From barricading herself in occasionally Grandma has now moved to flinging open the back door in all weathers. I arrive every day to find the outer door wide open, even if it is raining, and Grandma shivering in a corner. Charlie is going to have to fix some kind of mechanism to the door to prevent this. When I try to be cunning and scold Grandma for letting the heat out, pointing out that heat is expensive, she says she wouldn't dream of doing so and I must be thinking of someone else.

She looks so awful. As I dress her on these days, pull on the jumper and track suit again I find myself wondering if she ever looked attractive in vest and knickers. She must have done. I think how sweet children look in their little white vests and brightly coloured pants, how pick-up-and-huggable. And young women, like Hannah, how fetching those running singlets, *those* vests, with tiny satin shorts. Probably the elusive Mr McKay just longed to get Grandma thus, in vest and knickers. But they were Scots Presbyterians, probably had the light out for all dressing and undressing, probably took knickers off under a nightdress and the vest never. I met Grandma too late to make these obvious sweeping generalisations, though – how can I guess at her sensual past? She was fifty-three when I first met her and looked seventy, and had already been widowed nearly twenty years. She is fond of telling us she had her chances of re-marrying but 'couldn't be bothered'. Bridget says she doubts if there were any chances. She has no memory of her mother having a single male friend, not one. No man, not even a relative by then, ever came to their home and Grandma seems never to have left it.

It makes me despair, this sudden wilful making herself cold. Whatever her state of mind, is there no automatic animal response to cold? When she opens that door on those raw, wet autumn days we have had recently, does she not feel the blast of cold and want to close it instinctively? No – she opens the door wider, shivers and then takes her clothes off. Yet cold makes her miserable. She would never heat her home properly even when Charlie took over the bills, long before we brought her down here. That kind of obstinacy has just got worse, that's all, but it was always there, always part of her, moaning about the terrible cold yet too mean to have even one fire.

Meanness is not exactly the word. It is more that Grandma disliked excess and her judgement of what was excessive was always faulty. I used to have some ugly arguments with her on that. I would point out that there was something wrong with her values, surely, if she thought lighting a fire in the mornings, in a room where there was ice on the *inside* of the window panes, extravagant and yet lighting twenty cigarettes a day not so. Grandma would sniff and become distant. She would say she could manage fine without a fire till the evening and I would cut in and say 'but not without a ciggie'. She called cigarettes 'ciggies', being deliberately jocular or matey, but if I did, it was interpreted – correctly – as contempt. I did despise her smoking and I despised even more the absurdity of economising in ways that did not make sense – to me – and frittering money away in other ways. But Grandma would always win, absolutely always. Her house remained freezing until the magic hour of six o'clock. By eleven, when she went to bed, it would be warm enough to be tolerable.

The whole household smoked, even if Charlie were sitting among them wheezing with bronchitis. Grandma on her minimum twenty, Bridget on forty, Stuart on forty – all of them puffing away and saying poor Charlie, what an awful chest he has. My indignation only amused them, still does. Nobody smokes like that in my house, in Charlie's own home. I have every right to forbid it and I do. But Grandma and Bridget make me feel like a spoilsport, a prig, a fusspot, a silly, self-righteous do-gooder. They ostentatiously blow their smoke away from Charlie as though that made any difference. They smirk when they see me open a window – little Jenny being virtuous. And Grandma always did go into a huff if she asked to smoke and I pointed out that Charlie was chesty. I was implying that she, his mother, did not know what was good for him and I was wrong. Charlie himself did not help. His mother's refusal to accept that smoke caused him discomfort, made him so embarrassed that he encouraged her to go ahead, it didn't matter, he didn't mind. Then she would light up, smiling triumphantly at me.

Now, when I control Grandma's smoking to a large extent, I no longer care. I give her cigarettes when she wants them and derive a certain amount of shameful satisfaction from watching her ruin them. Because she is convinced people steal her cigarettes she hides them and, in hiding them, destroys them. She breaks them in half in her cardigan pockets, crumbles them to bits. It drives Bridget mad. She roars at her to stop ruining the bloody cigarettes and Grandma is outraged. Even when she does smoke them, she ruins them. One puff and she forgets she's smoking and the cigarette burns out. Dangerous. Of course – there are holes in her skirts, in the carpet, in the table-cloths. She can't be left with cigarettes on her own, ever. We keep them in a dish high up on top of the bathroom cabinet and dole them out when we are there. She gets through hundreds. We only have to put a packet of twenty on the table for one minute while we make tea and it will have disappeared. The only way is to take one cigarette, as required, from the bathroom dish and never let a packet near her. I am the most generous with them. Once, for sheer devilment, when she complained she hadn't had a ciggie for weeks, as she was actually smoking one, I gave her another just to watch what she would do. Could she smoke two at once? No. She let both go out and complained bitterly again.

These days I wonder where my compassion has gone. Hannah looks at me accusingly sometimes and I know she thinks I am being less than kind to Grandma. My irritation threshold gets lower and lower in proportion to Grandma's inability to control what irritates me – it is all wrong, I ought to feel *more* tenderness for her, not less. At least when I am with her on my own I do still find it easy to be gentle and I don't think I betray my irritation. It is when I am *not* with her that this unworthy feeling gets the upper hand. When Susan rings and says the cigarettes have gone and I know I put a new packet there the day before and I know they will turn up crushed and useless, *then* I am profoundly irritated. When I arrive to take Grandma out and I know I will find her with no clothes on, *then* I could scream – but I don't, not when I am with her. I can even pass the biggest test, changing her when she is wet, and remain soothing and calm. Oh, let me praise myself for something.

I think that when Grandma was small she must have been smacked or scolded severely for wetting herself because she is so alarmed now. She offers every sort of explanation for her state – buckets of water thrown at her, wet towels put on her seat, a leaking tap mysteriously attached to her chair – and, until I have accepted the excuse and agreed with it and said how careless other people are, she is terrified. She will even ask me not to mention it to her mother and I have to promise. I find reserves of patience I never knew I had when I actually have to deal with this kind of problem. But for the situation in general I have none. I want an end to it as much as Charlie does. Bridget, who never thinks more than a week ahead, does not know what it is like to be farsighted and fatalistic as a consequence.

Bridget is going on holiday tomorrow with Karl, for three weeks. First, to catch what is left of the late autumn sunshine (though she is mad to imagine it will be hot). They are going to the Black Forest and on a boat up the Rhine. Then they will spend the last week at Karl's home in Berlin. Bridget is excited and nervous and most of all amazed at her own daring. She has wasted every holiday she has ever taken. Mostly, she spends them at home, sleeping, but, when occasionally she has stirred herself and gone away, she has gone on dreadful package holidays to Benidorm – literally – it is not a joke – or else coach tours of Belgium. She has had awful holidays, truly. When I offer to organise a good holiday for her, she is quick to say she cannot afford it. Where does Bridget's money go? A Sister's pay is not high but Bridget is single and her standard of living very far from extravagant. She has a car, she smokes and drinks, but otherwise what on earth does she spend her salary on? She has no idea, resists all Charlie's attempts to sort out her finances and make some wise investments. He tries to get her to buy rather than rent a flat but she will have none of it.

She has been round to borrow things for her holidays. A case, for a start. She thinks she ought to have a decent case and of course would not dream of buying one – Bridget prefers borrowing. She would like to borrow my clothes but so few fit her since we are completely different shapes. She has taken a beach wrap which would fit anyone (though heaven knows what use she will find for that on this holiday) and a light dressing gown. I urged her to go out and buy some new clothes and she said she might if Hannah would go with her. I should think Hannah might – she likes to choose clothes and has a good eye for colour and style. But any outing of that kind will inevitably end in disaster. Bridget will ask Hannah's advice and then not take it and Hannah will get cross. To be as indecisive as Bridget is a state of mind beyond Hannah's comprehension.

I wish we were allowed to meet Karl properly. Now that his existence is acknowledged and we all know about the coming holiday, why not? I have formally invited Bridget to bring him for supper or Sunday lunch but she shuddered at the thought and made enigmatic remarks about this being 'too much'. Pressed to explain for whom – for her, for Karl, for us – she shook her head. She does not want to discuss it. Karl is hers and she is wary of showing him to us. She did once say he was 'too young for all this' – more mystery. I tried to reassure her, to say that Karl's youth would hardly be a handicap in our family or be held against him but, though she agreed, this did not alter her mind. I asked her if Karl himself did not think it odd that she kept him apart from a family he must know she was very involved with – she said yes, he was curious. Watching her carefully, I suggested that perhaps Karl might think she was ashamed of him or embarrassed to be seen with him because of what silly people might say about an older woman and a young man. Bridget coloured and said, 'Not at all,' sharply. But that can be the only explanation for declining an invitation to Sunday lunch, unless it is because Bridget does not want Grandma even to see him.

Bridget hates me to try and analyse her relationship with her mother, especially if I imply that there is anything abnormal about it. Then, Bridget jeers and accuses me of having read too many ridiculous pseudo-psychology books. Once, I went so far as to suggest Bridget had been more of a father and husband to Grandma than a daughter and that made her angry. She claimed her desire to protect her mother and look after her was every daughter's desire (is it?). She said I did not seem to understand how much she *liked* her mother for her own sake, quite apart from their relationship. And I suppose I do not. It is hard for me to believe Bridget chooses to be with Grandma not because she is dutiful but because she is amused and entertained and in tune with her. As Bridget points out, her life is full, she is no desperate spinster who has to cling on to her mother because she has nothing and no one else. It is very tempting to say that if things were so idyllic between Bridget and Grandma, why did she ever leave her? Why did not Bridget stay in Glasgow? Was lack of promotion the real reason? I doubt it. And why not, if it was, if Bridget had to move to London, why not bring Grandma who was well at the time?

Grandma does not know Bridget is going on holiday though she has been told often enough. It offends her. She is against holidays – 'Holidays, holidays, what does she want to be having holidays for?' When we say Bridget is going to Germany she is appalled and asks what is wrong with her own country, what is wrong with the Highlands? Adrian unwisely suggested the weather was wrong which brought forth a tirade against people who told lies about Scottish weather and how they used to *bake* in the sun on their holidays there. Hannah pointed out that Bridget might be going to Germany because she had never been whereas she was fed up with Scotland since she grew up there. Grandma was outraged – 'fed-up, fed-up' she screeched – and demanded to know how anyone could be fed-up with the most beautiful country in the world. She said that she wanted to hear no more about it anyway – 'Don't tell me, I don't want to know the half of it.' It was no use trying to get her used to the idea of Bridget's German trip. Constant repetition of the facts only produced constant fury. When Bridget has gone we will need to go through the whys and wherefores every hour in any case, I should imagine.

But we have a new helper. She even comes with glowing references and not from a newsagent's board or an agency. Dr Carruthers passed her onto us and we almost wept on his neck with gratitude. Her name is Mary, so Grandma will be sure to think it is her aunt and that will start every day off most satisfactorily as she remembers the Mary she once knew. And she is Scottish, what Bridget calls Edinburgh-posh. Her references show she has worked looking after elderly people for the last twenty years (she is sixty-two). Charlie pointed out that every job she has had has lasted a minimum of two years and has come to a natural end. Mary has never given notice. Either the old person has died or gone into a Home or hospital, with Mary faithful to the end. The only disadvantage is that Mary is lame. She has a club foot. Dr Carruthers did not even mention it so that when Mary called on us, we were taken aback, visibly. How could a fairly small, slight elderly woman with a club foot cope with a large, heavy even older woman who sometimes fell and needed to be lifted? It seemed impossible. Nobody dared say so. Bridget said later she wanted to laugh, it was so ridiculous, so farcical. But Charlie, who had seen a solution to our problem within his eager grasp, was not going to let it go. Boldly, he asked Mary if she thought she would be able to manage a fairly cumbersome old woman who often needed help getting up. Mary took his point: she said her lameness had never been a handicap in any of her jobs and that she was tougher than she looked.

So we have Mary, Mary Black. She starts tomorrow and will do all of Bridget's five nights leaving us only one each. God knows how it will work out, but, like Charlie, I am desperate to give it a try. Bridget, because she is going away, has had rather less to say on the subject than she normally would have. It is in her interests to be a mite more enthusiastic and she has tried to be. But she makes it clear that she realises it lets *us* off the hook. I think she was looking forward to Charlie having to do what she does week in and week out, just so that he would appreciate her more. If so, she is very silly. If Charlie had to do four or five nights a week with his mother, the effect would be to make him rapidly overcome those scruples he still has – he would have Grandma in some kind of institution within a week. He would refuse to endure that kind of tyranny, I know. So Mary has saved Grandma's bacon, for the moment. With Mary's help we may stagger on for some time yet. Until something new happens.

I fantasise all the time, to an alarming extent, about what that 'something' will be. I used to think it would be a heart attack, that I would go for Grandma one afternoon and find her on the floor, dead, and that would be that. How naïve of me. Grandma's heart beats soundly in her wretched body, sending blood reliably to her dying brain. It is not going to stop suddenly, that's for sure. So I dream of a fall in which she breaks her leg and in that fantasy I pretend to be a neighbour and ring for an ambulance because I do not want Grandma at home with a broken limb and I am terrified that if they see she has a daughter-in-law on hand, not to mention a daughter across the hall who is a nurse, then no hospital will take her. Once in hospital she gets an infection and dies. Equally unlikely: Grandma's falls, if they are falls, never seem to hurt her. This leaves me with the burglar fantasy which I do not like and rarely allow myself to resort to: a burglar knocks Grandma on the head – only a little tap, she hardly feels it (I don't want her to suffer) but her skull fractures because it is thin, and she dies. Only I bet Grandma's skull is as thick as brick and she would be so obliging with any burglar he would have no need to hit her. Lately, I have another quite attractive fantasy taking shape: Grandma thinks her pills are mints and takes a whole bottle which has accidentally been left around. She goes into a deep sleep and dies. But I see the flaw already: the pills are bitter – it is a great fuss to get Grandma to take any – and she likes only sweet things. She would never take an overdose.

No, the 'something' is impossible to envisage. It is more likely to be a growing nothing. Grandma will go on and on and on, able to do less and less and needing more and more and more care. It will all happen at home. I see it and groan.

155

Hannah

This Mary is unbelievable. She's too good to be true. No wonder Bridget is suspicious. The first time Mary met Grandma she kissed her and said the Lord loved her. Grandma said she was glad someone did as she was like the last rose etc. etc. Makes me suspect this Mary's Scottishness – Scots don't kiss on first meeting. Maybe it's just that she's lived in the soft South so long she's picked up our ways. But she has the accent all right and seems to know her Scotland and can even recite a few lines of Burns though only what most people can manage – 'My love is like a red, red rose' and that stuff.

Grandma is greatly affected by Mary's club foot. She whispers 'poor soul' in her hearing and wonders how it happened, people should take more care. Grandma's anxious, sympathetic eyes follow Mary's club foot in its polished boot-like shoe as she limps across the room. She tut-tuts and heaves herself up in order to persuade the Poor Soul to sit down and rest her leg. Mary has explained she was born lame, that her right leg is shorter than the left and was bent under in her mother's inside (she doesn't say womb) which made it worse and then she was a breech birth and the forceps got stuck – it goes on for hours and Grandma loves it. I shouldn't think Mary loves it by now, not after having to relate the saga so many times because Grandma greets her every day as a stranger. But Mary copes with this well. She's obviously quite familiar with senile dementia. And she has her own theories, does Mary. She's a diet freak. She thinks Grandma's memory cells wouldn't be dying off at such a rate if she ate the right food. She brings molasses and honey to replace the white sugar Grandma uses in such quantities and has substituted low-sodium salt for the ordinary kind. Mum says there's no harm in it and Mary's right. What Bridget will say when she comes back, God knows.

I do the hand-over every day at the moment. I walk along now with Grandma muffled up in shawls even though it's not really cold. Grandma is moaning like mad and shivering and saying the weather isn't fit for a dog to go out in and there is no rest for the wicked and what has she done to deserve this and then some mumbling about January's bitter blast o'wind. I say it's only just November, not January and the wind is not bitter, in fact there's no wind or that tree in front of us would be moving. Grandma says trees don't move where she comes from. I say she knows what I mean and by that time we're at her gate. We stop, I bend to open the gate. Grandma asks if I know the people here. I say yes, my Grandmother and Aunt both live here. Grandma says that's nice for them. There's a light on in the kitchen. Mary is always early, I never have to wait for her. She hobbles smiling to the door and opens it, ushers us in. She must've been here at least three quarters of an hour because she has baked gingerbread. It's standing on the table, steaming gently. Mary says she has just this minute taken it out of the oven and Grandma must wait till it cools. Grandma's greedy eyes light up, her big hand stretches out and she says quite distinctly, 'Get lost.' I remove the cake. Grandma glares at me. I tell her hot cake will give her indigestion and then she will have Mary up all night.

Who the hell's Mary when she's at home?
Grandma!
Grandma yourself. I want my cake.
In a minute, when it's cool.
You mind yourself, give it here.
No.
I'll take a strap to you.

157

Grandma!

So I will, bloomin' cheek, I never get anything, always the same.

Mary's made it specially for you.

I made it, I've slaved all afternoon and that's the bloomin' thanks I get, go away with you.

No, Grandma, Mary very kindly made it.

Who the hell's Mary when she's at home?

But Mary only has to limp over with some tea and the limping action arrests Grandma's attention and instantly she forgets about the cake. I know I'm just waiting to catch Mary out. I'm conscious of scrutinising her, of looking for the iron fist in the velvet glove. She's so tender with Grandma, even when Grandma is cross. She seems not to mind being mildly abused, only smiles. And now Grandma is allowed the gingerbread and gorges, ramming into her mouth with indecent haste and spraying crumbs everywhere as she says it's delicious. Mary invites me to have a taste. I say no thanks. Grandma goes into overdrive trying to persuade me. As I well know, she can't bear people not to like what she likes, she will not *believe* they don't share her tastes. I can see Mary thinks I could easily take a token piece to please my Grandma, to keep her quiet and I could. But I won't. Grandma is getting spoiled and it's not good for her. I don't want gingerbread, I happen not to like gingerbread and I absolutely refuse to pretend I do just for the sake of indulging Grandma. I am not like saintly Mary.

Mum is in love with Mary. Dad is in love with Mary. Mum says Mary restores her faith in human nature, just to know there are such good people in existence who only want to give. Mum says there can be no other motive for Mary's devotion. Who else but a saint would want to be cooped up with Grandma five nights a week, getting wakened half of them too? Dad agrees Mary is a saint but, being Dad, feels obliged to point out that money may well be a consideration. What other job could club-footed sixty-two-year-old Mary get? We give her £200 a week in smackeroos, Dad says. Mum points out that by the hour that is not so much because Mary starts at six o'clock when we take Grandma back and doesn't leave till Susan

158

arrives at 9 a.m., making her hours longer than those any other night helper has ever done. Dad launches into sums and calculations of every sort and still concludes Mary, in her circumstances, has a good deal.

Who cares? So long as Grandma is looked after and kept out of a Home.

★

Mum says would I like to go to St Alma's with her when she takes Grandma today. Would I *like* to? Does she mean as a treat? It isn't the sort of outing anyone would *like*, is it? But I say yes. I really should inspect one of these Homes if just to argue better against them. I have never been in one. Mum says St Alma's will not be typical, that it's the best, that she wouldn't dream of suggesting I visited the other place she and Dad looked at. She says I will see immediately how lucky we'll be if we manage to get Grandma into this very wonderful place. She has her fingers crossed.

Susan of course is given the morning off but not told why. Mum doesn't want her to know where Grandma is going or why. She says Susan is against Grandma going into a Home because she would lose her job. Mum doesn't want to have to put up with Susan 'in a mood'. It's important to keep Susan sweet so she's given the morning off with pay and Mum mutters on about taking Grandma into the country for a drive. Is East Finchley the country? Actually, it does look remarkably green as we drive along Totteridge Lane. We pass a horse, a pony, in a kind of paddock. There is a van parked in front of what must be stables and Mum has to stop until it has moved. Grandma has plenty of time to stare at this pony.

> Poor horse.
> It looks happy enough, Grandma.
> All on its own.
> Maybe it likes being on its own.
> You'd think they could give it company.
> Company?
> Even a chicken or two.
> Do horses like chickens?
> Poor horse.

159

The van moves, we move. We leave the horse behind. Grandma thinks it's the Highlands starting and peers out of the window to see if she can see any cattle. Mum says under her breath that she has never seen any landscape less like the Highlands.

St Alma's *looks* all right, I suppose. If only Mum would shut up, I'd be quite prepared to notice for myself the attractive house and pleasant gardens, the freshness of the paint and brightness of the knocker. Grandma thinks it's the manse and again Mum is irritated, casting her eyes to heaven and asking me if I have ever *seen* a Glasgow manse? It really annoys Mum when Grandma makes that kind of stupid comparison based on no connection whatsoever. Mum says it has nothing to do with Grandma's mental condition now, that this is part of the old Grandma. It just makes me smile.

Grandma is quite happy going into St Alma's because I'm on one side and Mum on the other. The floor is very shiny. Grandma says it must've taken some polishing, it's like a skating rink and she's afraid she'll slip. Mum says it isn't in the least slippy and demonstrates. It's true, the floor only looks slippy but isn't. Grandma refuses to be convinced. Every step we persuade her to take is followed by 'Oh help!' from her. She won't even try to walk properly. She says she should have brought her skates but then remembers she only has one because she loaned her cousin the other and never got it back, she wonders why, he has a damned cheek keeping it all this time. We get her across the hall to the Matron's office and Mum knocks as Grandma asks what in the name of heaven is going on, do we have to knock to get in our own house now?

I hate the Matron – on sight. She looks like Mrs Thatcher: stiff, smarmy, pretend-kind. She's even dressed like Mrs Thatcher with a floppy bow blouse and a greyish suit, and she has the cardboard hair and the bland smile. Grandma hates the Matron too. Grandma starts sniffing loudly, always a sign of her nervousness. She nudges me, I nudge back. This Matron is exactly the sort of woman who intimidates Grandma, though funnily enough Grandma loves Mrs Thatcher. What she likes best are Mrs Thatcher's harangues about working hard, and her jingoism, and her constant hypocritical harking back to Victorian values – Grandma loves that in a Prime

Minister. But not in this Matron. I'm not sure about Mum. Mum may not hate this woman, she can't hate her or she wouldn't have brought Grandma here or called St Alma's desirable. But Mum is wary of her, not at all comfortable. Lucky Bridget isn't here. She would immediately have said could Grandma have a seat. Bridget wouldn't be intimidated.

We do sit and tea is brought in. Grandma looks at the china and says who pinched her wedding china, she wondered where it had gone. The Matron says it is pretty isn't it. Grandma says it should be back in the china cabinet where it belongs, she did not give permission for it to be taken out, this is not a special occasion so far as she knows. Mum placates her. Grandma has great difficulty getting her fingers round the rather pretty delicate cup. She sips the tea and says in the name of God it reminds her of a friend she once had who could not make tea etc. etc. The Matron smiles and says does Grandma like her tea strong. Grandma is emphatic, she does *not* like tea strong, never did, but she likes tea that is tea and not coloured water and she likes it hot, it's no good if it isn't hot, and she likes a decent mug to drink it out of. The Matron copes well. Still smiling glacially she goes to a cupboard and gets a mug and puts her own electric kettle on and makes Grandma a mug of tea herself, using two tea bags in the mug. Grandma tastes, approves, thanks God but not the Matron.

The Matron asks Grandma if she would like to join the others.

What others?
The other ladies, they're painting at the moment, it's our painting morning.
I've done enough painting to last a lifetime.
You like painting do you Mrs McKay?
Somebody's got to do it and my lazy lot won't.
(*Mum explains hurriedly that Grandma thinks Matron means home decorating.*)
I think you'd find this sort of painting fun, Mrs McKay.
Fun? It gives me a bad back.
Shall we give it a try? Shall we join the others?
What others?

161

We all troop out and cross the hall and go through what looks, in passing, like a pleasant sitting room with chintzy chairs, into another room at the back. It has a black and white checked floor and is full of easels. At each easel there is an old woman, wearing a smock. Some have paintbrushes in their hands and are managing to dip them occasionally into paint and splodge on the paper in front of them. There is a vase of autumn leaves on a table in the centre of the room round which the easels are grouped. Three women in pink overalls are looking after the twelve artists. They make encouraging noises all the time, like coo-ing birds – oooh-ow, oooh-ow, they go. Grandma is totally thunderstruck. She just stares. Mum is taken aback. She says she didn't see this the last time she came. Matron says no, but then she came in the afternoon and afternoons are Resting, Reflecting and Ruminating. She laughs as she explains these three Rs are very important at St Alma's – the mornings are for stimulation of one sort or another and in the afternoons it is the three Rs for a couple of hours.

Grandma allows us to take her coat off and is quite uncomplaining about having a smock put on. One old lady who looks as though she has died at her easel is removed (remarks are made about Elsie having worked too hard but on her paper there are only two wavy green lines and a spot of yellow in the corner). Grandma is put in her place. Mum is finding this hard but not as hard as I am. We need Adrian. Adrian would laugh, he would have hysterics at the sight of Grandma-as-artist solemnly picking up her paintbrush – oooh-ow oooh-ow go those in charge – and dipping it in red paint and then very deliberately and unexpectedly putting it quickly in her mouth and sucking it. Consternation, squawks from the helpers, sniggers from a couple of the brighter old ladies and protests from Grandma who maintains she was just testing. Her mouth is cleaned, the paintbrush returned to her hand and all three helpers surround her. One guides Grandma's hand. A red line is made on the paper. Matron says shall we go? We go. Grandma, as effectively trapped in a smock as she would be in a straitjacket and with three attendants blocking her view of us leaving, makes no sound.

Mum asks could her daughter have a quick tour of the rest of St Alma's if it is not too much trouble. Matron says it is *never* too much trouble. As we walk quickly in and out of rooms, I think how utterly alien this place is to Grandma: it is pure Mum. Mum sees the beautiful paint, the flowered wallpapers, the rugs, the pale-patterned curtains, the polished tables, the loose-covered armchairs and she feels at home. Cleanliness, brightness, colour, a modicum of elegance and style – that is Mum. It is not Grandma. Mum must be mad. This place will not do for Grandma, even if they would take her. Its virtues would repel her. She likes shabbiness and mess and muddle and nothing too clean-looking because it will only get dirty. Grandma doesn't even like light, the sort of light that comes through St Alma's big windows. At home in Glasgow she spent her time crouching in her kitchen with lace curtains obscuring what light there was. But Mum is telling me to agree that everything is lovely, to join her in admiring the jugs of fresh flowers and the prints on the walls. And Matron is still smiling.

We are back at the front door. Matron says to come back at four o'clock. Mum says that if Grandma seems unhappy she'll come at once and collect her. Matron's smile broadens. She says there's no question of Mrs McKay not being happy, that the problem is more likely to be getting her to leave at four. Mum blushes. Mum says, hesitantly, that Grandma does need reminding to go to the loo especially if she drinks a lot of tea. Matron says there is no need to worry, that tea is controlled and all the ladies are potted regularly. Good job Bridget isn't here for that 'potted'. We leave. Mum asks what I think. It seems cruel to tell her but I do. I say I think Grandma will hate it, that no one in their right mind could think she would be happy there. Mum gives one of her bitter little smiles. She queries 'happy'. She says there are other considerations apart from happiness. She says she's not going to crucify herself trying to ensure Grandma is happy because happiness isn't measurable and can't be guaranteed for anyone. She says that on the other hand she sees it as her duty to make sure Grandma is properly cared for and treated with respect and tenderness. My turn, I query 'tenderness'. I say 'tenderness', from *that* Matron? Mum says OK respect and kindness. That's all we can do.

As we drive home, the vision of those old women plonked in front of easels stays with me. I can see it's a good try. I can see that it's much easier to push twelve old women into chairs and leave them for the day. I can see St Alma's deserves credit for trying. Maybe some of those old women will get pleasure out of splashing paint about, maybe some of them have wanted to all their lives and a great primitive artist will emerge. Maybe Grandma will think she's back at her beloved school, except probably they didn't have painting then, not in her kind of school. Who can know what Grandma will think? I say so to Mum.

Almost immediately I say I'm sorry. Mum says nothing for about ten minutes and then lets fly. She says what she is bloody sick of is criticism, that what she wants is constructive suggestions. What do I suggest? I say things seem fine as they are but Mum interrupts to scream that this is the point, don't I see, can't I understand, things are not going to *stay* as they are. We must plan, we must prepare, we are lost if we just wait for things to get worse. And she is the only one that sees it. Right. She has promised herself. There is to be a demarcation line beyond which she will not go. She will inform Bridget on her return. One, she will not clean Grandma up if she becomes doubly incontinent; two, she will not nurse Grandma if she becomes bedridden; three, if Grandma gets to the stage of not recognising her, she considers herself absolved from day-to-day care. She breathes deeply. She says all this will happen and it is better it should happen when Grandma is already in an institution because etc. etc. I switch off. There is no mistaking Mum's distress, but I have heard all this a million times.

What I want to know is:

What am I going to do with Mum when she's old?
Why is it all such a terrible problem and fuss?
Why doesn't someone *do* something?

Mum goes on her own to pick up Grandma. I don't want to go again nor do I want to be with Mum. She comes back quite cheerful. Matron said Grandma was very good and ate a good lunch and didn't wet herself and it had all been a great success. Her name is down, together with fourteen others. Great. Grandma may get a scholarship to St Alma's. *Will* Bridget be thrilled. Mum says there's no need to be sarcastic nor any need to tell Bridget. St Alma's is

164

merely a contingency plan which she, Mum, is greatly relieved to have. Dad praises her, he says he's delighted, he only wishes the waiting list was a good bit shorter and that he didn't have a nasty suspicion that by the time Grandma got to the top of it she might not score high enough on her reassessment. Still, Dad says, it's one small victory and a consolation. Grandma will be much better off when she finally gets into nice, bright, light St Alma's and has company all day long and plenty going on.

I take Grandma back home after her exciting day. She seems very, very tired. She trudges even slower than usual and sighs and has not the energy to bend and examine an empty cigarette packet in the gutter. I ask who stole her scone but she doesn't laugh.

> Where's that Bridget? Leaving me alone.
> She's on holiday, Grandma, and you haven't been alone.
> On *holiday*? What for?
> Pleasure.
> *Pleasure*? Whatever next, if we all thought of pleasure.
> You should have done.
> What?
> Thought of your own pleasures in life.
> That would've been a fine thing, who'd have done the work?
> Other people.
> Oh, aye, if you believe that you'll believe anything.
> What would've been your pleasures, anyway, Grandma?
> I wasn't wanting pleasure, I had my bairns.
> But what pleasure would you have liked for yourself?
> I've always had plenty of money.
> This isn't about money Grandma, it's about what you would
>   like to have had in life.
> I have my bairns.
> I *know*, but apart from that.
> I never wanted anything else, women don't do they, it's the men
>   always wanting, wanting.
> I want plenty.
> Oh highty-toighty, well I hope you get it.
> I will.
> Where's Bridget, the hussy?

She called for Bridget as we went into her flat. Mary hobbled through, smiling, and was met by a glare. Grandma turned round and said she would be going home, the men would be looking for their teas etc. etc. Mary said the tea was ready, poured out and waiting, nice and hot and sweet. Grandma said she supposed she could rest a minute to drink it as Mary had poured it out but then she must be off because the men etc. etc. The tea was heaven, it was delicious, it was just how she liked it, what did you say your name was but anyway you can make good tea. Grandma's feet are up, her kitchen is warm and cosy, it feels perfectly all right to leave her. There's no need, now we have Mary, to linger outside the door eavesdropping, no need to wonder how Grandma is being treated. Mary *is* a saint.

★

We're all going away tonight. Mum is so worried she's thinking of not going, she says we shouldn't all be away, because of Grandma. Dad is cross with her, he says he's paying Mary a fortune to stay with Grandma and what is the point if it doesn't free us. Mum says but what if anything happens, what if Grandma falls and Mary rings and no one is here, what then, what will Mary do? Dad says ring for an ambulance like anyone else. Under his breath he adds that it might solve a lot of problems. Mum hears, Mum pounces, Mum says what does he mean, it would *create* problems, not solve them, and what would Bridget say? Dad sighs, he says he will speak to Mary. He speaks. Mary says no one is to worry, she would cope. Dad does not ask how, he is triumphant, he repeats that Mary said she would cope. Mum doubts it, she says Mary is too good. Then she has a brainwave. She says she will give Stuart's number to Mary. In an emergency Stuart would *have* to come, even if he never came again, even if he only did it once. Mum says she won't ask him, she'll just do it. Dad says he doesn't bloody care, just so long as she's agreeing to go with him.

They are going to a Silver Wedding party in Cambridge. Dad's best friend is a don there. Dad is looking forward to it no end, Mum not so much. Mum doesn't really like Dad's old Cambridge friends and she certainly doesn't like the wife of this one. But it'll be a good party, no expense spared, champagne until the early hours and all that. Dad is as greedy as Grandma though Grandma wouldn't thank anyone for champagne. Adrian is going to the Barn, a place his school has in Somerset. He's doing some A-Level Geography field trip, will be away all weekend. All I'm doing is going to stay at Frinny's. I have to. I have no desire to stay at Frinny's but they will not leave me in an empty house. I've stayed with Grandma, the odd night on my own but apparently that's different. I say I'm seventeen, it's ridiculous. Dad says it's *because* I am seventeen that I can't stay in an empty house. He says I'm vulnerable. His head is full of scare stories about burglars and rapists. He's worse than Grandma. He goes on so much about the dangers of living in London that I sometimes think I should just go to bed and stay there until I am Grandma's age. So I'm obliged to go to Frinny's. She has a small bedroom and I have to sleep on the floor, and the flat her family lives in is too hot, always. I sleep badly there but I have to be grateful.

Frinny doesn't know what I'm talking about when I go on about Grandma. One of her Grandmas is only sixty-seven and takes Frinny on holidays. She took her to Venice for a week last year. Imagine. The other is a bit older and bossy but spoils Frinny and her sister something rotten. She's always buying them clothes, lovely clothes and she pays for their riding lessons. When Frinny's parents go away it's that Gran who comes and takes charge and does all the cooking and so on. I'm jealous. I would love a Gran to have fun with. But poor Grandma, it isn't her fault etc. etc. I think if Mum's mum had lived she wouldn't have been much better either but I can hardly remember her. My children will be lucky. Dad will be great as a Grandad and Mum taking charge will be heaven for me. If I have any children. If there's any point.

There was a postcard from Bridget this morning, from somewhere-on-the-Rhine. Bridget's handwriting is terrible. I'm always intending to get a book on graphology to try to interpret it. All their handwriting is terrible – Bridget's, Dad's, Stuart's. But what Bridget writes is witty. She mocks herself so beautifully, sends up her own ignorance. She's having a wonderful time though 'a little conspicuous because of my effortless German which naturally arouses comment'. No mention of Karl at all. The weather is great. Mum is pleased. She desperately wants Bridget to have a good time. It was such an upheaval for her to get away that it would have been too awful if she hadn't enjoyed it.

I show the postcard to Grandma who's having tea with us before we all go off. She handles it suspiciously. It is rather a lurid postcard, the blue of the Rhine a violent, unbelievable turquoise. Grandma stares at it.

> It doesn't look like the Clyde.
>
> It isn't Grandma, it's the Rhine.
>
> Rhine who?
>
> In Germany, the River Rhine, Bridget's on holiday sailing down it.
>
> In the name of God — what does she want to do that for, what's got into her?
>
> She's enjoying it.
>
> Some people have funny tastes, no need for it, what's wrong with her own country?
>
> She's seen it.
>
> What?
>
> Her own country. She wants to see other countries too.
>
> Why?
>
> Well, it's interesting, different.
>
> There's nowhere nicer than the Highlands.
>
> There is.
>
> There is not.
>
> It rains there and the food is awful.
>
> You mind yourself, you're ignorant.
>
> I'm not. There's nothing to do in the Highlands, nothing Bridget likes to do anyway.
>
> To do? To do?
>
> Look at the lovely blue in this card, you can tell it's lovely and sunny.
>
> It doesn't look like the Clyde.

I've made her irritable. Criticisms of Scotland have always made her irritable. When anyone mentions statistics from newspapers about Glasgow being the worst city in the world for drunkenness or

Scotland the worst country for lung cancer, Grandma goes mad. She says people will make up anything. She says she signed the pledge at ten and her father never touched a drop and she doesn't know what people are talking about or why they tell these lies. If I want to be wicked I say Robert Burns himself was a drunkard and a womaniser. Grandma sniffs and says if I believe that I'll believe anything, etc. I say these are facts, that Burns had at least five illegitimate children, including two sets of twins. Grandma says twins are bonny. She always ends up off the subject. Will never concede facts are facts.

But today I must keep her in a good mood so that Mary has no trouble. I take out the ironing board and become Mummy's Little Treasure. Grandma loves that. She sits with her feet up, watching, feeling she's doing it herself, I think. She hums 'The Skye Boat Song'. I iron a skirt, a black and white swirly silky thing I got off a stall last week. Frinny and I are going to a party so we thought we'd shock everyone and wear skirts. Grandma says it's nice, what is it, where did you get it, how much? I tell her. I tell her about the party. She says everyone goes to parties except her, it's years since she went to a party. I smile at the thought of what Grandma would think of the party Frinny and I are going to, of her vision of what a party is. I ask what she likes best about parties. She says the sing-song and the jelly, she's very fond of jelly, and it's nice if there's a fiddler or a piper. She sighs. She says nobody knows how to enjoy themselves these days. Everyone stays in their houses and they're bloomin' miserable and nobody cares. I say, Oh Grandma, and she says do not 'Oh Grandma' her.

Mum comes in to ask what I think of her dress for this Silver Wedding lark. It is black and she looks good. Usually, Mum goes for pale colours though I've told her and told her she looks awful in them, but tonight it's black and her skin looks milky and smooth and her hair gleams. It's a no-fuss dress, excellent. I ask where she got it. She says I'll only sneer. I say I will not, the dress is beautiful wherever it came from. She says Marks & Spencer's, so there (she knows I loathe M & S almost as much as I hate Laura Ashley). I say well, well, and what do you think, Grandma. Grandma says Mum will look very nice at the funeral but she will need a coat. Mum says it's a party she's going to. Grandma sniffs and says everyone except her is going to a party and she would have thought a nice red more like the thing. Mum realises all this is very tactless. She rushes off and comes back in her jeans and an old jumper and makes Grandma some more tea. I say I'll take her home afterwards.

Mary has brought with her a tape of Scottish music, dance music. It is playing as Grandma and I go into the kitchen. Grandma's delighted, does a little jig and Mary beams. Grandma says we could have a party, she could get some lemonade and crisps. Mary says that's a very nice idea and maybe we will. It's lovely to leave Grandma looking so happy. I make sure I tell Mum before she leaves.

*

I'm first back. I came back at noon the next day, Sunday. I'm going to go along and give Grandma her lunch. Mary will have left at eleven and won't return until six and I've told Mum and Dad there's no need to hurry, that I can look after Grandma until six. I will probably cheat. I'll take my Walkman and homework and do a lot of ignoring. But first I have a long, luxurious bath and then I have a sandwich. I don't like eating at Grandma's. I don't mind making her things but I don't like eating with her.

Just before one, feeling a little guilty because I said to Mum I would go earlier, I trot along the street. Almost at once I sense there's something wrong: the front door, the main front door which opens into a sort of small entrance hall, is open. The two doors inside are safely shut, one to the ground floor (Grandma's and Bridget's) and one to the first (the two actors we never see). But the front door is open and that is so unusual I'm alarmed. I hurry. I use my key and go into Grandma's flat calling her name. There's no reply. She's not there. I search thoroughly, including the garden, and then just as I'm beginning to panic the telephone rings. I dive for it. It's Mary. She's ringing from the hospital. She says it's a long story, that she has had a dreadful time, she's near to tears, she wants to know when my parents are back. I say not until late this evening but that I will come at once, but what's wrong, what has happened. The money runs out. I hesitate, I wait, the phone doesn't ring again.

I walk quickly to the hospital. It's not far. I'm inside within twenty minutes but then I don't know where to go. I give Grandma's name at the desk and after a very long time I'm sent to the seventh floor, to Ward G5. Mary is sitting outside, waiting. She looks agitated, she's clasping and unclasping her hands. I tell her that whatever has happened she mustn't worry. And then she goes over it, in bits and pieces. I want to stop her but she obviously needs to tell me it all in this jumbled way. I want even more to ask her to begin at the end, to tell me how my grandmother is, but there is no restraining her.

This is roughly what happened: Grandma fell at three in the morning. Mary could not get her up, Grandma complained her leg hurt and Mary was afraid it was broken. She rang Stuart, as directed, and Stuart said ring for an ambulance, that this is what he would do even if he came over. Mary rang, the ambulance came and Grandma was brought in. Nothing was broken. Grandma was now sleeping peacefully. Mary felt a fool. Stuart had been already. He was coming back when Grandma woke up to take her home. Poor Mary. She feels she has failed Mum. She feels she acted hastily. She wishes she had not rung Stuart. She wishes she had not rung for an ambulance. She blames herself for all this bother over nothing. I reassure her. I tell her if there's any blame attached to anyone, which there is not, it should be to us: we should not have left Mary to manage. I tell her my mother will be far more worried about her, about Mary herself, than about Grandma. I ask how she feels. I say she must feel shaken. She says yes, she does. She hesitates, then she says she's not even sure if she can manage to do tonight, she feels so tired and – I jump in, I say of course not, no one would expect her to and one of us will take her place.

I am taken to see Grandma. She has just woken. She smiles and whistles and raises her eyebrows. She looks so sweet in her hospital gown, her white hair on the big pillow. A nurse comes up and says Grandma can go home now, where are her clothes? I say I think she must have come in her nightdress. The nurse sighs and says, of course, and here it is and could you be as quick as possible, we need the bed. I feel so embarrassed that Grandma is a fraud. Mary and I draw the curtains round the bed and change Grandma's hospital

171

nightdress for her own. She is indignant, objects, wants to be left alone. We hustle her out of bed. The nurse says we can use a wheelchair. We push Grandma into a wheelchair. She complains bitterly. We hurry out of the ward, head for the lift. Grandma says repeatedly what's the hurry, what is going on, that there's no need for this.

Horrible Stuart is waiting downstairs. He is in his uniform. Grandma gasps at the sight of him and whispers, 'It's the Polis.' Stuart says he has to hurry, he's on duty, come *on*, Mother.

> Who are you mothering?
> You. Try to stand.
> Fancy, a policeman, the shoes on him.
> Stand, Mother.
> What size do you take? Was your father a big man?
> You should know.
> Who?
> You.
> What?
> For heaven's sake, Mother.
> Who are you mothering?

Stuart is furious. He manhandles Grandma into his car without speaking to her again and Mary and I get in the back meekly. I hate Stuart so much for his insensitivity that I grow bold. I ask him if he will please take Mary home first. Mary protests, she says she can walk. Stuart grunts then silently drives Mary home. I tell her to have a good rest as she struggles out, and I thank her profusely. The minute she has gone Stuart starts. He asks where the bloody hell my parents are. Grandma says heh, language. Stuart asks what they were playing at, why wasn't he told they were going to lumber him. Lumber, I query. Grandma says she's had enough lumbago to last her a lifetime. It was a chance they took, I say. Well, Stuart says, they better hadn't take it again because he's not having any, he's had enough, he's always made it plain that this kind of thing is just *not on*. Grandma says she should think not, people have no respect these days. By then we are home. Stuart shovels Grandma out as brutally as he pushed her in. He has no pity in him. The minute we

172

are in Grandma's kitchen, he says he's off. He says he will be ringing Dad. I say sarcastically that I'll tell him, that I'm sure Dad will look forward to it.

Grandma asks have the men gone now? I say yes. She says thank goodness, they're only a nuisance, we're better without them. I can't muster the energy to dress her. I put a shawl over her dressing gown and pull it tight. She says do I want to strangle her? I give her a kiss. She says oh, my word, is it my money you're after? I make tea and toast and put the radio on. It is 'Down Your Way', which Grandma likes. I feel quite shaken. The ward Grandma was in was full of such deathly ill-looking people, all lying pale in obedient rows. Some were groaning, the woman in the next bed silently crying. And there Grandma sits, at home, bright in her tartan shawl, slurping tea, crunching toast, talking back to the radio, quite oblivious to what has happened.

> I wish Mum and Dad were back.
> I wish Bridget was here.
> I wish Stuart loved her.
> I wish people didn't have to grow old.
> I wish I could stop thinking such stupid things.

Jenny

I knew it would happen. There can be no excuses for Charlie and me. It was unforgivable of us to go off leaving an old, club-footed, frail lady in charge of Grandma without adequate back up – almost criminally negligent. My God, how would it have looked in a court of law? Charlie was furious when I said that, he shouted that no crime had been committed and what the hell was all this about courts of law? He still doesn't see that anything the least bit dreadful has happened. Well, if Mary gives in her notice he will see it then.

I rang Mary at once of course, as soon as I had heard the whole dreadful saga from Hannah. I apologised, grovelled, begged forgiveness for exposing her to this ordeal and she in turn apologised for having misjudged Grandma's condition and for ringing Stuart. I did not talk about Stuart, I just ignored that. I really wanted to apologise for how Stuart had behaved, too, but I did not trust myself to start on that one. Mary said she was glad to have that night off and was sure she would be able to stay with Grandma after that, 'if you still think I am capable'. Did she mean that? Or was the poor woman trying to tell us as nicely as possible that she could not manage any more? Charlie says he has had enough of my crossing bridges before they are even in sight but I cannot help it. Mary is giving signals, I am receiving them.

I am receiving them from Hannah too. Even if, as Charlie

174

maintains, nothing dreadful has happened, surely he can see how very upset Hannah is. She got such a shock, arriving to find Grandma gone and then having that distraught call from Mary. She told me that as she ran to the hospital she was sure Grandma had been horribly injured and was dying and it would be her fault for arriving late and for not having offered to stay with her in the first place. And then seeing Grandma in that ward was a shock, too. Hannah said that, although Grandma looked so sweet and was quite happy, it made her seem so helpless and vulnerable. The signal was flashed unmistakably: in a Home Grandma would look even more so.

Charlie rang Stuart. I sat beside Charlie when he called Stuart and his brother's hectoring voice was so loud I could hear every word. The conversation went roughly like this:

> Stuart, it's me.
>
> You've taken your time.
>
> What?
>
> I've been waiting for you to ring, what the hell did you think you were doing?
>
> Well, we went to this Silver –
>
> I know where you went, I'm not talking about that, it's none of my business, what I'm referring to is telling that woman to ring me.
>
> Well, we had to give her someone's number in case of an emergency and we thought –
>
> You *thought*? That's what you bloody well didn't do, mate. You can't have been thinking at all because if you'd *thought* you'd have remembered I'm not in on this, I had enough a long time ago. I'm not having any more of my life messed up by Mother and I've told you straight.
>
> It was only –
>
> Never mind only, you've got yourself into this mess, I told you what would happen, you're a mug, Charlie, you should see sense and put a stop to it.
>
> Well, normally the system works quite well but with Bridget being –

175

Don't mention Bridget to me, don't try that blackmail.

Blackmail? I never even thought of it. I was just going to say that with Bridget being away we –

I'm not interested, if Bridget wants to be a martyr then that's her affair but count me out, don't ever do that to me again.

I won't.

Good.

I'm sorry you were bothered.

Now there's no need to be like that, I'm just giving it to you straight from the shoulder, I never did like hypocrisy, but there's nothing personal in it.

No?

No. You've got to be tough in this world, Charlie. You've only got one life and you can't afford to let it be spoiled.

She's our Mother, Stuart, and –

Good God, I *know* she's our Mother, what do you think you're telling me? You think I'm a brute, eh? Well, I'm not. I know she's our Mother, I know she's old and sick, I know she can't help it but it's the other bit I'm not having, the bit where Bridget says it's our duty to look after her. I don't see it, Charlie. I shored her up all through my childhood. Oh, I know it wasn't her fault, nothing that happened was her fault, and I admit she was a good mother, very good, but that doesn't mean I have to go on paying for it all my life. She should be in a Home and that's that.

There's not much point in me saying anything.

No, there isn't. You should ring the Social Services and get them to take Mother on.

Anyway, I'm sorry.

Why on earth should Charlie be sorry? Stuart is Grandma's son too, he is part of this whether he likes it or not. I was furious with Charlie. Suppose Stuart and Paula went off for a night and left a babysitter with our telephone number and there was an emergency and we were called, would we have been so indignant? Of course not. We would have flown round and been only too glad to take charge. The minute he hung up I asked Charlie why he was in such a hurry to apologise, why he was so nice to Stuart, why he even listened to him? He said Stuart was merely pointing out, yet again, that the whole Grandma situation is a nonsense, and that it should be sorted out. I asked sarcastically how this sorting out would be done and Charlie said by doing what Stuart said, by putting Grandma in a Home, now, before Bridget returned. That was the nasty bit. The idea of making any decision about Grandma without Bridget being party to it was wicked. I said so. Charlie said he wasn't particularly bothered about the wickedness so much as the imposs-ibility. Stuart had said the thing to do was ring the Social Services. Charlie was now thinking of doing this, of saying we couldn't cope any more – maybe they would be obliged to do something. Charlie said if you thought about it, it was true that we couldn't cope – there must be places for the senile demented who have no money and no one to care for them. Perhaps, Charlie said, we had to be cruel to be kind. The cliché left me speechless.

But Charlie acted on Stuart's suggestion. He rang the Social Services and said the support system for looking after his senile mother had collapsed and his sister was away and he didn't know what to do. To his astonishment a temporary place was offered at once in a place called Birchholme. They would take Grandma for a week to give us 'time to make alternative arrangements' until the sister came back from holiday. Charlie was elated, said he should have thought of this ages ago, blamed Bridget for not letting him enquire before. He insisted we must at least go and look at Birch-holme and, if it was half decent, give it a try. It would have been silly of me to object.

Birchholme was no St Alma's but then how could a Council Home be? (Actually, why not?) It was a large, Victorian building, quite unsuitable for old people because of all the stairs and rather daunting because of the high ceilings and long corridors. Yet it wasn't depressing – the walls were brightly painted with plenty of posters and there were nice touches like a piano in the corner of the main sitting room and a big fish tank and even a cage of budgerigars. The staff seemed young and did not wear those off-putting overalls so beloved of institutions. It was all, in fact, a little too casual, I thought. I could not see that there was any real supervision going on

– not that I wanted regimentation but I wanted Grandma to feel secure. The Matron, a mere slip of a girl it seemed to me, was alarmingly blunt. She said it was true, there was no close supervision, they did not have the staff for it, and it was also true the old folk had to be prepared to shift for themselves a bit. I said my mother-in-law couldn't shift for herself at all so what would happen to her? The Matron said they would get round to her in the end. What that was supposed to mean I didn't like to think.

Charlie put it to Mary the next day: he said we had an offer of a place in Birchholme for one week only and in view of the way things were going he would like to try it, but he certainly did not want to dispense with her services and would pay her for that week. Mary said she did not want to be paid and that she thought Birchholme was probably a good experiment because, with the best will in the world, she did not know if she could carry on indefinitely. Charlie was quite triumphant at the ease of these negotiations. It has all happened with such speed I do not know what to think. Tomorrow we take Grandma in. Charlie will come with me – he must, I could not do it myself. It was quite bad enough taking her, during that short period, to the Day Centre and leaving her. And Charlie can tell Hannah and Adrian. I cannot. Hannah will be so upset, she will see no reason for it. She will ask us if Bridget knows.

*

I had to pack a case for Grandma, of course, and there was no way of doing this without her seeing and misunderstanding. She said she had forgotten to save her comics and had nothing to read on the journey. I comforted her, told her I would find some comics and that the journey was not long. I ought to have emphasised that she was *not* going to the Highlands but I did not have the heart. Where was the harm? Well, I could have fathomed that for myself: the harm was in the excitement. She grew flushed and agitated watching me and worrying about where she had put all kinds of items that would be essential in the Highlands. Then she began calling for her brothers and her father. The feeling of deliberately misleading her grew and grew, and, in the end, I could bear it no longer. I sat her down and sat down myself in front of her. I held her hands,

178

sweaty with excitement, and looked at her steadily and told her that she was not going to the Highlands, I said she was going to a kind of holiday home for a week, to give her a little break. I said it was very nice and that I would visit her every day. She smiled and said, 'Right-oh, anything you say.'

It was the usual fuss getting her into the car, the usual agony getting her out. It exasperates Charlie though he is not generally an impatient man. We were all hot and bothered by the time we walked through the front door of Birchholme. Then, the minute we were inside, we were confronted by an old woman on a walking-frame coming towards us, inching her way painfully along the corridor. Grandma began tut-tutting and poor-souling and I wished we could avoid a confrontation. But we could not. The old woman pushed her walking-frame right up to us and said to Grandma, 'They put you in here to die – don't you believe anything they tell you – that's what they do, put us here to die.' At that moment a young woman in a bright pink boiler-suit came out of the sitting room and said, 'Oh, shut up Marjorie, you're an old moan.' As she said it, she smiled at Grandma and nodded and then led Marjorie, still crying doom, away. Grandma said she thought she would get off home because the men would be in for their tea.

We took her into the sitting room and took her coat off and found her a seat and then Charlie went to find some tea. There was nothing institutional about the way the chairs were arranged. They were grouped round small tables, some in threes and some in fours. We had chosen a threesome. Grandma sat in a comfortable wing chair, and I pulled up an extra stool for me. To her right was a very small, shrivelled old woman with a prominent deaf aid in her left ear and to her left a remarkably lively, straight-backed woman with a disconcertingly direct stare. She stared at me, then at Grandma. Grandma said, 'It's cold for the time of year, isn't it?' The starer said, 'No.' Grandma said, 'Please yourself,' then winked at me and began to whistle. The deaf old lady woke up and shouted, 'Cut that bloody row!' Grandma stopped, her mouth still shaped in a silent, shocked whistle. She mouthed at me, 'Is it time to go?'

Charlie came with tea. He pulled up another chair and while Grandma slurped the tea eagerly he tried to chat to the other two old women. But the deaf one had gone back to sleep and the starer would not talk to him. She turned aside and literally put her chin in the air. I looked around desperately for someone more congenial to sit Grandma beside. Across the room there was a group of four old women who seemed to be enjoying themselves in marked contrast to the other somnolent inmates. They were laughing occasionally and chattering and I longed for Grandma to be part of that group, even though I knew she would not be capable of making any new relationships or sustaining any kind of sensible conversation. I watched them and, when one got up and walked off and did not return, I nodded at Charlie. We helped Grandma up – she got up quite easily and smartly because she thought we were going home – and trundled her across to the other group. They went silent instantly. Charlie said this was his mother, Mrs McKay, and she had come for a little holiday. He asked their names: Alice, Vera and Mrs Dorothy Gibson. He asked each of them how long they had been at Birchholme – an unwise question I was sure. I was right. They all three seemed offended. We were making no progress whatsoever and there was the uncomfortable feeling of having intruded.

I left Charlie and went off to find the Matron. She was in her office, a chaotic cluttered place, unpacking what looked like trays from a large cardboard box. She was on her knees and, though she looked up and smiled distractedly, she carried on with what she was doing, making some comment that these were not the sort of clip-on trays she wanted. I said I was worried about leaving my mother-in-law who seemed so isolated in the sitting room. I said she liked to chat but she was quite nervous with strangers and sensitive to any hostility. The Matron brushed this fear aside. She said some of them were a little clique-ish, but it would be all right and she reminded me that Grandma wouldn't really know she *was* among strangers, that she would probably think she was back at school. She advised me just to go and, obviously trying to make it easier, she stopped unpacking and said she would come and sit with Grandma for a minute. I was so grateful. We went back into the sitting room where Charlie was now sitting alone with his mother. The other three had gone off, he said, arm in arm. For Charlie, he looked quite worried.

Matron brought over a dignified old lady whom she introduced as Violet. She told us Violet was ninety-two but had all her faculties. Violet promptly recited 'Come into the garden, Maud'. Unfortunately, Grandma, who was absolutely delighted, joined in and Violet was most offended. Grandma asked her if she liked poetry and Violet said it had its place. She was watching Grandma very closely. After Grandma had made some quite unconnected, inconsequential remarks, impossible to reply to, Violet turned to the Matron and asked, 'Does *she* have her faculties?' Grandma was startled and said 'bloomin' cheek' and 'faculties indeed' and 'some people are the limit'. Matron just laughed, patting Violet's knee and said 'How about a sing-song ladies?' Then she took them off, Violet on one arm and Grandma on the other, towards the piano, and called for someone called Freda. Freda, another jeans-and-jumper member of staff, rushed in and began playing 'My Old Man Said Follow The Van.' It seemed a good time to leave.

Before we left, I took Grandma's case up to her room. The woman in the pink boiler-suit showed me the way, chattering all the time about the difficulties of keeping all the Birchholme Ladies, as she called them, happy. She said the jealousies were worse than in a nursery class and as for the ganging-up, that was diabolical. It made it easy for me to confess my worries as to how Grandma would cope with this. The woman, called Sophie, said, slightly to my alarm, that Grandma might indeed never manage to make any friends but as she was only in a week it was nothing to worry about. I said I thought a week a long time if you were unhappy. Oh, said Sophie, she won't be unhappy, nobody's unhappy at Birchholme, except Marjorie and she's a misery wherever she is.

By this time we were in the room where Grandma was to sleep. It was a perfectly pleasant room with only two beds in it. I asked whom she would be sharing with and Sophie said no one, that they had a few empty beds at the moment. I hesitated, uncertain how to phrase what I felt I had to say: if I said Grandma really could not be left on her own without someone in earshot, they might not let her stay. And I wasn't sure, in any case, what exactly Charlie had said she was capable of. In the end, I explained that Grandma might wander and would someone be near. Sophie said, of course, there was someone on duty all night, taking half of them back and forwards to the loo. Which reminded me: where was the loo? Sophie showed me on the way back. It was miles from Grandma's room, she would never get there. I stopped and said to Sophie I really didn't think this was going to work. Sophie said I would be surprised and that I worried too much.

Charlie was in perfect agreement with this judgement, naturally. All the way home he lectured me on the folly of 'getting emotional'. He was even against my going to visit Grandma, tried to persuade me it would be far more sensible to leave her for the week. My visits, Charlie said, would unsettle her. Why didn't I just ring up each day and ask for a report? Bridget, I said. My one defence when Bridget finds out what we did while she was away is that I visited every day, that I saw her mother with my own eyes and was satisfied. And I want to, I said, on my own account too. I felt I had abandoned her brutally and could not live with this for a whole week. Charlie groaned. He said he could not stop me but I must promise not to do anything silly. When I asked what he considered silly he said bringing Grandma home. I said, if I found her unhappy, I would certainly bring her home without any permission from him. Charlie said very well, if I thought she needed bringing home, he wanted to be involved – I must tell him and he would go with me and see what he thought and if necessary we would bring her home together, was that clear? I said perfectly clear.

*

I brought Grandma home today, Thursday, without consulting Charlie. I could not stand her being there a second longer.

On Tuesday when I first went I could not find her. I went into the sitting room, looked around, could not see Grandma, could not think of whom to ask and so went in search of her. I went to her bedroom, so afraid I would find her lying in bed neglected and forgotten, but she was not there. The bed had been made, the candlewick bedspread pulled smoothly over it. There was no one about in any of the corridors. Wherever I looked, there seemed to be old women asleep and I started tip-toeing instinctively. I tried the Matron's office but it was quite empty. Finally, I heard far off clattering and banging and tracked the noise down to a kitchen. A boy of about twenty was washing tea pots out. I said I was looking for Mrs McKay, a new – and I hesitated, not knowing whether to say patient, inmate, guest – a new lady who had just come in the day before. He smiled, rather nastily I thought, and said yes, he'd heard of her, she'd been in everyone's room waking them up for work and she'd got pretty short shrift. I found myself flushing, half with shame (of which in turn I was ashamed) and half with anger. I asked curtly if he knew where Mrs McKay was and he shrugged and suggested I look in the dining room.

She was there. She was sitting, on her own, at a table for four. The room was empty, all the dozen or so tables cleaned and re-laid for the next meal. It was a dull afternoon and the room, although it had a large window, was quite dark. Grandma was motionless, staring straight ahead, slumped in an attitude of total dejection. I rushed up to her, saying her name, but there was not a flicker of response. I came right up to her and said, 'Hey, it's me,' and she looked straight at me with entirely blank eyes. It seemed to me that there was a faintly sickly odour about her and tiny flecks of what looked like foam in the corner of her mouth – but it was meringue, clinging to her incipient moustache. I wiped it away, far too energetically, still talking to her. It took a long time for any recognition to dawn and even then she did not know my name. I wanted to cry. I longed to go and shout at someone and blame them. But there was still no one about. I took Grandma into the far more cheerful sitting room and settled her in a chair and gave her a mint and some of the tea I'd brought in a flask. She was still like a zombie. It was at least twenty minutes before she spoke and then it was, 'Where's that Bridget, the hussy?'

Telling Charlie that evening brought little sympathy. He made nothing of her being on her own in the dining room, he said she was on her own at that time of the day in her own home. That was true but there was a difference which Charlie could not see. And, as for wandering at night, she did that too. I said that at home when she did it there was always someone there who got up instantly and attended to her. Imagine her terror when she found a stranger, a stranger who perhaps shouted at her to get out! Charlie sighed and said he'd had enough of my over-active imagination. He said I didn't know anyone had shouted at her, that I was only assuming it. And, anyway, even if they had, his mother would forget it at once. He rang the Matron, whom I had not managed to see before I left, and reported that she said his mother was fine although there had been some night disturbance. They would give her a sleeping pill that night and that would solve the problem. This had me screaming – Bridget has always been so proud that Grandma is not given sleeping pills. She had explained to me again and again that, although sleeping pills would give us all good nights, the side effects would outweigh the benefit of this. Sleeping pills will make Grandma more likely to be incontinent and it will make her more confused. Charlie said it was only for a week.

Yesterday I went full of apprehension. I went later, reckoning I had gone at a bad time the day before, at the post-lunch time when most of the Birchholme ladies were snoozing. At least, this time, Grandma was not on her own. She was in the sitting room, ostensibly grouped with two other women, but they had pulled their chairs round so that their backs were to her. She seemed asleep when I arrived. When I whispered in her ear, she tried to swat me away as though I were a fly and said she couldn't be bothered. She told me to go away, she was fed up, she wanted to be left alone. I coaxed and wheedled and tried to humour her into opening her eyes. When she did, I was alarmed. Her eyes were red-looking and a small amount of pus leaked out of one corner. She looked at me as blankly as she had done the day before and then she said, 'How long is this going on?'

I found the Matron and told her Grandma seemed very miserable and that her eyes looked inflamed. The Matron was quite open. She said yes, Mrs McKay was a little low but then that was not surprising considering she had been in a home environment up to now. She said they did their best but they could not compete with the one-to-one care people received at home. And as for the eyes, well there was unfortunately some mild conjunctivitis around and it was so infectious, they would watch it carefully. I asked if Grandma had slept and the Matron smiled and said they had made sure of that but I hadn't to worry, the pills they used were not strong and certainly not addictive. So I went back to Grandma and gave her a

Duncan's Walnut Whirl and tried to get her to talk. She wouldn't. One of the other women, not one I'd seen before, said, 'She's sulking, that one. It won't do, you know, won't do at all, will get her nowhere, she'd better stop it, stop it *sharp*.' Grandma opened one eye and muttered, 'Get lost.'

I stayed all afternoon. I gave Grandma her tea when it came round but, in spite of some delicious chocolate cake on offer, she would not eat. One of the young women helpers asked her if she was on hunger strike and told her to wake up, we'd got the vote. Then she turned to me and said, 'You've spoiled her, that's the trouble,' before she took the trolley away. I sat, holding Grandma's limp hand, and looked around. Twelve old women in that room and where had they all come from? I wondered how many had also been spoiled and how many, on the other hand, only felt spoiled now. I went round helping to feed them and was astonished at the vast amounts they managed to eat. Where had Grandma's greed gone? At this rate her great bulk would disappear and we would present a shrivelled shadow to Bridget on her return. When I left at five, Grandma had neither eaten nor drunk and had been barely awake. I sensed a growing dislike of her among all the other women – her despair made them frightened.

So today I brought her home. What was the point of sticking out another four days of this? What were we doing it for? Hour by hour Grandma was retreating into utter dejection and I was driven mad by the evidence of her suffering. I took one look at her today, an abandoned lost heap of years, and I went and packed her case and put it in my car and then told the Matron I was taking her home. The Matron was quite philosophical, not in the least offended. She helped me put Grandma's coat on her and we walked her between us to the car. Grandma knew she was going home even if she did not understand where from or even what home was now. 'Is it over?' she asked and when I said yes she opened both eyes and said she hoped they'd hurry up with the bloomin' tea after all this time and that she wasn't going to any more sales, they were a waste of time and she didn't like the people who went.

Hannah

Grandma is in fantastic good humour. I come in, chuck my bag in a corner, make some coffee, sit down beside her. She has her specs on, the funny round ones she bought in Woolworth's in 1930-something and will not be parted from. I tell her I'd forgotten she wore specs. She looks over them at me and says solemnly, 'Yes, surprising in one so young, is it not?' Then she holds her hand out to me, palm open and uppermost. She stares at it.

What's that?
Where?
There.
On your hand?
Yes.
I can't see anything, Grandma.
Then what are you looking for?
Because you told me to.
I did not.
You did.
Why would I tell you to look at nothing?
I don't know.
Do you think I'm daft?
No.
Then what's that?

186

Finally, she blows off whatever was supposed to have been there and laughs and takes her specs off. She says she will have to get new specs but they are such a price she doesn't think she'll bother. I say she'll get them free on the National Health and she says a likely story. But she is lively, whistling as she chats and making funny faces. It's quite fascinating, the difference. Mum thinks that in some unfathomable way those three days in Birchholme must have done her good. She has been so cheerful since and alive and trying so hard to join in. Even the old enquiry, 'Do you like school?' is said with some real interest and she struggles to take in the answer instead of going off into endless reminiscing. And Mum is more cheerful too. She's stopped going on all the time about whatever shall we do. Bridget will be charmed.

Bridget comes back next week. Four postcards altogether, between us, and good times being had on all of them. Mum is already making plans to drag Grandma to a hairdresser and get her tarted up for Bridget's return – she's dying to show off how well Grandma has been cared for. Nobody will mention the little episode in hospital nor the bigger one in that Council Home – dear me, no. Adrian and I have not exactly been told *not* to mention them but we hardly need warning. Mum says that she will of course tell Bridget everything but that she wants her to see what great form Grandma is in first. Well, on today's showing Grandma couldn't be playing the game better.

I take her home and she actually says it's nice to get in, nice to be in her own but and ben. I can hardly credit this. She surely has no more idea where she is than she ever had. When the faithful, reinstated Mary comes in, Grandma greets her like a long-lost friend. 'Hello!' she cries out. 'Hello! Hello! Who's your lady friend. Oh, you are a lady, pardon my French.' Mary says she is Mary and Grandma says of course she is and how is she and she's glad to see her back so soon. Mary raises her eyebrows at me. It's been like this all week, ever since Grandma came out of Birchholme. It's as though she's high. In which case, as Mum says, she'll come crashing down. But there's no sign of it.

Who'd like a handsome man and a thousand a year?
Not me, Grandma.

You don't want a handsome man and a thousand a year?

A thousand wouldn't even keep me in chocolate and why would I want a man?

A *handsome* man.

Handsome or ugly. I thought you hated men anyway?

What nonsense! The men all liked me.

That wasn't what I said – I said I thought *you* didn't like men.

Oh, I like the men, never had any bother with them.

What's 'bother'?

You know – bother. Though once an officer tried to be a bit funny, that time I worked at the NAAFI.

Oooh, Grandma!

He gave me a lift and started – you know – and I said I'd tell my landlady, she was famous my landlady.

For what?

Dealing with bothersome men.

And did you?

No. He left off.

And then you met handsome James McKay.

Who?

Your husband.

Would you like a husband?

No.

Would you like a handsome man and a thousand a year?

It's all silly but Grandma loves it. She looks at Mary and me coyly. I try to see her as a flirt sixty years ago. I try to see her walking home from the NAAFI to her lodgings and the army officer pulling up and offering a lift to the long-legged Scots girl and Grandma climbing in, thrilled and then the hand on the knee or round her shoulder and Grandma threatening the fellow with her landlady.... It doesn't work. I absolutely cannot see Grandma at all. And I cannot sort out this attitude to men.

It's very easy to go tonight. Mary is quite comfortable – she was nervous the first night back – Grandma is sparkling. She hasn't got up once since she came home nor has she wet herself. It has all ended so well. Mum says she's learned her lesson, that she will just let events take their course and stop trying to anticipate them. Bridget will be relieved. Dad says nothing. He was furious when Mum brought Grandma home but since then he has shut up. And he's pleased, himself, to see Grandma suddenly the life and soul.

*

At least it wasn't during the night. Mum finds this a comfort, God knows why. And no one was away: that's another proclaimed comfort. The only really awful bit is that this time it was Susan and not the wonderful Mary.

Eleven o'clock on a Friday morning. I'm at school, Adrian's at school, Dad's at work, Mum is shopping at Waitrose. Grandma falls. She is doing a Highland Fling to amuse Susan's nephews-of-the-day who are strapped into a double pushchair and bawling. Grandma does a little jig and catches herself on the wheel of the pushchair and she falls and as she falls she catches her head on the fender and there is a cut and it bleeds. Enter Susan, exit Susan, screaming. She screams all the way down our road and pounds on our door: no one in. So she screams all the way back and the nephews join in and for once in their lives the actors realise they have to involve themselves because someone is clearly being murdered. They come down, take in the situation. One tries to calm the hysterical Susan while the other rings for an ambulance. Grandma is carted off, alone, and one actor waits with Susan (poor him) while the other waits at our front door for one of us. Most unusually I come home at lunchtime to get a book I've forgotten. I go with actor number 2. He very kindly drives me to the hospital. It's the same ward Grandma was in before. A nurse tells me not to worry, my Grandmother is as tough as an old boot, she will be fine except she may have broken her ankle – they are waiting for the x-rays – and will have a very big headache for a while.

That's it. Here we go again. We should get a season ticket to that hospital. Susan makes a meal of it. We hear over and over again how it all happened. No one asks why a bloody double pushchair was slap in the middle of the cramped living room nor what it was doing there in the first place. No one asks Susan why she wasn't in the room. Susan rolls her eyes and says her heart will never be the same

189

and she will never be able to look after Grandma again because she couldn't survive another shock like that. That is that, Susan says, and waits. Mum gets out her purse. She thanks Susan, she pays her until the end of the month, in cash. Susan is mollified. She says she will miss Grandma. She says Grandma was very, very difficult to look after though she, Susan, had never liked to say so, but she will miss her. She hopes we know she always did her best. Mum says we are grateful. She runs Susan home (someone, certainly not the actors I'm sure, has already disposed of the nephews). Then we all sit and look at each other.

Dad says that at least Grandma is in hospital. Oh, great, Mum says. Dad stresses that for the moment there is no need for panic, that until Grandma's ankle is mended she will be kept in hospital. Mum says, 'And then?' Dad says that then we will have to have a conference and decide what is to be done. Mum says she will save him the exhaustion of any conference (she fairly spits out the word). She will tell him what cannot be done for a start:

One: Grandma cannot go into St Alma's because she's nowhere near the top of the list;

Two: She cannot go to Birchholme because she, Mum, let alone Bridget, would never stand for it;

Three: She cannot come home until we replace Susan.

Also, Mum says, we don't know what kind of shape Grandma is going to be in. Will her bones knit properly? Will she be able to walk again? She was walking badly, anyway: this might just be the end. And then that blow on the head. Will she only have a big headache? Maybe the confusion will be worse.

I don't say a word. There's nothing to say. Nobody is thinking of poor Grandma lying in pain in hospital – we're all far too busy thinking of our own inconvenience. Mum is right back to square one again, almost hysterical with worry, and Dad is acting as though he has been framed for a crime he never committed. He is sullen and moody and resentful. He seems to imply Mum is attacking him and it does look a little like that – her voice is rising and has a distinct note of accusation. I ought to be able to think of something to say to make them stop turning Grandma's accident

190

into some sort of private feud. I wish Bridget was back. They don't. Mum especially is dreading Bridget's coming back to such a situation. What price the haircut and new dress for Grandma now?

We all visit every day. That is the easy part. No family could be more devoted. Mum goes at two o'clock and stays until four when I arrive and I stay until five when Adrian arrives and Adrian either leaves at half past or stays a little longer if Dad isn't going to be able to get there until seven. Adrian asks me what I do. I say I talk. Adrian says he talks but Grandma doesn't seem to hear him and he finds it embarrassing. I can just see him. He'll mutter and mumble and then he'll just sit looking gloomy and watching the clock. But I'm not really much better. I talk all right but God how quickly I use the chat up. Adrian's right, there's absolutely no come-back, not even gobbledy-gook. Grandma is gibbering into her beard, as she used to put it. Her eyes swivel about and her mouth hangs open. They've taken her teeth out.

Nurses are supposed to be angels. Maybe they are angels in other wards but not in this one. Or maybe they just don't think Grandma needs any angel-ling when she has this devoted family. They hardly seem to come near her. They always seem to be in the office or sluice room having private jokes. Grandma loves jokes – if only they knew. Grandma will laugh at anything, she would love their jokes. Mum does all the asking how Grandma is, so I never do. The nurses tell Mum that Grandma will not try to walk or stand. They say her ankle is not broken after all, that it's not even sprained. They have x-rayed it and it's only a little bruised. But she will not try to stand on it. They get her up and she refuses to bear her own weight – she just goes slack. This is true. I've seen it. Nurses have come while I have been there, twice, and tried to get Grandma up. It was pitiful, I thought, but they didn't seem to think so. They spoke loudly, telling Grandma to 'come *on*' and warning her this 'will not *do*.' If that's how they speak to her when I'm there, how do they treat her when I'm not? Grandma just hangs between them and they have to give up. I'm so relieved when she's back in bed.

Sometimes I try to talk to the other old women in the ward. They're not all senile like Grandma. Two of them read, they have new books from the library trolley all the time. I ask about the books they're reading but they both, in different ways, get off the subject of literature pretty quickly. They get on to Grandma. They say she's a pest at night. They say she shouts and hollers, 'Bridget,' all night and wakes everyone up. One of them says that if Grandma is not all there, she shouldn't be in this ward, she should be put away with the others. What others? I'm so offended I have to leave. And I don't talk to my reading friends any more. This leaves only one other woman who is so attached to drips and things that I'm scared to approach her and two more who seem permanently asleep. It's not a lively ward.

I walk around every ten minutes or so. I patrol the corridors, I stop on landings and stare out of windows. Grandma used to rave about hospitals – she loves them. She told me they are more like hotels and she doesn't know why people don't like them. She's been in hospital three times and loved it every time and didn't want to come out. She told me she cried when the Sister said she was ready to go home after she had her veins done. It was such bliss lying in a lovely clean comfy bed and having food brought to her and just being able to read all day. She wanted to stay there forever even though she felt guilty about her children. Grandma said people don't know they are born these days they are so lucky having such hospitals. The extravagance of clean sheets and towels all the time thrilled as well as appalled her and she could never get over the luxury of constant warm baths. And the company, of course Grandma loved the company of other women and the gossip and the tales of home they all had to tell.

And now she doesn't even know she's in hospital.

*

This morning, Mum cries. She sits in the basket chair in our kitchen, Grandma's usual chair, and she cries. Dad tells her not to be so ridiculous, he asks her what on earth she is *crying* for, he says if anyone is going to cry it ought to be him. I really can't go near Mum when she cries. She is unapproachable. The natural thing would be to put my arm round her and comfort her but I don't do that. I can do it to Grandma but not to Mum. Not that Grandma

192

cries but she often looks as if she wanted to if only she could remember how.

The crying, which has stopped now, is because the hospital want Grandma out. They say there is nothing wrong with her that they can treat. They say the pressure on beds is tremendous, that they have urgent cases they must admit. They want Grandma out by tomorrow if possible, Monday at the latest. Bridget returns on Friday. Mum has asked for an extension until Saturday, explaining about Bridget, but the hospital have said no, quite out of the question. Dad, who never believes in these cases that Mum has really tried, rings the hospital himself and speaks to whoever is responsible for this ultimatum. He gets nowhere. He gets told a few home truths. He gets as depressed as Mum.

Adrian says they cannot just sling Grandma out onto the street, there must be somewhere for her to go. Oh, the charm of such innocence. Mum says there is: here. Dad groans, loudly. Mum says if anyone has any other suggestion she would be delighted to hear it. Dad leaves the room. Nobody says anything. We finish breakfast, bang stuff into the dishwasher, rustle newspapers. Dad comes back. He puts the kettle on. Mum says she knows what he has been doing. She knows he's been ringing Birchholme. She says she can tell by his face they won't take her and of course St Alma's won't and he's very lucky they won't, because if they had said yes, there would have been a big fight. Mum says there's only one choice: either here or back to Grandma's flat with us all doing round-the-clock care. Which is it to be?

I say here,

Mum says here,

Dad says there,

Adrian says he would rather say here, but he doesn't see how it could work if Grandma can't walk because we've nowhere on the ground floor to put her so he says there too.

Well, a tie. Who gets the casting vote?

I feel someone must try to say something cheerful so, hoping I don't sound like dear Adrian, I say maybe Grandma will walk and come to herself once she is home. Maybe she's carrying out a kind of rebellion without knowing it, a sort of protest against hospital.

Adrian says sarcastically that I am such a deep thinker but really that idea is crazy: if she's protesting against hospital, surely she'd choose a more logical way, one more likely to succeed. I say she isn't choosing anything consciously and Adrian says oh we're delving into the subconscious are we and we start bickering. Dad shouts at us. Then he gives his reasons for preferring Grandma to go back into her own flat. Mainly the reasons are to do with what Adrian has already mentioned, to do with layout and bathrooms and stuff. But Dad also tries to be cunning, arguing that in her own environment Grandma will be more likely to find her bearings. She may not know where she is but there's five years of familiarity in her surroundings which must have made some small impression. And then, in a moment of truth, Dad says he could handle it better if his Mother was not actually in his home.

It was wise of him to confess that. Mum says so, she says she knows that is at the bottom of it. Surprisingly, she says she feels the same. Her conscience would be clearer if Grandma was in our house but her nerves would be in shreds. She needs to escape too. She'd rather have all the inconvenience of going backwards and forwards just because it would always be such a relief to leave each time. She sums up. She says we *ought* to bring Grandma here but we'll all survive better if she's there. And it will alarm Bridget less. I protest at this: how? Well, Mum says, if Grandma is sitting in her own chair, looking normal, Bridget is less likely to think anything awful has happened. If she's been moved to us, Bridget will know something pretty drastic has taken place. Well, I say, it has. Mum says it is all a matter of breaking it to Bridget in the right way, that's all. Dad says if there is one thing he does not want to hear about, it is Bridget.

I go along to Grandma's flat. My part is to get it ready. Mum and Dad go to collect Grandma. They have decided there's no point in delay. I change the sheets on Grandma's bed first. God, she must be so hot. Bridget brought all Grandma's own bedding down from Glasgow when The Big Move was made. The sheets are thick flannelette and then there are about six old blankets, all heavy things, and an eiderdown. It takes hours stripping it all off and putting it back. Then I hoover, and wash the bathroom floor. I put some chrysanthemums, which I've bought, into a jug and stick it on Grandma's bedside table. Silly, really. Grandma is no lover of flowers, not bought ones. She says they're lovely but she's counting the cost. Then I give the living-room a once-over. Not much I can do about the carpet there. It's ruined. Grandma and Susan's nephews have dropped endless gunge on it and it's all trodden in. This flat really needs spring-cleaning. Nobody has time to care for it properly.

They arrive. Grandma has not walked. She's been taken from her hospital bed in a wheelchair and tipped into the car. Now, it's impossible to tip her out. The hospital have loaned us a light wheelchair until we can get our own. It stands on the pavement beside the car. Grandma is slumped in the front seat. Dad is trying to get her at least to put her feet out of the car. She won't or can't move them. Dad lifts her feet and tries to turn them round. Grandma cries out. Mum tells him to stop. We all stand back and look. Adrian is sent for. He crawls into the car and crouching at Grandma's other side, lifts her towards Dad who is on his knees on the pavement. Mum hovers with the chair. Adrian and Dad get Grandma out of the car but not into the chair. It just can't be done. They are obliged to half-drop Grandma onto the pavement. But they do it next time: they lift Grandma into the chair and away we go.

No one knows whether to put her to bed or not. Dad and Adrian go off. Mum and I stand in the kitchen looking at Grandma. She looks awful, terrible. She is all sideways, her head lolling horribly. Mum says let's get her to bed. We put her to bed. She seems to be asleep. I say I'll stay all afternoon until Mary comes. We've agreed with Mary that one of us will always be on call now, no going away and with that guarantee she is willing to help 'for a while'. Mum doesn't like the sound of that rider. And she's worried about the lavatory. Grandma can't get to it. In hospital she's been wearing incontinence pads. They've sent some home with her. Mum handles them with distaste. She doesn't know how she can ask Mary to do this. Mum chews her lip at the thought. I must say I don't want to change those pads myself. The thought makes me heave. Grandma as a grotesque baby, legs splayed apart for the clean nappy. Bridget would be scornful. She would be contemptuous. What poor specimens Mum and I are if we can't face up to changing an old woman and making her as comfortable as possible.

I know even before Mum leaves that I'm going to cheat. I'm not going to look again to see if Grandma needs changing. Too bad. Dad and Adrian won't be called upon to do any of that. The women do the nasty bits and aren't supposed to mind. It's all part of being a woman. Dad is arranging a proper nurse from Monday, from an agency. He's been told already that this nurse, who we will be very lucky to get, will not do any cooking or cleaning. She will attend to Grandma and presumably sit in a corner knitting like Madame Defarge the rest of the time. Mum and I will cook and shop, and clean. Mum says that in many ways it is easier getting a nurse than it ever was a companion. After all, a nurse nurses. She doesn't have to be nice or appreciate Grandma's witticisms. The job is clear-cut.

There's absolutely nothing to do. Grandma sleeps solidly. I read. I have my feet up on the bed and I read and read, about a hundred and fifty pages of *Bleak House*. Every now and again I squint at Grandma but there's not a hint of any awareness or movement. She's snoring, quite heavily. When I can't take any more *Bleak House*, I make some coffee. I sit with the steaming mug and watch Grandma.

Mary comes. She's nervous. She isn't at all her usual self. I explain that Grandma just seems to want to sleep. Mary nods, a little fearfully. I don't know whether to mention the incontinence pads. I can see Mary's gaze wandering to the packet. It's a very large packet, quite unmissable. Mary looks at me and asks 'Is she . . . ?' and trails off. I say yes. Mary hesitates. She says she feels bad about this but she does not know if she will be up to that kind of nursing. She is sorry, she is ashamed, but it isn't really in her line. She will try to cope, she would not wish to let us down, but perhaps she ought to hand over to someone else who is better at it. I am tempted to ask how one person can be 'better' at changing incontinence pads than another. I don't. Mary is lovely, she is upset at having to say this. I say I'll tell my mother and I quite understand. I say, quite untruthfully because I've never done it, that I don't like doing it myself, that it's unpleasant. Mary is grateful for my pious lie.

I go home. I tell Mum what Mary has said. Mum says she was

expecting it. Today is Saturday. Bridget returns on Friday, if Mary can hang on until then it won't be too bad.

*

Grandma is walking. She wakes up on Sunday morning and she gets up and goes to the loo and has a fight with the incontinence pad which totally baffles her. She is outraged, who played this joke, bloomin' cheek. Mary is relieved, we're all faint with relief, we all rejoice. Too soon. All day Sunday, Grandma wets herself. She can't find the bathroom and even when she's taken to it she stares at the lavatory and says she wants 'to go', and when we say 'go then' she asks where the lavatory is. She can't be forced onto it, she won't be pushed, she shouts at me and Mum when we try to jack-knife her. It's hell every time.

She walks but the walking is unsteady. She bumps into the furniture, she's very unsafe. She complains her legs hurt. She stands for ages looking down at her feet as though trying to work out what to do with them. And all pattern to her speech has gone. She's forgotten names of things and orders of words.

> Thingabobme up.
> What, Grandma?
> Up. I want up.
> Come on then, heave-ho.
> Under the whatsit where the you know.
> What, Grandma.
> Parrot.
> What is it you want?

And she rolls her eyes. No more going in circles even, just fractured sentences, meaningless jumbles of words. Most alarming of all is her inability to eat and drink. She looks at the tea, she feels the mug and then she just stares at it. Food gets flattened, squeezed, pushed round the plate, up her nose, even into her ears. It takes hours to get a tiny cube of toast into her.

What will Bridget say?

*

Things happen so fast now. Years, months, weeks when nothing seemed to change, when the changes were so gradual that it took an outsider to notice them. But now things gallop, every day is a new disaster area. Sunday night Grandma falls out of bed four times and Mary rings and Dad goes and on Monday who can blame Mary for saying she can't go on? Dad could hardly get Grandma up himself. She swore at him, Grandma who hates swearing, who never swears. She lashed out at him, her son, and screamed that men were all the same. I'm glad I didn't see it. I'm still 'pet' and with me, during the day, she's quiet, too quiet. Mum won't let me take my turn at night. The wretched nurse starts on Wednesday, the agency had no one 'suitable' available till then. Dad does Monday night, returns haggard in the morning as soon as Mum has gone along (with no Susan she has to). Mum does Tuesday and so it's to Mum that it happens.

At two in the morning Mum hears Grandma get up. She goes into her room. Grandma is in the bathroom. The door is closed. Mum tries the door, which is usually left wide open to aid Grandma in her search. It's locked, she thinks. She hears groans. She pushes the door and bangs on it. The door gives a fraction; it's not locked, it's blocked by Grandma's body. Mum rings Dad, who's in such a deep, deep sleep after his awful time the night before that he doesn't hear the telephone. Neither, I'm afraid, do Adrian or I. Poor Mum. She rings for an ambulance, half afraid they'll say they have had enough, they will not come again for this fool of an old woman. It takes so long for them to come that Mum thinks Grandma might be dead. The noise has stopped, there's no groaning. The ambulance arrives. The men say they will have to take the door off. They say it's not really their job, that really Mum should call the police or the fire brigade. Mum pleads. The men smash the hinges of the door and lift it away. Mum, telling me, does not go into details. She just says Grandma's mouth was oddly twisted, her face a terrible colour. The ambulance men think she may have had a stroke. They cart her off. Mum goes with her.

The rest I hear from Dad who doesn't tell things like Mum. He goes to the hospital in the morning but won't let me go. I have to go to school, he is adamant. All I do all morning is worry, I would be far

198

better off at the wretched hospital. I race home at lunchtime. Dad says Mum is still with Grandma, but contrary to what she told me on the phone this morning, Grandma has not had a stroke. She has not had anything. Once more, she is a nuisance to the hospital, once more we have cried wolf and they want her out. Dad says he is off now to see a man at King's Wood. *King's Wood*, I echo. King's Wood is a mental hospital, a loony bin, a nut house. Good God, *King's Wood?* Dad is grim. He says he knows perfectly well what King's Wood is, but there is no alternative. There is a ward there for the senile demented. Grandma will have to go there. Dad warns me – he says, 'I warn you, Hannah' – that he doesn't want to hear any self-righteous speeches from me. He has had enough. Mum is making herself ill, we cannot cope. Even when the nurse arrives, we still cannot cope. He has reached the end of his tether (picture: Dad as a goat at the end of a long rope). He says that before the blessed Bridget gets back he wants the deed done. I say Bridget won't let Grandma be in King's Wood, she won't tolerate it. She can bring her out, he says, but if she does, she looks after her herself. And, he says, it will be impossible to get her back in.

King's Wood. I've never been, but it's famous in our neighbour-hood, famous like Holloway Prison or Borstal, famous for being a kind of Bedlam. I've passed it often. It's a huge building with enormous grounds. Going past on a bus I've looked down over the high wall round it and seen people wandering about. It has a security wing where they take violent cases. Everyone is frightened of King's Wood; it's no good saying it's a psychiatric hospital. The stigma is awful even now. Bridget will go *mad*, she will be livid. She leaves her mother all jolly, if confused, leaves her laughing in her kitchen chewing biscuits and swigging tea and talking back to the radio, and she comes back after three weeks to find her a zombie in *King's Wood*. Who is going to tell her? It will be like those Greek messengers who were killed if they brought bad news. Dad must do the telling, the explaining. But Bridget will want the truth from Mum, and even from me. She won't trust Dad.

King's Wood will take her. The hospital is arranging a transfer tomorrow. When Mum comes home she is drawn and exhausted. She does not fight the King's Wood news. She has never been there.

She asks Dad what it is like. Dad pauses. Mum says there's no point in his lying because she will be going to see for herself tomorrow. Dad says it's awful to go into. The corridors are long, the paint peeling, the smell diabolical. The ward Grandma will go into is locked. Inside, there are three rooms. One is vast, the sitting room and dining room combined; one is medium sized, used as an extra sitting room; yet another is huge, the dormitory with twenty-four beds. The first sight, says Dad, struggling, is pretty bad. Old women sitting in chairs, the television blaring, half of them shouting out. But the staff seem kind and attentive. The inmates are all clean and their hair is brushed. There are plants and flowers everywhere and pictures on the wall. There is a garden outside with a door opening onto it. Once you're in, Dad repeats, it's not too bad. He seems a little distraught, for Dad, but ends by saying, firmly, that there is no choice. We have left it too late. It is King's Wood or nothing. He says when Mum goes tomorrow she has to remember that: there is no choice.

I bet there is. There must be. It's just that Dad won't devote himself to looking for it. He *thinks* he's looked but he hasn't looked far it seems to me. I know most private places don't take the senile and incontinent but there must be some specially for them. Or, if not, we could employ full-time people, night and day. That's what Bridget will say. But then Bridget hasn't any money. Dad has. It would cost, he says, £500 a week to have nursing care all round the clock for Grandma and still we would have the responsibility. He insists it is this, the hell of being responsible, that he wants to be rid of. And he doesn't want to pay £500 a week for maybe ten years or more. He says he isn't *that* rich, not by any means. He says Bridget will have to realise it and being a McKay she will.

Poor Bridget.

Jenny

Charlie was right, it is the going into King's Wood which is the worst. Can't something be done about those corridors? Other hospitals have no money either but the paint there is not chipped and dirty nor is it dark bottle-green. But then King's Wood is to be closed, there is no point in painting it. And Grandma did not notice the paint on her way in, she did not notice anything. I wished so much that she would be asleep and that they would carry her in on a stretcher but she was, for her, quite wide awake and I pushed her in a wheelchair. My heart pounded with fear. I was so afraid of taking her in. When I stood outside the locked door and rang the bell I was trembling with nerves. A man opened it. Grandma said, 'A man!' He did not attempt to smile at her or reassure her that although a man he was a friend. He just stood aside, tall and gaunt, his keys hanging from a loop on his grey overall.

No one came forward to greet us but then it was tea time, everyone was busy. All the old women were seated round a long table being fed. There were four staff for the twenty women. The noise was terrible – wild cawings as though a clutch of rooks had settled there. One woman banged all the time with a spoon on the table and another shouted, 'About bloody time! About bloody time!' over and over. I pushed Grandma to the table, glad that I was behind her and could not see her face. The four staff members, in yellow overalls, stared at us. I asked if the Matron was around. I said we were expected. One of them went off, grudgingly it seemed, and came back with a small, squat woman in a blue and white uniform who said she was Sister Grice, and she was in charge. (I only learned afterwards that her name was 'Grice' – she pronounced it 'Grease' and so did everyone else.) Sister was very heavily made up, with alarmingly marked black arcs for eyebrows and a red lipstick of such brilliance that it was right off any colour spectrum I had ever seen. She was loquacious but had an accent so thick – a Geordie accent – that it was almost impossible to make out what she was saying. While she addressed me, a white-haired, sweet-faced old woman got up from the end of the table and shuffled down to stand beside me. She put her hand on mine and made some sound I could not distinguish. 'Go away, Leah,' the Sister said. 'Go on, off with you, don't bother the lady.' I said she wasn't bothering me and asked Sister what she had been trying to say to me. 'She's deaf,' Sister said. 'Nothing she says makes sense, don't let her bother you. It doesn't bother us.'

When tea was over, the women were moved to chairs placed roughly in a circle. Some of them had trays clipped in front. I soon saw this was to prevent them falling out. One waved to me and called, 'Fiona! Fiona! I knew you would come, darling. I said Fiona would come, how are you, my darling, come here and let me look at you.' My hands froze on the handle of Grandma's wheelchair. Grandma asked querulously, as disturbed as I was, 'Who the hell is that? What in the name of God does she want?' Luckily, Sister summoned us to the next room. On the way we passed a row of six chairs. Upon each was what looked like a dead occupant. One was twisted into a grotesque attitude, head back at an unnatural angle, feet splayed out, arms flung wide. One was bowed over, head almost touching the toes. The others had their eyes open but did not blink or move. Grandma was muttering, 'Poor souls, poor souls,' over and over. Sister took us into a small room with two beds. She pointed to one bed and said it would be Grandma's until she had settled in. There was a glass partition beside it and Sister explained that the room on the other side was her office and she could keep an eye on newcomers. She said I could undress Grandma and put on a

King's Wood dress. She held up a strange florid garment and showed me with pride the Velcro fastening down the back and demonstrated several times how easy it was to open and close this.

Grandma was not actually dressed in any case. She had her coat on but underneath only her nightdress. Sister said she did not even need her own nightdress and I should take it home. As I changed Grandma I told myself over and over again that clothes do not matter and especially not to Grandma who had never given a damn about clothes. But I had. I had chosen that nightdress with such care. It was a soft Viyella material, soothing and warm to Grandma's skin, and it was a pretty lavender colour with lace at the neck and cuffs and lots of little pin tucks around the cuffs and across the yoke. What I replaced it with was a pink nylon monstrosity too short and too wide, which when fastened by the magic Velcro of which Sister was so fond left a gaping hole exposing Grandma's bottom. I pointed this out. Sister said cheerfully that no one would see it in bed and it made 'things' easier. It was five o'clock but Grandma was put into bed and was glad of it. She closed her eyes at once. I kissed her, said I would come tomorrow.

Sister took me into her office. She was sucking a large boiled sweet and offered me one. I declined. She asked me a few particulars about Grandma which I supplied, speaking like an automaton. Sister said it was upsetting for relatives bringing people in but that I should remember my mother-in-law was not seeing things as I saw them. She would not have a clue where she was and she would be well looked after. I said I wished I could believe that but that it seemed to me Grandma had already picked up several clues that told her she was somewhere strange and hostile. Sister jumped on that, she said, 'Oh, not hostile, we're very friendly here, more like a family than a hospital.' I stared at her, fascinated by the extent of the delusion, as she extolled the virtues of her ward where everyone loved the 'old dears' and treated them 'like their own mother'. Already, I was afraid I had offended Sister and that by offending her I would make things more difficult for Grandma. So I half apologised before I left and was craven and hated myself.

Charlie came with me the next day. He took the afternoon off work and we both went. Again, the ordeal of the corridor, of the awful smells which neither of us liked to analyse too closely in case we decided it was something a little worse than urine. Again, the ringing of the fiercely harsh bell and the wait behind the locked door and the jangling of the keys by the silent man who opened it. I saw Grandma immediately. She was sitting in a chair at the far side of the room with a tray clipped on in front of her. The television was not on as it had been the day before but the room was just as noisy. A woman was standing in the middle of the circle made by the chairs. She had a soft football and was throwing it to each old lady in turn and urging them to throw it back. Some did, with astonishing vigour. They became wildly excited at the success of their aim and at the accuracy of their catching. But some held onto the ball and tried to hide it under their dress and then those on either side berated them and pointed and screamed. Charlie said, 'You can't say they're just sitting like vegetables, anyway.' No, I could not. As we watched, the ball was thrown towards Grandma. We both tensed. Charlie even said under his breath, 'Come on, Mum.' Grandma didn't seem to see the ball. It sat on her tray and she didn't even knock it off. Again and again the woman in charge took and threw it and again and again Grandma ignored it. I could not stand it a minute longer. Charlie was annoyed with me for interrupting but I marched forward and said I didn't think my mother-in-law was up to this and I unclipped the wretched tray and beckoned to Charlie to help me get Grandma up and we walked her out of the circle.

I had no idea where to go except away from the noise. We passed the six chairs with the comatose patients in them. Grandma was groaning and wishing she had a cup of tea and saying her legs hurt. Charlie asked me where I thought I was going. I said I was just looking for a little privacy. I found it in Grandma's bedroom. There was no one else there. I put Grandma in the only chair and Charlie and I perched on the bed. 'Look at that dress, look at her hair!' I raged. Charlie said nothing. Grandma squinted at him and said, 'Got a light, mister, got a fag?' Charlie said smoking wasn't allowed in hospital. Grandma laughed and said, 'Suit yourself, you always have.' Charlie said it wasn't his fault. Grandma sighed and said, 'They all say that, all the men!' I'd dug out the walnut whirls from my bag. Grandma bit into the first and the cream inside exploded up her nose. She pulled what was left out of her mouth and with the other hand took another and did the same again. The lower part of her face looked as though it was covered with shaving cream. Charlie leaned forward to clean her up but she thought she was trying to steal the chocolate whirls and biffed him with both hands. I laughed. He said he hoped that meant I was enjoying myself. Grandma said, 'And what's wrong with her enjoying herself? You men are all the same.'

I sent Charlie off to take a walk round the grounds, told him to come back in half an hour. What was the point in making him stay? I was better on my own with Grandma, though God knows there was little enough I could do for her. After the walnut whirls she had some tea which I'd brought with me and then I cleaned her up. I'd just finished when the woman who had been in charge of the ball game poked her head round the door and smiled brightly. She said her name was Jane and she was the physiotherapist. She said she quite understood that as I'd come to visit I would want a little privacy and so she didn't mind a bit that I'd taken Mrs McKay away in the middle of a session, not a bit, but that she did think she ought to explain, in case I hadn't realised, that the object of what she'd been doing was to keep muscles in trim. Arms had to be exercised as well as legs and what might have looked silly and pointless, wasn't. I was quick to slobber. I said I was sorry if I had seemed rude and of course I appreciated the work she was doing, that I was *thrilled* to think anything at all was being done. All this time Grandma was saying, 'Is she going?' alternated with, 'Ask her if she has a fag.' Jane left, after a little more boasting on her part and a little more soft-soaping on mine.

I took Grandma back to her original chair, once more running the ordeal of what I was already thinking of as the Six Death Chairs and settled her down. I knew I must try to make friends for her – it was foolish to isolate her and make others jealous. I sat at her feet, holding her hand, and tried to talk to the women either side. One seemed remarkably sensible. She said her name was Ellen and that she had been in King's Wood a year and liked it very much thank you but missed her children. I asked how many she had and she said six. I asked whether they were boys or girls and she said that had never been made clear, the doctors were unable to decide. That stopped me. But Ellen was gracious, almost queenly and now that I'd got her going was not going to miss the opportunity to tell me the story of her life. I was quite happy to listen but Grandma was not. She tugged at my hand impatiently and asked when we were going home. She stared at Ellen, in full flow and interrupted her to ask who invited *her* here. The woman on the other side, to whom I turned for some relief, had very clear, alert eyes but could not talk. She tried to but all that came out was a mm-mm-mm sound, her lips working away desperately. Grandma said she wished this woman, on her left, would shut up and give her some peace. I realised I was surreptitiously looking at my watch, praying for the time to pass a little quicker. No one else was visiting. All the other women sat there staring at me hungrily. When Charlie rang the door bell I leapt up and had kissed Grandma and gone all in a flash.

We did not speak on the way home. There was no need to. Depression filled our car like a fog. I found myself thinking of that inane question which turns up in women's magazine quizzes or on radio shows: how would you define happiness? I had just defined it and wished to be asked: happiness is coming out of King's Wood. It was sickening, the feeling of liberation, of relief. Not to be in King's Wood was bliss. To breathe fresh air, see the trees, hear ordinary conversation. Not to be confronted by hopeless, despairing people waiting to die. Not to have to tussle with the hideous moral dilemma: why is this allowed? Why don't I do something? Oh, happiness was leaving King's Wood behind all right.

*

Misery is thinking of Bridget coming back tomorrow. Misery of every sort. Misery *for* Bridget and misery because of her. Pity and guilt, sympathy and fear, compassion and dread. She arrives at Gatwick at ten in the evening. It was agreed, before she left, that she would come for lunch the next day and 'hear all the chat'. She will not disturb Grandma at that time of night but she is bound to look in on her in the morning before she comes here. Bound to. So what shall we do? Leave a note? What kind of note would that be? I think I should go to Gatwick. Charlie is against this. He says Bridget will be so alarmed at the sight of us, she will think Grandma is dead. One of us will have to stay the night at Grandma's to avoid Bridget perhaps popping in and finding Grandma gone before we see her. So I will stay and when Bridget comes I will either ring Charlie or bring Bridget straight along. We have gone over what we will say. I have warned Charlie to stick to the bare facts, no justification at this stage for Bridget to fasten on and rage about and tear to pieces. We are lost if we get into an argument before Bridget has heard a word. Charlie says he has a warning for me too: I am not to be so bloody apologetic and nervous. I am to be calm and matter-of-fact, I am to act as though the idea of King's Wood is satisfactory. And above all I am to remember that there is no going back. Should Bridget fire up at once and turn on her heel and say she's going to fetch Grandma home this minute, then I am to stand firm. Charlie will say on behalf of us both that Bridget can do that of course but that she must understand we are withdrawing our support. No more money, no more help. She, Bridget, will be on her own from now on if she chooses to bring Grandma home.

He must be *mad*. How could Bridget be left, on her own? The idea is monstrous. I will have to desert Charlie and stand with Bridget if she goes ahead with this. If?

*

I lay awake most of the night, waiting to hear Bridget return. I slept in the front spare room, where the helpers used to sleep. The light from the headlamps of the taxi lit up the room and I heard that distinctive, deep purring London sound of a taxi engine running while the driver waited to be paid. Bridget would be counting the fare out exactly to get rid of her change, just as Charlie does, and then working out the tip. The cab door slammed. Bridget's key turned in the lock. She went quietly into her flat. No Karl, only one set of footsteps. The faintest chink of light showed under my door. She would be reading my note, propped against the packet of freshly ground coffee and the bread I had left. All I'd said was, 'Hope you had a good time. See you tomorrow.' Would she think it odd that I hadn't added, 'Grandma is fine'? She would be too tired to think about it. The faint line of light disappeared. It was straight into bed.

Bridget has Charlie's capacity to go straight to sleep wherever the place, whatever the circumstances.

So across the hall Bridget slept and I did not. I lay and thought about Grandma in that awful place, totally bewildered, handled brusquely, not known by anyone. In my head Charlie challenged me: 'handled brusquely' – how did I know that? I don't. But I have eyes and ears and feelings and they tell me, unmistakably. Grandma has never been 'handled' except with love and kindness and tenderness. I do not need Bridget to tell me those are in short supply in institutions however well-intentioned the staff. And I do not need Bridget to point out that even an animal knows when it is being treated with sympathy and concern. I do agree with Charlie, we are not willing to carry on caring for Grandma, but he is not going to force me into the lie that we *cannot*. We can. But we are choosing not to, and choosing for very good reasons.

Reasons which of course Bridget will knock flat. The hard bit for me will be agreeing with her but siding with Charlie. And I will. I have promised. It is the only sensible decision. I will visit Grandma every day in King's Wood. I will get to know the staff and become their friend. I will get to know the other patients and become their champion. I will be vigilant. I will overcome my instinctive desire to 'be good' when in such places. I will complain, criticise, fight to make it better. If there is a Patients-Relatives Group, then I will join and be active and if there is not I will form one. If I can find any other relatives. King's Wood, I promise, will not be the soft option. Grandma will not become one of the forgotten thousands.

And still I did not sleep. I went over and over arguments with Bridget till my head ached miserably. I had hundreds of imaginary conversations, giving Bridget different lines every time the better to prepare myself for action. When today is over I can sleep, whatever the outcome.

Hannah

What a lunch this is. Everyone is more or less silent, the kind of silence that comes after shouting but there hasn't been any shouting, not that I've heard anyway. Bridget smokes and eats. This isn't allowed and Bridget knows that and never does it, except now. Puff, bite, puff, bite. How can she taste the food? Does she want to taste the food? I don't think so. It's a pity because it's very, very tasty food. All Bridget's favourite foods (though, like Dad, Bridget loves all food). Garlic mushrooms, fillet of beef done in a delicious wine sauce, sharp Roquefort cheese – Bridget adores that cheese, she can eat half a pound on her own which Dad says is like eating pound notes except there aren't any pound notes any more, ha ha Dad. The wine is flowing. Puff, slurp, puff, slurp. And nobody says anything.

Am I supposed to disappear afterwards? I raise my eyebrows at Mum. No response. I say does everyone want to be rid of me. Dad says no, I'm not a child. I say I'm glad to hear it. I ask why the silence. Mum snaps surely it is obvious. Bridget says she assumes I know about King's Wood. She spits the words and coughs for minutes. When she stops I say I do. Boldly, I say it sounds hell. Dad makes an exasperated noise in his throat. Bridget says it is hell, that is a precise description, that is what it is. Hell. Her mother has been sent to hell. Never hurt a fly in all her life and her sentence is hell. She speaks quietly, for Bridget, but with great deliberation, with venom.

Dad says melodramatics won't help. Melodramatics, echoes Bridget, voice rising. Dad says King's Wood is a hospital and it has an excellent reputation. Reputation, echoes Bridget, what does Dad think he knows about reputation? Bollocks. *She* is a nurse, she knows about reputations and King's Wood stinks. Dad leaps on her, he says it was Bridget who once said that if it came to the worst and Grandma slipped into total senility then the psycho-geriatric ward of a mental hospital would be better than any Home. Bridget says that was years ago, before the Health Service started collapsing, before staff shortages, every kind of shortage, wrecked places like King's Wood. And anyway she disputes that Grandma has reached that stage. If she has, says Bridget, it's been bloody quick.

Mum lowers her head. I feel I should stick up for her. I agree with Bridget but she isn't being exactly fair to Mum. So I chip in. I say to Bridget that I saw Grandma in hospital and it *was* quick, she did seem to just change. I say it was nobody's fault she fell, Mary — Bridget brushes this aside. She says she isn't blaming Mary or Susan or Mum (she doesn't include Dad). She's heard the whole story and nobody is to blame and she's sure (no conviction in her voice though) she's sure she couldn't have handled all these accidents better herself. But, says Bridget, there's no point in going back over it, she's only concerned with now, with Grandma in King's Wood. She cannot believe that is where her Mother is, it is appalling. And she is definitely sure she could have done better, *will* do better. There are some things not acceptable and quite frankly King's Wood is one of them.

Dad says he expected this, he isn't surprised. He says he would much rather Bridget had been here and in charge but the fact is she wasn't. Bridget takes that as a criticism, flares up, says does Dad mean she shouldn't have a holiday once in a century? Dad says don't be stupid, of course he doesn't, that Bridget knows quite well he wishes she would have more holidays. All he means is that Bridget cannot possibly appreciate what happened, what the situation was. It's no good us telling her, she had to be there. And she wasn't, through no fault of her own. But Dad says he has had enough of being cast as the wicked and heartless villain of this piece, the monster with no feelings. It is, he says, a question of choices. Bridget flashes at him is he saying he *chose* King's Wood and my God how's that for a choice? Dad's jaw tightens. He says he is looking forward to seeing Bridget do better and good luck to her. Bridget says she *will* do better, it will not be hard to do better than King's Wood, and she hasn't Dad's resources. Dad says he thought it would come down to money. He pulls a bit of paper out of his pocket and says that as he thought this would be thrown at him he did his homework. He passes it to Bridget, he tells her to study it very carefully. Bridget does. She is visibly shocked. She even stubs her cigarette out. She breathes deeply. She says Christ it's a fortune, that Dad is right, she had no idea he had spent £140,000 on looking after Grandma in the last five years, *excluding* the cost of renting her flat.

Then Bridget rallies. She has never looked finer. She straightens her back, tosses her hair, puts her hands confidently on the table. She says it is obvious what she must do: give up her job. She will look after Grandma at home in her own flat and when her savings are finished, which will be in about two weeks because she hasn't any – she laughs – she will go on to Supplementary Benefit. Mum is aghast, she says Bridget wouldn't would she? Bridget smiles, nods. Dad says she is certainly crazy enough. He is watching her carefully, he is trying to spot how Bridget will get him. Bridget says he needn't look at her like that, she isn't going to try to make his heart bleed, she isn't interested in moral blackmail, she's just going to go ahead and do it. Dad asks why. Bridget says because she thinks their mother is worth it. She thinks if life is about anything, it is about caring for those you love who love you. Dad says well bully for you.

Mum is deeply unhappy. She is fiddling with the cutlery, toying with her wine glass (which is still full unlike Bridget's and Dad's which have been emptied and filled too many times to count). I know she would like to have said what Bridget has said, it's Mum's sort of speech. I think Bridget is brilliant but I don't want her to make Mum miserable. Bridget turns to Mum, she says, quite buoyant now, can she count on Mum's help occasionally. Dad says no. Bridget says she was asking Mum, not him. Dad says no again. Bridget waits, looks at Mum. Mum looks up at Dad. She says surely a little visiting would be all right, that she'd be visiting King's Wood every day, anyway, what's the difference? Dad says she knows the difference. Bridget says she doesn't want to cause any marital discord. Dad tells her to shut up. Mum says she can speak for herself. She says the thing is that regardless of what Dad thinks, *she* doesn't think it is right to let Bridget give up her career. She thinks that is quite wrong. Grandma could live for years in her present condition and Bridget's life is more important than Grandma's. Bridget says that is for her, Bridget, to decide not Mum. Anyway, says Bridget, she's sorry she asked, she doesn't need anyone's help, she can manage on her own if she has to and it looks as though she has to. Well, says Bridget, getting up, she's quite looking forward to it whatever anyone thinks. She's never been happy about all these wretched helpers anyway and now she'll be rid of them. And now she's going to King's Wood, to bring Grandma home. Dad says sit down.

I'm rather disappointed that Bridget obeys. Dad says sit down very angrily but even so I thought Bridget would just ignore him and sweep out. She sits down. I am even more surprised to notice that her hand shakes as she lights her next cigarette. Dad says this is no way to behave, Grandma would be ashamed. He says we've got this far, gone right through the last difficult five years without quarrelling, so why do we have to do it now. It is ridiculous. Mum shoots him a look of gratitude, even pride. Bridget says she supposes she spoke too hastily, though she meant every word. She says she doesn't want to fight either. Good God, Bridget isn't going to cry, is she? No. Looks bloody near it though. Even Dad has picked that up. He says how about some good, hot, strong coffee. Mum leaps to make it. We leave the table and go next door. I take the opportunity – well, it is a sort of natural break – to ask what Germany was like. Dad is terribly pleased with me, smiles his encouragement. He would much rather talk about Germany than Grandma.

Bridget puts her feet up on the sofa. She says she's exhausted, it was a long journey yesterday and she was up all the night before that. I tuck her in with the rug I used to put over Grandma. Dad asks would she like a nap. Bridget says no, she'll have some coffee (she doesn't say and then we'll go to King's Wood). She says that actually although the holiday was marvellous and she really enjoyed it she doesn't feel it's done her any good. She can't understand it, she feels sort of jaded and she has odd pains everywhere. Probably just her wretched rheumatism again. Mum, bringing in the coffee, says Bridget does look a little pale. But anyway, Bridget says hurriedly, seeing only too well how she is playing into Dad's hands, she had a good time. The boat trip up the Rhine, or was it down, she can't remember, was fascinating. Dad says cut the scenery, how was Karl's mother and how was Karl? Bridget smiles, makes a funny Grandma face. She says she and Karl got on very well, he was good company, and his mother was very kind and hospitable but really she could never live in Germany. Or with Karl. The relief when she was on her own last night, just to be on her *own*. Cheekily, Dad says does that mean it's over with Karl. Bridget bristles, says certainly not, she likes him very much, more than likes him, but she just wants the luxury of being alone a lot of the time.

I'm sure Bridget didn't mean to but straight after the coffee which she was so sure would perk her up she fell asleep. I tucked the rug more firmly round her. Mum gently slipped Bridget's shoes off. Dad took the phone off the hook. And we all crept out.

*

Bridget is ill, but not with rheumatism again. This time she has flu. She has a raging temperature and is hallucinating. The doctor has been and pumped her full of antibiotics and has said she's brought back with her some particular strain of flu now sweeping the Continent. She's here, of course, in our house, being looked after by Mum. And she's furious. She tried to get up this afternoon after the doctor had been and she fainted. Now, she admits she's so weak she can't move. She dreams she is in King's Wood searching for Grandma and when she finds her, Grandma's face is a skull. Mum says Bridget must just reconcile herself to a week in bed, a week at least. Mum doesn't add 'imagine if you had brought Grandma home first'. She doesn't need to. Nobody needs to say it. Bridget knows. When I sat an hour with her she said, 'It won't work, will it Hannah? I can't do it, can I? It's no good.' I didn't insult her by pretending I didn't know what she meant. I feel so sorry for Bridget. What can she do?

I think I should go to King's Wood. I think I should see it for myself. Adrian looks appalled. He says he certainly doesn't want to go, he dreads it. But I want to be able to decide whether it is, as Bridget alleges, hell. Mum is adamant that I should not go. Does that prove it is hell? She says it would upset me. Well, maybe I need upsetting. If Grandma is in there then surely I ought to be brave enough to go to see her. Mum says it will give me nightmares and Grandma won't know me so what is the point of my going through it? Dad says I can go if I want, he accuses Mum of being over-protective, points out I am nearly eighteen. I think Bridget would like me to go, it would somehow make her feel better. And I'm curious, very curious. I've never been in any kind of mental hospital. They fascinate me. It would be daring to go. So I'm going, for this mixture of right and wrong reasons.

*

I go with Dad. Mum wants nothing to do with it. Dad is quite calm. He has some football match on the car radio and is absorbed in it. One thing I can be sure of: there will be no messy emotional talk from Dad. That suits me. I stare out of the window. We seem to drive through a succession of dismal high streets, all empty and litter-blown because it's Sunday. Grandma would want to stop and pick up all the paper and put it tidily in a bin. She would wonder where all the people were and make me laugh when she said church. We turn into the King's Wood drive, go through huge iron gates. There are big trees either side and bushes and beyond those acres of grass. Nobody about but then it's cold and wet. Dad pulls up at the very end of the enormously long building. He sits a moment, waiting for the half-time score: first things first. Then we get out and he looks at his watch. He says twenty minutes is more than enough. He says he'll chat the Sister up and I can talk to Grandma.

Mum told me about the paint, the smell, the locked door. They're all as bad as she said but I'm prepared. I'm not prepared for Grandma though. My stomach churns when I see her. She is like a lump, a mess of tripe, all loose and collapsed and floppy. She has a hideous dress on and big fluffy pompommed slippers and half of what she's had for dinner is down her front. I collapse onto a stool

214

beside her. I say, 'Grandma,' and choke. She opens one eye, barely interested enough to look at me.

> Where've you been, you hussy?
>
> Nowhere. At home.
>
> At home, at home, Polly put the kettle on –
>
> – and we'll all have tea.
>
> Yes, please, I don't mind if I do, how's your father?
>
> He's talking to the Sister.
>
> Good luck to him, good luck to the boys in blue, yoo hoo.
>
> He's coming in a minute.
>
> Who?
>
> Dad.
>
> Dad, dad, mad, mad, pad, pad, had, had, have you ever been had?
>
> Yes.
>
> Well that's a relief, a bloomin' relief, of Mafeking, do you remember that?
>
> No.
>
> No, no, in the name of God, what's the matter wi' you, will you stop it.

The old woman on the other side of Grandma is pulling her dress up. Painfully, in little jerky movements, up, up, until her knickers show and then she starts to pull her knickers down and a girl in an overall shouts at her and says no Elsie, stop it Elsie, you're naughty Elsie. Elsie's dress is firmly wrenched down. The television is on very loud, it's the football match Dad is nobly missing. I look for him. He must be in the Sister's office, doing his bit. I look round surreptitiously. Two of the women are wandering up and down. They see me looking and come towards me. They stand in front of me and I don't know what to say so I say hello. One nods, one stares. What can I say? So I smile and wait. They go away, resume their walk. Twenty minutes did Dad say? Two have gone.

Grandma is clutching my hand.

> I can't be bothered.
>
> With what, Grandma?

215

Grandma yourself, where's her radiogram, who's pinched it,
    all that money, have you any money?
Yes, why, do you want some?
What?
Money.
Money, money, money is the root of all evil.

The Sister is here with Dad. 'Always worrying about money, Mrs
McKay, but you don't need any here, darling.' Grandma looks at
her sourly, asks who she's darling-ing, and she'll look after her own
money thank you. Sister laughs, says Grandma is a character. Dad
asks how she is, Sister says fine, fine, she wasn't sleeping but she is
now, they've given her something. She relates some vaguely smutty-
sounding joke about Grandma and a milkman which Grandma is
supposed to have told her and then laughs and says Grandma is a
scream. Dad smiles weakly. I don't. Sister asks if I'm Mrs McKay's
grand daughter and I'm obliged to say yes. Sister says isn't that nice,
we don't get many youngsters visiting and the old folk love them.
Dad, looking around pointedly, asks if there are many visitors of
any sort. Sister says oh yes, today is not typical, Elsie has visitors and
Leah and Vera and Ida, they all have visitors. But she adds that most
people start off well then get discouraged and it's either too painful
to keep coming or they start thinking it doesn't make any difference.
Dad asks if it does. Sister is emphatic: yes. And for the staff, she says.
They like visitors. It is not like a normal ward where visitors bring
nurses PRESENTS out of GRATITUDE (well, it seemed to me those
two crucial words were in capitals). It is not much fun, Sister says,
being on a ward like this. Nobody gets better. It is very depressing
being at the end of the line, no thanks, no rewards, all we can do is
make them comfortable and it is not pleasant work. Even Dad looks
appalled. Sister hasn't finished. She says they are helpless you see,
like babies but twice the trouble.

  We say goodbye to Grandma. She doesn't seem to care if we are
going or not. Her hand falls limply as I let it go. The door is unlocked
for us to go out. The man stands with the keys. Two of the old
ladies, the two who had come to stare at me, the two who patrol all
the time, try to go through the open door. A nurse rushes, says, 'Not

you Doreen, not you May, not today.' Doreen says she has a car waiting. May says she's just going to empty the rubbish. We go out. The door is locked hurriedly. Out through the smelly corridor, past a huge trolley laden with clothes, heaps of them, presumably on the way to the laundry. Oh, the fresh air! It isn't even a good day, it's almost dark and raining a little but the air is so sharp and cleansing. We get in the car. Dad puts the radio on and fiddles with it. We don't talk. I'm bursting with anger but we don't talk. Dad whistles, the music on the radio fills the car. I think of Grandma in that place. I think of her being given her tea, having bread and butter rammed in, tea poured down her throat. Then what do they do? Sit? Again? Until bedtime. Is there an electric blanket? Does she get a hot water bottle? What about her six big blankets? And does anyone say sleep tight mind the horses don't bite?

Mum looks at me anxiously as we come in. She asks how it was. I say, I hope flatly, that it was dreadful. I say I don't want to talk about it. Mum says she knew I shouldn't have gone. I say, furiously, that *of course* I should have gone and that I will keep going and that I have to know what it is like. Mum says I'm too young. I ask for what. Too young to know there's something nasty going on? Too young to know about the old? I say on the contrary, I'm not young enough. Maybe if I was it would seem nothing to do with me. But it is, it is to do with me. If Grandma's fate is what is round the corner then I'd rather not grow up, thanks. Mum says I am upset. I laugh. I shout *naturally* I'm upset. Dad says we are all upset and I turn on him. You? You're upset, I yell. Dad is firm. He says yes, he is. He might not shout or yell or cry but yes, he is upset. He says he is probably more upset than me because, whereas I am not in any way responsible for Grandma being in King's Wood, he is. So that upsets him more. But, Dad says, it doesn't make him change his mind. We have been through the reasons why Grandma is where she is a thousand times and he has had enough, he is not going through it again. He has made the decision: it may not be the right one but it is *made*. He goes out of the house, banging the door in the way he tells us not to.

Mum says I should not be so hard on Dad. She says he is no ogre and I know it etc. Then she says will I please go easy with Bridget. I ask her what she means, knowing damn well. Mum says there is no need to prejudice Bridget against King's Wood, no need to go into details or say how despairing and helpless Grandma seems. It will only distress Bridget who isn't well enough to go and see for herself. Mum says she isn't asking me to lie (not much) but just to be non-committal. She says it would be cruel of me to tell Bridget what I think. I say, okay. I will be as vague as possible but I tell Mum there's no hope of fooling Bridget. And when she does go and see Grandma she will hold it against me that I didn't tell her how she had deteriorated, she'll get more of a shock. Mum tells me not to be so silly. Nothing will prevent Bridget being shocked but it's something to stave off as long as possible.

*

The staving-off is over. Bridget is not exactly better but she's better enough to go to King's Wood or so she insists. But she concedes she isn't better enough to bring Grandma home. She agrees she isn't yet strong enough to cope, that a week in bed has left her shaky. She's only going to visit and then she will bring Grandma out next week when she has made arrangements. She doesn't announce what these arrangements are and neither Mum nor Dad asks her (though looks are exchanged). Mum says she will accompany Bridget. Bridget is quick to turn the offer down. She says Mum has done quite enough what with looking after her and visiting Grandma every day. I think I should offer, but of course I know Bridget will want to go on her own. I offer. Bridget accepts. I have to become suddenly very busy finishing my breakfast to hide my confusion. And Mum is not pleased. She hesitates, wondering whether to say anything. In spite of saying last Sunday that I would keep on going to King's Wood I haven't been since, not once this week, but then I have been at school. It's a genuine excuse.

Bridget says we'll go after lunch, at about two. Mum says that is actually not a good time to visit, it is an inconvenient time for the staff. Bridget rudely says, 'Bugger the staff.' Mum flushes, not at the swearing, but at Bridget's attitude. She says she would have thought Bridget, as a nurse, would understand the staff's point of view. Bridget says she understands it perfectly, she says throughout hospital wards in the whole country this idea of putting staff convenience first has been swept aside: the patient comes first in *her* ward and then the visitor and then the staff. A happy patient, Bridget says, is one whose relatives and friends are encouraged to support. So don't give her this stuff about staff convenience. Mum is even more annoyed. She says Bridget is just being awkward, that she never for one moment suggested staff were more important than patients or visitors. Bridget says it doesn't matter anyway, that she simply wants it made clear that she will visit her own poor mother whenever she bloody well wants.

Mum really hates Bridget when she comes on strong like that – well, maybe not hates, dislikes. She feels put down by Bridget and the injustice really goads her. It is true Bridget represents herself as the knight in shining armour, the person with high moral principles who acts on them too. The trouble is, that's the role Mum covets and she can't have. Dad, of course, doesn't try, he isn't interested in virtue or high moral principles, his dear sister is welcome to both. He's only interested in practicalities and Bridget has little grasp of those except in her professional life (Dad doesn't actually believe Bridget *can* run a ward). He half wants, I know he does, to see Bridget get in the most appalling mess over these arrangements to do with Grandma that she refers to. Then he will come along and say he told her so and enjoy picking up the pieces.

Bridget has dressed with care. This is not so much unusual as odd: why dress carefully for King's Wood? She's wearing very bright colours as though determined to be seen from a long way off – shocking pink sweater, purple skirt, pink tights, scarf patterned in mauve and pink and blue, and on top a white flying jacket. She's even put on make-up which she hardly ever does – the old eyes are weighed down with eyeliner and the lashes with mascara. As we get into her car her perfume is strongly evident. I ask her what it is. She says Chanel No. 5, Karl bought it for her on the plane, she would never have bought it herself, waste of good money. She is smoking, of course, gets through two cigarettes before we are half way to King's Wood. I have to direct her though she swears she has been before and knows the way. She has no sense of direction at all, always turns left if I say right. When we turn into the gates she says she's dreading this. She says she knows what it will be like and she's dreading it. She says once she's in there, it won't be so bad, but the first sight of Grandma is going to make her crack up.

I tell Bridget we have to ring the bell and point to it. She puts her finger down hard on it and says, 'Bloody bell.' The man takes his time coming and peers suspiciously round the door when he does open it – visitors to King's Wood aren't usually so demanding – Bridget smiles over-brightly and says good afternoon in what I know is her best sarcastic manner. She sweeps in, her eyes raking the chairs where the old ladies are sitting. She tightens her lips, looks furious, says, 'For Christ's sake where have they dumped her?' I touch her arm, nod over to the far corner. Bridget says, 'In the name of God, what have they done to her.' She marches across the room, me scuttling behind, embarrassed by her air of authority. Grandma is half in and half out of an easy chair, her right shoulder falling over the side and her head lolling. One leg is up on a stool, the other awkwardly splayed out under it. Bridget says, 'Mother! Mother! For heaven's sake,' and hauls her upright and into the chair properly and snaps at me to get a cushion. I haven't the faintest idea where to get a cushion from. I go to the Sister's office. I knock. There are four of them there drinking tea. One of them comes to the door reluctantly, but then I remind myself I'm interrupting a precious tea break. I say my aunt was wondering if there was a cushion around to make my Grandma more comfortable. I hate the sound of my apologetic voice, my Mother's voice and tone. I should be like Bridget. The nurse looks puzzled but in the background Sister says, 'Give her a pillow – won't do any good but give her a pillow.' I'm taken to the dormitory. My heart thuds, with fear, what else, as we pass six corpses in chairs. I dare not look at them. Is there no mortuary? But then a creaky-cry sound comes from one, the nurse says, 'Don't start, Ruby,' as we go on. She goes to what must be Grandma's bed and hands me the pillow.

Bridget snatches it impatiently. She pummels it and puts it behind Grandma's back and arranges Grandma against it and puts both her feet on the stool, neatly together. 'Leaving her like that,' Bridget says. Then she sits on another stool beside Grandma and talks to her, entirely uninhibited by the surrounding old women. Grandma won't open her eyes. Bridget pats her hands, which she is holding, both of them, in her own. She keeps saying, 'Mother, heh, Mother it's me.' Grandma makes no response. Bridget swears under her breath and then begins to rage about Grandma's clothes. 'What have they put on her? Where're her clothes? My God, what rubbish is this, where are her own slippers?' Grandma opens her eyes. They're bleary. Bridget peers at her, says, 'Heh, Mother,' again. Grandma stares. She struggles to speak but all that comes out is an unintelligible murmur. 'What Mum? What?' Bridget shouts, 'What was that?' Grandma tries again. To me, it sounds as if she is saying, 'low bridges' but Bridget is triumphant, says, 'There you are, she's saying hello Bridget, and hello to you Mum. What have they been doing to you eh? Eh? Mum? How are you keeping? Come on, tell me, tell me?' Grandma mumbles. I only catch, 'legs'. Bridget interpréts. Grandma is saying her legs are sore. Bridget examines them. (Grandma has stockings on but they're rolled down to the ankle.) She says, 'Bloody hell, she's bruised, she's *bruised*.' She stands up, flushed. She tells me to stay where I am, she's going to see Sister Grice. But at that moment Sister appears, a bag of jelly sweets in her hand.

It is a very awkward tableau. Grandma is in a corner chair with another occupant on either side and we are in front of her. I am by now on the vacant stool so Bridget and Sister seem to tower over me. Sister offers Grandma a sweet. Grandma doesn't respond (though only a month ago she'd have snatched the whole bag). Sister selects a red jelly — 'see, they're soft' — and shoves it into Grandma's mouth, expertly getting it through her closed lips. Grandma chokes slightly, but then starts sucking. 'There you are,' Sister says, 'she's happy.' And then it's like a tennis match. Bridget serves first.

My Mother doesn't seem happy to me.
Oh, goodness, she's fine, she's a bit in the dumps today, but they all have their days you know.
I'm a nurse myself, a Sister.
You're the daughter, then?
That's right.

221

The one that's been on holiday a month? Very nice, where did you go?

Germany. But what I wanted to ask you about were these bruises.

What bruises?

There, and there.

Oh, they're nothing, they bruise easily at this age, I expect she knocked her leg on a chair.

But my sister-in-law says she doesn't walk on her own any more.

That's true, but we walk her, we keep her going, don't we Mrs McKay, don't we, darling?

And I was wondering where her clothes are?

Being name-taped, they'll be back soon.

I'd like her to be in her own clothes.

But they're awkward, they're not as comfortable as these, not as easy, look you see, Velcro, easier for the old things.

How is she sleeping?

Fine. She was restless at first, but she's settled now.

How is she eating?

Not much, but she's plenty of fat on her yet, you don't need to worry, she won't starve.

Well, she won't be here much longer.

Won't she?

No. I'll be taking her home next week.

Will you now, well you'll have a struggle, she can't do anything for herself now, you know. It's a full time job.

I know. I'll do it. Just as soon as I'm properly better.

I thought you'd been on holiday?

I have but then I was ill, with flu.

Oh, bad luck. You won't have to be ill when you have your mother home.

No.

You'd be sunk then, but you've got your sister-in-law of course, you're a lovely family. I wish you luck, you'll need it. Another jelly, Mrs McKay?

All this time Bridget has been glaring and Sister meeting her glare and deflecting it and ignoring it and needling Bridget. It is game, set and match to Sister. She implies, without saying a single word, that Bridget is deluding herself, that she really knows she will never take Grandma home. And *she* isn't in the least worried at what Bridget implies, that Grandma is somehow being ill-treated or at least not supervised carefully enough. Bridget, I'm sure, expected Sister to be on the defensive but she isn't, not a bit. She doesn't give a damn what Bridget thinks. She wanders off, doling out sweets, going from one slobbery old mouth to another without once even wiping the finger she inserts into them. The television blares. Doreen and May patrol, Leah squawks. Bridget stands fuming. She makes a decision. She pursues Sister. I hear her ask if there is a wheelchair. Sister nods, points. Bridget gets the wheelchair and we try to get Grandma into it. We fail. Sister saunters over. She puts an arm lock on Grandma and has her into the wheelchair in no time. She tells Bridget there's a knack, that nursing the senile demented is a specialised skill. And she smirks. She knows Bridget doesn't possess it. We wheel Grandma away, but where to? I don't know, Bridget doesn't know. Sister comes to the rescue. She says we can use the office, she won't be in there for half an hour. Bridget is obliged to thank her but not in the effusive way Mum would have done. The office is quite pleasant. There are posters, plants and a few old, but quite attractive, chintz-covered chairs. It's obviously Sister's sanctum and we are privileged. I venture to point this out and Bridget snaps at me. She says it's a disgrace not to have some kind of day room. I say that is hardly Sister's fault, probably not King's Wood's either. Bridget says, 'Oh shut up, you sound like your mother.' I am startled to see tears in her eyes. Just as I'm wondering how to cope with this, Grandma speaks. She says, quite distinctly, 'Is there any tea left in that pot?' We both stare. There is a brown tea pot on Sister's desk and Grandma is looking straight at it. Bridget bounds up, feels the pot, looks around for a mug, finds one, fills it, finds milk and sugar and lovingly takes it to Grandma who slurps thirstily. Bridget strokes her hair as she does so, crooning over her. When the mug has been drained, Grandma looks at Bridget as though seeing her for the first time. She says, 'You took your time, you hussy,' and shakes her fist at Bridget in the pretend-fierce way she used to. She smiles. Bridget smiles. They are beam-to-beam, their faces very close together as Bridget bends down over the wheelchair. I feel an intruder. I should go away. This is private. They don't even notice me slip out or if Bridget does she makes no sign. And when I'm out, although still in the ward, I feel so relieved, like being really out, in the fresh air.

*

On the way home Bridget swears she will have Grandma out 'in no time'. She is flushed, at her most manic. I don't say a word. She changes gears with a crash. Before we are half way home, she has to pull up at the side of the road and light a cigarette with a trembling hand. She hits the steering wheel, bangs it, several times without speaking. She inhales deeply. Will I ever be in this state over Mum? No, I won't. I'll take Mum out and shoot her if I can find a gun. But why a gun? I'll give her pills, neater, cleaner, more suitable for someone like Mum. Why doesn't Bridget do that? She's a nurse, it would be easy. Why doesn't she do it? I'm afraid to ask. Maybe Bridget understands something I don't. Finally, I blurt out, 'Bridget, do you wish Grandma was dead?' Bridget laughs, she seems to relax. She says no, she wishes Grandma was well, that's what she wishes. She wishes Grandma could enjoy a decent, natural end. She wishes she could be cared for with love and tenderness until she dies. Even a dumb animal, Bridget says, recognises love and tenderness. And Grandma isn't getting it. None of them in King's Wood are getting it. They are cattle, shunted off to the slaughter house and given a long drawn-out tortured death. But not for long, Bridget says, I'll have her out in no time.

Bridget explodes into our house. She repeats to Mum and Dad that she will have Grandma out of King's Wood in no time. Then she starts shouting. Bridget asks how Mum and Dad can *stand* it, how as human beings, they can stand Grandma being put through all that, how *can* they? Dad says Bridget is exaggerating, he says Grandma is well looked after – this is a mistake, just what Bridget wants. She asks Dad to analyse 'well looked after', she invites him to say what this means in his opinion. Dad says Grandma is fed and

224

washed and kept warm and comfortable. Bridget spits at him. She says 'comfortable' with such a sneer it sounds like torture. She says comfortable is the last thing Grandma is, that she is covered in bruises and those bruises can only have come through rough handling. She says that far from being comfortable, Grandma is in agony. Mum demurs. She says Grandma got bruised even when we were looking after her, that Grandma's own joke had been she bruised easily, like gardenias. Mum says if Bridget really thinks Grandma is being roughly handled, she must report it. Bridget says she wouldn't waste her time. Dad says she shouldn't waste it shouting at him either. Bridget controls herself, says very well, she won't. She says she is going home now to her own flat. She is better. She thanks Mum for looking after her. She turns to Dad and her parting shot is that he can give notice to the landlord of Grandma's flat, and save some money. Dad says there's no need to be insulting, that he doesn't give a damn about the money and he has had enough of Bridget's insinuations. 'Bring Mum home then,' Bridget flashes at him, 'and pay for her to be properly looked after in her own home.' Then it's Dad's turn. He shouts. He roars, 'No!' He says no money in the world would be enough to balance the awful responsibility. He yells at Bridget that *that* is what he wants to be rid of, the sheer crippling responsibility of organising and coping. 'And we,' he finishes, '*we*, Jenny and I, *we* have borne most of that.'

The relief when Bridget has gone . . . But then the depression. Several times Mum asks, 'What do you think, Hannah?' As if I know what I think.

> I think it's all a mess.
> I think old age is a mess.
> I think Bridget is right.
> I think Dad is right.
> I think it should be ended as soon as possible.
> I think there's no need for all this.
> I think there are a lot of clever people around.
> I think they should apply themselves to this problem.

I think if Bridget brings Grandma out and gives up her own job, goes onto Social Security to look after her, then she is mad. The question is: is it better to be mad or is it better to be sane and cruel?

Jenny

I rang Bridget before I set off to visit Grandma but there was no reply so I was half expecting to find either that Grandma had already been removed from King's Wood when I got there or that Bridget would be at her side. But Grandma was there and Bridget was not. Grandma was in her usual seat – so quickly, in such a short time, it has become 'usual' – surrounded by pillows. A pillow behind her head, one behind her right shoulder, a third under her right leg which was resting on a stool. I crept into the room, after the man on the door had let me through, worried that Bridget might have made trouble the day before and we would all be branded as a nuisance in consequence. But Sister Grice bounced out of her office, all smiles and welcomes.

'There's a little problem with the breathing,' she said and gestured towards Grandma. 'She's got a touch of cold on her so we want her propped up, you see, don't want her lolling all over, she's a devil for the lolling.' I made some kind of concerned sound. 'Oh, you don't want to be worrying, she's a tough old bird, we take good care of her.' I said I was sure they did. Sister Grice drew attention to Grandma's hair. 'There, you see, shampooed. We don't run to a set, this isn't Vidal Sassoon, eh, but we've shampooed it, lovely don't you think?' I said I did. Grandma's hair was indeed very white and clean-looking. I ventured to wonder aloud how they'd managed the

227

washing since I knew Grandma was not co-operative. Sister Grice said it was no problem. She explained to me they had a hoist. The old women got strapped safely into the hoist and lifted – 'gently, mind' – into a bath. 'They love their bath,' Sister boasted. 'Oh, it's a struggle getting them out once they're in. Some of them haven't had a bath in years when they come in, not in years.' I said we had been unable to get Grandma into a bath ourselves and had had to be satisfied with all-over washes. 'A bath's best,' Sister said. 'It's a luxury, they love it, you love it Mrs McKay, don't you, eh, you love your bath?'

Absolutely not a flicker of response. Sister marched off as the telephone rang in her office. I drew closer to Grandma. I could hear her laboured breathing above the noise of the television and the caw-cawing and sudden bursts of frenzied shouting which punctuated the background noises every few minutes. It was very hard to believe Grandma was aware of anything at all around her. But was she suffering? How was I to know? Then I took her hand, expecting it to be limp and was shocked at the strength of her grip. She clung to me, her nails digging into the palm of my own hand. It changed everything. Wherever Grandma was in her mind, she needed someone to hang onto. I bent my head, not attempting to speak, suddenly twice as confused as I already was. I dreaded Bridget arriving and finding me there but with my hand in such a trap I could not bring myself to move. I was still motionless half an hour later when tea was brought round.

Grandma's tea was in a feeding cup with a spout. Last week, I'd seen her drink from an ordinary cup, holding it herself once it was put in her hand. Now she had it in a feeding cup. The nurse gave it to me. I tried to insert the spout into Grandma's mouth but she flinched. I tried again. She let her mouth hang open, slack, and the tea dribbled out. The nurse came back, seeing my inexperience. She put one hand under Grandma's chin and tipped her head back very slightly and then controlled the flow of tea to a merest trickle. Grandma swallowed. It was all done, if not with the love and tenderness Bridget looked for, with patience and expertise. The nurse gave me a smile as she handed me the cup back. She was not young herself, older than I am, and her face had the same worn look

Grandma's had always had. I could read no expression in her eyes. I suppose I looked for contempt or even resentment but her look was quite bland. She was making no value judgements, or not letting me see that she was.

Bridget still had not come by the time I left. I didn't ask anyone if she had already been, because I did not want them to think our family was not in perfect harmony, but I felt Sister Grice would have been sure to tell me Grandma had already had a visitor that day. When I got home, I rang Bridget again, though the last thing I wanted to do was speak to her after the scene the day before. Charlie had said I should leave her to stew in her own juice, as he so inelegantly put it, but I had no intention of obeying his callous instruction. Bridget was suffering, something Charlie did not take into account. I could not desert her even if she did not want me. So when she still did not answer the phone I went round. Karl was there. He opened Bridget's door but made no move to step aside or to ask me in. I felt embarrassed. I hardly know Karl, I was not even sure how to address him. I asked him if he had enjoyed his holiday and he said yes, he had thank you. He was quite amiable but still blocking the door. I was obliged to ask if Bridget was in. Karl said no, she was just next door in her mother's flat and I felt immediately and foolishly relieved that he had not after all been told by Bridget to keep me out.

Bridget was packing. Grandma's flat was in chaos, with every drawer and cupboard tipped out. 'Don't worry,' Bridget shouted, 'I'll clear it all up. It will be left spick and span.' She looked immensely cheerful. 'I'm getting everything organised,' she said, 'all the rubbish can go to a jumble. I'm being ruthless, I have to be or there won't be room for the two of us in my flat.' I followed her through into Grandma's bedroom. The bed had gone. Bridget said Karl had already moved it. It hit me for the first time that Bridget was *serious*. My face must have been a study. Bridget said, a little grimly, 'You didn't think I meant it, did you? Well, I did. I do. I feel better already. I'm not going back to King's Wood till I'm ready to bring Mum out. I can't bear it. I can't bear going. Just give me a few more days and I'll be ready.' I said nothing. Absurdly, my heart was thudding and I felt shaky. Meekly, I helped Bridget carry Grandma's awful blankets through to her flat. Karl had set the double bed up in Bridget's sitting room. We put the blankets on it. I sat down, weak at the knees. Bridget was singing, she was happy. I wondered why Karl let her carry out this plan, why he wasn't objecting. I had never done more than exchange pleasantries with him – he had been entirely peripheral to Bridget's life. The holiday seemed to me to have made no difference: he still was. It was Grandma who was central to Bridget's life and Karl was either so stupid he could not see it or so in love with her that it made no difference.

I stared at the two of them, not knowing what to say, observing them minutely. Bridget bossed Karl but at the same time was lavish with the kind of endearments I had never heard her use. It was 'honey' and 'sweetheart' and 'angel'. And she had such an odd expression on her face as she bustled about, issuing directions. A sickly kind of expression, unctuous and unnatural as though she were trying to make up to him at the same time as dominate. It made me uneasy. I felt suddenly that physical attraction was all that kept Bridget with Karl. But did he know? He seemed so intent on pleasing her. Nothing was too much trouble, he hurried to carry out every task, his face serious. He struggled to hold her eyes occasionally but never managed to do so – she was off and away. All the time Bridget kept up an inane prattle, at her most infuriatingly repetitious, but Karl hardly spoke.

He was making a cupboard to put Grandma's things in. Planks of wood and a sheet of hardboard lay on the floor. Bridget praised him, told me how wonderful Karl was at carpentry. She laughed and teased him and told him to get on with it, all hands to the deck and a string of Grandma's other clichés. I said I'd been to King's Wood but Bridget stopped me, she said she did not want to hear the wretched name, she begged me to tell her nothing because she was pretending King's Wood did not exist and her mother was not there. I sat on the bed, bewildered. 'She's going to be so happy here,' Bridget enthused. 'It will be lovely, I'll make her so comfortable, I know all the things she likes, all the little treats.' An inexplicable anger towards Bridget caught me by surprise and I said, 'All on your own?' Bridget was not a bit put out. She said I was right. 'And if you're ill?' I asked. 'You've been ill twice recently –' 'Thanks,

Jenny,' Bridget said, 'I had noticed. If I'm ill then the Social Services will have to take over.' 'They'll put her in King's Wood,' I said. 'Well,' Bridget replied, quite composed, 'so they will. But at least she will have been *out* of King's Wood longer.'

There was no arguing with her but why should I wish to argue? My need to do so puzzled and distressed me. I felt locked in a contest with Bridget and I was envious that she was wiping the floor with me. I was the one who went to King's Wood and held Grandma's hand and condoned her situation, while Bridget moved beds and prepared a nest for her. I ought to be admiring Bridget. I ought to be clapping my hands and marvelling and praising but I do not. Instead, I am appalled at what Bridget is doing, it seems not magnificent but almost obscene. But *why*? Because it feels so. The facts of Bridget's action are admirable but the feel of it repulsive. She will give up her job, a job which is no ordinary job, one to which she has given her life and from which she derives great satisfaction, and she will wait on her mother who cannot walk or talk and may take years to die. Bridget cannot know these are Grandma's 'last days': look at the Death Chairs in King's Wood. With the kind of care Bridget plans to give her, Grandma could last another decade. And of course, while she does, so does my shame and guilt and confusion. Bridget knows we will never be 'out of it', as she says. Never. With Grandma in our street, in Bridget's flat, we will be sucked in once more, not having hearts of stone. How long will it take before we are back to rotas (to give Bridget a break), back to the supporting we have done so long, but supporting Bridget now, in this folly.

As I left, Bridget said, 'Don't worry, Jenny, I'm not going to be a burden, this is going to be *my* affair, I promise. I know what I'm doing and I can cope, I've got it all thought out, honestly. There's no need for you to fret. And thanks for visiting Mum till I can get her out, thanks Jenny, it makes a difference, don't think it isn't appreciated, you're very kind.' I suppose I made some expression of derision. 'No, really Jenny, you are, very kind, you always have been, Mum always said how kind you were and still are. You shouldn't upset yourself. It's Charlie's concern if anyone's, not yours.' That focused the anger I was already feeling. I told Bridget, coldly, that she couldn't separate Charlie and me like that, she was always trying to do it and it didn't work. Charlie's mother was like my own mother, we took each other's family as our own. Bridget shrugged. She really did not care, I could see, what I thought nor did she believe my high-sounding sentiments on marital accord. How could she? Suddenly, I despised Bridget and her Karl. She used him, tolerated him, enjoyed him but when it came to love, there was only her mother.

★

Today when I went to see Grandma she was not in her chair, nor was Sister Grice in her office. Another Sister was there, far preferable in demeanour, gentler and quieter. She said Grandma was in bed, that the doctor had been round and thought it advisable because the breathing was worse, there was some sign of infection. We went together to see Grandma who was in the small side ward where she had started off. She was propped up on huge pillows and turned onto her left side. The new Sister left. I sat beside Grandma's bed, so relieved not to be sitting in the main room, so pleased to have Grandma actually lying down and tucked up. It was quiet, peaceful. Grandma slept and wheezed. Her colour was dreadful, a dirty grey lying under her usual yellow pallor. Then, to my surprise, she opened her eyes and stared at me. I bent forward and said, loudly, who I was. A faint flicker of a smile came and went and an attempt at speech. I took her hand – again, the strong grip, fiercely strong – and another mumble. My ear almost against her lips I distinctly heard 'thank you'. Thank you – for what? For putting her in here? For discouraging Bridget from taking her out? For putting myself first? I wanted anything but thanks from her, thanks were unbearable.

Then she seemed to sleep again and looked, for her, at rest. There was little point in my sitting there – her hand no longer gripped – but I had only just arrived. I got up. There was nothing to do in that room. In my bag I had brought a packet of those soft jellies I had seen Sister Grice dole out. I took them out and decided to be bold, to try to use my time usefully, to remember there were other old women there who had no visitors. And it was a matter of being bold and even brave when it came to the Death Chairs. I was so afraid – afraid to look properly, afraid to talk in case it released a flood of

232

gibberish I could not understand, afraid to touch. It was no good offering the packet for the Death Chair occupants to help themselves. They could not. Sister Grice's method was the only way: ramming the jelly in, hooking my finger briefly over the flap of skin that was a lip and into the sickly-soft hole that was a mouth. I rammed, I hooked. The jellies went in and down. The big sitting room seemed by contrast suddenly full of splendid specimens of womanhood. There, several women could and did select their own jelly and several more were able to exclaim with delight. All except two said thank you, over and over again, thank you, so polite in the midst of senility. One said she was very hungry and took two in each hand.

And then there were the nurses. Two were sitting at a very long trestle table sorting stockings out, heaps and heaps of lisle stockings. They were both black, both tired and drained looking. I hated my Lady Bountiful role with my wretched little sweets. They had watched me doing the rounds but I could not tell whether I had been watched cynically. I sat down and asked if I could help. They shook their heads, said there was no need. I ask how long they had been there, where they lived, what kind of shifts they did. I said it must be very hard working in this kind of ward. They nodded, warily. They didn't ask me a thing but then why should they. To make conversation, I asked questions about the various patients and heard such a catalogue of woe, all delivered in a dead pan monotone, that I wished I had not enquired. One nurse looked me straight in the eye as she finished, 'but the poor souls wouldn't be here if there was anyone to look after them, would they?'

No, they would not. I went back to Grandma who still slept. As I left, I stopped at the door of the Sister's office, feeling I should make some enquiries about Grandma's condition. The relief Sister was there, busy with paperwork, but she invited me in, indicated a chair. She said she had wanted to catch me anyway, just 'to make things clear'. Grandma was not eating, and more important, hardly drinking. The infection of her lungs was worse. The Sister was watching me closely as she said, 'The doctor isn't sure if it would respond to antibiotics.' Messages seemed to flash from every movement she made – the lowered head, the careful outspread hand, the gesture she made with her pen. Nothing explicit was said at all. I said I thought it might be better to wait, to see if nature would clear the infection on its own and what about something for the pain. Sister raised her eyebrows. She said that perhaps that might be a good idea but she didn't think Grandma was in any pain at the moment. Then she asked if all the family were in agreement. I struggled. I almost assured her they were but of course it could not be done. I confessed. I said my sister-in-law was coming to take her mother home, probably in a few days. Sister was of course taken aback. She asked if my sister-in-law had visited today. I said no, she was busy preparing her flat to take in her mother and that she did not intend to come until she was coming to remove her. Sister said that in that case my sister-in-law should be told her mother was very ill. Moving her might kill her. 'So might leaving her,' I said. The Sister nodded agreement but had the last word. 'So might neither,' she said. 'You never can tell.'

*

Charlie was adamant: there was no need to tell Bridget about Grandma's condition. She had said she did not want to know, did not want to hear King's Wood mentioned, and that would have been sufficient justification in itself for me to keep quiet. But Charlie was even clearer. He went himself to King's Wood that evening as soon as he got home and saw the Sister – by this time, Sister Grice again. She said Grandma was very ill but still very strong. Her heartbeat was amazing for a woman of her age and her pulse steady. Sister Grice was of the opinion that Grandma would rally, that she had a long way to go yet. So, Charlie argued, why bring Bridget into it? It would only complicate matters. Bridget would have her pumped full of antibiotics at once. Nature should be allowed to take its own course, said Charlie. I put this into different words and presented them to him. 'You mean,' I said, 'nature might kill her, whereas science might save her, so let's give nature a chance.' Charlie was not ashamed to say, 'Exactly.' And he pointed out that once Grandma was under Bridget's care, nature would be fought tooth and claw.

So we did not report back to Bridget. I did not see her yesterday.

Today, she rushed in to borrow a step ladder: Karl was painting the sitting room which was now to be Grandma's room. 'Pink,' Bridget said, 'I thought a nice, cheerful, warm pink – what do you think?' I said I thought pink would be lovely and Bridget beamed. I even said I would make some new curtains, that I had some pink and white flowered material rejected by Hannah and always intended for curtains. Bridget kissed me. She was so happy, so girlish in her delight. As usual, her delight made me miserable. I didn't even tell her that I had visited Grandma only half an hour before. I didn't tell her that Sister Grice had checked she had our night-time number. I didn't prepare her at all.

Sister Grice didn't ring in the night. She rang in the morning just after Charlie had left for Munich on business. She told me Grandma had had a very bad night and that she was very ill indeed. I could not go on my own. It was very unfortunate that Charlie had gone, so unfair this had happened on one of his rare absences. I could not leave Bridget ignorant any longer. I could not deprive her either of the chance to see her mother before she died or of saving her. So I had to go along to Bridget's flat and ring the bell at seven in the morning. She took hours to come to the door and when she did she was bleary-eyed and stupid with sleep. I hoped she would look at me and realise at once the significance of my coming unannounced at such an hour but she did not. Or if she did, she pretended not to and really pretence is not in Bridget's line. She rubbed her eyes and yawned and said, 'Oh Jenny, come in.' But I stood still, determined to get it over with. I said, in a most false and rehearsed way, that I had just had a call from King's Wood and that Grandma was very ill indeed and I was on my way there now. Bridget stared at me, clutching her dressing gown round her fiercely. 'Ill?' she echoed. 'What the hell have they done to her now?'

I drove her there. All the way Bridget cursed King's Wood and everyone in it. She kept up a non-stop tirade against the institution and ranted and raved about the injustice of its existence. I said nothing. She did not once, thank God, ask me why I had not told her sooner. When we drew up outside the ward, she jumped out and ran as though catching a train. I mechanically locked the car doors and followed, dreading the scene I was about to witness. The thing for

235

me to do was keep very, very calm. I took deep breaths, breaths of the awful corridor smell. Bridget had her finger down hard on the bell but nobody had yet answered. When the door finally opened she swept in like a whirlwind, with me following sedately in her wake. The patients were all at the trestle table having breakfast and her passage alarmed them. By now I knew Ida and Doreen and Leah and May and most of them and I saw how each reacted true to type, how each had her own individuality, after all, even if senility had blurred the edges.

Grandma was still in the little room, next to the Sister's office. It was six days since Bridget had seen her but, even in the twenty-four hours since I had visited, there had been a further dramatic change. Her breathing was harsh and labouring and around her nostrils was a blue shadow. Her mouth was wide open, a great, ugly, slobbering dull-pinkish cavern. Her eyes were closed. Bridget's fight went out of her in a moment. She said nothing. She sat down on the left hand side of her mother and took her hand and leaned over her and said, 'Mother! It's me, Bridget.' The eyelids trembled, the vaguest hint of white eyeball glimmered for a second then disappeared. The mouth tried to close and failed. But the hand gripped. I could see it did. I saw how startled and then how pleased Bridget was, how feverishly she applied herself to that living hand, how she stroked and squeezed and caressed it. I sat timidly on the other side, not knowing if Bridget would prefer me out of the way. I, too, took Grandma's hand. We each sat with one hand in ours with this rasping, struggling carcase between us.

Bridget talked at first. She told Grandma about painting her room pink and the new electric blanket she'd bought and how she'd washed all the other bedding and how she would be home soon. But she stopped after a while. Instead she patted Grandma's hair and touched her face. There were no tears. After an hour, Bridget had to go out for a cigarette, right out into the corridor. She had not yet looked at me or spoken to me. But when she came back, the smell of cigarette smoke was suddenly welcome because it blocked out for a moment the rotting stench coming out of Grandma's mouth. She said as she resumed her post, 'Well, this is it, no doubt about that. In here, in this place after all.' I felt that whatever I said was going to be

236

wrong so I said nothing. 'She doesn't even know me, she doesn't know I'm with her, she's already dead, she's died on her own.' Then, it was easy to be swift with reassurance. I gestured with my hand to Grandma's in my other one. 'Look,' I said, 'feel – the grip. She knows she isn't alone. She knows that you're here, of course she does.' 'Too late,' Bridget said, 'kidding myself and knowing, knowing I did.'

It was a long, long day. We were at least left in peace. Occasionally May and Doreen, ever patrolling, would shuffle in and stare and cluck and go away. A nurse came from time to time to offer tea. Bridget and I talked, mostly memories of Grandma. We even laughed at remembered jokes. And all the time, the horrible, heaving breathing like a creaky pair of antique bellows. Each time one breath was over we waited for the next to begin. It always did. The rattle in the throat increased hour by hour until breaths and rattles were competing with each other for mastery. Once, when Bridget went for a cigarette, I tried to close Grandma's mouth. I could not. The resistance to my attempt was so determined, the jaw fighting to remain as it was. Dying was proving so hard. I thought of the natural childbirth exercises I had conscientiously done. Where are the natural death ones? Grandma did not know how to die and she did not want to die. There was no giving up, no surrender. She worked hard at staying alive all that long day, she laboured devotedly as she had done all her poor life, and nobody helped her, nobody even *tried* to help her. Nature had its evil way and was brutally cruel. Kind science never got a look in.

At eight in the evening the nice relief Sister suggested we went home. She said Grandma's pulse was still strong and invited Bridget to feel it – Bridget agreed, but said she would like to stay the night. Most people died in the night, Bridget said, and she wanted to be there. But we agreed we would go home for an hour and eat and wash and then return, fortified for the night ahead. We went and hardly were we inside the front door than the telephone rang and of course she had died. Grandma had died as we drove home. Only another half an hour and it would have been over, with Bridget there as she had so passionately wished to be. Thirty minutes, each one of them in Bridget's eyes a betrayal. We went straight back, against all my inclinations. Even in death, the jaw had not yielded. The hole was still there. Sister Grice, back on duty, said she would put a strap round it.

*

Bridget rang Stuart. She insisted. She was very calm. There was neither rage nor bitterness in her voice nor any apparent devastating distress. On the telephone, she could even have been described as quite bright. She told the news in a matter-of-fact way, without evident emotion. There were no euphemisms – 'Mum is dead,' she said, straight out. There was no staying up. We were both exhausted and after Bridget had finished we both went to bed and we slept deeply, to our joint surprise.

The next day, we were busy. Death made us very busy. We had the death to register, an affair of great time-consuming tedium. We had the undertaker to see. This at least was a livelier affair. We sat, Bridget and I, in a small sitting room at the undertaker's premises, a room eerie in its brown tastelessness, and were lectured on prices and types of coffin, prices and varieties of funeral car, prices and differences in clergy and their services. It was all done with the greatest and the most sincere, and therefore the most ridiculous, consideration. And the undertaker need not have bothered; we did not need kid gloves and the constant anxious eye for tears. That part of it was not upsetting. We fixed the cremation for the following day and left.

That morning, Charlie, whom I had failed to contact the night before, rang at last. I told him his mother was dead. 'You're joking!' he said, startled. What an extraordinary reaction – 'you're joking.' No, I said, I was not. Then Charlie said, 'I just never thought it would happen, I'd given up hoping.' I said his hopes had been answered. He said he would come home straight away. I thought of saying there was little point but then decided he should be at his mother's funeral, for Bridget's sake if not his own. I made a good meal that night and Bridget ate heartily – why not? I was not so stupid as to take this as a sign she did not grieve. Who, after all, would have expected Bridget to cry or wail or collapse? Not anyone who knew her. What I had expected, and feared, was anger and thankfully it had not come. I had expected it to be turned against me. Instead, Bridget was particularly friendly towards me. I thought maybe she would like Karl to be with her, but she shook her head emphatically and said, 'No, I just want my own family.'

And of course that is us: we are Bridget's family now. Husband-less, childless, Bridget, now motherless too. What would she have without us?

Hannah

Mum is not religious, Dad is not religious, Stuart is certainly not religious and Bridget hates religion. Yet here we all are, in a church, at a funeral. It's silly. I don't understand what this is for. Mum says it's for Bridget, Bridget says it's for Grandma. But Grandma is dead so how can it be for her? Bridget says un-Bridget-like things, such as, 'Grandma would be black-affronted not to have a funeral and a proper service.' When I say Grandma is dead Bridget smiles in an odd way and says she knows but it feels right.

It feels wrong to me. And absurd. We all sit in this awful waiting room at the crematorium. A large party of mourners has just left. We are not a large party. There are only seven of us, it's pathetic. Only Stuart and Paula are dressed for a funeral. Stuart is wearing a dark grey suit and an almost offensively white shirt with a stiff collar and a black tie. His black leather shoes are very shiny and his hair well brushed. Paula has a black coat with a discreet silver-and-black scarf at the neck, and black boots, also well polished though not as gleaming as Stuart's. Dad is quite funereal too but then his everyday work suits are all hideously drab. He has a dark blue suit on but his shirt is pale blue and his tie striped blue, white and gold. Mum is in grey, her grey skirt and jacket, with a spotted thing underneath. Bridget is in red. She says it was Grandma's favourite colour. She is wearing a scarlet dress with a black jacket over it. The jacket has a red carnation pinned to it. Adrian and I let the side down. There were heated exchanges over what we should wear. Dad thought I should wear a skirt or dress but I only have one skirt, and he didn't approve of it. I thought I should just be normal but normal means jeans and even Mum said no. So I'm wearing black trousers and a white sweater and since it's cold and I only have one warm jacket they have had to let me wear my bomber jacket. Adrian hasn't got a suit. He is wearing black trousers too and a white shirt but he adamantly refused to put on a tie. He has his horrible anorak jacket on top.

I have all this time to look at our clothes. There's nothing else to do. Bridget has just said she dreads this service being pathetic. How could it not be? With seven people present, only seven, who never go to church. Hours and hours have been spent on this wretched service. Bridget wanted rousing hymns. Rousing with seven singers? She says Grandma liked 'Fight the Good Fight'. She and Mum dredge up all these hymns from the past. Bridget is shocked that I do not know the words to 'The Lord is My Shepherd'. She keeps asking me, just like Grandma, if they teach me nothing at school. Then there is the music. Apparently, two pieces of music have to be chosen, one for the coffin coming in and one for the mourners leaving at the end. Bridget wanted 'Charlie is My Darling' for the first bit but the funeral director – funeral *director* – said it was 'inappropriate'. Bridget said she didn't care, that was what she wanted. The funeral director said the organist couldn't play it. Bridget was sure he bloody well could but Mum suggested 'The Skye Boat Song' which the funeral director passed and the organist could manage and so Bridget gave way. Mum says the funeral director doesn't like Bridget. It's all to do with the coffin. Bridget queried the cost of the coffin. The funeral director said it was the cheapest wooden coffin available with brass handles and a polished finish. Bridget said forget the brass and polish and why can't it be hardboard. The funeral director was obliged to reveal there was a plywood coffin with a cloth top but was sure Bridget would not want a cloth top. He was wrong. Bridget did. Bridget also wanted Dad, Stuart and Adrian to carry the coffin instead of the funeral director's lackeys but Dad refused. He said his back wasn't up to it and that he was paying and Bridget should stop fussing about cost. Bridget said she was doing it for Grandma's sake.

It is five to two. Our funeral is booked for two and there's another at two-thirty. The funeral director, looking like someone straight out of Dickens, from central casting anyway, comes in to this waiting room with another man. It is the minister, a Scot called McKay like us. He is very old and grizzled and sour-looking but he has a lovely accent. He shakes our hands and says he is from the Western Isles. Bridget has spent ages on the telephone filling him in on Grandma so that he can talk about her. I heard her tell him three times, but then Bridget tells everyone everything three times, that she doesn't want any fulsome speech about Grandma. That was the word she used: fulsome. Bridget said it would be embarrassing, 'know what I mean?' The minister must have said yes because she seemed reassured. Now that Minister McKay is standing in front of us I see he could never be fulsome. He hasn't got it in him to be anything but taciturn and grudging. Apparently he only gets £25 and even that probably goes to his miserable church and he has come all the way from East Barnet to officiate.

We troop out of the waiting room and across a yard into a small chapel. A large party is crossing to get to another chapel and we wait, in some confusion, to let them cross. They have right of way. There are many of them and most are weeping. The women are actually heavily veiled which fascinates me. Two are so grief-stricken they have to be helped along. White handkerchiefs, proper ones, not Kleenex, are held to red eyes. Then when they have gone, we continue, feeling hopelessly inadequate. The chapel is very small indeed, much smaller than our living room. Its maximum capacity is twenty-five so we're not too lost in it. It's really quite pretty. There is one stained glass window, circular, over the altar and the walls are dark wood. There are white chrysanthemums in a big urn thing (Mum's doing). Charlie, Stuart and Bridget sit in the front row with Mum, Paula, me and Adrian behind. The minister takes his place. I can feel the cold air rush in so I know the doors are open behind us but I am not going to turn round to watch the coffin being brought in. But Bridget does. She swings right round, defiantly, and stares. Her face is tight. No tears. There have been no tears at all that

242

anyone has seen. Her lips are twitching from side to side, first to the left, then to the right, as though they are winking. To avoid looking at Bridget's face I decide to look at the coffin too, even if it means breaking my resolution.

Four men have it on their shoulders at the door. It is such a surprise to see that it is draped in tartan. Bridget hadn't told me. It has Grandma's shawl, bright red and yellow and black, over the top and sitting on the shawl is a bunch of heather. I knew about that. It isn't heather, Mum couldn't find a florist who could get heather in December. Instead, it's some purple heather-substitute. Bridget smiles and turns back. The minister starts to speak. What he says is predictable, that Grandma was a good wife and mother and had led a good life, but his accent is beautiful. All the 's' sounds are long drawn out, his intonation rhythmic and hypnotising. Then we sing 'The Lord is My Shepherd', well, four verses. Bridget sings lustily and so does Stuart. Behind me I can hear the funeral director belting it out too. The prayers are just mumbo jumbo to me. Bridget gets restless during them but goes through the motions of head-bending and hand-clasping. We sing 'Fight the Good Fight'. Surely it can't go on much longer? Then we have what I take to be a concluding homily. It seems to me to be a dig at us for not being religious, ending on a 'how can anyone know' note and a reminder that God works in a mysterious way which we should never try to judge. Then there is silence, a bit of creaking, and the coffin starts to move between some discreet little curtains. Now that does seem dramatic, for a moment. I can't see Bridget's face. She is directly in front of me. But I can see Dad's left profile and Stuart's right. I am amazed to see a tear trickling down Stuart's cheek. Good God. Has Mum seen it? Dad isn't crying though. But he does a nice thing. As the coffin disappears I see him take Bridget's hand. That's it, then.

We have to go through a ritual outside. There is a place at the back of all the chapels, between the crematorium buildings and the gardens, where flowers are laid. There are dreadful little wooden markers in rows with the name of the chapel on. Some markers are nearly obliterated with flowers, mounds and mounds of them in every kind of shape. MUM is there in three foot pink flower letters and GRAN and there's a whole motorbike done in red and white carnations. On our marker there is at the moment only our bunch of heather-substitute. We're all proud of this except Stuart and Paula who cringe. They wanted to send a wreath but Bridget said Grandma would have been furious at the waste. Then there's nothing left to do. We shake hands with the minister and the funeral director. We get into our two cars. We go home.

*

It's a good meal. Bridget wanted it to be a Scottish meal in Grandma's honour so there is haggis and neeps and tatties and several very sickly puddings which have nothing to do with Scotland but which she loved. And there's whisky, best Highland Malt. As soon as we were in the door Dad said would the men like a whisky and Bridget said what about the women so they all had whisky. Dad said he only asked if the men wanted it because at real Scottish funerals it was only the men who went to the graveside; they came back chilled to the bone after most funerals and needed whisky. Bridget said it was amazing how men used tradition to exclude women. Dad just handed her the bottle.

She has drunk most of it but she doesn't seem drunk. We're still at the table and it's two hours since we returned. Everyone seems to be waiting for something but I can't imagine what. It's very rare to have the whole family round a table (the whole family except for Stuart and Paula's children, thank God). I can't help noticing the physical resemblances between the McKays and their individual likeness to Grandma. It's more in the facial expressions than the features and of course their very different colouring tricks the lazy eye into thinking they aren't alike. Bridget is looking closely at everyone too. She says Grandma would have loved this. Everyone agrees. Bridget says she loved her family around her. Everyone agrees again. Bridget says it's such a pity she hardly ever sat at a family table like this. Nobody says anything. Bridget asks, mock-innocent, when was the last time we all gathered like this? What event? What year? Can anyone remind her? No, nobody can. Bridget says it was such a simple thing, too. Grandma didn't want gold-plated yachts or diamonds or luxurious penthouses or fur coats – all she wanted was her family around her. And she didn't get it. Bridget raises her voice as she says her family were no bloody good to her in the end.

Looks are exchanged all along the line. Mum looks at Dad, Dad looks at the whisky bottle, Stuart looks at Paula. Nobody looks at Bridget. Everyone is ready to go. Stuart gets up first and thanks Mum for the meal and says he and Paula must go and pick up the boys. Bridget blows a smoke ring. Paula has gone for her coat. Stuart says, to nobody in particular, that he is glad it is all over and that we all did very well, very well. Bridget says praise from the mighty is praise indeed. Stuart should ignore her, but he doesn't. He is standing beside Bridget's chair. He touches her lightly on the shoulder and says he is grateful to her. Grateful! Bridget flinches, she asks what the hell he is grateful for. Stuart says for looking after Mum. It all fell on you, he says. Oh, so you noticed, Bridget retorts, that is a miracle. Well, Bridget says, you must be feeling very pleased now with Mum out of the way, with Mum obliging you by dying, conscience comfortable, is it? Stuart says that as a matter of fact no, it isn't, it never was, but that he put up with it, his conscience, niggling away. He decided a long time ago he'd had enough and was going to have the courage of his convictions. Courage? Convictions? Bridget squawks the words. She says she didn't know Stuart had either, it is news to her. Stuart says, quietly, that she likes to see things her way. Bridget snaps what way? Stuart says she liked to see him as a cold-blooded monster who didn't love his mother and didn't care what happened to her so long as it did not inconvenience him. Correct, says Bridget. Wrong, says Stuart. Dad interrupts to say they've both gone far enough and it is unseemly and we've all had a long day and we're all upset – but he is silenced. Bridget says this is the first time Stuart has said anything interesting in his life and she wants to listen. She invites Stuart to continue. But Stuart says he's finished, he's had his say. Bridget says that in that case it didn't make sense. Is Stuart saying he loved his mother? Yes, says Stuart, once. Oh, *once*, says Bridget, how funny, she thought love that meant anything lasted forever or is Stuart talking about men's love? Stuart says it has nothing to do with being a man: he loved his mother once but it just seemed to fade at the same time as his mother's for him faded.

Now he has done it. Bridget is on her feet, we all quail. She tells Stuart his mother *never* stopped loving him, how can he be saying these things. Stuart says no, it is Bridget his mother never stopped loving. He says Bridget could give because she received, it was an on-going thing all her life. Stuart says he and Charlie never got a look in from the moment they were grown-up. He says his mother didn't like men, she saw them as enemies, as nuisances, as tyrants. She saw them as spoiling her life. She only liked women. And that, says Stuart, made a big difference. He tells Bridget not just to blame him for his so-called indifference to his mother: blame her too. Bridget says this is obscene, she cannot believe her ears and Stuart is *mad*. Stuart shrugs. Paula is signalling to him frantically. He says he's going now and he's sorry if he's upset Bridget but it couldn't be helped and *then he kisses her*. And he goes. And Bridget slumps into her seat, stunned.

*

After Stuart and Paula leave, everything is different. We clear the remnants of the meal away. It's still early. Adrian goes out after worrying about whether it is appropriate (that funeral director's language had been catching). Mum lights the fire and we all gather round it. Dad stays an hour or so and then leaves to do some telephoning. We three, Mum and Bridget and I, go on sitting there, drinking coffee. Bridget drinks gallons of it. She says she will stay the night if that is all right and Mum says of course, she's been expecting her to. About nine o'clock Mum asks Bridget how she is feeling. Bridget says she's fine, just tired. Mum persists. She says to Bridget that she hopes she is not blaming herself for how and where Grandma died or for her having died at all. Bridget smiles slightly. She says no, she isn't thinking about that, there's no point, though of course she does blame herself for all those things, how could she not. But what she is thinking about and what is depressing her is what Stuart had said. She's worried that there is even the smallest grain of truth in what he said? The interrogative note was there in her voice.

Mum says she didn't know Stuart as a boy. She didn't know Charlie or Bridget either but I suppose that isn't the point. Mum says, from what she's heard, Stuart had a bad time as a child, what with his father's death when he was twelve, a bad age because you understand so much, and then that move to Newcastle and then back again. Mum says Grandma always told her how good Stuart was as a boy, how he helped her and looked after her and had two jobs, papers and messages, at the shop and he gave her all he earned. Mum says she thinks maybe Grandma didn't behave too well over Stuart's divorce and Stuart was hurt. Bridget snaps that Stuart didn't behave well either, that Grandma was quite right to be furious with Stuart. Mum says that that is her point, that Grandma made her disapproval clear and, however right it was, it angered and hurt Stuart. And then Grandma wasn't very nice to Paula. Bridget laughs nastily. She says oh come on, my mother was nice to everyone, and anyway – Paula! Mum says firmly that Grandma was *not* nice to everyone, that she had her ways of being mean, maybe not very serious ways but they were there. Mum says Bridget never did realise how cliquey she and Grandma could be and how they terrified Paula. Bridget tells Mum not to be so bloody ridiculous, that Grandma couldn't terrify a fly, that she was the kindest, gentlest, most harmless woman in the world. Mum says possibly, but she made Paula suffer. Bridget absolutely screams 'suffer!' Mum says Grandma was sly, she mocked Paula's clothes, she made her feel even more inarticulate than she was, she didn't treat her as a new daughter.

Mum has certainly roused Bridget from her lethargy. She is furious. She glares at Mum. She tells her that next thing she'll be saying Stuart was right. Mum is quite plucky. She says Stuart may well be right about his relationship with his mother being determined by her and anyway he can't be blamed, as Bridget is blaming him, for no longer adoring her. Mum says she actually quite admires Stuart for coming out with it because most men don't. Their 'love' for their mother is only a nice memory, superseded by their love for their wife and children, but it isn't done to say so. Mum says Charlie wouldn't say it but she knows he feels it. But as for the other part of what Stuart says, Mum goes on, she doesn't agree with that, she definitely doesn't agree with how Stuart behaved towards his mother. He more or less abandoned her and that was cruel. He wanted her 'put away' years ago and he was wrong to want that when the quality of her life was still good. Mum says that kind of behaviour is no good, it negates all that has gone before. Bridget looks a little happier. This is more what she wants to hear.

Now Mum is trying to be encouraging. She reminds Bridget that it's all over and her life can change. Mum says Bridget is free, that she can do what she wants without organising her life round Grandma. Days off will be real days off, nights no longer interrupted twice a week. Mum presses Bridget to say she's glad about this. Bridget won't. Bridget shrugs. Bridget says she never minded spending her days off with Grandma and she was hardly interrupted at all. Mum says Bridget lies through her teeth. She says Bridget is already romanticising the last five years. She asks her if she's forgotten the fuss if she had to work late, the frantic phone calls to get a helper to stay? She asks why Bridget doesn't remember moaning she couldn't even read a line of a book all evening because of Grandma? Or her exhaustion on bath nights? Or the tedium of having things repeated over and over when she was tired? Or not being able to sleep until noon? Bridget says none of that really mattered. Mum says whether it mattered or not, it is over and you are free so relish it. 'Relish what?' asks Bridget. 'Freedom,' Mum says. Bridget repeats the word. She says she supposes that's what it is. Mum says it certainly is to her, that she is going to capitalise on it at once, and that the biggest freedom will be not worrying about the next stage for Grandma. Mum says that in the end we were lucky and does Bridget realise that? Grandma went from being moderately, manageably senile to dying in a few months and that makes us lucky. Bridget should be glad.

Bridget isn't. She says she can't think of anything to be glad about. She says now Grandma is dead there is no one she feels 'like that' about. Mum asks like what. Bridget says she was so proud of Grandma, she just loved people to admire her. She says she supposes she was possessive and there isn't anyone she wants to possess or be possessed by now. Mum says she thinks that is a very strange thing to say. She says Bridget talks of Grandma as though she, Bridget, was Grandma's mother instead of the other way round. Bridget says not at all, Mum is getting carried away. Anyway, she doesn't want to talk about it. Mum says fine, neither does she, what she wants to talk about is Bridget's future. Bridget asks irritably what that means, what future, what is there to talk about for heaven's sake. She will carry on as usual, what else? They never believed on her ward she'd leave, anyway, so rescinding her notice was easy, they were delighted. Mum says what about Karl. Bridget says so what about him. He's still around, she still feels the same, nothing has changed there either. Mum reminds Bridget she's forty-three. Bridget says she's well aware of that, thank you. Mum says Bridget hasn't even got a place to live that belongs to her, is she going to pay rent all her life? Bridget asks why not, she likes her flat, she has no desire at all to be a home-owner or -maker or any of those things. Nor has she any desire to marry or have children before it's too late, well it's too late already, really. Mum says does Karl mean nothing then, that she had hoped etc. Bridget says she knows what Mum hoped and it was her own fault for hoping. Mum says that there will be no gain from Grandma's death for Bridget then. Bridget says no, no gain, only loss.

Then she goes to bed, leaving Mum and me. Mum is upset. She prods and prods the fire and frowns. She asks me what I think of how Bridget is reacting to Grandma's death. I say that Grandma has only just died, I don't even know how I'm reacting myself. It seemed so sudden. After all this time it's a shock even though she'd been ill so long and was old. I say maybe Bridget is shocked. She doesn't really seem to have taken it in. She hasn't cried or anything. She doesn't seem anything but the Bridget she's always been. I tell Mum I don't think she should have nagged Bridget about the future like that. I say she probably can't bear to think about it, surely we don't want her to think about it? Mum asks why not. I say that it doesn't look too appetising to me, Bridget's future. What will she have? Work? Oh, yes that's good, it's a real career and she loves it, it would be terrible if she didn't have that, much, much worse. But what else? Did Bridget have masses of close friends? Did she hell. She had Karl and she'd just told us what she thought of him and how much he doesn't mean to her. And she has us but how much is that? We're not going to be a substitute, for Grandma. She doesn't love us totally, completely, as she did Grandma. And I say to Mum that I wish she wouldn't keep using words like lucky and glad and relief about Grandma dying, even if they're true. I tell her *I* don't like it, never mind Bridget. It's horrible. Mum says she's sorry. She says she was only being honest, that she feels lucky and glad and relieved now Grandma is dead. But she says she feels a coward too because now Grandma is dead she can ignore the problem of all the other Grandmas and she shouldn't, she should be inspired to do something and she knows she isn't going to. She's going to dodge the issue now. It's selfish but that's what she is going to do. She doesn't want to think about senile dementia or hear about it or read about it ever again. She isn't an activist and she can't help it. But somebody, somewhere, will have to do something soon. They'll have to. We've tinkered around enough with the start of life, we've interfered with all kinds of natural sequences, and now we'll have to tinker with the end. Mum says, 'Your generation, Hannah, will have to have pro-death marches, you'll have to stop being scared to kill the old.' Will we?

★

Sunday lunch is abolished. Mum says so. She's wanted to abolish it ever since Grandma went into hospital but she says she didn't quite have the nerve. She has it now. Today she says, 'No more Sunday lunches,' and Dad and Adrian have a fit. Dad says it's the highlight of his weekend. Mum says that is pathetic, and get another. Adrian says he's always starving after his football and what will he do. Mum says she doesn't know and cares less, that there will be food in the fridge and he must help himself. Adrian says all right he will, but it won't be the same and he would have thought Mum would be the very one to want to keep an old tradition going. Mum says that the old tradition was that she spent all Sunday morning in the kitchen cooking the sort of meal she doesn't even like to eat at a time of day when she is never hungry. It was a tradition kept up for Grandma's sake because there were so few she was still able to appreciate and enjoy. Mum says she loathed the sight of the big hunks of meat Grandma loved, they made her feel sick, she would also rather have a tomato salad with a sprinkling of fresh basil and some good bread. Dad groans, he asks why can't Mum keep a tradition going for him?

He loves joints just as much as Grandma did, isn't he worth a tradition? Mum says no, she's had enough.

But what about Bridget? I ask Mum, what about Bridget? Where will Bridget go on Sunday if there's no big lunch, no focal point? She will feel she hasn't a family. Dad leaps on this, he says I'm quite right, that we have a duty to keep Sunday lunches going for Bridget's sake. Mum says rubbish, Bridget prefers eating in the evening too. Dad brightens, he says he has misunderstood, if Mum means we will eat on Sunday evening instead of at lunch time, then that's different, he can cope, he can adjust. But Mum says no, she doesn't mean that. Sundays are going to be no-formal-meal-at-all days. Bridget will come on a weekday evening and have supper with us instead. Dad subsides back into gloom. Why does he mind so much? I can't imagine. I'm glad. I never liked Sunday lunch anyway and without Grandma it would be a mockery.

So that's it. There's no one old in our family now. No more grandparents, no elderly relatives we're close to. There's no more of that hideous disintegration to watch. I can't mourn the loss. I can't even mourn Grandma, I would not truly wish her alive and here and round our Sunday lunch table. Not knowing what lay ahead of her. Even when she was reasonably *compos mentis* it was painful. She had no real life, not for ages. It can't be meant, intended, that people should die like that, can it? I wonder if being religious makes it all simple and acceptable? If you can say everything is God's will and he moves in mysterious ways his wonders to perform as the Rev. McKay said? I suppose that's a relief, if you're a believer.

When my time comes I'm not going to allow it.

When my time comes I won't trust to mystery.

When my time comes I will say I have had enough and go.

That is, if my time comes like Grandma's time, if it is the same sort of time.

But if it is, I won't be able to, will I?

Margaret Forster

DIARY OF AN ORDINARY WOMAN

'Extraordinary'
Observer

Margaret Forster presents the 'edited' diary of a woman, born in 1901, whose life spans the twentieth century. On the eve of the Great War, Millicent King begins to keep her journal and vividly records the dramas of everyday life in a family touched by war, tragedy, and money troubles. From the bohemian London to Rome in the 1920s her story moves on to social work and the build-up to another war, in which she drives ambulances through the bombed streets of London.

Here is twentieth-century woman in close-up, coping with the tragedies and upheavals of women's lives from WWI to Greenham Common and beyond. A triumph of resolution and evocation, this is a beautifully observed story of an ordinary woman's life – a fictional narrative where every word rings true.

'A highly enjoyable read; well-informed, gripping . . . an overview of the period seen from the underside'
Sunday Telegraph

V

VINTAGE

Margaret Forster

THE SEDUCTION OF MRS PENDLEBURY

'Beautifully written and a joy to read'
Auberon Waugh, *Evening Standard*

Rose Pendlebury has little in common with her Islington
neighbours. Her street has been invaded by young,
confident, upwardly-mobile people without, it seems, a
care in the world. She keeps herself to herself, and only
her husband Stan is aware of her bubbling anger, her
terrible prickliness and her ability to take offence.

But when Alice and Tony move in next door with
their enchanting toddler Amy, Mrs Pendlebury
begins to come out of her shell, as gradually her
new neighbours undermine her traditional,
cautious privacy. Mrs Pendlebury may not be ripe
for transformation, or even happiness, but she is
not too old to change.

'She charts real people and touches her harridan with
genuine pathos . . . nothing of hers that I have read
has satisfied like *The Seduction of Mrs Pendlebury*'
Guardian

'Margaret Forster's heroine is quite unforgettable
. . . Often splendidly funny . . . In an admirably
unpretentious way Forster has written a painfully
convincing tragic-comedy'
Nina Bawden, *Daily Telegraph*

V

VINTAGE